Transient Time Traveller
by Melissa Sweeney

This is a work of fiction. Names, characters, places, or incidents are either products of the author's imagination or are used fictitiously. Any resemblances of people, living or dead, is entirely fictional.

Chapter 1: Two Weeks Before 3
Chapter 2: Two Weeks Before, Continued 15
Chapter 3: Meeting of the Mind 24
Chapter 4: Aida's Second Letter 45
Chapter 5: One of the Boys 58
Chapter 6:Nighttime Wandering 66
Chapter 7: Investigations 71
Chapter 8: Unfamiliar Faces 79
Chapter 9: Familiar Faces....................................... 88
Chapter 10: Escape Plan 100
Chapter 11: Breadcrumbs 108
Chapter 12: Welcome to Roma 120
Chapter 13: Missus Sharma's Cottage 131
Chapter 14: Zaahir, Two Days Before 145
Chapter 15: Beatrice, Two Days Later 153
Chapter 16: Nighttime Highs 164
Chapter 17: Bookstore Date.................................... 175
Chapter 18: Baking up a Plan 186
Chapter 19: A Decision between Royals..................... 197
Chapter 20: A Welcome in Ruins 208
Chapter 21:A New Side to Eve................................. 223
Chapter 22: Royal Affairs 235
Chapter 23: Royal Fray 247
Chapter 24: Two Turtle Doves 260
Chapter 25: Talk with Yourself 273
Chapter 26: Good Deeds... 286
Chapter 27: Second Chances 296
Chapter 28: Getting Bored 313
Chapter 29: Log Cabin 332
Chapter 30: Forest Scuffle 346
Chapter 31: Home 355
Chapter 32: En Tempore Rose 369
Chapter 33: The Clock Tower 390
Chapter 34: Wedding Pep Talk 398
Chapter 35: Trying on the Dress 404
Chapter 36: Ballroom Whirl 410

Chapter 37: Back into the Catacombs 418
Chapter 38: Lost Found Family 424
Chapter 39: Circa's Decision 430
Chapter 40: Aftermath 449
Chapter 41: Rediscovery 460

For Mari,
my love

Chapter 1: Two Weeks Before

She never received letters. Being adopted into a small family on a smaller farm didn't bless her with mail of any kind. She'd theorized that no one besides her stepmother and her stepsisters knew of her existence, so she ghosted through life without much interference.

But she knew this letter, had been anticipating it for weeks since she'd sent in her application behind her mother's back. It was handwritten on high-quality paper and branded with the seal of the Roman lion. She'd dreamt of getting these royal letters in the mail, hope turning to dread come nighttime, but she hadn't thought she'd get a reply, let alone a letter of acceptance.

She'd been tending to the cows. The chickens, pigs, sheep, and goats had been taken care of and her family had ridden their horse-drawn carriage to the village, so all that was left to handle was their highland cows. Big, burly creatures more fur than hide. Aida needed more time to heave the heavy bales of hay into their stables, to groom them, wash them, clean out their troughs. She hadn't even heard the post carrier arrive, she'd been on the other side of the property. She was hurrying to get everything done so her stepmother would be in a better mood. Well, a less shit one.

There was one piece of mail that day, and it'd been addressed to Aida.

When her mother and sisters had finally come home and found Aida on the floor, frantically rereading the letter with the envelope torn with her teeth, they must've assumed she'd had jumped and was writhing in pain as a result.

She was writhing, but not because she'd travelled backwards into time. Her brain was spinning, eyes watering due to an emotion she couldn't name. After fighting for years, she'd finally earned this damned six-year scholarship to Durante Academy.

Not like wanting to dorm at a school named after King Durante's lineage excited her. She detested almost everything the royal family did, and she didn't even live in Roma. Roma, and Roma City, were hundreds of kilometers away, across the sea and doing far better than her home country of snow-covered farmlands. She should've loathed becoming a student in the country with the bloodiest warpath, most prejudiced ruler, and shittiest military since the time of gladiators.

But how she'd dreamed of walking through those academic halls, taking in the lessons in fervor and staying up late to perfect her homework. Schools here in Bĕlico, you were expected to drop out after primary school to work the family farm. It made sense for the people. Agriculture was the biggest export, so families expected many hands to tend to the fields.

But that wasn't Aida's path. Ever since she'd been adopted, Aida Mirko had set her sights on becoming a historian, and that path was only attainable in the sparkling, problematic country of Roma.

It was after her mother slammed the door did Aida realize her mistake: being too indulgent.

4

"What're y'all doing?" one of her stepsisters—Ekaterina—asked.

"You tracked in mud. We're not cleaning that up," her other sister, Olga, said.

Her mother looked over the mess Aida had made, then at the letter still in her hand.

She slapped Aida across the cheek and sent her glasses across the living room.

She should've expected it. How dare her. Here she was, trying to better herself in a world where most people wanted her kind dead, and she'd been accepted into the best academy in Roma. It had a seven percent acceptance rate. To any parent, that would've been cause for celebration.

Her mother grabbed Aida by the collar and dragged her upstairs to her room. Her mother and sisters lived downstairs near the fireplace, gifting Aida with the joy of taking the stairs. She had a fucking cane and limp, for Circa's sake. Her family couldn't have cared less.

"Mo'mma, wait—"

Her mother slammed the bedroom door behind her. "How *dare* you?"

Aida fell backwards into her bed.

"You ain't going," she decided. "You have obligations *here*. You work the farm, you care for us. How selfish can you be, leaving all of that to become a damned academic?"

"I wanna be a historian," Aida said, trying so hard to explain a goal she'd wanted to achieve for years. With her limp, it was difficult to do any sort of manual labor. She got tired easily, her dizzy spells were becoming more frequent.

Her sisters, they weren't expected to do half the chores she was expected to do, yet she did them. She hated it, but she did what was asked of her because it gave her a roof over her head and food on the table and a bed to dream of a life better than this. In the rare hours she had for sleep, she studied and over-worked her abilities to prove that a Visatorre deserved to learn, something that'd been barred from her people for cen-turies.

She didn't expect praise, or validation. She couldn't dream like that. All she wanted was for her mother to stop hitting her. She didn't know why that was a selfish ask.

Her mother stood over her. "You ain't going."

Aida fixed her broken glasses over her nose. "I was accepted."

"I ain't paying for it."

"I know that."

"What do you mean, *'I know that'*? You *won't* be able to afford it. The journey 'cross the sea alone is ten gold."

Unbeknownst to her mother, Aida had been saving up, hid-ing her childhood allowance underneath her bedroom floor-boards. After turning fifteen, her mother had stopped paying her for her work. Aida had thought it was because her mother had seen her as a daughter more than a servant. Then she found out Ekaterina's and Olga's allowances had doubled.

So, she'd taken to writing school papers for the local kids. She wrote top-grade essays about history, war, massacres of her own people and the rise of dictatorships she hated. If her mother had found that out, she would've thrown Aida into the village stockades for lying because "Visatorre folk ain't smart like normal folk."

"I have the money," Aida summarized.

"I don't care if you got a *fortune*! Y'all ain't gonna throw away your life and waste it on an academy when you're needed here."

"I'll be gone, isn't that what you'd want?" The fear of speaking out pitched her voice. "I'll be gone for six whole years, and I swear, whatever money I make—"

"*'Money I make'*, she says. What money you gonna make there? You know Romans don't take well to you folk as well as Bělican people do. You'll be laughed off the continent. You'll be ostracized."

"So how would it be any different than living here?" Aida wanted to ask. Gods, to be brave enough to say that sober. If she'd been high, that defiance would've come out, but it would've resulted in her being hit harder.

Aida lowered her head, feigning a defeat.

Her mother harrumphed and tied up her hair in a messy bun. "That's what I thought. Now." She held out her hand. Aida flinched. "Give me that letter."

"No," Aida said. "Please, just...let me keep it. For memory's sake."

Her mother rolled her eyes and wiped her hands on her apron. "Get up and help with the groceries, since you didn't want to help when we came in. The rest are in the carriage."

Aida nodded and went for her cane. It was a dark stick carved from a scavenged tree branch.

Her mother kicked it into the bedside table. The force tipped and spilled Aida's drinking glass from last night.

Aida froze.

"Know your stance in this house," her mother warned, "and stop making stupid decisions behind my back."

"Okay," Aida said, and waited for her mother to leave down the stairs, where her sisters were whispering about what their mother had said to their servant daughter.

Aida gripped her cane firmly as she stood back up. The one thing about being in your twenties was that, while you might've been afraid of your parents, if you had the money and the drive to defy the Gods, you could change your future.

After listening for her mother to return, Aida went for her travel bags.

———◇———

Bedtime at the Mirko household came early, as they—she— had to get up at four in the morning to take care of the livestock. Feed them, gather the eggs, change the hay, sweep out both barns, weed out the gardens. Aida half-expected her mother to put more energy into their own livelihood instead of working on how to destroy her daughter's confidence, but she couldn't expect much of anything from them anymore.

Aida *knew* she was smart. She wouldn't have gotten her scholarship otherwise. All the years of extra credit and letters of recommendation had paid off. It didn't matter what her mother thought. This year, she'd reclaim her dignity. Without her family's help.

That night, or morning, Aida awoke and began packing. It'd take a chunk out of her savings to leave now, as she'd planned on leaving later towards the school year where travel costs went down, but she'd manage. She always did. She currently had seventy pieces of gold lyria to her name with handfuls of silver and bronze pieces separated into different bags. It wasn't much—it'd buy her an old horse or a few week's stay in a seedy inn—but if she used it right, she'd make do.

Because, in all her twenty-three years of living, she knew that "family" could go fuck themselves with how good they were to her.

She dressed in a black dress fit for nighttime escape and braided her hair in her favorite way, down her front in two braids that were never even. She was bigger than most girls: both of her sisters' weights combined. She hoped the school uniforms could accommodate her, and that they weren't tacky. She needed a self-esteem boost, not a downgrade from what clothes she'd been given.

After packing her non-essentials, Aida got to packing the more important items: her journals, thick with cut-outs and pictures she'd glued in; her history texts on the once luxurious country of Siina and its murdered queen; the first novel in the *En Tempore Rose* sextet, *Pinnacle Isle*; and her signed playbooks from its opera-ballet adaptation she'd traded for a twelve-page essay.

She'd seen the opera of *En Tempore Rose* once, and by "seen," she meant she'd snuck into the theatre for ten minutes during a family trip to Roma City when she was eight. It'd been during a trading festival in which her family had participated. Aida had snuck into the massive theatre constructed within the Colosseum and caught the last few minutes of the performance before being discovered.

She'd been beaten so hard that she didn't remember much of the opera, but she remembered loving it. Those few minutes near the stage made her heart stop and restart with the love for her favorite stories, both real and imaginary. The ballerinas, dressed in snow-white lace, the glitter that danced from the rafters. It'd sparked her desire to be a ballerina before she found out that Visatorre were neither allowed to be stage performers nor were they allowed to watch an opera to begin with. They were a "risk" to those around them if they travelled backwards into time.

At least she had her journals. She had a dozen or so hand-bound journals she'd made herself because Circa knew her mother wouldn't have bought them for her. They detailed her favorite moments in history. Nothing of wars or tyrannical, egotistical kings she couldn't stand learning about. She was interested in the people, the interpersonal relationships between the royal families and their citizens. Their dresses, the food they ate, the ways they lived their menial lives a millennia ago.

And Eve, a magnificent, tolerant queen to a dead city-state that once held 100,000 Visatorre within its peaceful walls. Aida loved her, knew everything about her life from the minute she was born to the day she was executed. Her city-state, Siina, had once been a well-established, Visatorre-owned community within Roma City that could've easily rivaled the Goliath of a city.

History said that Eve had murdered the Roman king's wife, so in retaliation, he'd killed her, her lineage, and all 100,000 Visatorre of Siina, burying them in the Catacombs beneath Roma City.

Aida knew for a fact that that part of history was wrong. She'd written papers and thesis on Eve, and she couldn't see her murdering someone she should've seen as an ally. She'd been a young, proud Visatorre woman that housed the largest population of Visatorre the world had ever seen. Yes, she was rash, and she might've been labeled "eccentric" in today's terms, but to murder someone so significant for no reason, it didn't add up.

So, Aida was bent on becoming a historian, to rewrite the history books with the truth rather than the propagated schlock crammed down their throats.

After zipping up her final bag, Aida readied her three-kilometer-long walk to the village. It was mostly leveled terrain, but still, it burdened her legs. One bad jump into the past when she was a teenager had fucked up her hips, or her back, or her spine, or all three, given her exceptionally bad luck, and it made walking hard.

Scholars had theories as to why a time traveller jumped, and doctors have tried their damnedest to find a solution to why travelling hurt the traveller once they returned. They only knew that the farther back you travelled, the worse the injury. Five years back would get you a bad cough or throbbing joint. Fifty years and you'd end up with a permanent injury, like her shitty leg or a fucked up eye. 200 years back and who could say? You could lose your leg, your head might fall off. Aida had known a girl who travelled back 150 years, give or take a decade. She had regular bleeding from the brain. It lasted two months before she died in her parents' arms.

Aida, with all that was stacked up against her, considered herself lucky that she only needed a cane to get around.

All signs as to why Visatorre got fucked over by fate pointed to the Heavens above. Those who still believed in the Gods—very few in her generation—believed that these things happened because the Gods willed them to happen. Why did the Gods take away children right when they were born? Why couldn't humans live as long as trees or Aldaían turtles? It was nature, a nature human beings had yet to understand.

She closed the garden gates slowly, taking the back entrance so she didn't wake the easily spooked ducks. No more farmlands, no more chores done by six and being hit behind closed doors. Despite years of fucking up, making her think she was useless, too slow, too stupid to be anything more than a servant in her own home, Aida was to mentally burn this place to the ground with her accomplishments.

She paused at the start of the cow field, eyes darting left and right. While she wouldn't burn down the farm—she couldn't hurt the animals—she could do something else. Something more.

She crept into the chicken coop and burgled two dozen of the largest eggs she could find, enough to keep her fed for a few days, and another six for the carriage.

Keeping her movements quiet, she cracked her extra eggs and smeared them into the carriage seats. She got the yolk into the fur, over the handles, the steps. Then she took charcoal from her pocket and graffitied one side of the barn. She dumped out the milk she'd gotten for that day, she let the chickens loose from the coop. Dumped the drinking water over the hay, overturned the trough. Everything she could do to make her family's life horrible, but not enough to send an officer after her.

If they connected it to a *Visatorre's* doing, she might've had one on her tail. Luckily, she wasn't planning on ever coming back.

She paced herself as she made her way into the village. Idti, a racist outcropping of 500 farmers who'd sell off their own daughters for a lick of gold. She kept a knife in her pocket when walking down these dirt roads.

She made it close to the sea. The salty water replaced the smell of horse manure: a freedom not many around these parts could find.

Near the piers was a horse stable to rent out horses and their services. One driver was smoking near his carriage, reading the paper with his boots kicked up. As Aida neared with lantern and cane in hand, the driver made no attempt to hide himself gawking at her Visatorre marking: a white circle engraved in the middle of her forehead. Every Visatorre obtained one the first time they travelled, but that didn't stop non-Visatorre from staring like she had three legs.

"I need a ride to the export harbor," Aida said, keeping her face devoid of emotion.

"Now?" the driver asked.

"Not yesterday," she said, and gave him three of her gold lyria coins. "The quicker, the better."

The driver sat up and folded his paper. "You're the Visatorre girl who works up at that cow farm, ain't you?"

"Aye." She took out one of her own cigarettes and had him light it for her. She needed one after this week, and her mother hated the smell in the house. "Let's say I got fired."

"Didn't you live there?"

"Didn't you need to bring me to the harbor?"

The man clicked his tongue and helped her with her bags. "You Visatorre, y'all are something else."

She let the backhanded compliment slide and got into the carriage. She took one long inhale as she surveyed the land from this height. The morning birds had yet to begin their songs, and the lack of light let the Moon and stars shine over the country, dyeing it a deep blue.

"Did you hear the news?" the driver asked, making unneeded small talk. "The princess of Roma, Lucia, she just went missing. Papers're sayin' she vanished from that wedding she was having, saying she got kidnapped."

"Wouldn't be a change from what we see," Aida said. While dead monarchs got her on tangents, the alive ones didn't do much for her. The dead ones had a history to them, a certain taste of a past she couldn't reach without her head exploding. Plus, she hadn't seen the twin princesses. One had been married off to Bělico's shit stain, King Dmitri, as a kid, the other barely left the palace. What was the difference if she went missing?

"Do you think they'll find her?" asked the driver.

In the distance, Aida saw the faint outline of her home. Her *mother's* home—it had never belonged to her. Her mother had *tried* to be a good mother when she'd first adopted Aida, but the years had tainted her into a villain Aida couldn't wait to see get their comeuppance.

She gave her home the finger and got into the carriage. "Who cares about some dumb princess?"

Chapter 2:
Two Weeks Before, Continued

Lorian had dreamed about breaking out of the palace through the window. She hadn't thought it would be her last-ditch effort to save her life.

She wasn't in life-threatening danger. She wasn't going to die if she stayed the night. Acted proper. Went back downstairs and apologized to her wedding guests, and let Prince Zaahir take her hand like she'd been destined to do since she was six.

That wouldn't kill her per se, but if it came to that, she'd kill herself. No remorse, no second thoughts. She'd warned her parents that if they followed through with the marriage, it would've been the final straw out of the many they'd already broken.

Well, her father had. Everyone knew that despite being the reigning queen, her mother wasn't in charge. It was Lorian's father who governed their choices.

That night, after ripping up her wedding dress and wrecking every last piece of notable art she had left in her bedroom, Lorian had collapsed in her bed and sobbed so hard, she'd thrown up. Out of everything her parents imposed on her, this marriage was the one constant. Let her ruin her dresses, let her throw her infamous temper tantrums hidden from the country. But this marriage, like her sister's, would happen. Alliances needed to form between the three major countries of the world to keep war at bay, so it'd happen whether she liked it or not. Country before individual. Alliances before children.

The only way out was death.

Lorian had contemplated it, then kicked herself and fought for another way out. She couldn't end it here. She had to show her parents that she did have aspirations, just ones outside of royal duties.

The giant clock outside her room chimed for eleven. Per Roman customs, the wedding kiss would occur at the stroke of midnight, and so far, Lorian hadn't let any of her maids or officers touch her. She'd run from the buffet when guests were still arriving. Nobody had gotten her to come back down, though they'd tried.

First, her mother, whose frail knocks almost broke Lorian's heart. Then Lorian's sister, Beatrice, born twelve minutes sooner and thus married off first to a man older than their father. She'd given Lorian a methodical explanation as to why she needed to follow through with the marriage. It dashed all hopes Lorian had for her to understand her. Like they'd ever agree on anything, anyway.

Carmine was the last person to try. He was the queen's right-hand man—a constable, the highest rank an officer could receive—and childhood friend of the queen. He was the most sympathetic man about Lorian's plight, she'd give him that, but he, like the rest of them, told her to come downstairs and finish what was destined for her. He used to be better, back when he was more of a family friend who wasn't weighed

16

down by medals of honor, but those days were gone, as was Carmine's carefree nature. It'd been replaced with duties that outweighed Lorian's happiness.

Her father hadn't come up to check on her.

The only one Lorian had let come near was Missus Sharma. She'd been Lorian's and Beatrice's nursemaid since they were in the womb. She'd taught Lorian mathematics, both the piano and violin, and had guided her through speech therapy to try to get rid of her lisp. She knew almost all of Lorian's secrets, the ones her parents didn't know about.

Last year, Lorian told her she no longer wanted to be a princess.

"I understand your frustrations, Your Highness," she'd said, this sixty-year-old maid who deserved so much more than what Lorian gave her.

She *didn't* know, however, so when Lorian explained more, that she didn't want to be a princess, or Lucia, and not just a woman but something else, that'd puzzled her. Her generation still lived in the mindset that'd fizzled out during this ruling— people could be who they wanted to be, whether they were a boy, girl, neither, or something in-between.

Those rights weren't given to royal heirs, especially when it involved the procreation of royal children.

Lorian held her stomach as she thought of a way out of this. Even though she was still figuring out her identity, she was sure as fuck not marrying Zaahir for the sole purpose of bearing children. That thought was so far out of her comfort zone, it made her ill.

Frustrated by her dwindling time limit, Lorian groaned, took the last pillow she hadn't torn, and threw it against her writing desk. It scattered the letters she'd tried to write to her parents only for her to rip them up. Her mother might've heard her out. Her father would've lost his voice from screaming.

A letter fell to the ornate rug. It was hidden behind one of her jewelry boxes. It didn't have a name on it, but it'd been stamped with her family's seal.

Curious, Lorian picked it up.

Out the window & down to the forest.
Good luck.

She flipped over the note to read the rest, but that was it. It wasn't even signed. She inspected the handwriting, but that didn't click either. It looked like the person, whoever had written it, had concealed their own personhood to make the letter untraceable.

She looked back at her door. It was locked, as well as barricaded with her wardrobe. Nobody was coming in any time soon.

She crept towards the window that faced the outer walls. In the past, they were meant to keep enemies out, like the fallen city-state of Siina. It'd once been a wealthy state where most of the Visatorre population lived some 1,200 years back. Tensions back then had been high, she'd been taught. Visatorre were seen as part-God, part-monster, these people who could time travel or "jump" back in time to witness a single moment in history. Stories had been written around them, depicting them as nosy, voyeuristic ghosts that deserved all the pain their jumps caused them.

Her father despised time travellers for their unpredictable powers, but he seldom brought it up in public. They were a reminder of a bloody history most Romans wanted to forget, but Lorian hadn't forgotten. She knew that the queen of Siina had murdered the Roman king due to some type of disagreement, and as punishment, she, her lineage, and all 100,000 Siinans had been brutally slaughtered in an unjust bloodbath.

Lorian gritted her teeth. She hated it. She'd hated it ever since it was taught to her by her scholars and meant to sound like a victory. It wasn't. It was the royal family's insatiable bloodlust, and it was all the more reason for her to escape this prison.

The orchestra from her own wedding ceremony echoed from outside. 600 people had been invited and were likely placing bets as to whether or not Lorian would come back to the party by midnight.

So it was odd that out of all of these guests and bustling maids and officers, nobody saw Lorian's horse, Ether, nibbling on the flowers next to the palace walls. She was bridled and had on her saddle, but it wasn't the official, royally-sanctioned one with all the gold and rubies stitched into it. It was Lorian's personal riding saddle made of coarse leather.

And attached to Lorian's windowsill, weighted down so as not to blow in the summer night air, was a silk bed sheet tied into other bed sheets: a less than perfect escape ladder.

Lorian pressed her lips together. She touched the start of the makeshift ladder. It'd been tied several times behind her window and secured behind the jewelry box. Not even Missus Sharma would've seen anything awry.

Lorian packed what she considered to be her real clothes. No dresses, nothing too uncomfortable to wear. She did pack her corsets to bind her chest and hide her hips. She didn't hate her body. Her boobs were fun to play with when she was in the bath or getting ready for bed. They just meant too much to her past self, and she didn't want to remember that.

She would no longer be Lucia Maria Carolus Durante di Romano, future princess to the country of Roma and Aldaí.

She would be Lorian. Lorian...

Something. If she was going to run away, she'd have to change her surname. She'd chosen the name "Lorian" as a child, a nonsense name she'd made up to sound cool.

She had nothing of real importance in the palace. Clothing that displeased her parents, 350 pieces of gold lyria she kept in case she ever decided to run away, utensils—she ate quite a lot in her room. She grabbed documents with her mother's and father's signatures on them for forgery purposes, and she kept her signet ring and skeleton key because she was sentimental like that. She had her dagger because rapiers would be too excessive. She wouldn't need a map because she knew Roma City's layout by heart. As for her underwear...

She looked at the dagger in her hand, then at herself in the mirror. The blond hair she'd tied up in a ponytail to get it out of her face still curled to the middle of her back. It was a staple for Roman women to keep their hair long. Her mother's must've been worth thousands of lyria for how beautiful it was, reaching her thighs in elegant waves, and her sister's must've taken hours to prepare every day with all the braids and swoops she kept it in.

Nobody could know she was tied to Roman women. If she were to live as Lorian, Lucia needed to die.

Her locks fell around her in spirals. Her head felt lighter than it had in years, but she knew it didn't look right. One section was uneven, the next cut too close to her scalp. She didn't touch her bangs, as Missus Sharma had styled them the day before, and when she was done, she didn't look back in the mirror. She retied it into a small ponytail. Her neck felt free yet cold.

Someone knocked on her door.

She hid the dagger against her thigh.

"Your Highness, are you alright?"

The voice, so sweet and motherly, Lorian knew it better than her own mother's.

"Yes, Missus Sharma," she called out, and opened the window all the way.

"I don't want you to feel alone right now. I know this's terrifying for you, and unfair. Can you talk to me, please? Can you eat something?"

Lorian lifted one leg over the windowsill. She'd once climbed out of this very window to the clock tower above. When they'd found her, her father had slashed her palms. Everything seemed so much easier as a thirteen-year-old. "I have, and I'm alright now." She dared a peek down the four stories and closed her eyes. She wasn't that high up. She wasn't. "I'll be okay."

"Do you need anything from me right now? What can I do to help?"

She swung the rest of her body out of the window. Vertigo hit her like a crashing wave. She wrapped both arms around the tied-up blankets and gave them a firm tug. "No. You've done enough for me this week, and I do appreciate all that you've done." She put more of her weight on the bedsheet ladder, then more. "Go tell my mother and father that...I'm contemplating coming down."

"Oh, you are?" Missus Sharma asked, hopeful yet confused. "Let me bring them up."

"I-I'll need a minute," she pressed, hoping her voice wouldn't travel. "Do give me that, okay, Missus Sharma?"

"Of course, Your Highness. Oh, their Majesties will be so thrilled."

"I'll bet," Lorian muttered under her breath, and looked down. What was four stories, really, other than a two-second drop to your painful death?

She bit her lower lip, said a prayer to any God that would hear her, and let gravity take her down.

Her boot snagged on a jutting brick. She anticipated hitting the ground but didn't expect the dizziness once she hit the Earth. Her feet gave out from underneath her and she rolled over like a turtle. Ether looked down at her, chuffing.

Lorian stayed on the ground, fingers curling into the cold grass. She counted the eerie seconds of silence. Every time, someone in the palace knew when she acted out. She'd get caught, reformed into what her father wanted.

Nobody came. Missus Sharma didn't run to her bedroom window and call out for her. No patrolling officer asked what she was doing.

She breathed in fresh air, then slowly lifted herself up with her horse. She pulled on her reins and waited. She climbed onto Ether's back and waited.

Nobody was coming.

Nobody knew she was here.

Lucia had been killed, and Lorian had taken her first step.

She blinked back the tears. She didn't know what had brought them on. Her cutting her hair, her knowing that this one decision might strip her away from everyone she loved for months, years. If this worked, if she pulled everything off, she might never see them again. Beatrice, Carmine, her mother, Missus Sharma, the maids and officers who'd raised her, her father...

She violently turned her head away and broke Ether into a gallop. She tore through the gardens, through the first gate. A lone officer on duty hadn't been expecting anyone to pass through here and certainly wasn't prepared to stop a galloping mare running past him. He hadn't been expecting to see Lorian bounding for freedom, crying.

She knew *she* hadn't. Isn't this what she'd wanted? To be free from a marriage to a man she'd met three, possibly four times in her life? To be free from her father's expectations of being a subservient princess and to finally do what she wanted to do?

She ran Ether as fast as she could into the Roman night. Whatever she was feeling, tonight, she was Lorian. And tonight, she was unshackled.

Chapter 3: Meeting of the Minds

The second Aida stepped off the boat, she was struck with awe, an intense yearning of something grander than she'd ever thought was possible.

Then the seasickness sullied the occasion, but she wouldn't let her bodily issues mar this once in a lifetime experience.

You could *feel* when you entered Rome, when you officially made it to the country you'd been dreaming about. The air was different, the energy warmer. Unlike Bělico, which sprawled out into farm valleys and snow-capped mountains with the occasional farm, Roma was anything but. The people here had a place to be. They hauled barrels of water onto carriages, they sang for money, they bartered and sold their wares with the utmost power to their actions. The streets always seemed to be *moving*, something Aida had sought for in Bělico. But as a Bělican bumpkin, she didn't know how to hold herself in the space.

After exiting the carriage that brought her deeper into the city, Aida kept herself small, the grip on her cane and rucksacks making her hands sweat. The buildings were ancient and tall, and the noise overwhelmed her to the point of freezing her in place. She knew there were taverns near the center of the city, which was where she was going to sleep until the semester started, but why couldn't she move to find them? All at once, it felt like people were staring at her and ignoring her, like she was an uninteresting problem they couldn't be bothered to solve.

She took a breath, leveled her weight onto her cane, and carried on.

The architecture was dazzling. Rich period houses with visible timber frames and red roofs, cottages built around markets selling fish and sugary sweets. Unlike her time as a child, when she thought food was free and people were kind, she now knew what to use her money for and bought cheap food to keep herself alive.

The streets were decorated in triangular pennant flags, not for a festival, but to preserve traditions, and in the center of the intersections, written on that rich paper Aida fancied, were illustrations of that princess that went missing.

Aida heard Lucia's name whispered in the streets. Women with their hands over their mouths. Men with their hands on their hips, nodding about the obvious as to why she'd left. There were officers walking around everywhere, the men in the red jackets and black hats who kept Roma safe. They patrolled the streets with vigilant eyes, waiting to spot the hidden princess in her wedding dress.

An arranged marriage. Aida didn't know much about the people of Aldaí or their prince, Zaahir. He sounded like an average fellow with above-average values. Though, if she were to re-examine the predicament, she couldn't blame the princess for escaping such a marriage. If Aida had been arrange married, she too would've run, though probably not the day of. The girl must've either been a juggernaut for chaos, or an incredibly indecisive person.

The streets winded and were made of cobblestone that Eve herself must've walked. It was hard discerning which parts of the city belonged to Siina and which streets had been swallowed up by Roma after the city-state's destruction. Down certain roads, the city had white, ancient columns, fountains with Circa's statue atop them, and even a few buildings preserved from the Classical Era. They must've been 1,000 years old, so close to Queen Eve's timeline yet too far away for her to have ever seen them. Aida would've had to plan a full day just to explore.

No true Roman paid attention to the history around them, but the tourists were looking up at the columns with the same fervor as Aida. She would've dipped into the depths of the infamous Catacombs that lay underneath her feet, but she couldn't make a spectacle of herself. She saw Visatorre roaming the streets, those with the circles over their forehead and those who were hiding them in head wrappings. Most looked unfortunate, dirty. Some were begging for bronze lyria. Aida gave them what she could, knowing she should've kept all of it for herself, being that she was, in a sense, homeless as well.

As she toured the shops and eyed sugar bread cooling off in bakeries, she came across a deserted shop with its windows boarded up and door signs dangling. It looked like it hadn't been touched in years, so she rested against its walls to catch her breath. How far had she made it, two kilometers? It was another three to the nearest taverns. Should she've called for another carriage? Would they stop for her? She needed to read up more about the unspoken rules in Roma, not ones from a millennia ago.

She went to clean off her glasses when a figure in white caught her eye.

The poor beggar resembled more of a pile of laundry than a woman in need. She was hidden in a white cloak that covered everything but her shoeless feet and face.

Aida walked up closer.

The woman's eyes were completely bound by bandages. She wasn't injured—they weren't bloody or stained—they were just to show the public that she simply did not have eyes.

Taking in the woman's differences, Aida made her presence known and offered her the coins. She helped the woman take it. "Here," she said, "it's ten bronze lyria."

The woman lifted her head, showing Aida a wide, wicked smile that reached from ear to ear. Her teeth were stunningly white for being homeless. They were almost blue.

Aida just nodded and left quickly. Roma was incredibly different from Bělico. It was grand as well as poor. Interesting as well as confusing.

She couldn't imagine what she'd find near the palace, and the Colosseum.

Where Siina once lay.

— ✧ —

Students were allowed into Durante Academy a day before classes officially started. This was mostly for students and their families to tour the campus and feast in the dining hall together. Aida had no family to see her off and she'd already known everything about the campus, so she'd taken to moving in without any spectacle. Alone. Up four flights of stairs. Without anyone to help her.

It was fine. She was fine. It didn't matter that nobody helped her or that her mother hadn't come looking for her. It'd been two weeks, sure, and maybe communication between Bělico and Roma would take that long. And it could've snowed, so the post might've been halted.

Maybe her mother hadn't searched for her, and who cared? Finally, Aida had become unburdened by the weight of family life. It was all she'd ever wanted.

She only wished, against her better judgement, that she had somebody to pay and help her. She'd spent most of her savings on lodging at a nearby inn before the Academy opened. She would've paid for the help with what little money she had left, but she was carrying the weight of every Visatorre in Roma City. Out of the 2,500 people attending this Academy, she'd sniffed out that six of those 2,500 students were Visatorre. .2 percent. Ten years ago, no Visatorre had the rights to attend higher education. She couldn't let this opportunity be tainted by her own selfishness.

Stepping onto the soil of the Durante Academy didn't feel real, like she was stepping into a painting. It was built up like the Roman Palace, with arches and red brick holding centuries' worth of knowledge. It'd been built at the turn of the Neoclassical Era—the Era they were in now—but it was still more than 200 years old. It'd been named Scoppio Erutus Academy in honor of the first king of Roma, but then King Durante had been so arrogant, he coerced his wife to rename a historic foundation after himself. What Aida would do if she met that man.

She touched the iron-clad gates, then where her acceptance letter was in her bag. She'd done it. All without her family's help.

She'd taken all but four steps through the Academy gates when she felt her body tense. She'd familiarized herself with her normal bodily aches apart from these ones. When she felt like this, when the world shifted around her like someone was tilting it with both hands, that's when she knew. That's when she knew a jump was about to occur.

The first thing she did was take off her glasses. Nothing came with you when you teleported into the past, not even your clothes, so it did right by you that you secured any loose valuables or breakables on your person before you left. Stumbling across piles of clothes was commonplace and a jackpot for thieves.

When she travelled backwards into time, her only concern was someone stealing her books and throwing them into a fountain.

A loud zap of energy stole her from the present. The travelling itself didn't hurt, not at first, but it left you feeling floaty. That's the only way she could describe it. You left the Earth that grounded you and were brought somewhere, somehow, against your will and into Circa's hands. It was magic, Aida knew that, but everything magical about going into the past was robbed when you knew it'd leave you with a bloody nose or worse.

She dropped into a forest. Nothing spectacular, just an endless sea of unclaimed land and pine cones. She would've preferred something a little more interesting like a town or even a house. When you went back in time, you couldn't interact with anything around you, so if you jumped into someone's room, there you were, stuck until someone from that time period happened to open a door or window big enough for you to squeeze through. Open spaces like this, while bereft of anything eye-catching, made Aida thankful that she hadn't jumped into a crying baby's room or carriage.

She wandered. It was all you could do in the moment. She heard the birds chirping, the skittering of squirrels and rabbits who didn't know a Visatorre was meters away from them. She felt the wind through the leaves and branches, but it was strange, distant. And smell, that was something you had trouble with in the past. You were there, you were exploring, but you were a ghost. You couldn't be seen or talked to, you weren't acknowledged. It was better, in that sense, if you came across something important. A meeting between generals, an unsolved murder with a new eyewitness. You could learn about the world in a way most people couldn't.

And all she got was a forest. Just. Her. Luck.

She did come across something prominent in her travels: a crystal lake that sparkled with the bright blue sky. It reflected the white clouds like a mirror. Frogs leapt atop lily pads. And curled within the lake's natural perimeter lived a cabin that looked like it'd seen better days. It was modern, giving Aida context as to how far she'd jumped back, but some of the windows had cracks in it, and a natural ecosystem was growing where its lawn should've been. It looked cozy, if not a little worn.

The sound of hammering skipped across the lake. Without her glasses, Aida could only make out that two people were sitting on the roof, patching up a hole.

She circled the lake. She heard them speaking, but she couldn't make out their words or accents, leaving her lost as to who they were and where she was. She almost called out to them before remembering neither of them would hear her.

She tried anyway. "Hey," she called out. "Where are you in the world?"

Just as she was able to make out their faces, she felt her body being pulled back into the present. She tried to step out of the pull, to find out more about this cabin, but no Visatorre could do that. They could only go where Circa desired them to go and left when Circa wanted them gone.

When she fell back to the present, reality slammed down with her. Her aches, the weight of being alive. She was a mass that affected the world, and it sucked and hurt. She was dizzy and it was hard to keep her eyes from crossing, but all in all, she was fine, meaning that she'd only travelled a short way for an even shorter time.

Then she tried to sit up and immediately crashed back down, her legs too tired to hold herself up. Yeah, she wasn't dead, but check back in two hours when she had a bag of ice on her lower back and a migraine beginning to form.

The Sun had long since set. Night bugs chirped from the bushes and most of the lanterns had been doused. With the Moon's help, she patted the ground for her glasses, and found them and her bags, shoes. They were all still there, but she'd have to double-check to make sure. She'd needed to know her books were still with her, otherwise, what was the point of all this? If she lost her journals...

"Miss, are you alright?"

She lunged for her dress. One-pieces were the easiest for Visatorre to wear to regain their modesty, or what they had left of it, but someone had already seen her, and they sounded like her age. What a great first impression.

The person coming up to her was a blur without her glasses, but she saw that they were tall—everyone was tall to her—and they had blond hair and fair skin, wearing...

An officer uniform.

Just. Her. Fucking. Luck.

"Here, let me assist you," they said, this time with a noticeable lisp.

"I can assist myself fine, thank you. Sir," she added. She had to watch her mouth around here. She couldn't get written up for being too crass with an officer.

She got dressed in front of him. She didn't worry about her undergarments or socks, but she needed to cover her body in front of this person.

A piece of fabric draped over her shoulders: his jacket.

"Please, allow me," he said, and now, he was way too close. She had a thing about that, about people touching her without her consent.

"Not helping." She shrugged it off to button up her dress. "Give a woman some privacy?"

"Oh, of course." He turned with his hands behind his back. "My apologies. I was keeping watch over your things in case you came back. I heard a loud *zap*, then saw these clothes on the ground. I thought it'd be best to help you once you returned."

"Were you expecting me to disappear?" She flicked out her glasses and put them back on.

"No, I just didn't want you to be frightened once you returned."

He was indeed an officer, wearing that gaudy nutcracker fit the crown made all officers wear—a red jacket studded with gold buttons, black boots that reached their knees—but he was an officer in training: no medals or aiguillettes to signify rank, a short rapier attached to his belt as opposed to the long ones real officers used. He was another young fool pulled into a system to serve a monarchy who hated its people.

His green eyes shot down at her naked legs. A hint of red scratched across his long face. "Forgive me, Miss. This's the first time I've seen a time traveller jump into the past. It's like you were there, and then you were taken away."

"A time traveller." Not a Visatorre, their true moniker, but a simplified version of what they were. Rich, non-Visatorre called them that. Aida saw his whole life: sheltered, spoiled, kept away from real life. Most Visatorre weren't rich, so you either saw them on the streets, working in the fields, or doing manual labor to get by. Given that, and by how clean and posh this boy sounded, he'd probably never fought a day in his life.

He stepped back, taking her in from a different angle, then gasped and knelt down to collect her things. "It must be hard," he said, "disappearing like that and all." He handed her her shoes, taking note of her right one that weighed heavier than the other. He checked inside for any rocks.

"It's fine," she said, and put them on. If the cane didn't give away her ailments, her mismatched shoes would've. "The right one has a larger heel due to my limp. Keeps me balanced."

"Do you need help carrying anything?"

She sighed. She didn't need this kid's pity tonight, but her leg *was* beginning to pulse with pain. Sometimes, it radiated its anger up her spine and left her toes numb and body with feverish aches. This boy didn't need to know that, he didn't need to know anything about her. Lucky for him that he'd just seen a part of herself that she hadn't meant anyone to see. She picked up her bags, her upper lip curled.

"Please, Miss, it's no problem at all," he said. "I can help you take them to your dorm if you'd like. Which house is it?"

"...Willows," she said, but she was nervous about telling a boy where she now lived.

"That's across the campus. Here." He swiftly picked up all three of her bags with one arm, as well as her books and uniforms she'd received earlier that week. The Academy almost sent them to her stepmother's house before she'd intervened.

Aida stepped away from him. "Why're you helping me?"

"I'm an officer."

"But..." She sighed again. It was too late and she was too tired to argue. "If you do anything insidious, I'll scream so loud, I'll make you deaf."

"Oh, please don't think so ill of me, Miss..."

"Aida Mirko," she said, and curtsied. "What a first impression to make, 'ey?"

The boy chuckled, then bowed, a hand over his stomach. "Lorian Ashwell. A pleasure to meet you."

Aida started walking towards her dorm, her bloomers tucked underneath her arm. "What a bastard of a way to see your first jump."

"I've heard many different tales of it, no doubt. My father is rather...orthodox when it comes to the views of time travellers."

"So he's a cock."

Lorian burst into a laugh that Aida couldn't help but read. Slight dimples, with bright white teeth and hidden freckles around his scrunched nose. "How bold of you! I've never heard a woman speak as crassly as you do."

"Must not meet many girls."

"That is true, yes. Where are you from? Your accent is quite unique."

Aida arched a brow at him. "And you call *me* bold. First, you ask for my name before giving your own, then you ask where I'm from based on my accent? What about *your* accent? Wouldn't it be invasive if I asked you about that?"

Lorian lost a step behind her and touched his lips. "My lisp isn't something I can control, Miss Mirko, though I have been taking speech therapy to correct it. I'm sorry if it offends you."

Aida cocked her head at the sudden dip into aggressiveness. "When did I say anything about your lisp? I ain't that rude despite what people think of me. I said 'accent'. You speak proper, so one can assume you came from wealth, but I wasn't gonna say that out loud."

"Oh." Lorian's smile returned. "You are quite something, Miss Mirko."

"I get that a lot. And you just met me, *Lorian Ashwell*, so cool it with the conclusions."

"Do forgive me. I haven't met many people my age. I'm still getting used to the acclimation."

"Were you living under a rock up until now?"

"You could say that, yes."

Aida harrumphed. Rich *and* ignorant. She didn't know a worse combination.

But she couldn't knock him. He was kind, doing this for her. Her hands almost relaxed out of their fists, but she kept her guard up. She still had her cane to dig into his eye sockets if he fucked up.

He helped her all the way up the spiral staircase, stopping whenever she needed to. He hadn't mentioned her cane or how she sometimes walked into him due to her balance problem. For a boy who hadn't met a Visatorre before, he was taking it better than most. Most threw questions, insults. Rocks, if they were so primitive.

Her dorm room was small and cornered on the edge of the building, giving her an extra window that showed off the nearby city. She also had a writing desk, poster bed, wardrobe, and armchair. Her radiator had been polished and her bedsheets smelled of freshly cleaned linen. It didn't smell like her yet, but it would, in time.

No longer would she shiver upstairs in a house she didn't belong in, waiting for a better tomorrow. She'd finally woken up from that nightmare.

She turned to Lorian, who'd invited himself in.

"You can go," she told him. "Don't need you sniffing my clothes and seeing my journals."

"Journals?" He dropped her bags. One of her thickest journals fell to his boot.

"Hey, watch it."

"My apologies." He picked it up and smiled at the drawings she'd carved into the old binding.

She'd gotten that journal from school in which to write assignments, but she'd used it to write down her actual thoughts instead. In weeks, she'd torn out the older pages and spliced in new ones about her interests in history. Timelines, character sheets, her own theories about what she thought might've happened to Eve and her city-state. It was near bursting now, the original pages yellowed and loose, with thousands of furious writings smudged around crude drawings.

Lorian picked up a dried flower she'd bookmarked between the pages. "What a beautiful memory."

She grimaced. He didn't even know why she'd placed it there.

He didn't know, yet he still called it beautiful, this hand-made book that meant so much to her.

"Thanks," she said. "It's what I do when my brain isn't broke."

"Is it for school?"

"No. It's my thoughts on history."

"Which part?"

"Everything, I guess? But mostly Roma. Mostly Siina."

"May I?" He went to open the first page but waited for Aida's consent.

She didn't know. Back home, her sisters didn't care for her work, and her mother hated that she wasted her time writing when she could've been working.

No, she had to stop thinking that way. That place was no longer a home, it was a place, a memory.

"If you can read my handwriting," she said.

He crossed his ankles as he flipped through the first few pages, skipping over the founding of Roma, then Roma City, then Siina, then the erasure of Siina. He focused on her doo-dles of all things, the clothing styles and landscapes she thought Siina would've had based on paintings she'd studied. Not that she was embarrassed because she wasn't, she just thought words told a better picture than the, well, pictures.

When he didn't say anything, Aida took to decorating her space to fit her needs. She stuffed her clothes into her drawers and organized her books onto the shelves. She stacked her playbooks on the table and centered a figure of a glass balle-rina on the windowsill. After getting everything out of her bags and with Lorian still reading her brain, Aida caved to her desires and lit a blunt she'd pre-rolled for the trip.

When she struck her lighter and realized that there was, shockingly, still an officer in her room, she took the blunt out of her mouth. "Fuck."

Lorian checked that it was indeed a blunt and not a cigarette that might've gotten her off easier. Then he chuckled that damn chuckle of his. Was it irritating? She couldn't tell. "Fuck, indeed."

"Oh, come on, don't nark on me. I thought you were cool."

"And what if I do? It's in my job description that I relay all illegal activity to Dean Falco, and I obtained this job on a whim. I wouldn't want to disappoint anyone."

"Nor would I. I have a reputation to uphold. So." She crossed her arms, joint in-between two fingers. "Whatcha gonna do, officer?"

Lorian's smile widened, something Aida noticed about him more than anything, and he held out his hand. "I've been meaning to let off some steam."

Aida smiled back as she handed him her joint. "Haven't we all?"

——◇——

The hours kind of...passed, which was rare for Aida. She usually had her daily chores that dictated her day. Wake up, feed the animals, make breakfast, do dishes. Work, clean, attend. Only at night could she use her sleeping hours to do what she wanted to do, and that was to get high and study her craft.

Things were different with Lorian. He wasn't an officer. She didn't believe it. Officers were prissy rich boys who wanted to fight because of their affluent childhoods. Lorian didn't give off that vibe. He didn't reprimand her about the blunt, and he was *interested* by her take on history. She ended up rambling about her life, her mother, her sisters, her desire to become a historian, and she didn't fear that she was speaking too loudly or too much. What was this, a set-up? Good things rarely came her way, especially in the form of people. Maybe it was a dream.

"So, you've tried Nectar before, I reckon?" she asked. They were both on her bed, but she didn't feel embarrassed by that, either. Lorian wasn't. His cheeks had returned to their normal shade, though his eyes, like hers, were a glossy red.

"I have dabbled in it, yes, though I'm more used to drinking it rather than smoking it."

"Isn't there less of a high when you drink it?" she asked. Nectar was the golden honey that came overseas from Aldaí. When mixed with the Aldaían poppy flower that often grew near the beehives, it left you with an incredible high that could last for hours.

"Yes, but I lived in a household where it was frowned upon to smoke," Lorian said, "so I snuck it in with luncheons and dinners. I feel like my mother knew about it, but as long as my father wasn't aware, I was fine."

"And the raw shit is more expensive," she noted.

He shrugged and motioned for her joint, which she gladly passed to him. "My household was...it was fine, you know? Once you strip away its policies and protocols, we were whatever. But sometimes life's, like, you know, shit? Like it's *all* shit, like you can't get out of it, no matter what you do. You're always in the shit."

"I absolutely hear you," Aida said. "My mo'mma's the same way. When I become queen, all this? Changing immediately. Effective immediately. Life's not gonna be what we thought it was."

"Oh, *you're* going to be queen?" he asked.

"Absolutely."

"Good. You can take that shitty Lucia's place. Did you know she's missing? Can't find her. Never will."

"Wouldn't know. Don't follow the royal family now. Just their predecessors."

He paused. "Wait, you can't *become* a queen. You must be *born* into it, unless you marry someone who's high enough in *rank*, but why would you?" He kept using air quotes as he talked, like it wasn't obvious that that's how you became an official royal person. "Royal life sucks."

"I can take it. I ain't gonna be like those other two. One's off in Bĕlico, the other's off...somewhere."

"What if she were dead?"

Aida craned her neck over to Lorian.

He took another drag, his eyes half-closed. "Wouldn't it be nice if Lucia was dead?"

"The king and queen wouldn't think it."

"No?"

"Yeah. Hey, you know what? You don't seem like an officer to me."

Lorian dropped his hand. "I am."

"How, then?"

"I received a recommendation from His Majesty The King that the dean stupidly took. It was very generous, and I'm not letting the opportunity of a lifetime go to waste."

"But—"

"I'm an officer."

Aida glanced back over to him, curious that *that* was what got his reaction. Here she thought he was a prissy officer, but now, not only was he a stoner, he had a mouth.

He was looking over at her, his cheek pressed against the ruffled covers. "I'm an officer now," he said, adding on the adverb. "I know I may not be as refined or as skilled as the others, but I'm trying my best, and I want nothing more than to show what I can do."

Aida's lips parted. Finally, something she understood. "Good," she told him. "Maybe you'll be the officer to finally fuck over the king and make Roma a better place, because I know I'm going to be the historian to rewrite this country's history."

"I thought you were going to become a queen?"

"Same difference. I know so much more than any historian in Roma, and I'm going to change the world with what I know."

"What *do* you know, Miss Mirko?"

She got up and started pacing. "Well, I know that Queen Eve's full name is Eve Hyuang Costa, 'Costa' coming from her Siinan heritage, and 'Hyuang' coming from a province in Aldaí, specifically from the eastern provinces, meaning she was multi-racial. Not many historians bring that up, but I've cross-referenced diary entries from King Julius II and his wife where they both cite her middle name in passing, and how she truly was 'a blossoming flower', which is what 'Hyuang' translates to. Her full name means 'a blossoming flower in the river of life'. Isn't that pretty? They also wash her mother's heritage from the history texts. I've even read texts where they change her surname from Zhao to Zangari. Isn't that messed up?"

Lorian nodded along to everything. "It is, but, pray tell, who is Eve?"

Aida's jaw dropped.

"Did I offend—"

"Yes!" She swiped back her joint. "How *dare* you say that to me? All of my work rests on that woman's shoulders. She's the reason I want to be a historian because the history books have her history wrong—No, sit down," she said as he began to stand. He plopped back down. "Unless you have somewhere to be at—" She checked the watch that wasn't on her wrist. "God knows what time it is, you're sitting your ass down and listening to me."

Lorian immediately did as told. That blush returned to his cheeks. "Please, continue," he begged, and she did.

She spent the next two hours talking to him about Queen Eve's reign. She pointed out her upbringing and her beliefs, and how her older sister was supposed to have married King Meyeso but Eve had persuaded him to marry her instead. She was passionate, outspoken, energetic, youthful, and she never let any ruling stop her from achieving what she craved. And she'd done it all as a Visatorre, before the Roman king had murdered her for allegedly murdering his wife.

"Isn't that fucked?" Aida asked, needing some sort of validation from this boy.

Lorian continued staring at her. His hand stayed on his lips.

"Well? Isn't it?"

He kept staring at her.

"What?"

"I like the way you speak."

She faltered. Scratch anyone listening to her rambles, nobody had ever told her they liked the way she spoke, or thought, placing value on her brain.

She pulled down on her dress cuffs, feeling exposed. "Okay."

"You know so much."

"It's one of the things I pride myself in."

"Do you pride yourself in many things?"

"Of sorts."

"What about this?" He pointed his boot at her playbooks. *En Tempore Rose*. What a collection of playbooks."

"Whoa, wait." She invaded Lorian's personal space, the ends of her newly done braids tickling his nose. "You know about *Pinnacle Isle*?"

Lorian melted deeper into her bed. "Not the, uhm, book series, no. But I do enjoy the opera—"

"I *love* the book series!" Aida interrupted. "I have a first edition in my bag. What's your favorite chapter? Who's your favorite character? Mine's the Goddess, but Pinnacle is a close second, as is with Red Dragon, of course."

"Sorry, I only know the opera. My parents took me to see it when—"

"Oh!" Aida moaned. "Oh, for *shame*! For shame that Roman sensibilities have prevented you from indulging in the purest form of art that is *Pinnacle Isle* and the utter perfection of the hero's journey."

She stepped onto her bed. "Pinnacle, our orphan boy dropped on a desolate island. He thinks he's alone and so unbelievably screwed, but at the end of chapter three"—she pointed at the toy dragon Lorian had helped place on her shelf—"he finds a feral dragon being kept at the top of the island's tower. What's he to do, you might ask. Well, he's not alone on the island. Sempre, the Goddess, is also stranded on the island, and they, possibly with the help of Red Dragon and her babies, must find a way off the island before the summer storms come.

"How could you only indulge in the opera, a mere fanfare of what the books truly mean to us readers? Have you no shame, good Sir?"

Lorian looked Aida up and down. He sucked in his lips as he gave her a shrug. "Not really, no."

She pointed down at him. "You, Lorian Ashwell, are a fake fan, watching the enormously inaccurate opera instead of enjoying the pages of Pinnacle's and the Goddess' story. I need you to stay with me tonight so I can tell you the greatest story told on Roman soil. Do you hear me? You're staying with me."

"I wouldn't mind that in the slightest, Miss Mirko."

"It's Aida," she reminded him.

"Aida, then," he said, and she didn't know why, but she liked the way that sounded in his mouth.

Chapter 4: Aida's Second Letter

Aida flipped through the third history text she'd finished that week, trying to find any clues she'd missed. It was lunch time, so she'd yet again found herself in the campus library instead of the dining hall or open *piazzas* with the other students. Very few librarians walked this corner of the ancient building. She was able to eat her lunch of bread and butter in peace.

She pushed up her glasses as she leaned over her spine-broken books. It'd been three weeks since the semester started and she'd already had a head start on her future projects, giving her ample time to read up on her new home's history. One of the key aspects of wanting to get into Durante Academy was this library. More than 40,000 books archived. Everything from Pre-Classical recipes to first editions of history texts. She'd discovered a new biography on Eve's life. Her favorite color? Burgundy.

But she was getting nowhere today. Not only did this volume not have the answers she was searching for, there was a bug burrowing in her brain.

She hadn't spoken to Lorian since they first met. It shouldn't have mattered, being that he'd only done her a favor. She couldn't remember a lot about what they'd talked about because she'd gotten completely baked, but she remembered that they'd bonded, right? That's what people did, right? Or acquaintances at best. Her sisters often talked to one another about school, boys, girls. The actors they wanted to marry and what they wanted to be when they grew up. They'd never asked Aida about her passions, but this boy had. That had to account for something, didn't it?

So why hadn't they talked since?

And why the fuck did it bother her so much?

Someone giggled. Down the aisle of books, three girls from one of Aida's history classes were hiding. They had their hands cupped to their mouths as they whispered and pretended not to be looking at Aida. As a distant grandfather clock chimed for one, they ran off, their black dresses catching on their long legs.

Aida bit hard into her bread and chewed the tough crust so she couldn't hear her thumping heart.

It didn't bother her.

They didn't bother her.

Her stomach growled in upset, so she readied to leave. All she'd managed to find today was a new spelling of Queen Eve's name—"Eta," though scholars said this might've been a nickname used only by her loved ones—and, unfortunately, a new drawing of the Colosseum's interior, where Eve had taken her last fighting breath.

"Aida?"

She started. She knew that voice, and all of her nagging fears disappeared with her upset stomach.

Lorian bounded up the library steps two at a time to meet her. He was waving, like she wouldn't see an officer coming at her. Well, officer in training; she couldn't let him get a big ego around her. "There you are!" he said, and took off his hat in a bow. "Good afternoon. Did you have lunch yet?"

She shuffled her books together and wiped any sort of emotion from her face. "How do you keep finding me? Are you spying on me?"

"I heard that you enjoy spending your afternoons here, and I had a free hour to myself, so I came to find you." He looked around without his eyes catching on anything. "A little medieval here, is it not? Different from the upgraded buildings."

"A building built 200 years ago with history dating back to the Classical Era is medieval? *No.*"

He smiled that smile of his. "You have me there. So, have you learned anything more about Eve?"

She was surprised he remembered that. "Not much." She checked her notes. "People who loved her called her 'Eta', like how some Aldaíans call their spouses 'amar' for 'beloved'."

"Interesting. I didn't know that, and I've been taught a lot about Roman history. You know, I didn't know that she'd killed King Julius II's wife. I was taught *she'd* killed *him*."

"He killed himself a few days later from grief. That's what the books say, anyway. What books did you read from? I'd like to cross reference. Most books say the opposite." She started putting away her books. "Back when we were indulging in unfavorable substances, I pegged you as someone who didn't care much about history."

"I was...incapacitated at the time. I don't remember much of what happened. Please keep that night confidential. I don't want it harming either of our reputations."

"What, two young people enjoying one another's company with a natural reserve akin to morphine?"

"I mean two young people spending their time in… a woman's bedroom. At night. It's highly provocative, and I didn't mean anything by it."

"It *was* my dorm room, but sure."

"Please, don't think I'm immodest, Miss Mirko. Aida," he corrected when Aida gave him a look. "That had been my first day on the job. I'd…left my home quite suddenly not too long ago, and I was still getting my bearings. I sought only to do the right thing, though I did enjoy your company that evening."

"The evening spent with me talking *at* you for three hours straight about shit only I find interesting."

"On the contrary. I found much of what you told me quite interesting. I was true to my word about never meeting a person as outspoken as you are."

"Because the upbringing was that bad?"

He only nodded. "Very."

"Then that's something we have in common." She stood on her tiptoes to put away a book. Lorian went to help but stopped once he saw that she had it.

"Were you taught history in school?" Aida asked.

"In my teachings, yes. I didn't go to school, I was home-schooled. Why?"

"Because not many of us were lucky enough to be taught history. The good stuff. The shit that makes you think. A lot of what's done in Bělico is taught orally. That's how it was with me before I applied for secondary schooling. Some of the schools don't accept Visatorre into the school system. They're still stuck in the past. I was the only one in my graduating class. It's why I care so much."

"That's credible. Not many people our age are adamant about getting the word out. Most people learn what's needed to pass and forget the rest."

"It's what everyone should know. What else we gonna learn about? The current royals? Gag me, I can't stand them."

Lorian offered to place one of the books. Aida tried first before lending it to him.

"Do you know if...the Bĕlican queen has done anything?" Lorian asked. "You're from Bĕlico, right? Is she alright?"

"Queen Beatrice?" Aida asked. "Fuck no. I haven't seen her in person and I lived there all my life. She's like the queen here. Queen Rosalia."

"How so?"

Aida gave him a curious look before carrying on. He was in the royal guard, how did he not know about political affairs? "All they do is sit on the sidelines while their husbands do all the work, and it's foul work. Absolutely dreadful. If I were queen, I'd be like Queen Eve, who got shit done during her lifetime. Irrigation? Reconstructed. Trade routes from here to Aldaí? Reinvented. She'd helped to fund the first school for the blind, did you know that? She wanted to help people who couldn't see during a time where eyeglasses had yet to be invented. Roman scholars would lead you to believe the good and loyal Romans did all that, but no. It was done by a queen whose city no longer exists. I'd honor her by doing everything she couldn't do and more. I'd rework the entire system of the world."

"Will you now?" Lorian asked.

She tasted a tang of sarcasm on his tongue. She fought against it and stared into his eyes. It was hard, doing that with some people, but not so much with him. "Yeah, I will."

"How?"

"I'd fix the school systems. All children deserve to be taught, and it'd be the easiest change from a financial standpoint. Aldaí is progressive when it comes to this, so we can leave that to Prince Zaahir and that new princess he married. What was her name again? Beatrice and Lu..."

"I-I agree with you," Lorian said. "Aldaí is very progressive."

"So then, if we can work out a secure alliance with them, we can work on local modernization. We can show that the crown gives a fuck about us. We don't see the royals, ever."

"They do make public appearances from time to time," he defended.

"Yeah, bullshit, I've never seen them. If anything, they only visit the biggest, most influential cities that're pouring lyria back into their pockets."

Lorian shrugged in agreement. He looked like he had more to say on the matter but kept quiet so as not to interrupt her.

"So, I'd make them do more public showings. It might anger the extremists, but monarchies have to show that they're fighting for us. It's exactly what Eve did in Siina. She was such a vocal, public figure, visiting street markets and meeting with the people. And how do they do that?" She pointed at Lorian.

"I haven't the faintest—"

"By listening to the people, yes, thank you. Open up more administrations and city councils so the people can be more in charge of their fates than the fucking officers and constables frightening us into submission. No offense."

"None taken."

She looked down at one of her history texts. "We're in a golden age of the world. No one is fighting one another. We're not wasting hundreds of gold lyria on war strategies or extra officers. The last one was back in, what 1137? Twenty-two years ago? Back when we were babes? And that was just a fourteen-month fling where important Bělican crops weren't being regulated across the sea because of trade agreements. It left Roma without sugar for nearly a year. You see, *I* could change the world if I was given the *chance*, but I can't *do* that because I have a fucking *circle* on my forehead!"

Her voice travelled across the library, down the stairs and through the aisles of hidden knowledge. Lorian pressed his thin lips together, pretending he was an officer for the crown and did not enjoy breaking the rules.

Aida cleared her throat. She was getting ahead of herself again. She was going to push him away by being herself. She dialed it back. "The only chance I have is to become a historian. I might not be able to get a job right away, but when I graduate with a diploma from this Academy, I know someone out there will take me seriously."

Lorian gave that considerable thought before speaking. "Well, for what it's worth, I take you very seriously."

"Course you do. The first time we met, I was fucking naked."

"E-excuse me, I averted my gaze. I have values."

"Like a true gentleman."

Lorian opened his mouth to say more, then caught on whatever she'd said and smiled. "Yeah, I suppose so."

She didn't know what she had with this officer in training and why they clicked as well as they did. He was charismatic, helpful, charming, kind, easygoing. Everything she wasn't. She hadn't seen him in action, but he was probably good at his job, and had more friends than he knew what to do with. Total opposites in every regard, aside from the fact that they could share a blunt and be content with being near each other.

She frowned, not knowing why that made her so sad.

The wooden double doors leading to the main halls opened, and one of Aida's advisors, Mister Omar, came in. He had a note in hand and was sweating from getting from his office to the library before lunch period ended.

Lorian stepped back from Aida. "Well, I should be off, then." He bowed. "Farewell, Miss Mirko, Mister Omar."

"Farewell," Mister Omar said, and waited for him to leave before speaking. "Miss Mirko, I just received a letter from the dean. He said he needs to speak with you as soon as you're available."

"What does he want to talk about?" Aida asked. "I was getting back to my classes. You can't penalize me for choosing to spend my lunch break here."

"I don't believe it's about your elongated breaks in this great Rosalia Library," he said, trying to be funny and failing. "Uh, no. Well, here. You can read it for yourself, but it came with a message saying to come to him before the end of the day."

Aida took the letter.

In Regards to the Termination of Aida Mirko's
6-Year Scholarship

Something inside of her, something she'd been building up with little hope, split open and leaked a foul rot into the pit of her stomach. Her hands went cold, her face hot. She strained her eyes to see if anything more had been written on it, but that was it. A simple declaration that took all of her dreams and threw them out like an unwanted child.

She ran. Fighting on her cane to make her go faster, she broke around the corner and ran out of the library. She wouldn't read the rest of the letter. There wasn't any time. She'd go to the dean and fight. She'd demand her right to be here and fight. They wouldn't take this knowledge away from her, not now.

She pushed through the pain and jogged down the marble steps from the cloister to the open courtyard. Here, students in black and white uniforms continued their lunch in peace. Girls braided flower crowns and boys tackled one another to the grass like toddlers. A couple flirted with one another near the well in the center of the yard. Aida ran past them all. This was a mistake. It had to be.

The dean's office was one of the older buildings covered in ivy beside a church that students seldom used. At the front gates, two lion statues acted as guards for the door. Two actual officers stood watch over the building at all hours of the day. One yawned.

Aida forced the wheeze back into her throat. "I have…a letter from the dean. Open the gates. Please," she added.

The two men looked at one another, then shrugged and went to open the gate.

She barreled in before they fully opened the gates and knocked on the door. Beside the dean's home was a carriage engraved with the Queen's Lions: a constable carriage.

"Shit." She knocked louder. "Dr. Falco, it's Aida Mirko. I'm a freshman who started this year. You called to speak to me. May I please come in?"

The door unlocked twice, and one of the dean's maids welcomed her with a bow. "Hello, Miss. What was it that you wished to—?"

Aida let herself in.

"Excuse me, Miss!"

It was a magnificent house that smelled of syrup and old collections. Books on shelves she could never reach and busts of naked men and women from a tainted royal line. Walking around a gaudy zebra pelt, Aida snaked through the main room and knocked on the door labeled with Dr. Falco's name.

It opened upon her third knock.

The dean was sitting in a large chair behind a mahogany table. Around him were papers and texts with the map of the world centered between two windows. Bělico in the west, Aldaí in the east, and Roma centered amongst it all, even though the Earth was a sphere and nobody was in the center of anything.

Between Aida and the dean stood three men. Two wore the same uniforms as Lorian, but their ages and medals prized them as actual officers.

The other man, one with curly, brown hair and a short mustache, wore golden aiguillettes and sashes across his jacket, and a large, black hat.

The Constable looked down at Aida as if she were a sheep ready to be slaughtered. He set down the document he was reading. One hand went to his waist belt, to his rapier handle which shone gold in the sunlight. "Welcome, Miss Mirko," he said.

Aida gulped at him knowing her name. Constables were leaders of twenty, sometimes thirty men in Roma, and with the air of stuffy egoism on him, this man was probably high in rank.

She kept down her fear. "Why was my scholarship terminated? What have I done wrong?"

"Have a seat, my dear."

She didn't.

The Constable waited. "My name is Carmello Carmine, right-hand Constable to Her Majesty The Queen. Please."

She didn't.

The Constable narrowed his eyes, then focused on her cane. "I've been informed that your scholarship to this school was for six years based on your excellence in history and language as well as your race and upbringing."

"And?" she said, itching to fight him on how he said that.

"*And* a law has just been put into place to make amendments to that initial proposition. Under the new, current law—"

"What law?" she interrupted. "I haven't heard anything about a new law."

"The law," he said, "stipulating that it is unlawful to allow a student favorable advantages to their acceptance to Roman academies based on their race."

Aida looked over the letter. "So what does that mean? I'm still enrolled into the school, aren't I? I earned it. I left everything I had for this."

"The dean and I were going over your academic records and attendance rates."

"I've been to every class!" she said. "I even started doing extra credit!"

"And," he said, ignoring her, "unfortunately, we've concluded that your grades do not meet the qualifications to earn the scholarship for the next six years. Unless you can come up with the funds to attend this coming year, which we've estimated would be 1,510 gold lyria, we cannot enroll you into Durante Academy at this time."

Aida tried doing the math in her head. She thought it cost 1,450 gold lyria per semester, not 1,500 and change. Her mother didn't even make that in a year with the farm. For six more years...

She dropped her head. "I don't have that kind of money."

"Then I'm sorry to say that—"

"But that's not fair!" she exploded. It was like fighting with her mother. Her eyes were watering.

"—that after this semester—"

"No!"

"You will no longer be able to attend Durante Academy as a student."

Aida tried to read her letter for a loophole, but she couldn't think. No matter how much she fought to be an equal, it wouldn't happen. It's what Queen Eve had fought and died for. It's what people like her had fought for for centuries and died for. All because of these monarchs and rules bent to make the world more hateful.

In history, they said that the Visatorre queen had killed the king's wife. Others said she'd killed the king. Aida hadn't believed either statement, but now, feeling the anger pulse in her eyes, she wouldn't have blamed her for wiping people like this off the fucking planet.

Holding back tears, Aida threw her walking cane at the Constable, spooking him backwards. "Fuck you! Fuck you and the crown you serve! All of you deserve to be buried in the Catacombs for the amount of shit you do for us!"

"Good Gods, Miss!" he said. "Control yourself!"

The other officers unsheathed their rapiers, but the Constable held out his hand to make them put them away. "Miss, do you realize what you've done?"

She spat on the ground, cursed their mothers, and left, tears steaming from her bloodshot eyes.

"Miss!"

It wasn't fair. It wasn't *fair*. She'd worked for years to get here, she'd dedicated her life to it. She was to uncover new information she'd put together about Eve for this stupid country, but she hadn't done shit.

Her mother had been right.

She left the dean's house through the back near the horse-drawn carriages. She didn't want those damn officers seeing her like this, and she didn't want to be seen leaving the dean's home in tears.

The chickens in a nearby coop clucked at her. Hens pecked at the ground while their rooster counterparts watched from the roof.

The door to their coop was left open, letting them roam the contained land.

Aida cast a seething glare at the house behind her, then at the carriages left unattended.

She started collecting her throwing eggs.

Chapter 5: One of the Boys

As Lorian walked into an empty classroom and waited for Aida and Mister Omar to leave, she pressed her back into the door and utterly lost it.

She covered her mouth with her gloved hands. She'd done it. She'd finally talked to Aida again. And she hadn't been as crass with her as she'd been. The first time had been a complete disaster. With Aida being naked and Lorian open-mouthed staring at her, the curves of her wide hips and ass, her breasts, her face, her *eyes*. Gods help her, she'd never seen a woman's body so openly before. All she'd wanted to do that night was let Aida slam her down and do unspeakable things to her virgin body, yet what had Aida wanted? To talk about fantasy novels and a queen who'd been dead for 1,200 years. What had Lorian even said that'd led her up to Aida's bedroom? She'd need to write it down for reference.

Despite being betrothed for more than half of her life, Lorian hadn't a clue how courting worked. The girls she'd met in the palace were diplomatic and groomed to please her, all peachy smiles and saying whatever they needed to make her happy. She'd tried to court an Aldaían knight a few years back, but she'd only earned her name and her preference of cakes before they'd parted ways.

Aida's attitude was so inappropriate that it would've sent Lorian's father into hysterics. And she wanted her for that. She wanted to crack her open and explore her mind and passions and give it back to her ten-thousand fold.

Lorian dragged her hands down her face. Maybe she'd buy her a history book or ticket to *En Tempore Rose*. The official one, the one they performed in the Colosseum. She'd have to schedule a trip to the city center. She'd wear a hooded cloak.

After Aida ran off somewhere, Lorian re-entered the library and backtracked for the books she'd been putting away. They were old and leather-bound, with yellow pages that smelled of mothballs: *History of Roma: From the Perspective of King Julius II to His People* and *Hidden Dangers of Visatorre in Roman History*.

Lorian put that last one back. Aida was brave to read about history that was so rarely taught in class. Lorian had read about it behind Missus Sharma's back. She'd learned about the lost city-state of Siina and the belligerent queen who killed one of the dead kings, and how they killed and tortured those poor people as punishment. Thrown into the Colosseum with a pack of lions without any weapons with which to defend themselves. In this aisle alone, Lorian saw four other books detailing what a bad omen the time travellers were to Roma.

The power to go back in time, acting as a ghost to witness history in the raw way it was intended, only to come back and harbor the pains of going backwards. She couldn't understand their full pain. She could only educate herself and hope that that amount of injustice would never happen again in her history.

After skimming through more of Aida's books and realizing how little of it she retained, Lorian picked up the shortest read and went near the windows for light.

She got to page ten, most of which was a glorified chapter about how great the Roman kings were and are, when someone called her name.

"Lorian, you fuck!"

Between the library and the writing hall was a strip of muddy grass. It was a shortcut between the buildings for her and other officers to travel. Two officers were there, calling for her: Alessio and Matteo, the two assholes she'd befriended that month.

"There he is, little bugger," Alessio said. He climbed up a rock wall to get closer. "Get out of there and come down. Lunch's almost over!"

"Alright, alright," Lorian said, and slotted the book for later.

They were good boys, these two. She liked them enough to hang out with them while not on duty. They didn't know this, and they wouldn't, but she'd actually known them back at the palace. All officers in training had to go through a mandatory training program overseen by a constable. Lorian had always favored officers for their rowdiness. She'd watch them work out and sneak peeks at their shirtless bodies. When she'd found out that both Alessio and Matteo were working as security details at this academy, her decision had been made. A few faked letters of recommendation and her crafty ability to lie through her teeth and she was enrolled as an officer in training in a week.

They'd never know that she was actually the missing princess every Roman boy wanted to fuck, but she liked to tease them every now again with knowledge she shouldn't know.

"Hey, Alessio, have you ever been persuaded to eat worms?"

"Matteo, didn't you pee yourself after seeing a real lion in captivity?"

"Have you two ever kissed on a dare?"

She'd lied to them, calling herself a good guesser.

She walked out of the library and turned the corner to find her boys, but they weren't there. The yard was quiet; she heard the teachers writing on the chalkboard from the writing rooms.

She stilled her steps. From her knowledge, she knew nobody could truly vanish from the world for good. Something would bring you back to where you were meant to be.

A twig snapped behind her and she was put into a chokehold that stole away her breath. She could've gotten out of it easily, but she didn't want to hurt her boys. Alessio was a redhead with pointed nails. Matteo had dark, floppy hair to hide his innocent eyes.

Laughing along with them, Lorian took out her rapier and used the pommel to knock the wind out of Alessio.

Alessio dry-heaved and let her go. "Ow! You ass."

"You attacked me." She lightly kicked him for good measure. "What're we doing now?"

"Late lunch," Matteo said, and shared a loaf of bread with her. They weren't students, but through their enlistment, they were given a dorm room and three meals ordained by their royal regimen. Sometimes, if they romanced the right girl or boy, they'd get sweets and even alcohol, something that was forbidden from officers. The three of them had already gotten drunk that month.

They walked to their preferred eating space that the Academy cheekily called "The Defense Wall." What used to be a formidable, three-meter tall fortress from a time period Aida probably knew about was now a fence for the academy's livestock.

Lorian climbed up a dilapidated wagon to scale the tall wall. Alessio followed her, and they both needed to help Matteo up due to his size. There, they shared their bread and butter and made horrible jokes for hours that, if any other officer heard them say, they would've had their hands caned. Lorian had had her fair share of that back home and was keen on not getting struck for misbehaving again.

As Lorian dined, Alessio asked her, "Why do you always spend your time in those libraries? You never read."

It was true, Lorian wasn't the learned soul her mother and father had boasted about to the public. She seldom read for pleasure. She'd done so for Aida. Her first attempt to find and talk to her had failed miserably and she was left hiding behind a bookshelf to spy on her. The other try and Aida hadn't even been there. The girl kept Lorian on a leash and Lorian had no problem with that. "I *do* read. I know a great deal of things, much more than you do."

"Then name two books you've loved in the past year. No, five *authors*, and no poets."

"You try that. When's the last time you ever picked up a book?" Lorian reached for Alessio's hair, but he jerked back and stuffed his mouth with bread.

"That Miss spends her time there, doesn't she?" Matteo asked. "That Aida girl."

"The traveller?" Alessio asked. "She's an odd one. I've talked with some of the girls in her class, and they say she's off. I heard she's gonna get the nix, you know?" He made a mark across his neck. "Cut out."

"What do you mean?" Lorian asked.

"My father heard it from Constable Carmine. Word from the Lion is that he's gonna bar those people from secondary education."

Lorian's ears heated up. "Carmine said that? And the king agreed to it? Did the queen say anything?"

Alessio slowed his chewing at Lorian's mention of Carmine's name without his title. She had to stop doing that, being so informal about a man she shouldn't have known so personally. "That's what my dad said, so I think it's true."

"Did the queen rule against it?"

"You know the queen doesn't say shit against her husband. She's afraid of him."

"I feel so bad for her," Matteo said.

Lorian rubbed her neck. She'd grown up with Carmine, but after being promoted to a constable, she couldn't say if this was something he'd enforce under the queen's—king's—orders or not. He'd exchange his heart for his duty.

But she wouldn't have put this past her father. He was the most racist, hurtful, selfish person she'd ever known, and she hated that parts of his speech and behaviors had sunk into her. It took a great deal of unlearning to undo all of those negative stereotypes he'd tried to instill in her, and it took her finally leaving the palace and joining the ranks to realize how real Visatorre lived and how wretched the world was to them.

"What's to happen to her?" Matteo asked when they went silent.

"Dunno," Alessio said. "Kick her out? There's only a few of those people here, it's not like they'd notice right away."

"But that isn't fair," Lorian said. "She hasn't done anything."

"That's not gonna stop them, you know that."

"Then...I'll stop them," she promised, and tried mimicking how confident Aida sounded whenever she spoke. "It's not right. Do you know Miss Mirko uses a cane because of her illness—" She bit her cheek. "Uh, affliction. Can you imagine walking around with a cane at our age? It's uncouth to belittle those who're born different."

Alessio pulled a face. "Don't act high and mighty to me. This wasn't my decision, I'm just the fucking messenger. And it's not like we can change it."

"Say I become a leading constable, then," Lorian argued. "I'd rewrite the rules to make them fair for everyone."

"*You* wanna be a constable?"

"Don't you? Isn't that the goal of being an officer, to one day become a constable?"

"Eh, not really. Not for me, anyway. I needed to get away from my family and this was the only option I had. To be a constable means you have to put in twelve, sometimes fifteen-hour-days and be on the king's every beck and call. Thanks, but I'm good being ordered around for uninvolved things."

"And I wanted to become cool like my brothers, but I don't think I'm strong enough to be a constable," Matteo said, and he looked across the field towards the water well. "Oh."

Alessio and Lorian followed his gaze.

"Speak of the devil," Alessio said.

Stomping down the fields, dress lifted to keep from stepping in cow shit, was Aida on a mission. Her hands were bunched up in her dress and she was mumbling something to herself. She'd lost her cane. It shortened her steps.

Lorian brushed the crumbs off of her chest and stood up higher to see her. She walked with such determination, like she truly did not care how other people saw her. Lorian wanted to walk like that one day.

"Do you need a hand, Miss?" Alessio called out.

"Fuck off!" Aida yelled back.

Alessio tensed. "What the fuck's her problem?"

"S-she isn't allowed to talk to us like that," Matteo said meekly. "What should we do?"

"We need to stop her. Hey—"

Lorian palmed Alessio's chest, almost knocking him off completely before clutching his jacket and keeping him vertical.

"Ow! Lorian, what's with you today?"

Lorian stared intently at Aida.

Silent tears were running down her cheeks as she walked. She wasn't sobbing or weeping, the tears were just there, though it was hard to tell why she was crying in the first place. It looked like she was off to kill somebody.

When she was out of sight and then some, Lorian got up, told her friends that she was thirsty, and secretly tailed Aida down her chosen path.

Chapter 6: Nighttime Wandering

She didn't know what time it was. After egging the Constable's carriage, she'd found a tree to cry under, then a wishing well to throw rocks in as hard as she could. She'd passed by those officer boys, whoever they were, about an hour ago, but she honestly didn't care at this point. In her mind, her life was over.

"You will no longer be able to attend Durante Academy as a student."

She breathed hard through her stuffy nose to keep from crying again. She wasn't *qualified*? On what grounds? She was the most hardworking person she knew. Getting into this school was the only way she could become a historian, a fanatic dream that now sounded so stupid in her head. Who was she, without her learning?

Dead, she guessed.

She'd found a good enough Nectar dealer her first month here. She had to choose her suppliers wisely and found one chef in the eastern dining area for her fix.

The dining area was closed for the night. Aida knocked on the back doors, waiting for that head chef to crack open the door and sell her something, but no one came. He must've gone home for the night.

She looked down. Beside the door was a half-pack of cigarettes. Not infused with Nectar, but they'd do. She'd run out of these two days ago and was starting to feel itchy.

As she lit one, something rustled in the trees behind her.

She pocketed the pack. The Moon was waning behind the cafeteria and she had no lantern with her, giving her little to identify whatever creature or person was spying on her.

She waited, hands in fists. No decent person would be out at this hour, but if it was some *thing*—a wild fox, wolf, even a bear—she could kiss more than her scholarship goodbye. Along with her weak legs and occasional migraines, she also had a horrible immune system. One bite or scratch would send her to the hospital, or worse, back home.

She shuddered, and it wasn't from the idea of hidden wolves.

When nothing jumped her, Aida haphazardly ran to her dormitory. She only made it about fifty meters before getting winded. She needed to find another cane. Circa knew she'd basically given up her cane along with her scholarship in the dean's office when she'd thrown it at the Constable. She wondered if there'd be consequences for that.

She braved the three flights of stairs to reach her room. She had to pace herself—one story, rest, one story, rest. She normally kept her head down, but who cared now? She had no one to impress anymore now that she was unwanted.

At least they hadn't changed the locks yet. If Aida was stealthy enough, she could've lived in the attics or basements, sleeping next to fireplace embers to keep warm. That's what she'd do. She'd show them.

Upon entering her quiet, lonely, shitty dorm room, Aida locked the door, double-checked that it was locked, then collapsed against the doorframe and sobbed into her hands.

She hadn't any money to make it in Roma City, and she couldn't work without a résumé. In a few days, she'd have to go back to her home village. Ekaterina and Olga would laugh, her mother would beat her. And that was *if* she'd take Aida back. Abandoning them for the fall and winter harvests could've been a death sentence for them. What if she was charged?

Her legs were tingling from sitting this way, so she fell to her bedside, emotionally and physically exhausted. She looked out one of her windows for comfort. Beyond the tree line were the blurry buildings of Roma City. If she squinted, she could see golden domes and stone columns. She couldn't see the royal palace—she'd tried; you couldn't see it from any point of the Academy due to the forest—but you could see the Colosseum. Great.

She finally lit one of her cigarettes and let the smoke sting her eyes. What would she do? Send a letter to her mother detailing her failure? If the dean was cruel enough, he would've already sent one. But then what? Return? Become homeless in Bělico, where the winters were unforgiving, or Roma, a place that she, even though she'd researched its history, didn't know a thing about?

The tears returned. She wiped them on the lace of her pillow. She hated Roma as much as she loved it, she just wished the city loved her back.

As she went to flick her cigarette bud, her head tingled.

She held her face in a groan. The tingling turned to fuzziness, then a sharp ache. Her feet disconnected from her nerves and left her feeling like she was sinking through the floorboards. She would've stayed on the ground, but she needed to reach her desk. Too many times had she jumped and landed on her glasses. She needed to put them somewhere safe.

She ashed her cigarette and grasped onto the edge of the desk, dropping two of her heaviest books. Now her eyesight was losing her, and she hadn't even taken off her glasses. Had she?

"Whoa, watch it!"

She turned, dropping her glasses somewhere on the floor. That wasn't Lorian's voice, she was sure of that. She didn't know who it was, but they were in her room, hiding behind her bed like a thief.

No, *thieves*. There were two of them reaching out to her. She hadn't seen them because she'd kept the lights off, but in the light of the Moon, she saw a person not much taller than herself, and then another, running up to her.

"Cripes, you're such a klutz," one of the thieves—a woman—said. She sounded familiar. Why did she sound familiar? "Hey, why'd you keep it so dark and dreary in here?"

"What?" The words slurred in Aida's mouth. She was tipping over.

A hand grabbed hers, then another on her side, dipping her dramatically as if she were a ballerina in *En Tempore Rose*.

The person's hair flew out in front of her, long wisps of brown locks. Her round glasses caught on the moonlight and showed off the whites of her wide eyes.

Her pupils were pure white, giving her a wild look. "Careful," she told Aida. "We can't have you getting lost now."

Aida gasped. This woman's face, and her Visatorre marking, two circles instead of one...

She gripped the woman's blue dress. She was desperate for answers, to anything. Who was she? How had she entered her room?

Why did she look like her?

An invisible thread of fate pulled Aida back, and then she was gone.

Chapter 7: Investigations

Lorian could not keep up with Aida. It was like she was on a mission to go nowhere. All afternoon and evening she stopped around the campus, skipping classes and dinner. Lorian had lost her for nearly an hour through the forest only for her to turn up around a stable. She'd stopped crying, thank goodness. Any more of that and Lorian would've blown her cover to ask if anything was wrong.

But then Aida might've thought ill of her. *"Why, because I'm a girl, you're asking if I need help? Don't you have a pig-pen to guard?"*

Not that she would've known about Lorian's gender to know that they were more similar than they were different. She'd planned on telling no one about it, but with Aida, she would've made an exception. She would've told her everything. If only she'd let her in.

She blinked. She'd lost Aida again. It was getting dark now, and Lorian didn't want anyone to see her following one of the only Visatorre girls on campus. Not that she was doing that. She was only protecting her.

She took to the western farmlands. From her sleuthing, she'd uncovered that Aida had grown up on a farm, so she might've found solace with farm animals.

Lorian couldn't relate. She'd hated farm animals since she was very little, all but the horses, like Ether, who was grazing in the pasture with other officer horses. But never had she worked hard for much of anything in her life, so she looked up to those who worked tirelessly for their country. If she were to ever adopt, she'd teach her children these ways.

When she hopped the fence, she was met with a group of cow asses and their piles of shit.

She gave them a wide berth. "Should I just tell her?" she asked the cows. "About the expulsion, I mean. She must know and that's the reason she's crying, but I don't want to be obtrusive. But I want to be there for her. That's what a boy's meant to do, is it not? To console a girl down on her luck?"

The cow she'd been talking at flicked its tail.

"Ass, that's it. It's all ass, isn't it? You know, she called me a stalker today. That's not true, is it? When she gives me nothing to work off of. Do you know how long it took me to learn her age? She's my age."

The cows decided that she made poor company and turned their full asses to her.

"You're not helping. What's the point of an animal if it doesn't listen to you vent?" She blew her hair from off of her face. She needed to find Aida again.

The clopping of horse hooves closed in around her.

She'd trained herself to distinguish between the types of horse hooves. Working-class horses usually carried a carriage behind them, or had a different-sounding gait than a royal horse. Royal horses walked with purpose, bred to be loved more than most human beings.

Lorian dove into the stables between stacks of hay and listened to those honorary gaits.

"Her performance should've earned her a striking, Captain."

"If word got out that I struck a defenseless girl, Her Majesty would reprimand me."

Lorian's mouth went dry.

"But still, Captain," the man went on, "it's the principle of the matter."

"And she went at you with a cane," another man said, "*and* she vandalized your carriage. That surely must be causality to defend yourself."

"We don't know if she was the one who vandalized my carriage," Carmine said. "We'll speak of this no more, Officer Dowry. I'm tired enough as is."

Lorian slid to her butt, covering her mouth so that she wouldn't be heard. What on Earth was *Carmine* doing here? She could neither see him nor his men from around the stable, but how, *how* could the Gods' timing be any worse? She thought she'd be free from his tyranny for at least another year.

She'd had a scrap with him a few days after she'd run away. She'd been ripping down her wanted posters in the fish market before applying to the Academy. That's when he'd cornered her, and she'd panicked, flipped him over her head, and plunged him into the harbor. He was so daft, not working out that Lorian was the little Lucia he'd helped raise so many years ago. Maybe his age was catching up to him.

She strained her ears. It sounded like he and his men were walking in a circle, their horses treading the same ground.

"What shall we do about her?" one of the officers asked.

"We need to find her first and take her in for questioning. I agree that she cannot get away with that sort of behavior, despite the...circumstances about her expulsion."

Lorian dropped her jaw. So Aida *had* known, and she'd assaulted Carmine for it. *And* vandalized his carriage. As if she wasn't charming enough.

"We do have a record on the girl, Sir. Fights in primary school, and she's estranged from her family. Her mother has been searching for her."

"What about it?" Carmine asked.

"I'm saying that she doesn't have a very reputable history. To be accepted to such an academy that you yourself have graduated from, it damages the school's reputation. Might we find her and make a spectacle of her?"

"What do you suppose we do?" Carmine asked. "Arrest her?"

The night wind shifted the dead leaves on the ground.

"I was thinking something a little harsher, Sir."

Carmine was silent, thinking about how to respond to such an inhumane thought. With his gut? With what the king wanted?

"I'll wait to hear her side of the story," he concluded. "For now, that's all I'm doing."

"Oh, well, I'm sure we can get His Majesty's opinions on these rejects."

Lorian almost gasped. These men were adults who were in charge of the safety of all Roman people, Visatorre and others alike, and this's how they talked about them? About young girls?

"Captain, if I can be frank with you," said an officer, "it seems like you've been quite lenient in your position ever since Her Highness Lucia disappeared."

Lorian's foot slipped out from underneath her.

"I can say that all of us are quite worried about her well-being, but I don't want to see her disappearance affect your critical thinking. You need to stand up to these people, otherwise—"

A horse jounced, kicking up dirt as it reared in a sharp turn. "Are you telling me how to run my job?" Carmine snapped. "Princess Lucia has been on my mind the same way she's been on all of our minds, but I'm disciplined enough to have it not interfere with my work in upholding Roma City's values. And if you think it is, you'll be sure to write it in to Her Majesty The Queen as a formal complaint, do you understand me?"

The men went silent. A horse chuffed, but even it seemed to understand Carmine's rage about this princess who wouldn't return.

Reigns were tightened, and the horses set off.

"We'll save this decision for Her Majesty," Carmine said, voice fading. "Come now. We need to find this boy on these godforsaken warrant papers. Where're the dormitories again?"

After Lorian could no longer hear the horses, she snuck a glance into the now darkening campus. Carmine was here, searching for a boy but more importantly Aida. And he had his officers with him. He didn't do that unless the operation was important, or deadly.

She had to do something. It's what a man would've done. But the inability to make a quick decision kept her from leaping into action. Damn this ineptitude and damn her mother

75

for birthing it into her. Everyone knew the queen was as meek as a trodden flower, and her own father hadn't helped with fortifying her self-confidence.

She pictured Aida's smiling face, how happy she looked in her dorm room that night, and contrasted it with the pain she must've been feeling, knowing her world was crumbling through her fingers.

Checking to see that Carmine had truly left, Lorian ran out of the stables and headed up the muddy tracks to Aida's all-girls' dormitory.

With the keys to every student building in her pocket, she accessed the antechamber and flew up the stairs with ease. The halls were silent apart from the floorboards creaking underneath her boots.

Should she knock on her door? Wouldn't that look bad, a boy knocking on a girl's bedroom door at midnight? Should she wait outside like this all night, becoming even more of a creep to Aida?

From inside Aida's room, Lorian heard a thud, followed by a much larger crash.

She unsheathed her rapier. "Aida?"

Another scuffle. Someone fell. Aida's faint, scared voice asked a question.

No longer able to stand by, Lorian shouted Aida's name and went for the handle. It was locked.

A metallic *zap* echoed through the room.

"Damn it," she said under her breath, and crashed her shoulder into the door. If only she'd let her *in*. "Aida!"

There was nothing. Silence.

Then footsteps. They walked towards the door quietly and unlocked it.

Lorian thrust open the still-opening door and struck the assailant with the butt of her blade, but with another *zap* of energy and magic, they were gone, and the room was empty.

Aida's bed was unmade and the room smelled of night air and cigarette smoke. Her clothes were scattered across the floor. Her glasses were not far off, next to the desk.

Lorian felt the center of the pile.

Warm. She'd just missed her.

A piece of paper pricked her finger. It was nestled within the dress pocket. She went to put it back, then saw the royal lion inked on the document and couldn't resist.

In Regards to the Termination of Aida Mirko's 6-Year Scholarship

The words hit harder than expected. Could scholarships be taken away so impersonally? To waste a whole student's career on the promises you'd awarded them? It made her stomach cold with guilt. How could a country treat its people so animalistic?

"Excuse me?"

Lorian whipped around so hard, her short ponytail hit her cheek.

Carmine and his entourage of officers came up the stairs to Aida's room. They all had hands on the hilts of their rapiers.

Carmine eyed Lorian with disgust, then slight terror at seeing her armed. "*You.*"

Lorian tried to hold back, but her fear made her spit out, "I've been called worse."

"Are you Lorian Ashwell, an officer in training of this school's recruits?"

"Did the uniform give it away?"

"We have no records that a 'Lorian' by any name is authorized to hold a royal emblem of the crown." He smiled, something that didn't fit his face. "How convenient that you managed to be here. You saved me a trip."

Lorian's heart stampeded through her. Carmine used to love to joke, but not like this. This felt so wrong.

Unsheathing his rapier, Carmine aimed his weapon down at Lorian. "Come with us, boy."

Lorian held his gaze. This wasn't fair, but that wouldn't stop them, and it wouldn't stop her, even though what she was doing was technically illegal. She was a bit deviant in that regard.

Standing up to her full height, Lorian clutched her rapier and crossed blades with Carmine.

Chapter 8: Unfamiliar Faces

Aida always tried to land on her feet when she travelled backwards into time, but she wasn't a graceful girl, so, like always, she ate complete shit.

And as if Circa couldn't be any crueler to her, she landed on cobblestone. It didn't rip up her skin—you couldn't get injured in the past—but it still hurt to have her brain rattle from the fall. Was it too selfish to ask to land on some grass? Maybe someone's bed?

She wound up in an alleyway between old, brick houses. It was light out, about mid-morning, but it was hard to tell by how the houses were angled. They cast her in shadows that left puddles in-between the stone.

She rubbed her eyes. She hadn't hallucinated it, right? Someone had jumped her in her room, which she'd locked the door to because what sane girl left her doors unlocked? And she'd been in there for several minutes. It made her itchy knowing someone had been watching her without her knowing. People had the same feelings about Visatorre. *"Oh, they can be watching you at any point in time!"* It's not like they had a choice when they jumped, and it wasn't like they were out to cause you harm. She'd have to look into the break-in when she came back. Not that the dean would be interested in making her feel safe and welcome.

Those unwanted feelings came back to her, but she swallowed them down. Right now, her expulsion wasn't her priority. What mattered now was her location in the timeline.

Commotion from the street over drew her from her alley. There must've been a street fair going on. She saw confetti flitter between the houses.

Once she met with the main road, and once she tasted the electricity in the air, she covered her breasts to retain her modesty.

This was no street fair, it was a street *festival*. Or carnival? Birth of a royal heir? Out on the streets, hundreds, perhaps *thousands* of people were flocked in large groups of cankerous celebration. Pennant flags of every color tossed in the wind as bags of confetti were thrown out of windows in bunches. The people were dressed in elaborate costumes, the women in tight corsets and incredibly tacky, pointy hats, men in tunics and also incredibly tacky, pointy hats. Street vendors packed the remaining street space, and between them, musicians played live music. Freely roaming children danced to the flutes.

Visatorre children. Alongside non-Visatorre children. And not just the children, the adults, too. There were mostly Roman people with a sprinkle of Bĕlican and Aldaían people here and there, but they were integrated like it was commonplace. There were no homeless, no mistrust. In this small pocket of time, there was peace between all people.

She stepped out into the street, her head turning like a mechanical doll.

The Colosseum, standing tall and in perfect condition, was decorated for whatever festivity was happening. It looked like it'd just been built, without chunks of stone broken off from the top. It looked new.

And the Roman Palace, off to the side of the Colosseum, was at once completely different and identical to the one she knew. Its lion flags whipped proudly in the wind. Its famous clock tower was a different shade of stone, unpolished, most likely, but the little nutcrackers that danced to each hour were still there, as well as the famous painted glass that twinkled at noon.

Instead of looking like relics, the architecture, the *feeling* of Roma City, looked intertwined with the time period.

Aida bit her lip. Her breathing hurt. How far back had she gone? Where on Earth was she? She needed to think, but she was drawing a blank.

She listened to the music. That should've helped. The men were playing ancient horn trumpets. They hadn't been used in nearly a century due to the invention of the sousaphone that the public thought was easier on the ears. Everyone was wearing pointed hats, which had also gone out of style nearly *two* centuries ago. The women wore makeup of deep reds, the men wore open-toed sandals instead of boots.

Aida walked up ahead and spotted an officer, or what she assumed to be this time period's equivalent of one. He wore armor and vambraces and carried a heavier sword on his belt than the standard rapier. The Classical Era called these men "gladiators."

But that couldn't be right. Gladiators had been abolished along with the city-state of Siina.

Nearly 1,200 years ago.

"Fuck," she cursed, and let the reality of her situation sink in. 100 years back in time would've severely damaged her body, but to go back more than a millennium, would she even return in one piece? Would she come back a mass of human skin, her organs spilling out of her stomach like warm porridge?

She held her intact stomach. This had to be a reenactment, right? But how had they fixed the Colosseum? Why were these Roman people speaking in an accent that sounded like a foreign language?

She journeyed through this new Roma. This celebration was more akin to a world's fair that'd been popular back in the day. Pavilions showed off inventions that caught the crowd's eye. An ancient form of the toothbrush, a new type of papyrus brought over from Aldaí you could reuse, a prototype of what they now knew as an aqueduct. Pieces of history Aida and the Neoclassical Era had been using for generations, and they had signs claiming these inventions were new.

She stopped at each tent, taking in the people and the costumes they wore. No, they weren't costumes, were they? They weren't playing a part in a play. These were their everyday outfits, sewn by their mothers in homes they'd built by hand, some of the only clothes they probably owned.

She touched a small dagger on a table. If only she could pick something up, even a stone from the Tiber River. How she'd treasure what a trinket was to these people.

"Heya!"

A loud crash of thunder behind Aida indicated that a Visatorre just jumped, but when she turned around, she saw no clothes on the ground, no onlookers distracted by the suddenness of the jump. A fully-clothed man jumped back into the world, landing on his feet with a surprising hop to his step. "My, what a night!" he announced.

Two of his friends, one Visatorre and one non-Visatorre, called for and met up with him.

"Took ya long enough, mate!" one of them said, his accent so thick it hardly sounded Roman. "Whaja see?"

"A brothel a 'omen, I stumbled into," he said. "What a scene I saw. Musta been 200 'ears back, and 200 trollops 'ere achin' for a man. Aye, the things they said were a head-turner."

"What a find!" the other man said, and the three of them continued their day at the festival.

Aida took in the city square in a more confusing light. To not only be unharmed from a jump, but to come back fully clothed, and happy...

She rubbed down her Visatorre marking. How had history gotten history so wrong? Where were the slaves, the poverty? People should've been dirty and ruthless. Weren't they at war with Queen Eve by now? Was this even Roma City, or was it Siina?

She kept going. Towards the northwest was the Tiber River that cut through Roma City. Down the way was a dam that shouldn't have existed, less the countryside be dry for years. They must've fixed that with time.

She turned, found a new invention, a new Visatorre whose children's children were probably dead, living happily, safely.

She covered her mouth, surprised to find her cheeks wet with tears. These feelings, combined with everything she'd been through that day, that pummeled her like schoolyard bullies. She sank to her knees. This was all she ever wanted, but like with Durante Academy, she knew it was too good to be true. She'd return to her timeline naked and bleeding, and that freakish stalker would be the only one to find her body and do loathsome things to it. This was it—her final jump.

She glared up at the sky. "Is this funny to you, because I'm trying really hard to find the joke, and I don't fucking see it."

Circa, her Goddess, did not answer.

"First, you give me a fucked up childhood that no child should go through, then you raise my hopes with a scholarship to my dream school only to take it away before the first semester even ended. Then, as if I'd done so wrong by you, you bring me back three billion years into the past I would've loved to visit and make it my death sentence. I'll return with my back broken or head cracked. And then that's it, isn't it? Aida Mirko dies accomplishing nothing, further proving that Visatorre have nothing to live for, huh? That we're meant to die without meaning. Is that it? Huh?"

Circa didn't answer, so Aida tried to pick up a stone to hurl it at something. She couldn't, but she tried. To besmirch the past and make her mark, for once in her damned life.

She growled in frustration and kicked a nearby fountain. "Fuck you! You're the Goddess of Time! You're the Visatorres' God. You're all we have, and you constantly fuck us over! If you really cared for us—" She held back her tears. "Give me *one* good thing in my life!"

The crowds suddenly burst into cheers. Families brought their children up onto their shoulders. Others ran out into the street. Gladiators began parting the crowds, but they couldn't see Aida, so they left her by the fountain. The rest gladly obeyed orders and shuffled around the street vendors to see what was coming.

Aida scurried up to the fountain's edge, distancing herself from whatever was about to happen. She hated crowds. Circa must've known that. What a prick of a God.

The clopping of horse hooves and a rickety carriage came her way. She figured it was the start of a parade. With her luck, it would be for something barbaric.

The carriage turned the corner, and the plaza erupted into deafening cheers. Visatorre who'd climbed up to the rooftops called for the people riding in the carriage.

"Your Majesty!"

"Congratulations, Your Majesties!"

It was a boy and girl riding in a carriage driven by Clydesdale horses. They were about Aida's age. The boy was Aldaían with dark brown skin and black cropped hair. The girl, Aida couldn't make out her origin, but she was beautiful. Tan skin with brown hair that turned red in the Sun, tied up in coiled buns. She wore a dark maroon dress cinched at her waist, and instead of a hat, she wore a golden crown that matched the boy's.

The crowd chanted the man's name: "Meyeso," "King Meyeso."

And the woman, with more power to her name: "Eve," "Queen Eve," "Our Beloved Queen Mother Eve."

Aida's hand shot up to her mouth as the Royal family of Siina made their way to her. They were coming right towards her, making the turn at the fountain. At the top of the fountain was a sculpture of Circa smiling down on them.

Eve, who'd been waving to the masses, stood up in her carriage. Her husband went to grab her dress in case she fell, but she raised it. Hopping over the railing, she jumped right out of the moving carriage and onto the statue of Circa.

Aida gasped as she watched her fly over her, water sparkling in the sky and creating a rainbow between them.

Eve hooked an arm around the Circa statue, spun in a circle, then laughed and waved to the masses, sending everyone into hysteria.

"Congrats on your pregnancy, Your Majesty!"

Eve turned to the brave person who'd shouted that over the crowds. "My thanks to *you!*" she called out.

None of Aida's history books said anything about Eve having an heir. Had she had a miscarriage? If so, why hadn't that been brought up in any way? It was a *royal* child; historians loved royal children as much as they loved war.

Another carriage came in from near the Colosseum. It was just as grand, with four magnificent horses carrying two equally beautiful heirs. They were of fair skin and blond hair, the boy growing out a beard that made him look older, the girl with freckles and a demure smile that invited Aida in.

Upon seeing the carriage, Eve squealed, climbed off the statue and touched down with a thud on the cobblestone.

"Wait!" Aida ran for her. She was *right* there, so *close.*

Eve climbed into the carriage and sat right between the two heirs. Aida recognized them as King Julius II and Queen Julia, the monarchs—or monarchs to be—of the Roman Empire.

Four of the most famous monarchs who'd been dead for centuries. And Eve had been friends with them. The man who'd murdered her for murdering his wife, who was now whispering a secret in Eve's ear and making her snort.

Eve snorted when she laughed.

Aida risked getting knocked over and climbed onto the carriage. Even though they couldn't see or acknowledge her, she needed this. If she were to die after this jump, let her meet her Queen Eve.

Eve, without the king's knowledge, was holding hands with Queen Julia. Eve played it off like the touch meant nothing, but it wasn't nothing to Julia. She kept looking down at Eve's hand, her cheeks flooding with confusing warmth. Both girls were wearing matching blue bracelets. The beads were bumping against each other.

"What happened between you three?" Aida asked, trying to read their subtle gestures. "What did you do to break the world?"

Eve made sure everyone's eyes stayed on her. Julia fidgeted from the touch of another kingdom's queen. Julius took in his people's adoration with a proud smile. Meyeso, he stayed back, for no one could stop Eve from doing what she pleased.

Aida pinched Eve's dress, the closest she could reach. "Did you really kill her?" she asked. "Did you murder this girl?"

The carriage bounced, and Aida's eyesight blotted out into spots. Her body dipped into the road. The last thing she saw was Eve looking over at her—the crowd *through* her—and waving like a true queen. Then Aida was whisked back into the present.

Chapter 9: Familiar Faces

Lorian stepped over the larger of the two unconscious officers. She had very little space in which to fight Carmine; both of his subordinates were clocked out on the ground because she refused to maim anyone. One quick hit with the end of her rapier and another shoved against Aida's bookshelf and they were out cold. Carmine had tried to run for help, but Lorian climbed over the bed and relocked the bedroom door, sealing the two of them inside.

"Y-you're mad," Carmine wheezed, and lunged.

Lorian parried his blade with hers. She had her free hand clutched tightly behind her back like she'd been trained to do so. Her fingernails dug hard into her palm.

"You know that, once this's over, you're going to be hanged. To draw swords with a Constable of Her Majesty—"

Lorian circled to his side and knocked him off-center. He tried to stab her in the heart, but he wouldn't deliver a finishing blow. All these years after being promoted and Lorian had yet to see him kill anyone under his command.

"Give it up," Carmine panted. He tried again for Lorian's legs. Lorian rolled across Aida's bed and pranced back up on the other side, sword still in hand.

Carmine wiped his lips. "Who taught you how to fight like this?"

Lorian cocked her head boldly. Would he believe that he *himself* had taught her, that she'd memorized his fighting techniques as a child because she'd admired him as a young man?

Carmine sighed when he knew he wouldn't receive an answer. "This act is growing old. Just end it now. I have three men waiting for my arrival. Once they catch that I—" He lunged again. He caught Lorian's vest and tore open her breast pocket.

Lorian jerked right, bringing her too close to Carmine's free hand. She jumped back, hit his wrist, and stole away his blade.

Carmine exhaled as he stood weaponless, and Lorian readjusted her grip on now two rapiers. All she needed was Aida and this fighting would be paused in lieu of a naked, defenseless girl on the battlefield.

The two stared each other down, timing what to do and how. Carmine should've been equipped with a dagger or bladed dart with which to defend himself. Maybe he'd thought a quick visit to a college campus wouldn't have called for more than a decorative weapon.

"Well?" he asked. "You killed my men, what's stopping you from killing me?"

"I didn't kill them," Lorian said. "See for yourself. They're stunned, not injured."

Carmine briefly glanced down at the nearest officer. The man moaned and tried turning.

"I don't kill anyone beneath me," she continued. "It's not right."

"'*Beneath you*'," he spat out. "How dare you."

"Well, you know, I'm kind of a bastard when it comes to choosing my words."

"Why're you doing this? What's your game here?"

"Never knew you were one to make polite conversation," Lorian joked. He was such an introvert at palace parties, guarding the queen without a word. "I want to be an officer, nothing more, and nobody's taking that away from me."

"Then why didn't you sign up? Every Roman boy dreams of this life, you didn't have to lie."

"That's what you'd like to think," Lorian said. "That's what I was taught to believe, that all boys my age dream of enlisting, but that's not the case. Most boys join as a last resort."

"It's not a mandatory draft."

"To certain families, it is. They expect extraordinary things from their children. Forced enlistment, forced apprenticeships...forced marriage," she added, "but you already know that last part, don't you?"

Out of everything she was saying, that last quip got a reaction out of him. His neck muscles bulged like he was against such marriages. Had he not gone along with her proposal as easily as her mother and sister had?

"*Enough*," Carmine said. "Since you haven't killed my men, I can only assume"—he took out a dagger—"that you shan't kill me."

Lorian backed up. "N-nor will you. You'd never."

"You've given me no choice." He circled in closer.

Her back hit the door. "Wait."

"I'm sorry," he said, and lunged for her one last time.

She shut her eyes. She hadn't the time to dodge, to escape. "Wait, Carmello—!"

The blade nicked her neck. She froze, as she wouldn't dare hurt him. Never kill. Never stoop as low as her forefathers. These were the promises to which she held herself.

Carmine, too, had frozen, his dagger a hair away from her jugular. His face, once hardened to take a life, was cracking in perplexity.

He leaned in. "Who are *you* to call me that?"

Lorian constricted her throat to keep herself from drawing blood. "Lorian...Ashwell, child of no one important, officer in training, and soon-to-be constable to right the wrongs of three generations' worth of sin."

He studied her face, her green eyes stolen from the queen. "Do I *know* you from somewhere?"

She faked a smile. Without her makeup, earrings, long hair, curves, and bratty attitude, she thought she'd changed enough to sneak by the general public, but had it been enough for Carmine? "M-Mafi Harbor," she came up with. "I was caught stealing some fish, I dunked you in the water. It was quite comical."

"No, I'm sure..."

Electricity zapped through the room, illuminating them for a blinding second. Then two eyes appeared from the darkness. "Leave them alone, old man!"

Something struck Carmine and sent him backwards. A figure with long, dark hair and a dress of multiple layers emerged from the shadows. Lorian couldn't even register that she had Aida's voice, she was too stunned by the sudden violence that'd just taken place.

Two more zaps and Aida's bed creaked with added weight. Two figures now appeared in the moonlight, their dresses and capes fluttering to a still around them.

"Appeared," because they did not climb onto the bed, nor did they crawl out from underneath it. One woman and another, they had *materialized* onto Aida's bed from nothing.

The woman stood wearing glasses like Aida, with tan skin and brown hair like Aida, who was as big as the stubborn and passionate girl Lorian had come to know over this past season, but this woman wasn't Aida. This woman was in her early thirties, and she had her hair down. Since Lorian had known her, Aida kept her hair in two braids that ran down her front. And to be wearing a dress that showed off her bare shoulders with a fluffy petticoat, this couldn't have been her.

But it was, from her eye shape to her hands to her nose. Nothing would've dissuaded Lorian from that.

The person to her left, on the other hand, was like looking into a mirror. They were a few centimeters taller than Lorian and had grown out their hair into a full-length ponytail, and they were dressed as a king with a cape around their neck. Other than that, this person *was* Lorian, just a little more masculine and with the confidence to hold Aida's hand like they were more than friends.

The Aida look-alike fixed her glasses with an un-Aida-like smile. "Well, then," she said, "I don't remember our introductions being so obnoxiously loud, but it's good to see you again, Little Lorian. A pleasure." She curtsied as if she was on stage. "And to Little Me." She looked around the room. "Oh, darn it, where am I? I thought I'd timed this out right."

"I told you we should've planned this out more efficiently," the other person said, very clearly in Lorian's voice but older. "We should've been listening through the door like I said."

"I was impatient!"

"Oh, *you*, impatient?" the Lorian asked. "I would've never known."

"Hey, you said Carmie attacked you, and it's not like I was here to judge the situation by myself."

"And you deal with it by kicking him?"

"I get a lot of leverage out of kicking."

Lorian's eyes darted from person to person, utterly bewitched by their existence. She felt like she'd travelled for the first time. What felt natural to them was inexplicable to her, and she couldn't comprehend the slightest bit of information. How, and why? What, and when? Were they even real? How had they jumped backwards into time like this?

She lowered her blades, lost of all answers.

Carmine sat up holding back a bloody nose.

"Circa, Aida, did you have to be so violent?" the Lorian asked.

"I didn't mean it. Carmie," the Aida said, "I didn't mean that, you know that, yeah?"

When Carmine finally got a good look at the two intruders, he scooted back. "W-who are you? How did you get in here?"

"Can ya guess?" The Aida—Future Aida—pointed to her face, which was so much like Aida's, it hurt. Her white Visatorre marking had an extra circle drawn inside of it, and her pupils were pure white, making her stare a thousand times more unnerving.

Carmine looked between Lorian and Lorian's doppelganger. "What on *Earth*."

"Luckily we're just dealing with earthen qualities," Future Aida said. "Now, I should be coming back soon, but I know that I don't like being excluded from any hearings, so in the meantime, let's catch up." She posed a hand underneath her chin. "How's the weather nowadays? How's studying going? How—"

Lorian's rapier was stolen from her hand, and Carmine stood up and aimed it at the two strangers.

Lorian doubletook Carmine's blade still in her hand. The thief. That was *her* rapier. Who was breaking the law now?

"I'm sick of these games," Carmine said. "You three are to come with me, to be questioned by Her Majesty's men under the charges of assault of a constable and two officers."

"Oh, enough of that act, Carmie," Future Aida said. "It grows old. Besides, we're not here for you, we're here for *them*." And she pointed down at Lorian.

Lorian didn't know if she should've drawn her weapon. She and Future Lorian were unarmed, but like Carmine, they could've had a small weapon concealed on them. And who knew? Perhaps they weren't even human, and mere swords and words wouldn't harm them in this realm.

"You, my little one," Future Aida said, "are in for a whirl-wind of a time. You and your missing, very beautiful friend have a task to accomplish, one you won't realize its importance until after it's done. From here on out, all Visatorre and Mediocris depend on your future actions."

"They don't use that word yet," Future Lorian whispered.

"What?"

"Mediocris. They don't use that word yet."

"Ah, right. Well, you're smart. You can pick up on context clues. Visatorre and *non-Visatorre*," she explained. "Anyway, Lorian, when Aida returns, go into the city. Follow the crowds. Follow my voice. Then—"

A spark of lightning crashed through the room, and Aida's body fell exactly where her clothes lay. Lorian turned away out of respect, but then she heard her gagging, floundering like a fish like something was malfunctioning in her brain.

Aida drooled as she convulsed. She looked in pain, the way her arms were tight and shaking, legs flailing, but her face was expressionless.

"Fuck," Future Aida said, her smile fading. "Ain't it different from the other side."

"Aida!" Lorian slid beside her and cupped her cheeks. "Aida? Aida, are you okay?"

She spasmed against Lorian's knee. It looked like she was being strangled by an invisible wire.

"What's wrong with her?" Lorian asked.

"It comes with the territory, I'm afraid," Future Aida said. "Keep her head steady. Both hands now. Help her out."

She hated the feeling of Aida's head trying to thrash against her hand, and she hated how she didn't know how else to help. She hadn't been this bad when they'd first met. Did all jumps end this badly, with gagging and coughing?

Carmine hovered over them.

"Do something!" Lorian pleaded. "One of you, any of you, please."

"She'll be alright," Future Lorian said. "She just travelled a long way. This'll hurt her for the rest of her life, but fear not. She's still the same girl you fell in love with."

Lorian faltered on that line and how strange it sounded when spoken aloud, then asked, "How do you know what's going to happen?"

Future Aida smiled dementedly. "Can ya guess?"

"This isn't the time for games," Carmine said. Despite wanting to kill Lorian minutes ago, he now knelt beside her to help Aida. He centered her head. "Easy, *easy*."

"Is she breathing?" Lorian asked.

"I believe so."

"She is," Future Aida said. "Look, you two, life's gonna be challenging from this point onwards. Your whole world's gonna fucking blow, but remember that this is going to be so, so worth it in the end."

"Shut *up!*" Lorian yelled. "Gods, just shut the fuck up and help us! You're not making any sense. She's dying! Can't you do anything else besides act like a fucking know-it-all?"

"Uh, she isn't dying, for one. I'm a good testament of that."

"Is this really a good time to be arguing?" Carmine asked.

"Shut up," Lorian groaned. Even though she had a thousand questions for this pairing, right now, she wouldn't have cared if she ever saw them again. The fewer bodies in this room the better. Then she could try focusing on the Aida that mattered. She'd stopped drooling but was now gurgling.

"Shit, no wonder they hate us," Future Aida said. "I can't think of anything to say."

"You had a whole speech prepared," Future Lorian reminded her.

"Well, shocking no one, I've forgotten it." She checked her watchless wrist. "I think it's time we scram. You ready?"

"Ready as ever," Future Lorian said. "Good luck."

"Like I need it." She turned to Lorian and bowed. On her left wrist, she wore a woven bracelet that matched the color of her dress. Its single amulet shone against the white of the Moon. "Fare thee well, *Your Majesty.*"

Lorian cringed. She had no idea what she was planning. In truth, this woman probably wasn't Aida at all, for Aida wasn't chipper. She didn't crack jokes, she wasn't as demented as this poor loon of a girl was.

Future Aida physically jumped off the bed towards them. Before landing on Lorian's head, she pivoted at the right minute and landed squarely into Carmine.

"Here we go!" she said, and taking a handful of Carmine's vest, she and he disappeared in a flash.

Lorian fell back on her butt. Once there and then not. Just like a Visatorre.

"It won't be any less surprising," Future Lorian said, still standing on Aida's bed. The room felt calmer now that a trickster god and the man seconds away from murdering Lorian were gone. Lorian finally heard herself breathe and Aida groan.

Still holding her, Lorian regained her composure and fully addressed her mirror image. They did look alike, like she was a real queen.

Or king.

"I...don't remember saying much here," Future Lorian said. "It's Aida who usually does all the talking. I apologize for not being much help."

Lorian wanted to ask at what point *had* they been any help, but then she took in their demeanor and contrasted it with her own. How they held themselves, how they hadn't learned to smile naturally. Even the way they stood, slouched a bit to keep their chest from being so pronounced. So much like herself.

"Tell me," Lorian said, "is what that woman said true? Are you really me?"

It sounded ridiculous when she said it aloud. How could she be talking to herself? She was right here, on the floor, and she wasn't a Visatorre.

Future Lorian nodded. "Very much so, yes."

She racked her brain to find a reasonable question to ask. It felt like she had one chance at this, like this impossible event could only last a moment before it disappeared. "Then... then tell me something only I'd know that'll convince me that you're me."

She regretted it. She had only one secret no one on Earth could ever know.

Future Lorian smiled warmly down on their past self. Their eyes looked like their mother's.

Placing one hand to their heart and one behind their back, Future Lorian bowed. "I believe we both know the answer to that, *Your Highness*."

That was it, wasn't it? What else had she been waiting to hear? What else had she been hiding since deciding that she'd no longer be Princess Lucia of Roma but Lorian fucking Ashwell, a person of her own design?

Future Lorian straightened. "She'll be back soon," they said, "she" in reference to Future Aida.

"Where did she take Carmine?" Lorian asked. She should've called him "the Constable," but with two unconscious officers and an unresponsive Aida, she knew she didn't have to be heedful with anyone but herself.

"Aida will discard him far away from here, giving you two a chance to escape."

"Escape where?"

"Into the city. What you and Aida did tonight is treasonous against the crown. Hitting a constable? Fighting Carmine and his dogs? The city will be after you, so you need to disappear however you see fit. I'd tell you what you decide on doing, but you seldom take good advice, do you?"

Lorian rubbed her lips together. "That attitude never goes away, huh?"

"Alas, it does not," they said, and turned as if ready to jump into time themselves.

"Wait," Lorian said, "how are you here? We're—you're not a time traveller."

"So long as Aida is touching you, she can take any living being into the past with her."

Lorian looked down at the Current Aida, her Aida. She was panting, each breath laborious, and trying to turn her shoulders to no effect. "How?"

"You won't believe me if I told you," Future Lorian said. "Just trust us. All of this is in Circa's hands."

"Circa?" she asked. "The Goddess of Time?"

A flash of lightning and Future Aida plopped back down beside Future Lorian. She almost fell before they caught her. Carmine was missing.

She turned to Lorian. "Good luck, little one, and take care of me! I'll wake up soon!"

"Wait—"

As if she could stop Aida, in any timeline.

Taking Future Lorian's hand, Future Aida threw up a peace sign and vanished, leaving Lorian with an injured Aida, two unconscious officers, and a kidnapped constable who wanted both of them arrested.

Chapter 10: Escape Plan

She breathed in, breathed out. Aida gasped in, weakly breathed out, eyes watering from staying open too long.

Lorian, still unable to properly move, took Aida's glasses and folded them into her pocket. Then she took Aida's school uniform and began folding that, too. She couldn't bother with her socks or bloomers. Her hands were trembling.

The unconscious officer nearest them moaned. Lorian stilled, then began dressing Aida as quickly as possible. She forced the white collar over her head, then the sleeves through her arms.

Aida sobbed.

"I'm sorry." Lorian lifted her upright to get the rest of her dress on. Aida was double her size, she couldn't lift her without the risk of dropping her. "Stay with me, Aida."

"Mm..." Spit rolled off of her lower lip.

Lorian wiped it with the back of her cuff. She needed Circa to freeze time so she could think things through. She needed a minute, an hour. She needed a clear head and steadier hands.

But she couldn't waste time with Aida like this. Action needed to be taken, whether she was ready for it or not.

"I'm sorry," Lorian repeated, "but you need to stand. Can you do that? Stand?"

Her chin stuck out, trying to speak.

Lorian worked with her and got her standing before any of the officers regained consciousness.

"She just travelled a long way. This'll hurt her for the rest of her life, but fear not. She's still the same girl you fell in love with."

Lorian teared up. Visatorre could travel ten, fifteen years into the past without much damage, so what had Future Lorian meant? How much of this Aida had been taken from her?

To check, Lorian lifted Aida's head.

She, too, was crying. Not in the normal way people did. The tears fell like raindrops without expression, like her mind was fighting with what she needed to express.

Lorian held her cheek and waited for her eyes to meet hers. "You're going to be okay," she promised, "but we need to leave now, okay? We'll leave together. I won't leave you behind."

Her mouth parted to speak. Her weak breath hit Lorian's nose in tiny puffs.

Then she doubled-over and puked. Lorian jumped back, then held back her curly hair so none of it stained. Without her braids, it was wildly curly and unkempt.

"Alright." Lorian helped her back to her feet. "One of the better times to have your cane and you, what, threw it at Carmine?"

Aida huffed on what sounded like a laugh as the two of them exited the room and fled down the stairs. Lorian found the servant stairwell easily—the old architecture reminded her too much of the palace. It helped them remain hidden.

"Your Highness."

Her future self wasn't a princess, or queen, or whatever they'd chosen to be. She would *never* return to that lifestyle.

They exited the dorm and broke for the tree line. She didn't know the extent of Aida's injuries, whether it originated in her back or her leg or somewhere deeper, so she went slowly for her sake.

It helped that she had no idea where the fuck she was going. She'd fought Carmine, incapacitated two officers. Future Aida had taken him somewhere, for which Lorian would no doubt be charged. With admitting that she'd been the one to knock Carmine into the Mafi Harbor that summer—it'd been the talk of the town, she relished in it—she was a dead man. Either her parents would identify her and lock her away with Zaahir in Aldaí, or she'd be hanged in public as a disgraced man, or woman. Maybe her father would still see her as a "disrespectful brat," just like on her wedding day. She'd been slapped in front of everyone for calling him a bastard.

Lorian rested Aida on a tree. She'd kept up, but her knees were now shaking and she hadn't spoken coherently. Lorian didn't know if she could anymore.

No. Aside from a few quirks, Future Aida looked healthy. If they were the same person, her Aida would be fine, right?

"Lorian?"

Lorian unsheathed Carmine's sword. It was larger than hers and didn't fit well in her scabbard.

Alessio and Matteo ran up to them. They were still in their uniforms, but their swords were missing.

"What're you doing?" Alessio said with a sleazy smile. "Running off for a quick session in the forest?"

"Not the time," Lorian said.

"Oh, not the time?" Alessio raised a hand to his belt, his smirk remaining. Then he noticed Aida's heavy breathing and he slouched his shoulders. "Something happen to her?"

"She jumped. Far. It's bad. I don't know what to do."

"Oh." Alessio stepped back. "Oh. Fuck, okay."

"What should we do?" Matteo asked. "Is she well?"

"No," Lorian said. "She was convulsing and drooling. I don't know how to help her."

"Do you know how far back she went?"

"I-I don't know. Far," she guessed. "Hundreds of years, I think."

"Isn't that, you know, serious?" Alessio asked.

"I think so," Matteo said. "Should we bring her to the hospital wing?"

"We can't," Lorian said.

"Why not?" Alessio asked.

"Because—" Aida began to fall. Lorian kept her standing. "Because I might've attacked Constable Carmine and two of his officers."

The boys' eyes went wide in shock. Ever since Lorian had been a child, she'd been abrasive. She was a bastard child through and through, and while Alessio and Matteo remembered Lucia as a princess that seldom left the palace, they only knew Lorian, a boy who sometimes got too in over himself, who couldn't act until anxiety blundered him into an unplanned action.

Alessio opened and closed his mouth, then squinted at the glint of gold in Lorian's newly acquired rapier.

"Stole this, from him," she explained, "though, in my defense, he stole mine, so I guess I got the better deal."

"Are you—Why?" Alessio came up with. "Are you mad?"

"He was going to arrest me. I'm not an officer. I'm..."

She almost said it, almost. She knew it'd do more harm than good, but she wanted to try and be truthful for once in her life.

She tucked it away. Another time. "I snuck into the training program. I never enlisted, or trained, or went to an academy for it. Carmine was about to take away Aida's scholarship, so I went to her room to see what I could do. Then he found me and killed two birds with one stone and tried getting at me, but Aida had jumped and I didn't want to leave her. So I freaked, panicked. I attacked him, and then she came back, and now I'm here and *fucked*. Totally, royally, absolutely *fucked*."

As she spoke, Alessio's upper lip curled. When she finished, he said, "So you lied to us? All this time, we thought you—"

"Yes, I did," she said. "I had to. I had to leave my home, otherwise my whole world was going to collapse on me." She sighed. "Hate me. Disown me as your friend. I deserve it. Just *please*, before that, help me help her. Help Aida."

Alessio didn't move or blink. He reconstructed the way he saw Lorian, an aggressive officer as well as a liar on top of all her bad traits. Friends didn't hide things from each other. Friends were honest.

She wouldn't know. The only friend she'd ever had was Missus Sharma, and she'd abandoned her to chase a freedom she hadn't yet found.

Alessio spat on the ground, then cursed and fixed his belt. "Fuck you. Fuck you and your mother. You're a piece of shit officer who I never want to see again." He helped take Aida in his arms. "There's a cellar in the barn next to our dorm. Hasn't been used in months. You can hide there for the night."

Lorian smiled. "Thank you."

"Shut up. If an officer comes by looking for either one of you, I'm not lying. Unlike you, I've fought hard to get this position."

"Um, ouch," Lorian said. "I've fought hard, too."

"Yeah, at lying."

"Oh, like officers don't lie."

"We don't!"

"Um, guys." Matteo brushed something off of Aida's lower lip. His finger came back red.

"Crap. Let's go," Alessio said, and the three of them helped carry Aida to the barn.

———◇———

"Hurry *up*." Alessio lifted the hatch and beckoned them down into the cellar. There were tall, wooden steps they had to take. Lorian made sure Aida didn't trip. Her eyes were going in two different directions.

Matteo retrieved blankets and pillows from their room and helped set up their beds. Alessio stayed up above, keeping watch with his arms crossed.

"I hope this's okay," Matteo said. "Is she going to be alright like this?"

Aida had gone down the second they pulled out the first blanket. She curled up in a ball like a child.

"Don't get comfy," Alessio called down to Lorian. "You can't stay down there forever."

"Bite me, okay?" she said. "Tough day."

"Yeah, whatever. Where're you from, anyway, since everything you've told us was a lie?"

"Not everything was a lie. I'm still from Roma City. My father's still a piece of shit. I still worked at the palace."

"Yeah, I don't believe that last one anymore," Alessio told her.

"It *is* a bit hard to believe," Matteo agreed, "you, working so close to the queen."

"Then don't believe it. It's the least impressive thing I've done. I was forced into that prison by my parents and did everything I could to get out."

Alessio scoffed. "Surprised you left."

"I'm surprised you got so far," Matteo said. "I could never."

"Okay, quit wasting time." Alessio called Matteo back up.

"Hey," Lorian said. "Thank you, honestly. I'll be sure to put in a good word with the queen so both of you are heralded for your heroism."

"Screw off," Alessio said. "You don't know any of the royals. You'd be lucky if one of the princesses spit in your face and called you trash."

Feeling like she'd gone too far, Lorian just said, "Yeah, right."

"Yeah, right. Night, asshole."

"Good night, Aida," Matteo said, but Aida was already out.

They shut the cellar door and covered it with a bale of hay. The only light Lorian had was a single stream of moonlight that illuminated the floating dust.

She stretched out her face and fell backwards into her pile of blankets. She'd essentially fucked over her life for the second time that year. She wondered if her future self had escaped her trail of bad decisions or if it got worse with age. By forty, she'd be putting countries to war with a drunk decree.

She turned to Aida. She looked so much different with her hair down like this, glasses off, her face not scowling at Lorian for looking. She looked peaceful, beautiful, in this limited light.

Lorian went to fix her curly bangs, then thought better of it and stayed her hand. What an earful she'd receive about this tomorrow.

She prayed Aida could speak by then.

Chapter 11: Breadcrumbs

Aida woke up. Then died. And on it went, until she was indivertibly pissed off.

The first time she awoke, the sky was spinning, stars falling and blurring together, her body ablaze. Then she felt someone close to her, but she couldn't think, let alone demand that whoever was touching her better knock it off before she started kicking.

This went on for several days, her dipping in-between being alive and being something else. Her one constant was that her head hurt and that someone was watching her, always watching her. And the bluebirds. They were singing lullabies.

Sometimes, she felt a large hand cup her cheek. It felt nice, but she didn't know to whom it belonged. Queen Eve? Her mother? When had she returned to Bělico?

Around the third day of tossing and turning, she willed herself awake. She couldn't keep like this. She needed to wake up and figure out where she was. By how hard the ground felt, she kept envisioning a dungeon.

The ceiling opened and blinded her with sunlight. "Aida!"

She fell backwards and covered her eyes. She wiped down her skin of flames.

Someone touched her. "Are you okay? How do you feel? Are you hurt?"

She covered her ears. Why were they shouting? She did what she had to and shoved them away.

Lorian fell on his ass. "Ow."

In a rush of muddled memories, Aida spat out, "What on Earth are you doin' here?"

"I...sincerely apologize. Did I frighten you? It seems you have your strength back. That's good." He looked closer into her eyes. "My goodness, your *eyes*."

"Where...where am I?" She touched her throat, surprised to find it so dry. They'd hung out that night, right? She'd talked about *Pinnacle Isle*. No, that was earlier.

"We're beneath one of the stables near the training officer dorm. What happened to your eye?"

She smelled it now—the horses and their thick, wet hay—but around her was also a lantern, a kettle of water, and most of her belongings: a satchel with her clothes, a bag of her books, her cane, her glasses. Next to them were two other bags filled with Lorian's officer clothes.

Her breathing hitched. "Did you kidnap me?"

"Oh, no."

"Oh, Circa, you kidnapped me. Why would you do that? I don't have anything. I don't—I—" She felt an airiness between her legs. Aside from a white nightgown, she was completely naked. With a boy.

Her blood went cold. "You sick *fuck*."

"Aida, you're mistaken."

She brandished her cane as a sword. "I knew I shouldn't have trusted you. To think I thought you were one of the good ones."

"I didn't kidnap you," Lorian said. "Please, listen to me. I can explain everything. I'd overheard Carmine—the Constable—talking about arresting you for assaulting him. I got worried, so I went to your room to tell you. I heard a scuffle, I knocked until someone unlocked the door, and you were gone—you'd jumped—and then Carmine—"

"Liar. I didn't jump. I would've remembered that. I would've..."

She stopped. *Had* she jumped? Her, ambling over cobblestone...

"The Constable had been searching for me," Lorian continued. "You see, I'm...I'm not a real officer. Or one in training. I'd forged the papers to get into the training regimen..."

What streets had she walked through? She remembered a toothbrush. Maybe some hats? A brothel?

"...didn't hurt him, but I did, well, *duel* him."

"Who?" she asked.

"The Constable."

She stared at him. "You fought a constable?"

"The queen's constable, yes. When you came back to us, when he cornered me and was about to kill me, I was..." He bit his lip. "You won't believe me, I know you won't, but right before I was outmatched, you and I...came from the future."

Lorian stammered, "I know it sounds ridiculous, and it is, but these two people appeared from nothing. They looked like us but older, in our thirties or so, and they were spouting absolute rubbish, and then they, well, *stole away* the Constable. Or you did. The one who looked like you jumped towards him, snatched him up, and vanished with the future me. And you were convulsing so terribly when you came back, I thought you were going to die. So, without any real plan, I took you

110

down here, and, well, here we are." He opened up his arms. "In hiding."

He bowed his head. "I'm sorry for these inconveniences. I know you must be upset and hurting."

No, she wasn't upset. She'd been looking for something, and she'd found it, but like everything else in her life, it'd been taken from her...

She slapped a hand over her mouth. *Eve*. Her husband. King Julius II. Queen Julia. And all those happy Visatorre. In Roma City. No, *Siina*.

She'd gone into the past. And the distant past, too. Ancient, during Queen Eve's time. How had she forgotten something so important? What was wrong with her brain?

She began to sweat. She gathered her belongings in a rush, clumsily putting on her glasses and strapping on her heels. Why hadn't she remembered a meeting so crucial?

"Wait," Lorian said. "Don't move around too much. They'll be looking for us."

She'd been looking for Eve, and she'd found her. She was beautiful and liberated beyond her years. And she'd been pregnant.

She looked down at her hands. 1,200 years into the past and all she felt was a little haziness? Had her luck finally turned around?

She dropped her hands. "Wait, what did you say?"

"The officers," Lorian said. "Carmine. They're all looking for us."

"Why?"

"Because I attacked them."

"So? That has nothing to do with me."

"It does, in a way. You were in the room when it happened, and that woman—I've been calling them Future Aida and Future Lorian—sort of *kidnapped* him. He was dropped somewhere in the palace. Because of this, and because they've found neither you nor I nor our future selves, they've been posting wanted posters of us across the city. At least, that's what Alessio told me. I haven't been out too often. I went out to steal back your cane and some of your belongings from your dorm room. I have some cheese somewhere. Are you hungry?"

"Wait." She held her head. "How *long* was I out?"

"Two days. Your jump left you shaking and unresponsive. When we set you down, you passed out. I didn't know what to do. I didn't want to leave you alone."

Despite sounding genuinely concerned for her, Aida didn't chance it. He'd gone through her room, but he'd saved her when she was hurt. He'd lied to her, but he'd defended her.

This was all too confusing, and it wasn't getting any clearer with him. "I don't believe you," she said. "You said this 'Future Aida' jumped around in time? That's not possible. And you're not a Visatorre."

"I know it doesn't make sense. I'm as lost as you are."

"It *doesn't* make sense, so if you'll excuse me." Aida redressed herself, leaned on her cane, and left through the cellar door.

"Wait!"

If her botched memories were anything to go off of, he was right about one thing. She, as of this semester, was no longer a student at Durante Academy. Her scholarship, the tests she'd been studying for, none of that would ever matter again. To ensure that it was true, she took out her expulsion letter from her dress pocket.

112

She tore it to shreds and let the pieces drift behind her. She needed answers, and she needed to find a new future.

She sorted through her bags. She had a good chunk of the clothes she'd brought from home, and Lorian had packed away her books, journals, even her signed playbooks. How considerate, the liar.

"Aida, wait!" Lorian appeared by her side, taking her arm. "It's not safe."

"Let go." She shoved him off and continued en-route to her dorm.

"Stop being stubborn. Didn't you hear me?" He looked nervously around the grounds. "We're *wanted*. A dozen officers have been scouring the campus looking for us."

"Well, I don't know why they would be, considering I'm innocent."

"Not in their eyes, you're not. You attacked the Constable."

"Oh, for Circa's sake, I threw my cane at him."

"And you egged his carriage."

"They can't prove that last part."

"Nevertheless, they're connecting you with this Future Aida. Apparently, she's been toying with the Constable, stealing his hats and freeing his horses. Everything she's doing, it's falling onto you."

"You're talking as if I believe you. It sounds like you're making it up. Which, given that you're a known liar, I wouldn't put it past you."

Lorian threw back his head. "I didn't know you were this...this..."

She waited for the insult and to throw a worse one back at him.

"Strong-willed," he chose.

Her eyebrows shot up. How rare it was for someone to give her a compliment.

"Fine. If you're not going to listen to me, at least let me walk you to your dorm," he said. "That's where you're going, right? They've been through there, looking for clues to where we went."

"The nerve of this Academy. Why did I ever want to come here in the first place? I heard it was elite, but I didn't think it'd be this forward with immorality."

"Welcome to Roma," Lorian said, "where the people are vile and the history's—"

He jerked back, grabbed Aida by the arm, and brought her around the building they were about to pass.

"What?"

"Shh," he said. In the distance, two men were arguing and growing louder.

"I said I don't *know*, Sir. I'm sorry I can't tag along on this ghost chase."

Taking a peek, Aida saw a red-haired officer in training and an officer arguing near one of the school's wishing wells. The boy was about their age and had his chin held high, hands defiantly on his hip bones.

"I already told Officer Vato," the redhead said. "I saw Lorian and that girl leave through the forest. By the time Matteo and I came out to investigate, they were gone. It was as if they'd both jumped."

"We searched the forest top to bottom. Their footprints end at the tree line. Are you sure they went in?"

"I never said they went in. Look, Officer, do you need me to give another account about what I saw? I've already done so with three officers, they have everything I said on file."

"Do you believe me now?" Lorian whispered to Aida. "We need to be watchful. I can't be found out. I'll be killed, and you'll be thrown in jail without having a witness to defend you."

"Trust" wasn't something she gave out easily. In fact, she didn't know if she'd trusted anyone in her life. Her sisters? No. Her mother? Absolutely not. Who else did she have to put her trust into?

Lorian, she guessed.

She found herself nodding against her better judgement. "Okay," she said. "Where should we go? Back to that crummy barn?"

"I think, for the time—"

"Hey!"

The larger officer was looking straight at them, sword drawn for attack. "You two, stay right there!"

Cursing under his breath, Lorian unsheathed his own rapier. "Aida, go! Take my horse!"

"What?"

"The horse stables behind us!" He ripped something off of his neck and threw it at her. It was a necklace with an old-looking key, a silver ring, and a horse whistle attached to it.

"Go!" he yelled when he caught her examining it.

He was insane. An absolute nutter. To attack not only the queen's most-trusted constable but also another officer in the same week, for her...

The corner of her mouth twitched into a smile as she took off towards the pasture. What a lad.

A stupid lad. "Wait, which one's yours?" she called out.

"Ether, the palomino one!" He said more, but the clash of steel against steel drowned him out.

Aida didn't look back. She spotted the golden mare grazing by herself near the fence. Luckily, the door had been left open, so Aida ran down the hill and entered the field.

She'd ridden a few horses in her life. When she'd been lighter and her mother kinder, she'd ridden for practice, then fun, when nobody was in the house to ridicule her. But then her anxieties built up, along with her weight, and now she was nervous about getting back on.

She circled the horse, testing its friendliness. "Hey there."

It bucked its head.

"Oh, c'mon." She dangled the horse whistle. "This what you want?" She blew into it.

The horse's ears perked up. She looked Aida right in the eyes, then sniffed between her ear and temple.

"Overly-friendly. Just like your owner, 'ey?"

The horse chuffed.

"Okay." She tried mounting her. "Don't buck me, I swear to the Gods."

Out on the main courtyard, Lorian called out Ether's name.

Trained to his voice, the horse obeyed and galloped out of the pasture.

Aida hunkered close to the horse's center. Why was she going so fast? She must've been well-trained, and well-bred. The rich bastard.

"Aida!"

She turned around. Lorian had found himself another horse, a dark brown colt with white spots. He galloped towards her with Ether ready to follow.

"Hey!" the red-haired boy shouted. He was standing beside the officer, who was now unconscious. "Stop! That's my horse!"

"I'll return her, Alessio, I swear!" Lorian said. "I'll drop her off at the Colosseum! Find her there in a day's time!"

"Fuck you, Lorian!"

Aida just waved to him as Ether ran after Lorian. While she justified certain "borrowing," she couldn't condone stealing someone's whole horse. She supposed this was a special case.

"You, Lorian Ashwell," Aida said, "are an incredibly desperate, stupid man, and you're gonna get both of us killed."

"Thank you," he said, "but if you choose to believe me, I did see our future selves this week, so there's a chance you and I continue to make bad decisions for a long time."

Aida concealed her smile by staring up into the sky. "Fuck you."

They rode down the path into the denser part of the forest. Here, the trees curved in around them, the branches masking them from the Gods judging their recklessness.

"So," Aida said, "in the case that I do believe you and that you're not a sword-wielding nut who'd lie to a fair maiden such as myself, what on Earth am I going to do with you?"

"With me?"

"Yeah, our situation."

"Oh. Well, when I left my home, I hopped from tavern to tavern, doing labor work to earn my keep. I made a list of the safer inns we can stay in, but they're closer to the sea than the city."

"I'm not sleeping with you," she said, then corrected herself by saying, "not in the same room, and I don't have any money. If I can't go back to my dorm, this"—she showed him her bags—"is all I have now, thanks to you."

"Thanks to me? You're lucky I went back to collect them."

"You're right. I'm the luckiest dame in the country."

"Are you seriously mad at me?"

Aida looked up at Lorian's hurt face, and she backpedalled. That wasn't the reaction she wanted. She thought she was being funny. Wasn't this what friends did? "No. Sorry. I've been through one fucking weird week, or lifetime. Oh!"

Lorian flinched. "What?"

"My trip! My *jump!*" she said. "Fuck me, fuck seeing our fucking future selves, I saw *Eve!*"

"That queen you like?"

"'*That queen*', he says. Yes, you dolt, the queen! *My* queen. Good God, how did I forget to mention that?" Her mouth hung open, trying to decide where to start the story.

"Hey!"

The sound of electricity cracked and ignited so close to her ear that Ether whinnied in alarm.

The Visatorre jumped right in front of their horses, but she hadn't come back the way you were supposed to, naked and delirious. She'd come back like that man had done in Siina: fully clothed, wearing a beautiful blue dress that sparkled like a summer ocean, and she was smiling. Her grin was manic.

She was Aida. Or her future self. Her mirror image, doppelganger. While she did wear her hair down and smelled of vanilla, whatever Lorian had poorly explained to her, all of it was proven true upon her arrival, a catalyst to chaos.

"Hey, little me," Future Aida said. She teleported again, this time to Aida's right, and her bags were robbed from her. Another jump and she was back in front of them. The booms from her jumps crackled in the air.

"Hey!" Aida said.

"Hey again!" Future Aida said back. "And no, you're not getting these back unless you chase me for them. Come on!"

She jumped back farther and farther down the path, her presence fading as quickly as it came. "Hey, don't you want these back?" She took out a handful of Aida's playbooks and spread them out like playing cards. "If you don't want them, I'll be happy to dump them in the Tiber River for you. And you *know* I will."

"Wait!"

"I'm not waiting, Aida, you know I won't! Come now!" She laughed. "Off to Roma City!"

Chapter 12: Welcome to Roma

Aida steered frightened Ether back on course. "Wait! Give me back my things!"

"Careful!" Lorian said. "She might be dangerous."

"She's me," Aida said but didn't know how much weight that carried. From years of being alone, she knew herself inside and out, and never would she've been this loud or *annoying*. What a child this "Future Aida" was, playing keep-away when she should've known she was still recovering from her jump.

The Aida jumped down the road like a carefree rabbit. With her extra lead, she stooped in trees like an owl and pretended to bide her time by kicking stones. This was all a game to her. It made the veins in Aida's eyes throb.

As they descended into Roma City's farmlands, Aida noticed that Future Aida was pacing out her jumps. At times, they lost sight of her for minutes, only to find her sitting atop a farmer's shingled roof. When they got close enough, she saw Future Aida panting, a haggard expression making her smile look all the more fake.

"She's baiting us," Lorian said.

"I know, but I can't imagine her hurting either of us. You saw the two of them in my room, didn't you? So we know we aren't going to die now."

"But we can't trust her."

"*Do* you?" she questioned. "She's wired. I just want my things back."

"Well, it *is* hers."

Aida rolled her eyes. "We're not doing this. From here onwards, she is she, and I am me. We are not the same."

"Whatever you say, *Current* Aida."

Her jaw clenched to keep from smiling.

Farmlands growing apples and peaches circled the stone walls of Roma City. It was all Roma City, but the closer to the palace you got, the fewer farms you saw. Vineyards ended at the gates, growing the grapes that'd soon be in the bellies of Their Majesties.

It was massive, the entrance marker. Pillars the size of redwoods holding up ancient concrete archways. They dated back 3,000 years, before Eve and the growth of Siina. It used to bring travellers to their knees, thankful to have finally made it all this way, while slaves had told horror stories about crossing this no man's land. Now, nothing but weeds and dandelions grew around the stone, dating it as a forgotten piece of architecture.

They lost Future Aida in the crowds. It must've been a market day, for hundreds of shops had their doors open for customers. Street carts sold everything from bread to ice to meat to Aldaían bugs kept in wooden cages. A musical group played music near a fountain, and children danced while their parents bid and bartered.

Déjà vu patted Aida on her back. The street layouts were different and the buildings had either been redesigned or torn down, but the *feelings* were there. Around every corner, Aida anticipated seeing Eve or free Visatorre relishing in the joys of being alive.

The Visatorre people were still in the city, but they didn't make her feel any better. They weren't the ones manning the shops or entertaining the crowds. They were hiding in alleys and sitting on planks of wood without jobs. Those who were brave enough to be in the sunlight were dressed down. The Visatorre children were skinny and the women skulked in alleys. Some looked okay, which comforted Aida, but it hadn't been like this in Bĕlico. In Bĕlico, everyone worked. Visatorre overworked because they needed to, tending to crops and herding the sheep for their employers. In Roma, it felt like they were undesirable vermin.

What hurt the most was that Aida found herself looking away from them. She didn't want to see them this way, she wanted what their great-great-great grandfathers once had.

After recognizing what she was doing, she cursed herself and went to the first Visatorre she saw in need. She offered what she had left: a few bronze lyria. The man gave her a short nod, clutching the coins like diamonds in his gloved hands.

"Aida?"

"I'm coming." She guided her horse back to Lorian, who was watching her intently.

"Do you do that often?" he asked.

"When I can. Do you?"

He thought on it, then said, "I always thought my contribution as an officer was enough, but after living in the real world, I now understand that I've been ignorant to my people's plight."

"Officers aren't necessarily on our side. They regularly fuck us over because their leader lets them."

"Do you think ill of me for wanting this life for myself?"

"No," she said, "because I expect you to change it."

"How am I to change an entire system of—" He cut himself off. He looked a tad bit embarrassed. "Never mind."

"What?"

"Nothing, but thank you. For thinking so highly of me. I do hope things change, and that I can become a constable who'll be seen as a savior rather than an oppressor."

"I never said I thought highly of you, I said I think you're better than most people, which isn't really a compliment because most people are shitty to begin with."

Lorian's cheeks went red from unwarranted praise.

"Hey, stop that. Here, let's start fixing things from the ground up. You got any lyria to throw their way? And don't say you don't because I know you do."

He smiled. "A few coins, yes. Once we settle down, remind me to make a donation to a shelter."

"And find my bag. You're tall. Do you see where that woman went?"

He peered over the heads of the crowds. "I do not."

They decided to get off their horses and weave through the streets on foot. The crowds made Aida fold in on herself. She tucked her head close to her horse and stared into its side, hoping nobody would look at her.

A sneaky arm wrapped over her shoulder.

She looked up at Lorian. "'Ey."

"Where to, Miss?" he asked.

"What a gentleman," she said sarcastically, but she couldn't find what was sarcastic about it. True, he was smiling, and she was, too, so why was she against this? "Would you be doing this if I was a boy?" she asked him.

"Well, it'd depend on the boy."

"How about that boy back there at the Academy?"

"Oh, definitely not." He scouted up ahead. "Do you not like crowds? I can drive us down a different route. I know these streets very well. We're close to the palace."

"I'll be fine. We'll get out of here soon. I'm just not used to it, so I can fix it with practice. But we shouldn't walk near the palace."

"No tour around the palace gates?"

"Eyes ahead, officer."

He obliged. "Oh, speaking of eyes, do yours feel any different?"

"What do you mean?"

"Well, your right pupil is completely white."

She stopped dead in her tracks, startling their horses backwards. "What?" She tried opening her eye, then gave up and went to the nearest fountain sputtering out drinking water. There was no reflection in the bubbling pool, so she looked into the metal pipe.

She tried to blink it away. It looked like a smudge of a cloud in her eye, but it followed her reflection, glued to her retina.

"It must've appeared after you came back from your jump," Lorian explained. "After you met Eve, was it?"

"Yeah." She tried rubbing it out. "Am I diseased?"

"I've never heard of a sickness dyeing a pupil white. Your future self has it in both of her eyes."

"Then I'm definitely diseased. Gods, that's great. You know, just tack it onto the list, why don't ya?"

Lorian met her in her reflection. "Was it everything you wanted?"

"What?"

"Meeting Eve. Was it everything you wanted?"

She should've said yes. Saying she'd gone back in time to meet Eve would've made Past Aida break down in happiness.

"I don't know. She wasn't anything like I'd built her up to be in my head. She was our age, jumping around her carriage and fountains. And she was a lot shorter than I imagined. She was a bit like..." She stopped herself. "She was different."

"But not bad?"

"She's Queen Eve. She'll never be bad in my eyes." After splashing her face with water, Aida set off. "If every day I grow closer to looking more like that woman, I'm gonna throw myself off the palace clock tower."

"Eve, or your future self?"

"Can ya guess?"

"I think she's rather charming, in a crude sort of way."

"She's deranged, Lorian. Don't tell me that's your type."

He laughed as he walked, the street layout somehow memorized in his mind. Then his face fell. "Uh-oh."

"Don't 'uh-oh'," Aida said, then looked to see what he was "uh-ohing" about.

Tacked onto a bulletin board were two expertly drawn pictures of Aida and Lorian. They were the newest, covering posters of murderers and tax evaders.

"Uh-oh," Lorian repeated.

"Stop that." She grabbed his horse's reins. "Come on. We're going this way."

"I wouldn't."

"Why not?"

He pointed ahead.

When Aida's family had visited Roma City, she hadn't known the wrongness of glorifying the Colosseum. As a little girl, seeing a wonder of the world had blown her tiny mind. She'd wanted to touch it and take tours through it like all the adults were doing.

Now, she knew its history. It loomed over her and Lorian, blocking out the clouds with its height. The Sun shone through its hundreds of arches. They were broken like they should've been, devaluing it to a tourist trap.

Aida held her heart. Countless people had been slaughtered here for sport in the jaws of lions and inhuman men.

And parents wanted to take their children here to check it off their bucket list.

The plaza outside the Colosseum held more people than Aida could count. Food carts, fountains, statues, benches, patches of grass and trees where children and dogs played. Bĕlican farmers in their sheep-wool ponchos, Aldaían families wearing their headscarves made for the desert Sun. Tour guides, families on vacation, carriages stationed so their horses could drink from their troughs, Roman Visatorre.

Her light-headedness came back. The run from Durante Academy had her blood pumping, but now it was draining to her feet. So many people, so much noise...

"Aida?" Lorian asked.

"I'm fine," she said. "Let's keep going."

"Are you sure?"

She closed her eyes and let Lorian lead her. "When I saw Eve, there was a festival going on. Visatorre and non-Visatorre were mingling like friends. I didn't even see slaves or Visatorre being treated unfairly, which I should've seen for the time period. I saw one Visatorre jump 200 years back."

"How do you—"

"I saw it happen. He told his friends. I saw him jump fully clothed and come back perfectly fine."

"Just like your future self?"

She didn't say no. "Lorian, history as we know it is completely wrong. Visatorre were a free people, well-integrated into Roman society, who were able to jump without pain. Something happened between now and Eve's death that fucked us over. Your history, my people, it's like they were cursed. I mean, who knows if Eve or Julia even died, you know?"

"You think they're still alive?"

"Preferably, yes." They entered deeper into the crowds. "If my future self can jump into the future, why not her?"

A man bumped into them without apologizing.

"There must be something going on today," Lorian said. "It's never this busy. Perhaps there's a town meeting, though my...the monarchs don't work on Sundays."

Aida stared at her feet to keep focused. She felt nauseated and didn't know how far she'd be willing to go to get her possessions back.

The crowd nearest the Colosseum started a low cheer that infected the rest of the plaza with noise. Someone had left the Colosseum, someone important.

Aida cursed her small height. She hopped to see over a man's head. "What is it?"

Someone Lorian could see but Aida couldn't made him withdraw. "I-it's nothing. We should leave. It's not safe."

127

"But what is it?" Aida crouched down, hands on her bad knees.

"No, Aida. We *have* to go." He grabbed her. "*Now.*"

She didn't listen. There must've been a reason why he was avoiding the answer. She moved in closer.

"Aida, no!"

The royal flags, that's what she saw first. Those yellow and purple stripes in the air. Then the officers—constables—atop their horses, wearing their medals and black hats.

Constable Carmine, who stood in front of the platoon, gazed into the rambunctious crowd like a guard dog protecting his family.

Beside him, why the crowds had gathered that morning: Roma's own King Durante and Queen Rosalia; their daughter and former heir of Roma, Queen Beatrice; her husband and the Bĕlican king, King Dmitri; their daughter, Princess Nina; and the future king of Aldaí, Prince Zaahir.

"Holy shit," Aida breathed out. She recognized Zaahir from the portraits her sisters would swoon over, and Beatrice and Dmitri from the Bĕlican currency, and who could not know Queen Rosalia? Her beautiful blond hair reached the floor when out of its braids, and King Durante had this ugly face that screamed, "I own my title like a god."

This must've been the first time in decades where so many monarchs were together in public. They were *waving*, like they gave a shit about their people.

"Hey!"

They both turned, Lorian with a hand on his sword, Aida's on her cane.

Two Visatorre kids were staring up at them through the crowd, holding each other's hands. One little boy and girl, the boy a bit older, the girl a bit taller. They stared at them with sparkles in their innocent eyes.

"Aida, we need to go. Now," Lorian pressed. He kept looking between her and the two heirs up ahead. His hands were sweating.

"Aren't you the one from Mama's picture?" the little girl asked.

"No, we aren't," Lorian said halfheartedly, then to Aida, "Aida, we need to *go. Now.*"

"No, at our house," the boy reiterated. "We have pictures of you all around the living room."

"I-I don't know what you're talking about. Go off and find your Mama." Lorian backed up and Aida went with him.

She'd never seen him so off-kilter before. She thought him a servant to the crown, not a person with such a wealth of emotional range.

Lorian, stuttering on more excuses, walked backwards into a woman carrying a basket of pastries.

"Oh my!" She gasped and almost took a header on the cobblestone, but Lorian caught her.

The little children ran to her side.

"My earnest apologies, Miss," Lorian started. "I wasn't looking where I...was..."

The old woman fixed her glasses. She was a little grandma with greying brown hair and a soft face. She had on a knitted cloak that she wore over her shoulders and an emblem of a lion on her breast.

When she got a good look at Lorian gaping at her, she lowered her basket until it dropped and spilled her pastries. Those two little kids bent down and helped pick them up. Their eyes never left Lorian's face.

The grandma covered her mouth with one wrinkled hand. "Lucia," she gasped in a whisper. "Lucia, my love, is that *you*?"

Lorian kept staring at her, too stunned by their meeting to talk, too terrified by this older woman who thought she knew him.

Lucia. Aida had heard that name a hundred times before but thought very little about her. The tall beauty with golden curls and fair skin, the one who kept silent in public beside her beautiful twin sister.

What the public didn't know was that both of their royal heirs had come back to them today, though the infamous Lucia was now an officer who went by Lorian Ashwell.

"Oh, fuck," Aida said, her realization coming weeks too late.

Chapter 13:
Missus Sharma's Cottage

No matter how far she strayed from her past, Lorian could not part from Missus Sharma.

She'd tried to with her sister, who was thirty meters away on horseback and had thankfully not looked this way. Zaahir, they'd only met a handful of times. While he'd agreed to the marriage, he seemed uninterested in her overall.

Her parents were complicated. Like Carmine, she used to like the adults in her life. Then things changed. Her mother now looked weak, her father had become disgraceful. And Carmine was...

Different.

But Lorian couldn't leave Missus Sharma. She smelled like home, like sweet pastries and lotion. It looked like she'd aged ten years when it'd only been a season. Her hair held traces of white streaks like clouds through a sunset sky, and her hands felt colder and more cracked than usual.

Missus Sharma hugged Lorian like she'd never see her again. "Oh, *mi dolcezza*. My baby."

"I know," she said, unsure of which emotion to feel. "I'm here."

"But why? What happened? Where did you go? Are you safe? I saw the posters in the square." She pulled away. "What've you done?"

Shame Lorian didn't know she still had filled her stomach. She hadn't told anyone that she'd run away. She didn't think Beatrice knew, though she found out most things before Lorian had even thought of them. She'd wanted to tell Missus Sharma, but she couldn't do that to her. If Missus Sharma had been involved and her father found out, she would've been punished for withholding information from the crown. Lorian didn't think she'd have to face this disappointment so soon.

"I apologize," Lorian said, "but we can't stay here. Mother and Father are here. They can't see me like this."

"Oh. Yes." Missus Sharma looked past the crowds to Beatrice. "Do you have a place to go, a place to hide?"

Lorian shook her head.

"And your friend?"

She turned to Aida, who had an uncertain, irritated look on her face. Yet another lie she'd chastise Lorian for. They'd never cease.

"Her name's Aida," Lorian explained. "Missus Sharma, do you live close?"

"I do. Dear, are you okay to walk?"

Aida, who was leaning on her cane with both hands, straightened up and nodded once.

"But we didn't get everything on the list," the little boy said. He, like the little girl beside him, were time travellers, their marks scarring their foreheads.

"Hush, Onti," Missus Sharma said. "Take Chrissie's hand and be soft and quiet."

Lorian, Aida, and the two little ones followed Missus Sharma down an eastern alley. Lorian didn't dare breathe until the crowds dwindled. The cheers from whatever Lorian's family was doing faded behind the brick buildings.

"Your parents were introducing Bea and Prince Zaahir to the public," Missus Sharma explained. "Your father asked that they come on urgent matters. According to reports, there're two Visatorre who can jump in a special way. I don't know too much about it, I was out getting groceries. Such a maelstrom of news. Lucia, dear, how have you managed to keep hidden for so long? With all these officers about, I was sure that they'd find you."

They passed a hidden cafe with outdoor seating. A few people were dining out.

Lorian ducked her head and continued on before speaking. "It's not safe here," she whispered.

"Oh, yes," Missus Sharma said, downcast. "Of course, yes."

Lorian's guilt ate at her with every step. From Missus Sharma's bad back to the little ones to Aida's legs, they had to walk at a snail's pace, giving the shame time to augment. Shame for running away, for lying, for endangering Aida and hurting Missus Sharma. She'd hoped to have more time to sort this out, but the broken pieces of her choices needed to be picked up.

Why hadn't Aida said anything? Neither a question nor utterance of dismay. Somehow, that hurt the worst, knowing how distrustful she must've been but choosing not to speak about it.

Missus Sharma's wealth from the crown showed in her house: a farmhouse cottage with a large yard surrounded by a stone wall that looked to be from the Classical Era. The bricks were overtaken by vines. A giant lemon tree grew behind the house. Flowers were everywhere, adding spots of color to the yard.

"Here we are," Missus Sharma said, lifting up her heavy dress. "Please mind the mess, your Highness. I would've cleaned up if I knew I'd be having company."

"It's quite alright," Lorian said. The "mess" came from the front lawn: hula hoops and play swords, dirtied rabbit dolls and gladiator toys. Both Onti and Chrissie looked away like they weren't the ones to blame.

As Lorian followed Missus Sharma down the drive to the cottage, Aida stood back by the iron gates.

"It's okay." Lorian reached out to her. "You can trust her. She was my nursemaid from before. She's kind."

One of Aida's eyebrows arched, questioning her.

"Please. If you can't trust me, I understand, but trust *her*. She's a good person who won't hurt us."

Aida challenged her with her eyes, unconvinced and waiting for her to prove her wrong.

To test her, Lorian kept her hand out, pleading with her eyes.

Aida shifted her cane from one hand to the other. "Your name."

Lorian nodded.

"Which is it?" she clarified. "Which do you prefer? Lucia or Lorian?"

"Oh." She hadn't expected that name to leave Aida's lips. It didn't sound right. "Lorian."

"As a girl? Or a boy?" She looked away. "Or something else?"

"I don't know," she said honestly, "but not Lucia. That's not me anymore.

"That was my last, most protected secret, and now I have nothing left to hide from you. I'm stupid and impulsive and don't think my actions through. I want to be better, and that starts with leaving that life behind. I'm sorry I broke your trust, and I'm sorry my actions led us here. It was unfair to you, and for that"—she bowed—"I apologize."

Aida kept staring at her. And staring. And Lorian was realizing how much power this one girl had over her. Everything she thought about her dictated her worth. She had been a princess meant to rule in the most powerful ally Roma had, and this girl held more authority over her with a stare.

"Okay." She handed over her horse's reins, then walked over the grass to meet with Missus Sharma.

Lorian watched her leave, everything unsaid building. How she wanted to hug her and thank her for accepting her misdoings. She tied up the horses alongside Missus Sharma's, a shy smile escaping her trembling lips.

Missus Sharma's cottage had as much clutter on the inside as it did the outside. Vegetables lay in iron pots on the counter. More toys, packed between couches and underneath rugs. A few candles had been lit in the kitchen, but a generous amount of light came in from the front windows. Muffins were set out on the sill to cool.

A woman was sitting in a well-used sofa chair, reading a gardening book. When she went to greet Missus Sharma and saw Lorian instead, she gasped. "My *word*, would you look at that."

"Iris, darling, put the tea kettle back on the stove for me," Missus Sharma said. "Aida, Lucia, please, go sit in the living room. Chrissie, put away your treats in the proper cabinets. Onti, make sure you put away your shoes."

"I always do," he whined, and launched his boots at the front door.

"Please don't run about for our sake," Lorian said.

"Oh, Lucia, sit, please. You poor thing." She took Lorian's officer jacket and began folding it. "I have so many questions for you, Lucia. I'm so confused."

"She doesn't go by Lucia anymore."

They pulled back.

"The name's Lorian now," Aida said. "Not that other name."

Lorian wet her lips, more unease spreading through her.

Missus Sharma inhaled, then exhaled with a pained expression. "Oh. Yes, I...Forgive me. I do remember you mentioning something like that. My apologies, Your Highness."

"And it's not 'Your Highness' anymore," Aida said. "It's just Lorian."

"Oh..." Less enthused with that answer, Missus Sharma went into the kitchen.

With formalities out the window, Aida flopped down next to Lorian in a groan.

"Are you alright?" Lorian asked.

"Yeah. Sore, but I'll manage."

"That's good. I mean, better. I mean..." She gulped. "Thank you," she whispered, "for understanding."

"Oh, we'll talk about that later, don't you worry," she said, but Lorian didn't hear any malice in her tone. She wondered if it was from a change of heart or Aida's lethargy catching up to her. Even though she said she was fine, Lorian saw the sway of her body. She needed two more days of rest.

Iris came back with a plate of tea and some crackers. "Here you are, babies. My, if I thought we'd be hosting guests, especially *you*, I would've dolled myself up."

She already looked beautiful in Lorian's eyes. She was Aldaían, with dark skin, wrinkled eyes, and her natural hair pulled up with a headscarf. Lorian hadn't recalled Missus Sharma talking about any relatives from Aldaí. She'd thought she lived alone.

Missus Sharma came back in with Chrissie and Onti on her heels.

"It's a great honor to finally meet you," Iris said, breaking the tension. "My name is Iris, but you can call me Mi'Sharma, uh…"

"Lorian is fine, and this's Aida Mirko, my…friend."

Aida side-eyed her.

"How did I meet you in the Roman Plaza?" asked Missus Sharma. "You've been gone nearly two months. Where were you?"

"I was with her," Lorian said, and after a sip of tea, she explained her summer away from home.

The children grew bored and took to the floor to play with their toys, but Missus Sharma and Mi'Sharma listened as if they were hearing a fairytale for the first time. Lorian could see how someone could be enrapt by her tale, but she didn't feel hopeful about it having a happy ending. From the moment she fled her wedding, deceit darkened her heavy soul, and now, she felt like half a person on the run, waiting to be caught.

When she finished, Missus Sharma began fanning herself. "Goodness gracious."

"I was about to say," Mi'Sharma said. "That's an adventure if I ever heard one."

"I'm deeply sorry for all the heartache I must've caused you," Lorian said. "How are my mother and father?"

"I'm not sure. The day you ran away, I was fired from my position."

Lorian sat up. "They *fired* you? How could they? You were with my mother before Bea and I were born, they couldn't—"

"Unfortunately, with Beatrice now in Bělico and you leaving us, they had no choice. I was ready to leave as soon as your wedding day was coming up. I just thought it'd be under better circumstances."

"She worked for them for nearly twenty-five years," Mi'Sharma grumbled. "I wanted to walk right up those palace steps and give them a piece of my mind, I did."

"I had no place there without Lucia and Beatrice. They thought my time had been served. It's no problem, though. Mi'Sharma here tends to the animals out back and sells goat milk to get us by, and I've allocated most of my earnings, so we'll be okay."

Lorian couldn't imagine the Roman Palace without Missus Sharma. She did the laundry, baked the pastries, made sure Lorian was cared for the way a mother would've done.

"And so," Missus Sharma said, "Carmine—excuse me, the Constable—is now looking for you, because of this woman and her partner, and they're...you?"

"It sounds very nonsensical, I know, but both of us have seen them in action. She—Future Aida—is able to carry herself through time without injuring herself. She said we had a mission to reshape Roma, but now that we're here, I feel more lost than I was two months ago."

"Well, our doors are always open. You're more than welcome to stay with us for as long as you need."

"But—"

"No buts," she said. "I lost you once. I won't lose you again."

Lorian's jaw strained to tell her otherwise, but what was she to do, now that she'd made herself more of a target? "Thank you," she said.

"Of course. Onti, Chrissie, is that okay with you? These two older kids are going to stay with us for a while, okay?"

Onti pressed his Visatorre marking into the table corner. "Is it true you're a king?"

"No, he's a prince," Chrissie corrected.

"I'm neither, actually," Lorian said. "A pageboy, if anything."

"Pageboys are lame!" Onti said. "My brother was a pageboy before he died and it was lame."

"Onti, hush now," Missus Sharma said. "Please forgive him. He does mean well."

"Who are they, if I may ask?" Lorian asked. "Are they your children?"

"Oh, yes. I adopted them from off the streets years and years ago. And this's Iris, my partner. We met almost thirty years ago when she was visiting from Aldaí."

"Really?" Lorian asked. "I never knew. It's nice to meet you."

"It wasn't good for servants to talk about their family life when not prompted, Your Highness."

Lorian almost bent over with how much guilt she was now carrying. Had she ever asked Missus Sharma about her family life? She'd assumed she lived by herself.

"But we know all about you," Mi'Sharma said. "Cara here has told us countless stories about you and your sister since you were mere tots. You're practically family as is, like you're my little godchild. N-not that I'd impose such a title on you, Your Highness! Er, Lorian. Sir—Miss—" She covered her face. "Golly me, I've never been in the presence of royalty before. I'm not as equipped as Cara."

"Please, don't think of me so highly," Lorian said. "Most of that is in my past now. And it's a pleasure to meet you all. Aida, this's—"

"I know," she said flatly.

Lorian faked a smile. "Uh, please excuse us, but would you mind if I spoke to Aida privately for a moment?"

"Of course not," Missus Sharma said. "Take your time. We'll make accommodations for you two in the meantime. Iris, can you help me bring down some blankets?"

Instead of staying in the living room, Aida left towards the backyard. She closed the screen door but not the main one, leaving it ajar for Lorian.

Outside was that lemon tree Lorian had seen from the front lawn, along with a garden, a pond where two ducks swam, and a chicken coop built against a goat pasture.

Aida found a hammock tied to the tree and climbed in. Her feet dangled above the grass.

"May I?" Lorian asked.

She stared at her tiredly, then tried scooting to make room. She kept sliding into the middle.

Lorian got in next to her. Their hips touched. She pretended that they weren't.

"So," Aida said, "escaped-princess-turned-officer-turned-criminal."

Lorian added it up. "Throw in 'runaway fiancée' and you should be good."

"*Wow*," she drawled. "What a troublemaker."

"Unfortunately. Are you sure you're alright? You seem different."

She blinked slowly. "I think something's wrong with my brain. When you were talking back there, I don't know, but my head seems clouded, like I can't concentrate normally. It's been like this ever since I saw the Colosseum for some reason."

"I'm sure it's just a temporary haze from your jump. You'll feel better in a few days."

She didn't look optimistic. "By the way, uh, you're married? To the prince of Aldaí?"

"He's my fiancé." She showed off her ringless hand. "I've only met him during parties I had to pretend to be interested in. I didn't know him at all. It's why I left. They wanted me to be sent off to his country to bear his children. I wasn't doing that. My country's here, and my choice deserved to be heard."

"Way to stick it to your father."

"We've never seen eye to eye." She smiled as a memory tickled her brain. "I got the idea from that opera, of all things. *En Tempore Rose.*"

"Oh, I have no idea what that is," she said, "it's only my favorite opera based on the book series that I clung to since I was six. Pinnacle, the Red Dragon, the Goddess and her beautiful, long, blond hair. I know that bitch like the back of my hand."

"I need to take you one day."

"Visatorre aren't allowed in the theatre."

"They aren't?"

141

"You really are a royal heir, ain't ya? We're not allowed into a 'professional' setting, else we might cause 'risk' to the performers. It's not a rule that's set in stone, but most bigoted people don't wanna see a Visatorre jump in the middle of the performance and get mildly spooked."

"Oh." She laced her fingers in her lap.

"So," Aida said, "how did *En Tempore Rose* change your life?"

"Right. So, you know how the main boy—"

"Pinnacle. Pinnacle Pescatore. A fifteen-year-old emotionless asshole when the series starts but a twenty-three-year-old considerate god when the series ends."

"Right. So, towards the end of the opera, Pinnacle is faced with a decision: to hop on the dragon's back and leave the island or stay behind and be with the Goddess."

"You know, in the book, both he and the Goddess hop on Red Dragon's back only for the Goddess to tell Pinnacle that he'd just gained back part of his humanity and disappears. He spends the next five books earning back each piece: friendship, family, love, community, death, and sense of self. His whole journey about regaining his humanity is summed up in a two-hour opera. But yes, go on, continue."

Lorian chuckled at her passion. "Yes, yes, I'm a fake fan, but in the opera, he wields a sword, and looked so much like a gladiator from the Classical Era."

"Don't even get me started on that technical inaccuracy."

"Oh, I won't, but the way Pinnacle held himself, I saw myself as him. I want so badly to be a knight and slay the dragon, but I'm chained to my island, unable to reach what I want. It's why I wanted to be an officer. I wanted to be a gladiator."

"I love the, uh, what's her name?" Aida tapped her foot in the air. "What on Earth's the Goddess' name? Why can't I—*Sempre*," she yelped. "Fuck, how did I forget that? Anyway, she's given this long, beautiful hair that the ballerina has to work with. Usually, they keep it in buns and gel, but she's supposed to stand out. They often keep it braided down her back." She played with one of her braids. "I always thought that was pretty, but it was hard for me to braid it that way without help, so I do them down my front."

"Well, they look beautiful regardless."

Aida stuck out her tongue.

"I mean it, they do."

"And what, am I supposed to give you a compliment in return?"

"It's not manda—"

"I like," she said, freezing Lorian, "that you were able to run away. I'm glad you didn't let yourself get married to someone you didn't love."

Lorian settled more comfortably next to her. "Thank you."

"'Cause I know it must've been hard for you and all." She fiddled with her hands. "It's not like your compliment, but, you know..."

Lorian had to better control herself. Aida, nervous? Her pouty lip did something to her groin.

"We should go see it," Aida then said, "the play, when we're not running from the law."

"We will," Lorian promised, and cleared her throat. "It's a date."

Aida lifted her leg onto the hammock. "Yeah, I'll sit next to the Constable, you with your family. Beatrice, yeah? That sister with whom you have no qualms."

"Oh, absolutely none. We're the model siblings."

"And Prince Zaahir."

"Happily married."

"With kids."

"Wonderful," Lorian said, and fell back into the hammock. She squinted through the lemon tree branches. "Uh-oh."

"Stop 'uh-ohing'. What is it?"

She pointed above her.

On the highest branch hung Aida's stolen bag.

Chapter 14:
Zaahir, Two Days Before

"What do they mean it can't be done?" Zaahir muttered as he exited the meeting room. "They're such...this's so..."

His knight gave him a look.

"Absurd," he said, because any stronger language would've crossed his mother.

Two hours of discussion and none of his council members had budged on his proposals. While he thought the school expansions, heightened naval support in the north, and the opening of a new food pantry were beneficial to his country, the older party affiliates didn't seem to think so. He was left looking like a fool in front of his own cabinet.

He didn't know how else to help them. If he was to take his mother's place in a few years, he had to be more persuasive with his people. Aldaí was the most powerful, progressive country on Earth. He was sure to keep that promise for the next century.

If he were to have any heirs. Twenty-four years old without a presentable suitor and his people had begun doubting his politics.

"My Liege."

Kadar, like always, was right by his side, standing alert with a hand on his scimitar belt. He and Zaahir had been coupled since Zaahir was ten years old. He needn't look far for his forever companion.

"I know," Zaahir said. "No use fretting over what cannot be fixed at the current time. Let's be off."

They left down the hall. It was an aisle of gold, of bright pillars holding up the Aldaían Citadel. Above them were portraits of Zaahir's past family members, his mother, and their three Gods: Circa, Tymos, and Ukrei, dancing in fields of pastel flowers. To his right grew the royal gardens built by his great-great-great grandfather, and the ocean, bright blue without a cloud in the sky. The Sun sizzled over the water.

Beyond it, though Zaahir couldn't see it, lay Roma and all of its gifts.

"You did well in the meeting, My Liege," Kadar said as they walked. "I was quite moved."

"You always say that. I need to be better for Aldaí."

"Your passion for a kinder world exceeds you, my Liege."

"Yes, but those people don't take me seriously, not without my current future set in stone. My mother wants to hold another search party to find her."

Kadar's eyebrows shot up. He wore the signature headscarf all Aldaían knights wore, so only his eyes were visible. They were an expressive gold Kadar loved.

"Does she believe Princess Lucia will return?" Kadar asked.

Zaahir shrugged. Two months ago, he'd been left at the altar, waiting for a wife who hadn't wanted him. He'd had a sinking suspicion that that night would go awry when she'd cursed out her father before the hors d'oeuvres arrived.

Even if they were to find her, wherever she was, Zaahir couldn't imagine her coming to Aldaí to weld their two worlds together. Poor girl.

Poor person, rather.

"You said you don't know where she went," Kadar continued. "She never informed you?"

"No, she only told me that she wanted to leave. That, and her...declaration."

"Of being gender-nonconforming."

Zaahir looked up. "What an interesting way to describe it."

"It's how Mohona lives by." Mohona was his little sibling. "They're only sixteen, but they knew what they wanted early in life. In all honesty, you can see the signs at a young age."

Zaahir smiled fondly at the few memories he had of the Roman heir. "Like I know her myself, though the few times we met, she was such a firecracker of a person. I was charmed by her."

"Hm," Kadar said, and said nothing more.

That dip in his low voice stirred butterflies in Zaahir's stomach. He came closer to his guard. "Is that a hint of jealousy I hear in your voice?" he teased.

"Of course not, my Liege. I was incredibly happy for your wedding and I was disappointed to see it come to a striking end."

"Were you now? What a relief. I was very ready to wed her and bear many children with her."

Kadar walked a little faster ahead.

"Excuse me, Sir Kadar, wherever are you going? I wish to retire early today."

"Of course, My Liege," he said, and the grumpiness Zaahir rarely heard from his knight made him giddy.

He jogged up the stairwell and beat Kadar to his room by a hair. Typically, his knights would open and close every door for him, making sure the royal family was guarded, but today, Zaahir wanted to surprise Kadar, and he wanted to see his face when he did it.

As Kadar reached for the golden handle, Zaahir wrapped his own hand around Kadar's.

Kadar eyed him, those sharp eyes melting Zaahir in his slippers.

"You wouldn't believe how hard I worked on this," Zaahir explained as he opened the door. "It took meticulous planning to gather the rose petals without you knowing."

Scattered across Zaahir's bedchamber were red flower petals plucked from the blooming trees outside. He'd lit candles around his bed and clawfoot bathtub. The windows let in the scent of the sea. It was exactly as he'd imagined, but Kadar's stunned expression was the sweetest cherry on top.

One would've expected the petals to lead to his bed, which Zaahir was no stranger to, but he'd wanted to be frisky today. He knew these meetings had been stressing both of them out, so what better way to relieve themselves than taking their loved one on the balcony?

With seldom rain in Aldaí, Zaahir was able to keep fainting couches and cushions outside. He'd often sleep out here, listening to the waves crash on the cliffs below.

Zaahir took advantage of Kadar's surprise and whispered in his ear. "Will you take me up on the offer?"

"Hmm." Kadar moved his head to meet Zaahir's lips.

Zaahir kissed the fabric shielding him from his soft, brown skin, and sat him on the couch. He straddled him. "This alright today?"

"What exactly are you insinuating?" Kadar teased.

To show him, Zaahir began unbuttoning his tunic, his hands slow in case Kadar wasn't in the mood.

Kadar got comfortable. "Not often I see this side of you."

"I wanted to treat you today. So many talks of Lucia this month, I know it troubles you." He brought his lips to his ear. "You know that no matter who I'm engaged to, to me, you'll always be my husband."

Kadar, who'd taken to roaming the curves of Zaahir's hips, looked up.

"I know you hate it. I do, too. If I wasn't obligated to bear sons, I'd marry you in a heartbeat. You know that, right?"

He nodded. "*Amar.*"

The roll of his tongue sent a shiver down Zaahir's spine. *"My love,"* used only between spouses.

Zaahir couldn't undress his *amar* quickly enough.

———◇———

The next morning, Zaahir awoke entangled around Kadar. They'd ended up in bed that night, but between here and the balcony, they'd ventured to the floor, the bath, up against the wall. They didn't often have the time to indulge in one another so intimately, as Kadar had training and Zaahir's schedule was peppered with meetings and lessons and travel. But sometimes, Zaahir was selfish. Sometimes, he fell in love with his own love.

Zaahir tossed and turned from the morning Sun until he found Kadar's lips.

"Mm," Kadar mumbled into him. "Good morning."

"Good morning, *amar*." He kissed his Visatorre marking. It was a faint circle he often bullseyed his kisses.

"What time is it?" Kadar asked.

"Do you have someplace to be?"

"*You* do, so that means I do as well."

Zaahir moaned and rolled onto his back. "I do not want to."

"You have no choice."

"Says who?"

Unable to technically order him to do anything, Kadar gave up and flopped a tired arm over his bare chest. His stubble tasted sweet on Zaahir's lips, and he played with his curly hair that was so often hidden from him. When he was like this, fully exposed without any coverings, Zaahir lost himself to lust.

A knock rapped on the door.

"Do forgive the interruption, my Liege. It's Hana. I have an urgent letter from the King of Roma requesting your response as soon as possible. May I come in?"

"One moment," Zaahir called out.

Kadar yawned and hid his head underneath the covers.

Zaahir waited for him to be fully burrowed before saying, "You may."

Hana came in with a bow. "My apologies for intruding so early in the morning, my Liege, but the king requests that you answer posthaste." She looked at the lump of covers beside him and bowed. "Kadar."

Keeping with his modesty, Kadar stayed covered in the presence of someone he didn't consider family. He did give a sleepy wave from the covers. "Hello, Hana."

Zaahir rubbed his tired eyes as he opened the letter with Hana's letter opener. He hadn't spoken to the Roman king since he left the wedding. He'd asked Zaahir to forgive them for Lucia's outrageous behavior. The only thing outrageous about the wedding was the lack of flavor in their hors d'oeuvres.

He read the letter while petting Kadar beneath the covers.

Halfway through the letter, he stopped and devoted all of his attention to the letter.

After reading it twice, he said to Hana, "Schedule a meeting with my mother at once."

"Yes, my Liege," she said, and left.

Kadar, curious, peeked his head out. "What did he say?"

Zaahir went to give him the letter but feared the words stained on it. "They found a Visatorre who can control her jumps without harm."

In Aldaí, they had a prophecy. They had many prophecies that spanned across generations, ones that were rescripted, ones that were left to time as they no longer fit the current beliefs. But one remained with them.

Their Gods, with powers greater than any king or queen, were able to teleport between realms. They could skip around centuries, take you on spiritual journeys to teach you lessons depending on what vices you carried. Visatorre were seen as people blessed with such powers, but because of these powers, they were weakened as a result, as no mortal was able to hold the full duties of a god.

The prophecy foretold of a Visatorre breaking through these limitations, becoming god-like without pain. They said when that happened, the world would either vaporize or be born anew in gold.

Now, Zaahir wasn't a spiritual person, but he knew that when fate announced herself so blaringly, you didn't ignore her arrival.

Zaahir turned to his *amar*. "I think we need to pay another visit to Roma."

Chapter 15:
Beatrice, Two Days Later

Beatrice was staring out of her carriage window, chin propped up on the windowsill, utterly indifferent to the world.

She wasn't *feeling* indifferent, just masqueraded it. In fact, as their carriage journeyed down the familiar path of tulips, she was feeling all sorts of ways. She was back in Roma, back for another meeting issued by her father with her husband and not her. She came to Roma once or twice a year for council meetings. Her husband, as usual, would do all the talking, so Beatrice would smile and nod and pray that her sister wouldn't fuck anything up.

But this was the first time she'd be coming back home without Lucia. She didn't know why that relieved her and also made her want to throw herself out of a moving carriage.

She didn't know if she should've been calling "Lucia" "Lucia" anymore. She hadn't denounced her name publically, doing the paperwork to change her name and gender to whatever she wanted, but in the weeks leading up to her wedding, her sister had become somber.

She'd brought Beatrice into one of their spare drawing rooms. She'd been high, eyes red and bleary, and was crying into her hands, not on Beatrice's shoulder. Not that she'd expected that—they weren't that close—but she'd wanted to help her, or at least make her stop crying, so she'd listened.

"I hate myself," Lucia had said. "I don't want to be known as Lucia or have all these expectations laid upon me only to be wed off to a man I hardly know, and I can't *stand* hearing them talk about how exciting this fucking wedding's going to be. Nobody cares about how *I* feel."

Beatrice had hated herself, but she'd shrugged off those complaints. She was used to her sister's antics to get out of duties, but she knew how much she hated this wedding, so why had she been so obstinate in hearing her out? "So, who *do* you feel like?" Beatrice had asked. "Who do you want to be?"

"Lorian," Beatrice mouthed in the carriage. Pretty, just like her old name. Prettier, even.

But Beatrice had yelled at her. It'd upset her knowing their family meant so little to her that she'd throw everything away to be someone new. Lucia was their grandmother's name.

Should she've been more supportive? Yes. Should she've accepted her sister at her worst? Also yes. But she wasn't a Visatorre. She couldn't go back in time and fix her and Lucia's relationship. She could only do what she thought was right going forwards.

And seeing their twin's smile seemed pretty damn right.

"Mo'mma."

Beatrice looked down. Her daughter, Nina, was playing underneath her yellow dress. She rested her chin on Beatrice's knee.

"Nina, get off the ground," Dmitri said from across the carriage.

She and Beatrice ignored him.

"Am I going to see Lucia today?" Nina asked her mother.

154

"I don't think so," Beatrice said.

"How come? How come they haven't found her yet?"

"Because she doesn't want to be found."

Dmitri's fuzzy upper lip protruded out like a llama. "You aren't to meet with her, Nina."

"She can meet her if she desires," Beatrice said.

Dmitri crossed his legs. Beatrice did the same.

"Don't bring me any trouble," Dmitri warned. "I do *not* want to deal with either of you today."

"Yes, let's not," she said.

Dmitri said something under his breath and stared outside the window instead of engaging with his own family. If they were even that. Beatrice knew he had courtesans he loved more than her, so she let it go and played with her daughter's pigtails until the carriage stopped.

Two officers welcomed them I nto the palace. She'd missed these men, with their silly black hats and long swords. Her Bělican guards wore thick furs for the harsh winters that smelled worse than their horses. It was nice seeing these men in their tight, black pants again. She could see the outlines of their willies.

While the officers helped them with their luggage, Beatrice looked up to the six stories of her childhood home. Each window sparkled, yellow and purple flags of Roma waving on the pointed towers. How she'd loved walking through the halls with her mother, and running through them with Lucia. It must've been years since then.

"Where are my mother and father?" Beatrice asked one of the officers.

"Forgive me, Your Majesty. There was an unforeseen circumstance in the main foyer that required His Majesty's attention. I do not know of Her Majesty's whereabouts. If you follow us, we can direct you..."

Breezing past them, Beatrice took her daughter by the hand and walked herself into the palace. They knew she didn't need an officer telling her what to do or where to go. She was a queen now, and the only person who could stop her was her mother and her tears.

Her high heels echoed down the marble floors. Nothing had changed since she'd left. She still passed dead family members in gold frames. They were so much larger in her memories.

"Where are we going?" Nina asked. "This place is so big."

"We're going to see your grandmother," Beatrice said.

"Your Majesty."

She turned to Prince Zaahir walking up to meet her. He was wearing the royal robes custom to his family, and his knights were safely a few steps away. Unlike Roma and Bělico, Aldaían officers—called knights—were expected to accompany the royal family everywhere they went, even to the bathroom. Kadar was at his right, his personal knight and partner. He copied his Liege and bowed.

Beatrice returned their bows. "Prince Zaahir. It's a pleasure to meet you again. And Sir Kadar, good morning."

"The pleasure is all mine, Your Majesty." Zaahir reached for her hand and kissed it, then air-kissed both of her cheeks.

"Have you heard anything from her?" Beatrice whispered into his close ear.

"Not yet," he whispered back, then fell back into line and cleared his throat. "And a good morning to you as well, Your

Highness," he said to Nina. "I hope the carriage ride from your ship was to your tastes."

Nina hid half of her face in Beatrice's dress, staring up at the man she saw as a stranger.

"She's a little under the weather," Beatrice explained, not wanting to go into detail about how her husband had made her cry twice on the boat ride here.

"I see. It seems we've come to this palace at rather inopportune moments."

"You can say that again," Beatrice muttered, then clearly, "How do you mean?"

"There was a commotion in the main foyer. I'm sure it's nothing," he said, though his eyes said everything but. He nodded his head an inch to the left. "Your mother is in her study."

"Perfect," she said, but it wasn't. Her mother being in her study meant only one thing: she was deep into one of her depressive episodes and needed help crawling out.

Zaahir offered his hand, and the two of them walked side by side. Kadar followed behind his monarch-to-be. Nina watched them over Beatrice's dress.

"How are you, truly?" Zaahir whispered to Beatrice.

"Wanna slit my throat and be done with this," she said. "Dmitri's getting on my nerves and I'm ready to murder someone."

"I hear you. I came in last night. Your mother has been...bad, honestly. I won't sugarcoat it."

"I figured. I tried writing to her, but her letters come farther and farther apart."

"I think it'll do right by you to see her. I've tried to talk with her, but she's been taking Lucia's disappearance hard."

Beatrice walked a little faster to get to her mother.

Her mother had held herself up in this study since Beatrice was small. It was full of artwork and vases, of bookshelves and quilts she'd knitted herself. She did her work here, read here, relaxed when the world expected so much from her. As a child, Beatrice would run in and sit on her dress while she looked over documents. Sometimes, her mother would braid her long hair, making it look exactly like hers.

Beatrice steeled herself as she knocked on the door. The officer guarding it didn't even try to stop her.

Her mother was sitting on one of her fainting chairs, one hand over her eyes, the other absently playing with a braid in her hair. Once she heard company, she sat up and folded down her dress, but Beatrice saw the bags under her eyes. She knew that look.

"Bea."

At the nickname, Beatrice let down her guard and ran into her mother for a well-needed hug.

She inhaled the scent of her powder, how rich and at-home she smelled and felt in Beatrice's arms. She wasn't as tall as her mother, but in their heels, they almost stood like equals, though she couldn't imagine being on equal grounds with her mother.

"I'm so glad to see you again," her mother whispered. "I've missed you so much."

"Don't worry," Beatrice said, "we'll find her."

Her mother pulled back, sniffled once with eyes closed, then nodded with a more at-ease smile. "Of course. Have you met with your father yet?"

"No."

"Oh, alright." She dropped the subject. Neither of them wanted to see him if they didn't have to. "Well, have you eaten anything? Either of you?" she said to Nina. "Are you hungry? I believe the cooks were making dinner for your arrival. I haven't been out much, but Carmello said he needed to work on something and left a while ago."

"Let's see what he's been up to. I've missed him."

"He's been doing well. He's been helping me so much with everything. He keeps me going. A-as well as your father," she stuttered. "They've both been well."

"Please, don't bring him up. Let's wait until we're forced into his company."

Her mother caught herself from laughing too loudly. "Of course."

From outside, Zaahir and his knights introduced themselves with bows.

"Your Majesty, it's a pleasure to see you again," Zaahir said. "It's good to see you up and about."

"Yes. It's good to keep going, even when it seems impossible."

"Even when the world's going to shit," Beatrice mumbled.

"Have you heard anything about those future selves?" her mother then asked.

"Huh?"

"It seems like they're more of a problem than we expected," Zaahir said. "I saw the woman a few hours ago."

"Future selves?" Beatrice asked.

"Didn't you receive a letter about it from your father?"

"I haven't heard from Father in months. Dmitri said he had a business arrangement with him that needed our attention.

Damn man doesn't tell me anything. Zaahir, be the only helpful royal man here and tell me what's going on."

"Well, your father sent me a message describing an incident that happened at Durante Academy. Constable Carmine had been assaulted in a dorm room, and then he'd encountered two...They've been calling them 'future selves' of a student and officer in training that'd been at the school. They seem to be the older versions of these two and have been causing a ruckus around this kingdom."

"That sounds..." What did it sound like? A fairytale? A horror? Impossible? "Uh, I haven't heard anything about this. Have you met with these people?"

"*Halt!*"

Kadar appeared in front of Zaahir and defended him against the wall. The other knights and officers aided in Beatrice's, Nina's, and the queen's protection. A man's voice travelled down the hall, sounding irate and out of breath.

Keeping Nina back, Beatrice broke all defense measures and peeked out the door.

A woman dressed in blue skipped down the hall like she owned it. Her dress said as much, for as she ran past, Beatrice placed the diamonds sewn into the fabric as Cyro diamonds from the southern caves of Aldaí. It might've been more expensive than her own dress, though she'd never met this noblewoman before.

The woman caught Beatrice staring. "Oh, Bea!" She twirled around, then teleported to stand in a window not too far off. She hiked up one leg as she commended them. "What a sight. So many royals all in one room!"

Beatrice blinked at her. She could see her bloomers. She didn't know if the girl knew she could see her bloomers.

"Wait!" Carmine was ten seconds behind the woman, face red from the chase. He had his sword unsheathed. "Get away from them!"

"Oh, hush." The woman stood up on the windowsill and, with an extravagant bow, disappeared into another jump.

Carmine caught his breath on the hallway corner, then saw two queens and one prince watching him make a fool of himself. He sat up like he hadn't been running for his life. "My apologies, your Majesty, your Highness, Your—" He checked down the hall. "I-I didn't mean to interrupt you."

"Are you alright?" her mother asked.

"Yes, Your Majesty. It's just that woman again."

"Who is she?" Beatrice asked.

"She's a criminal with a bounty on her head for assaulting me and a handful of my officers. She's the one who can jump freely from place to place without harm. I don't know how she does it. All the information I have on her comes from eyewitnesses and her need to cause me grief in my own country."

He bowed. "Please excuse me, Your Majesties, Your Highness. While it is lovely to see you again, I need to... I need—" He fixed his hat. "I need to capture this girl."

"Don't let us hold you up," Beatrice said, and gestured down the hall for the chase to continue.

"Thank you." He bowed once more, shared a concerned look with Beatrice's mother, then took off, fixated on keeping peace in the palace.

Beatrice gave the scene a beat of silence before she lifted up her dress and ran after Carmine and the mysterious girl.

"Bea, wait." Zaahir caught up with her, as did her mother and their entourage of guards.

"Was that the girl?" Beatrice asked. "The future self?"

"Yes," Zaahir said. "She's been coming and going within the palace. Your father is furious with her existence. He says that she's a threat to our civil unity, but she seems so...childish."

Beatrice swirled her tongue in her mouth. That sounded like Lorian.

The hallway led them into the foyer connecting the first floor to the music room. Around them were a dozen officers staring up at the foyer chandelier. The shadows and light were dancing around the portraits and people.

Hanging on the chandelier, bending the candles still in place, was Carmine, jacket askew, hat now gone. He was bracing himself on the light fixture so he didn't fall.

After flailing and ordering his men to grab a different ladder, the chandelier swung clockwise, and he saw Beatrice, her mother, and Zaahir staring up at him.

"Your Highnesses...es." He gave the best bow he could. His breath was shortening. "Forgive me, again."

"How'd you get up there?" Beatrice asked.

"That woman has an agenda on placing me in very precarious situations with her jumps. She touches me and whisks me away—Where is that ladder? Someone get me a ladder!" he shouted at his officers, and six of them ran about to find a ladder.

"We must find her," Carmine said. "Her name is Aida Mirko from a small farm town in Bělico, and her accomplice was...I believe his name was Lorian Ashwell. Queen Beatrice, have you heard of two such people?"

Beatrice looked up. Blinked. Looked over at Zaahir who was looking at her. He blinked.

"No, I have not," she said, and wondered what her sister had done to humiliate their royal family this time.

She couldn't wait to find out.

Chapter 16: Nighttime Highs

Missus Sharma continuously told them that moving in wasn't a big deal and that they didn't have to worry about it.

It *was* a big deal, and Aida was very worried about it.

A family, caring for your well-being, asking if you've eaten enough and if they could do anything to help? She'd never heard of it. She had to be careful when Missus and Mi'Sharma inevitably betrayed her in some way. It'd been three days and neither of them had slighted her, but still. You never knew with grandmas.

By adding two new mouths to their family, Missus and Mi'Sharma had completely renovated their home. They got up earlier and worked twice as hard. They cooked meals as if Lorian was still a royal kid. Porridge and biscuits, toast and homemade jam, fresh fruit from the nearby market. Aida had never eaten such meals before.

They rearranged furniture for them. They didn't have a spare bedroom for them to hog and Onti and Chrissie had a child's bunk bed that fit neither Aida nor Lorian.

So with Missus Sharma's permission, Aida and Lorian pushed the living room couches together to form one bed. They didn't know why they'd done this, but after their first night of sleeping separately, they mutually agreed on Together

Couches. Aida had learned that sleeping with someone wasn't as scary as she thought. In fact, knowing Lorian was close to her made her sleep better.

She didn't know why.

And she didn't know how, but these two women cut their own firewood. Aida had tried to cut wood back at home, but it threw out her back and made her bad leg numb.

A few days into their stay and Lorian discovered that these older women were chopping their own wood by hand.

"Missus Sharma, please."

"Oh, Lorian, sweetheart, don't even think it. Go back inside, dear. I'll be done with this in a second."

"I don't mind." She unbuttoned her jacket and hung it up on a nearby rake, exposing her shoulders and upper chest. "I'd love to take out some tension in my back."

"Dear, you don't have to."

"You don't think I can do it? You put so little faith in me, Missus Sharma!"

"Oh, it's not that, love." She handed her the axe. "Do be careful."

Aida watched her. Secretly, of course, with her nose hovering above the windowsill. Without Lorian's uniform and the corset she wore—Aida hadn't known she wore one—she saw the curves and dips of her hips, the posture that might've deemed her a princess as she split the wood in one strike. Sweat jumped off of her curly bangs as she worked.

She had a tattoo on her upper forearm. It looked like she'd done it herself, tiny stars and moons like a child's doodles. Aida knew that any royal family from any time period wasn't allowed to have tattoos. It didn't surprise her that Lorian had somehow inked one onto her rebellious body.

Aida still couldn't believe that she was the lost heir, and that she wasn't dead in a ditch or kidnapped. She was so normal in a way Aida favored, yet her mannerisms could've marked her as upper class.

She kept watching, perplexed, until Missus Sharma came over to dust the window Aida was peeping through. Aida excused herself and helped Chrissie clean the fireplace.

Missus and Mi'Sharma gave them no actual chores to work on. They offered, and sometimes they were allowed to work, but what sucked was that Aida kept forgetting what to do and where to go. She was having difficulty remembering Chrissie's and Onti's names. She blamed it on both of their names ending in the same sound, but she knew that something had permanently messed up her brain. She had trouble concentrating and remembering. She kept forgetting where the living room was when she slept in it every night.

To keep her brain sharp, she kept repeating the things she struggled with over and over in her head, relearning the simple things. She couldn't lose her mind to her powers. She wouldn't.

Lorian didn't seem to mind their sleeping arrangements. She must've acclimated herself to moving around at a moment's notice, whether it be for crown-related business or from her time running away. She seemed happy now that she had a small part of her family back.

On their third or fourth night, Aida rested in her makeshift bed, smoking a spliff. Lorian, after making herself some tea, took a seat beside her. Wearing only a tank top and baggy pants with her hair down, she looked very at ease, very cozy.

"Do you smoke Nectar every night?" Lorian asked.

"It keeps me calm. How'd you smoke it and get away with it in the palace?"

"I drank it."

"Oh, I think I remember you mentioning that. From Zaahir, right? Your fiancé."

"Don't say it like that, but yes. Turns out most royalty needs to calm down every now and again with some illegal substances. Legal, in his case. It's recreational there."

"Maybe you should've married him. You could've gotten high every night." Aida offered her her spliff.

She took it and relaxed with her.

"So," Aida said, "can I ask how the king and queen are behind closed doors?"

Lorian took in another inhale. "What do you think of them?"

"They're cowards."

"I still can't believe how frank you are with them."

"What? It's true. They've been a wreck ever since you died, or ran away, I guess. There's been no interaction between them and Bĕlico or Aldaí until our future selves came into the picture. They're like King Julius II. Gods." She pushed back her bangs. "We need to find out why everything got so fucked. The day I travelled back, everything was so different. And *Eve*." She flung up her hand. "What a queen."

Lorian hiked up her legs, getting even more comfortable. "I can't go back to royal life. I'll be swiped up into the monarchy again, used as a pawn for my parents' greed. I know it's selfish of me."

Aida sat up. "Just because I like Eve doesn't mean I expect you to become a queen like her. You aren't obligated to do anything your parents demand of you."

"They're the leading—"

"You're your own person," she stated, "so if you want to be an officer and live with your grandma, then fine. They shouldn't be able to stop you, even if they're royal."

Lorian went to argue but stopped herself. Her face looked different tonight, and it wasn't from the drugs. "What do you think," she then said, "about your jump?"

"What about it?"

"To jump so far, and with the arrival of our future selves, do you think they're connected?"

"That...would make sense, I guess. The timing is..." She held her head. A headache was forming behind her eyes. She took a drag to calm it down.

"Are you alright?"

"No. I think that jump really fucked me up. I thought the pain would be gone by now, but it's not."

"I'm sorry."

Her headache panged. "I hate when people say sorry when they weren't the ones to hurt your feelings. You didn't do anything wrong."

"I believe people say it because they're sorry that someone they like is feeling anything other than happiness."

"Well, I'm never happy, so you're gonna be saying that often."

"Is that a challenge?"

"It's a threat."

Lorian just laughed.

She didn't understand what Lorian was doing. This wasn't the Lorian she'd come to tolerate. She was so carefree tonight, like they hadn't been through the weirdest week in Roman history. She was...at peace, here, with Lorian.

Aida craned her neck over her pillow, spliff teetering out of her mouth.

"Yes?" Lorian asked.

"How come you have a tattoo?"

"I'd asked for one on my sixteenth birthday. When I didn't get what I wanted, I destroyed a painting of my great-grandmother and gave myself one."

"Bit of a brat, ain't ya?"

"A *bit*?"

"Yeah. Hey, Lorian, what're we doing? Are we living here now? Staying in hiding? I don't want that. I want to learn more about this side of Eve and this Julia person she was so close to. And she had an heir. Can you believe that? They must've killed it, the assholes."

"What about our future selves? They said we had to do something to protect Visatorre history."

"Those future selves can go jump off the Roman cliffs."

"Don't say that."

"Why not? Why do we have to listen to ourselves—or us? Fuck. Okay." She sat up to make her point clear. "For all we know, they could be some kind of trickster gods, or demons. They could be shapeshifting into us. Like, do I seem like my future self?"

"I very much believe *I'm* my future self. They knew I was Lucia. They wouldn't have known that if they weren't me."

"But if they're all-knowing gods, they would've known that about you. And if they wanted to be helpful about the future, wouldn't they just tell us what we need to do? Why string us along like dogs?"

"I do see your point."

"I don't think they're us. Not 'us' us, not in this timeline. I think they're either demons or another universe version of us, bent on making us fail at something important."

"I hope we see them again to put that to the test."

"Put those words back into your mouth, I swear to the Gods."

Lorian laughed again and got ready for bed. She undid her hair from her ponytail and let it flop around her shoulders. Then she turned backwards on her side of the couch, feet by Aida's head, her head near Aida's feet.

"Is this how royals sleep?" Aida asked.

"No. I thought sleeping side by side would make things...uncomfortable."

"You know, you don't have to treat me like some fair maiden. I wasn't the type of girl who swooned over your picture in the paper."

"Not many girls swooned over me," Lorian said, "though... I did yearn for their attention."

Aida's ears piqued. "Did you now?"

"Yes. It made my father even more furious with me. I neither wanted to marry a man nor intended on marrying one."

Outside, the crickets seemed to chirp louder than they had a few minutes ago.

"So you like girls?" Aida asked directly.

"Of sorts," she said. "I seem to be attracted to most people, but girls always seem to catch my attention."

"What's your type?"

"Short, with a tough personality to rival my own. I like passionate and strong-willed people who know what they want and will do anything to get it. Looks also play a big factor."

Aida exhaled in relief. She almost had something to worry about. "Then, I guess if we're being extremely and uncomfortably open with our feelings tonight, the same goes for me."

Lorian's couch shifted.

"I guess," she added. "I've never been caught up in the cycle of being liked and liking someone back. It doesn't cross my mind as often as most people, though I suppose if I were to settle for someone, it'd be the same for me. I think."

Lorian was looking at her now, arms crossed to hold up her head. She tilted her cheek against her knuckles. "Never?"

"Ever. And don't convince me that it'll happen because I spent all of my teenage years waiting for it. I tried everything. I read romance novels, I watched operas about young, beautiful people falling in young, beautiful love. I've even tried it out to see what I was missing."

"How bold."

"I know, and it hasn't happened. Once again, Circa fucks me over for no reason at all."

"You know, if we're taking the whole world into account, there's more than one god."

"I only revere Circa."

"Goddess of time."

"Goddess of Visatorre," Aida corrected. "Back when people actually devoted their lives to the Gods, Visatorre only revered Circa. Tympos and Ukrei were considered the non-Visatorres' Gods and not part of the culture."

"If that's the case, you don't seem to favor your God."

"I greatly dislike many of her choices."

"Well." Lorian lay on her back, drawing circles over her stomach. "I favor them if it meant I ended up meeting you."

Dormant feelings kicked at the gates of Aida's ribs. "Pardon?"

"If the Gods control fate, then they helped me meet you. It's true, you're unlike any girl I've ever met, and that's not a bad thing. Back at the palace, they all acted like dolls. And who could blame them? It earned them advantages to be fake. But ever since I met you with your books, I knew you were different."

"What, because I read? Newsflash, Your Highness, but a lot of girls like to read."

"That's not what I meant. I meant *you*, throwing your cane at the Constable. I meant *you*, being so capable despite the world constantly fucking you over. You *challenge* me, Aida, and that's something no man or woman has ever done before." She laughed. "Goodness, you're so guarded. Take a flirty compliment when you get one."

Aida gawked at her. *Compliment*? When had Lorian given her a *compliment*? She'd just accused her of being odd, and she heard that enough times in her life to know it was true. And she wasn't *guarded*. She never held anything back and she always spoke her mind. But flirting? No, no way. Why her?

Not that people couldn't. Good for them for trying. She even encouraged it at times. When she'd spent most of her days without speaking to a single living soul, she sometimes pictured a person by her side. Being married to them and cooking for them. Having a child with them or finding ones to have like Missus and Mi'Sharma. But she also pictured a cat in this scenario, though having a person did have its charm.

She supposed.

She covered her mouth as her brain shamefully went against her will and imagined such a life with Lorian. Sleeping on one couch instead of two. Maybe in the same bed when neither of them were high and they just enjoyed being near each other. Having sex.

She hated it. She wanted to stitch herself up and keep that discomfort out. She was born different, she couldn't give Lorian what she needed. Why was she doing this to her? And why was she insinuating that she wanted to pursue her? Nobody *pursued* her, who would?

"Anyway," Lorian said, rolling over. "I'm gonna turn in for the night. Goodnight."

"...Night?" she said in a question. Their conversation was hours away from being over.

But the words slipped away. Night settled in around them, and the time to question Lorian's wording faded into the next morning.

———◇———

They awoke to the smell of eggs cooking and the sound of bacon sizzling in a skillet. Mi'Sharma had breakfast duties that morning while Missus Sharma readied the children for school. They went to a thirty-kid school that only taught Visatorre children down the road. Aida knew they existed, just not in Bĕlico. There, most Visatorre either dropped out or didn't enroll due to peer-pressure. They kept working the land or took on an apprenticeship to pay to be alive.

"Is there anything I can help with?" Lorian asked. She'd dressed and cleaned herself for the day. Aida was still waking up at the bathroom mirror. She kept admiring her new, wonky eye. Every time she caught it in the mirror, it freaked her out. Nobody mentioned it, but it was like getting a spot on your skin. It might've not been dangerous right now, but give it a few days in the Sun and it might turn fatal.

"Oh, dear, sit down. Chrissie and Onti will be heading off to school in—Goodness, now! Off, you two, hurry, or you'll miss roll!"

"Wait!" Mi'Sharma swung around her skillet and divided her eggs onto two plates. Chrissie and Onti gobbled them up as politely as two hurrying children could.

Aida hid her amusement by braiding her hair. Back in Bělico, her sisters would hog the bathroom for hours and make her get ready in her room with a hand mirror. She'd never started off the morning so warmly, with a family not yelling at each other for stupid reasons. This family, she decided, was pretty alright.

Someone knocked on the door. Lorian, who was closest to the windows, went to answer it.

She froze mid-stride.

Aida exited the bathroom, brandishing her cane.

Lorian gulped. "It's Carmine," she said. "He found us."

Chapter 17: Bookstore Date

Onti covered his mouth to keep from yelping, but his eyes couldn't hold back the fear. When Carmine ordered that they open the door, he shrieked through his fingers and jumped right out of the kitchen, clothes thrown off of his body in shock.

Lorian would've stayed frozen like a deer to a huntsman's dog if not for Aida. She yanked her back and hid her in the bathroom so she didn't get them arrested.

Carmine knocked on the front door again. "Her Majesty The Queen's Constable Carmine present. May I speak with whoever is in charge of the household?"

Missus Sharma turned slowly to the door. "One moment, please!" she called out, then whispered to Aida and Lorian, "Come with me."

She led them to a cellar door etched into the floorboards. Lorian grabbed her rapier from their Together Couches before heading down.

"Hide in the storage closet," Missus Sharma said. "When they leave, either Mi'Sharma or I will come get you. If you hear footsteps coming down and don't hear us calling for you, I need you to stay hidden. Do you understand?"

"Yes." Lorian kissed Missus Sharma's cheeks. "Thank you."

"In and out," Missus Sharma promised. "I won't keep him long."

"Make haste!" Mi'Sharma looked between them and the front door. "*Hurry!*"

They descended down the tight stairwell into damp darkness. The door slamming shut behind them startled Lorian into Aida.

"We're screwed, we're screwed, we're screwed," Aida muttered.

"It's not the ideal situation," Lorian said.

"Really, it's not? We're cornered."

"We'll be alright."

"I know when you're lying, Lorian. Don't do that with me." She headed for the back door, bypassing the musty storage closet. She listened through the screen, then poked her head out to scan outside.

Footsteps creaked the floorboards above them. A muffled voice asked someone a series of questions.

"Our horses are still up there," Aida whispered.

"I know. Hopefully my horse knows not to recognize Carmine."

"How would a horse recognize an officer?"

"Carmine trained her as a foal."

Aida brought her head back in. "She's a *royal* horse? Like, bred in the palace?"

"Yes."

"Like a totally trackable, well-known, stupid horse that Carmine would easily notice? Are you serious?"

"Hey, don't call her stupid. You're going to apologize to her when we go back up."

"*If* she's still there when we come back."

"Are we going somewhere?"

Aida unlocked the door. "If you think I'm staying trapped in another basement where we can get cornered, you have another thing coming."

They both knew to walk on the grass and hide in the shade of the tree to avoid detection. Lorian kept looking over to the house. Aida kept her eyes forwards.

Not much of a "forest" grew behind Missus Sharma's home. The trees were sparse and held pockets of daisies and mushrooms around their roots. Half a minute of exploration and they came out on the other side. A stone wall blocked them from the street. There were no horses or carriages, but down the way were pedestrians going about their morning routines. If they were wearing any cloaks to disguise themselves, disappearing into the crowds would've been a sure way to keep concealed.

Aida bumped into Lorian. A root had tripped her. "Sorry."

"No need to be sorry," Lorian said. "You're quite clumsy, aren't you?"

"Well." She tapped the thick heel of her shoe with her cane.

"No matter. I don't mind." She offered her her arm. "May I?"

"I shouldn't. One might think we're lovers out on a mid-morning stroll, and we're supposed to be wanted criminals, are we not?"

They looked over to the less crowded part of the street.

"I mean, the farther we go, the better," Aida said, reading Lorian's mind.

"Let's go down here," Lorian said, and helped her off the stone wall by taking her hand. "It should be less crowded this way."

Down that very way came the clopping of horse hooves. The gait was unmistakable, but Lorian checked anyway, as did Aida.

A lone officer was patrolling the busier street.

"Shit," Aida cursed, though a smile was curling on her lips. If they didn't leave soon, she'd likely mess with the man in ways they didn't need right now.

"Keep it moving, Miss," Lorian whispered, and gave her a pat down the safer route.

They merged onto an open pavilion hugging the eastern cliff side. Some Romans swore you could see the outline of Aldaí from here. As a child, Lorian would make up lies about seeing the white flags of the Aldaían Citadel from the clock tower. She and her sister and mother would take trips out here to their private beach. They hadn't gone in some time, and now, the threat of Aldaí being so close to her frightened her.

Aida strolled over to a bookstore and checked out the books on display. Many of them had gilded edges or were signed by their authors. Aida's eyes fell to one particular box set—the six-book box set of *En Tempore Rose*. With its childish lettering and red dragon soaring across the title, the series looked a bit juvenile, but it was in the storefront for a reason. It'd captivated readers of all ages for the past seventy-five years. The box set even boasted that each book had the author's signature inside.

Aida's eyes sparkled as she looked at the building itself, feeling the grooves of the stone like a map.

"We shouldn't go in," Lorian advised. "We'll draw attention."

"I know that."

"But do you want it? The box set?"

She looked down at the price tag. "No."

"Because I have the money."

"I have my pride. Leave me with something."

Lorian recalled the first night she and Aida had spent together. She wanted that smile back. "I want to buy it for you."

Aida squashed her nose against the glass, staring into the eyes of a young Pinnacle. "I always connected with Pinnacle in the first book. He was untrusting, standoffish, he factored in reason and logic to every decision he made. For Circa's sake, he named a red dragon 'Red Dragon' and calls her nothing else for 1,200 pages. But as the books continued, he started learning more about himself, learning how to love the Goddess and the people on the separate islands. I had trouble relating to those parts. It's like Pinnacle became a whole other person, becoming more outspoken and fun-loving. That's why I like the first book best. He feels the most like me in that one."

"I'd like to read it," Lorian said. "It sounds interesting."

"The author's wife died while he was writing the fourth and fifth book, and I feel like the story took a turn after that, though some people like them." She sighed. "Lorian, do you think Eve was a good person?"

"Pardon?"

"Eve. Back when I saw her, she was so much...different than what I'd thought she'd be. She acted so wild. She acted like my future self. Do you think I painted her in the wrong light like I did Pinnacle? History says she killed King Julius's wife. Do you think that's true?"

Lorian respected Aida's question and didn't answer right away. She didn't know everything about history like Aida did, but she did have a gut that she trusted and the perfect historian from whom to learn.

Aida scoffed at her silence. "I shouldn't have asked."

"No, I was just thinking it over. I know you regard her in a high light. I didn't want to say anything to upset you."

"Why?"

"Huh?"

"Why're you so careful with me? I don't understand. Do you think I break easily?"

"On the contrary. I think you're incredibly smart and resilient. You think over your options more than I do, and you're book-smart as well as street-smart. That's why I don't want to say something off the cuff of my sleeve to invalidate you."

"You wouldn't invalidate me. You don't have to sweat that small stuff."

"Do you want me to upset you?"

"I don't want you to think I can't handle it," she said bluntly. "No more of this pussyfooting around, worrying about this and that. You're—"she mouthed the word 'royal' "—ain't ya? Surely, you've dealt with worse. You've escaped a marriage and a toxic living environment. You survived your father. You joined the ranks. That's not something most people can do. So, keep that energy with me. Fight me if you don't like my ideas. Argue with me if you think I'm wrong and encourage me in the right direction. If you don't, then I'll stay stuck in my own head and end up with answers only I think are right."

In truth, Lorian *was* being careful with Aida. How many people had she pushed away due to her mouth, her actions? She didn't want that with Aida. But how *could* you be careful with someone like her? She was as sharp as her rapier. If she wanted to be pampered or taken care of, Lorian would do that later. Now, as she was still getting to know Aida, giving her what she needed was best.

Lorian stuck up her nose. "Then I think you should put more faith in me, and trust me more as a friend. I'm not going to hurt you. Sometimes, I think you treat me as a pet. Don't do that."

"Okay, I won't. You need to tell me this shit clearly, otherwise I won't understand."

"I'll keep that in mind. And to answer your question, no, I don't think she killed Queen Julia, because from what you've told me, it sounds like she liked her a great deal."

"So we're on the same page, then." She walked towards the sea. "By the way," she said, "I don't think 'friends' say what you said to me last night."

Lorian's face flushed. How bold of Aida to bring that up. She barely remembered what she'd said, she'd been so nervous. All she remembered was the intent: to show Aida the slightest hint of her interest She'd complimented and praised her. She hadn't made any physical move on her because of course she hadn't, but even then, had she gone too far?

"Take a flirty compliment when you get one."

She might've not known what a flirty compliment sounded like. Lorian liked playing around with her friends and teasing them. She'd have to be more direct with Aida.

"I've liked you for a while."

"I'd like to get to know you more than a friend."

"I love you."

She shivered at the last phrase. She liked many people over the years, some officers, some maids, but she knew she'd never been in love. She didn't even know if she was in love with Aida, she just knew that the dream she had about her last night left her aroused.

Aida went to the merlons and looked out to sea. The tiny curls around her forehead tickled her thick brows. Lorian had to steel herself from fixing them behind her ear.

She looked down at Aida's hand, aching to hold it. Her arms were crossed and hiding her fingers.

Biting her lower lip, Lorian scuffled in her boots until her shoulder kissed Aida's.

Aida looked at her, eyes half-lidded not in lust but tiredness.

Or slight intrigue. "What's this now?"

"You told me to be more direct with you," she said, "so this's me being direct."

"Direct about what? You're being direct about vagueness."

Did people their age even say it openly? Could she even go on a date with Aida? Where, the beach? She wouldn't like that. The library? She'd spend more time with the books than with Lorian.

"What I said last night, I didn't mean to make you uncomfortable. I only wanted to let you know...where I stood, and shot my shot with you. I told you my feelings," she said, now shaking, blushing. "That's all."

Aida looked back out to the ocean. "What am I meant to do with that?"

"Nothing. Well, when you're ready, you can give me an answer so I don't fold in on myself wondering how you feel about me." She cleared her throat. "If you have any feelings for me in the first place."

"Feelings," she repeated. "Look at me."

She did. Had been. "Yes?"

She lifted a hand dramatically to point at her Visatorre marking.

"I see it, Aida. I see you."

"You don't know me."

"And I'd like to. If you don't like me, Aida, you can say it. You don't have to toy with me. But if you *do* like me, or if you want to try something with me, you can. Nothing about the way you look or think will stop me from thinking you're beautiful."

Lorian clenched her jaw. What was she doing? This was too soon. It wasn't the right time.

"It's not like I want to keep myself from anyone," Aida said. "I told you, I've tried falling for people. I just don't want you to—"

"You don't want me to *what*?"

"To get *fucked up* by me." She began talking with her hands. "Look, I saw how panicked you were when I jumped. I know a lot of what you're doing right now is because of me. And truthfully, Lorian, I don't know if I *can* fall in love. It's like that switch is turned off in my brain, and I don't want to betray anything we may or may not have, *if* we have anything, you know? It's confusing to put into words," she ended with. "I'm sorry."

The anger that was always on the surface of Lorian's heart fizzled away. "No. Forgive me. I don't want to put you in a compromised situation. We can take our time with this and see what you can stand."

"Don't put your expectations too high."

"I'll be sure not to. Here." She held out her hand. "Back in your dorm room, our future selves were holding hands. They said you can travel with other people while touching them. If you're to become her, you can start with a handhold."

"Thanks, but I'm trying everything in my power not to be like her."

Lorian retracted her hand. She'd promised she'd work with Aida's pace, she needed to be prepared for this rejection and fear.

She hadn't fallen in love, but she'd tasted it, and damn it, she wanted more. Love was a selfish thing to place upon someone and she didn't care. Teased with the promise of trying, Lorian wanted to be ravaged by Aida and be left a shaking mess of feelings.

Aida owed her nothing, yet Lorian was willing to give her everything.

Aida nudged Lorian with her shoulder, and her soft, plump fingers intertwined with Lorian's long ones.

Her cheeks were pink. "I guess I can handle this much," she said without looking at her.

Lorian's cheeks hurt from smiling so hard. "I would assume so, but you did go a thousand years into the past a few days ago, so maybe things are more complicated for you."

"Oh, like trying to be a monarch was so complicated that you fucked off out of a window?"

She clicked her tongue. "Okay. Touché."

"That's right."

"Lorian?"

Lorian's heart leapt over the railing and plunged itself into the waters. The voice came from behind them, a sneak attack she wasn't prepared to meet again.

Alessio was standing behind them. He was armed with his rapier like a true officer, but it was sheathed, and his hair, which usually stuck up with the product he used, was now cut shorter.

"Cripes, Lorian." Alessio checked behind him before running up to them. "Where've you *been*? All the officers in Roma City are looking for you, and you're, what, having a date with this girl?"

"I have a name," Aida said.

"I know you do, they've been making rounds across the country. They're printing wanted posters of you, you know. Have you seen them? I've been trying to tear them down, but two more get put in their place."

"Wouldn't be a first," Lorian muttered, then, "Is that so?"

"Don't act like a snob, you're in danger. They took me and Matteo and all the other boys off the campus to look for you. Do you have a place to lay low?"

"We do. Your horse is also taken care of."

"She better be." He looked behind him again. "Okay, you two need to leave, now. Every constable and officer has their sights trained on finding you, or these future selves, or whatever the fuck they are. Do you know what's going on with that?"

"We're as lost as you are," Aida confessed. "Aida Mirko, by the way."

He gave a quick bow. "Alessio. Now go, before someone sees you. I can only stick my neck out for you two lovebirds so many times."

"I'm glad you do it at all," Lorian said, and raised his fist at him.

Alessio hesitated before crossing his wrist with Lorian's, their bond frayed but not torn.

Chapter 18:
Baking Up a Plan

Despite everything in her brain telling her to find a Plan B, Aida had become accustomed to Missus Sharma's and their setup in the living room, or as Mi'Sharma put it, their "Nest."

The doily-covered room of a nicely furnished home had become a pile of blankets, old food dishes, and books, stacks and stacks of thick books. From being a part of the royal family's workforce, Missus Sharma had amassed a collection of history texts that could've put any library to shame. She graciously let Aida borrow them.

Two days after Carmine had searched the cottage, Aida had read through the thickest texts Missus Sharma owned. Royal lineage spanning back to the end of time, ancient maps with individual house markings. She'd learned Lorian's full name, something kept within the royal line out of superstition of witches knowing a person's full name. Aida, even though it was in her nature to, kept that knowledge to herself.

In-between reading, she started a new journal not about dead royals but about her own life. It felt pretentious, but she only wrote down mundane details. Things like the street she grew up on and the first day she was adopted into her bullshit family. The number of freckles on Lorian's nose got written down on the top of a page, and Pinnacle's character growth from book one to book six took up three pages. She had to reference the books at times, which made her nervous—she used to know everything by heart—but she carried on. She wouldn't forget her favorite book series if she had her notes to look back on. Everything was fine.

It was easier with Eve. Aida had written down every paragraph mentioning her in her own words. She memorized how the past talked about her. She was "a newly budding royal" when she'd married Prince Meyeso. It'd been expected that her older sister was to marry him, but Eve had pulled the strings to make Meyeso fall in love with her. She was "licentious," "rowdy," "surprisingly intelligent despite her natural upbringing." The last one was the way older authors put in their not-so-subtle biases towards Visatorre.

The other two adjectives, however…

She turned the page to a new illustration of Eve and Meyeso—wildly inaccurate to what she'd seen in the past—alongside two blond-haired royals.

King Julius II and Queen Julia.

"The one who murdered her," she muttered, then, looking at the blond-haired woman, "and the one who liked her."

She paid closer attention to the two women. They were standing next to one another, their husbands farther off, coupling them. Their pinky fingers were touching as if they were meant to be holding hands. They had on matching blue bracelets that looked familiar.

Aida kept reading. Underneath the picture, the author made a note saying that this artwork was seen in poor taste, as it depicted both queens in "unfavorable suggestion."

The full piece was in the Catacombs, a place where "unfavorable" beings lived.

"Whoa," Aida breathed out. She'd known the Catacombs themselves were ancient art pieces, but she hadn't known people kept *artwork* down there.

She flipped the page to a chapter dedicated to all the statues and paintings made exclusively for the Catacombs. She hadn't known they existed. They weren't in any history books she'd read.

If they had all this hidden in the Catacombs, what else was buried down there?

Aida touched where the two women connected, wondering what sort of relationship they had, how they did it.

And why the fuck was it so hard for her to reciprocate the same feelings? Lorian had outright declared her feelings to her. What was she supposed to do with that information? Reject her? Accept her? You couldn't say, "We'll see about that," because that sounded like a refusal and it'd hurt Lorian's feelings. She equated it to her acceptance to Durante Academy. Everyone wanted to hear a, "Yes," nobody wanted a, "No," and hearing a, "We'll see," was no doubt the worst answer one could receive.

She didn't know how she felt about Lorian. She liked being around her and how she treated her. But that was the same with Missus and Mi'Sharma, and with Eve, though she hadn't formally met the latter. At what point did appreciation for a person turn to romance? In novels, it happened so fast, and Aida didn't know if this was too fast for her liking. She wanted...

She wanted to meet Eve again. She felt like she could teach her a lot on this topic.

Running herself into the ground, Aida fell back into her chair. After slouching for six hours, she couldn't take her back and leg pain, but she didn't want to stop researching. Her mind was just somewhat damaged. She lifted her bad leg and gave it a good stretch.

"Aida?"

She slammed her thigh back down and flattened out her dress.

Lorian came out from the kitchen. She and the kids had been fiddling around on the second floor. Lorian was a natural with kids. She kept them busy while Missus and Mi'Sharma tended to the house or the animals. She played jacks and hide-and-go-seek with them without acting embarrassed. Aida was impressed. She didn't think Lorian had much experience with children. Maybe she was generally a good person.

"Onti and Chrissie and I are making sugar bread," Lorian said. "They wanted to know if you'd like to join us."

Aida checked the kitchen. The two kids were spying on her behind the wooden column, waiting to see what she'd say.

"*Huh*," she drawled. "Sugar bread, huh?"

"Yes. It's a traditional Roman dessert."

"I've had it. Where do you think the sugar is grown, Aldaí?"

She expected her to laugh. She didn't, just continued smiling down at her. "Of course. Do you like it?"

"Why don't you ask the question you want to ask," Aida said, "because I don't think those kids were the ones to think about inviting me to *make bread*."

Lorian laughed. "Ah. I've been caught."

"I can read you too well."

"You can. Then, Miss Mirko, may I cordially and *personally* invite you to our exclusive bread-making event as my charming plus one?"

"There we are. What happened to being upfront with me? You know I have a problem with that."

"I apologize. I'm still learning when not to lie."

"Yeah, I bet." She nudged her in the hip. "Come on, then. Bread takes hours to prove, it's a horrible thing to wait on."

"You do have to admit, it's quite fun."

"I wouldn't know. My mother never let me cook. One wrong travel and boom, house in flames from an unattended fire. And you talk as if you've spent your days cooking for yourself."

"Hey, I'm a great cook! How do you think I made extra meals for myself when my father sent me away from the dinner table?"

"What, were you caught playing with your food?"

"More like threatening to abdicate."

Onti climbed into his chair. "What does abdicate mean?"

"It means she wanted to quit being a royal kid." Aida put on one of Missus Sharma's spare aprons. "Can't blame her for wanting that."

"So it's true," Chrissie said. "You're a real prince—" She winced. "Prince? Princess? Mama said not to talk about it, but if you were a princess, that'd be cool."

"I suppose it would be," Lorian said. "I *was* a princess, but I don't know if that lifestyle is right for me. You, on the other hand, would make a remarkable princess."

"I would?" Chrissie asked.

"Of course. Some girls are born to be princesses. I wasn't meant to be like that."

Aida helped navigate them out of that difficult conversation. "You can be the princess of Siina."

"What's Siina?" Chrissie asked.

"Oh, don't get her started," Lorian said, but Aida was already started.

"Siina was a city-state in Roma almost 1,200 years ago. A city-state is a city surrounded by an entire other state. It was a place where hundreds of thousands of Visatorre lived peacefully under two Visatorre leaders, King Meyeso and Queen Eve."

"What happened to it?" Onti asked. "I've never heard of this place before."

"We don't know for sure what happened, but it's believed that Eve and all of her people were killed by the Roman king for murdering his queen. I don't believe it's true, so it's up to us to find out what really happened and avenge her."

"You're gonna avenge her?" Chrissie asked. "That sounds so cool. You're like a superhero."

"I'm a historian."

"Aren't they one in the same?" Lorian asked.

"No, queens are cooler," Chrissie said. "I wanna be a queen so badly."

"What's stopping you?"

"Her name," Onti said.

"Her name is lovely!" Lorian said. "Here, what color dress would you wear as queen?"

"Oh, a pink one!" Chrissie said. "Like Mo'mma's night-gown!"

"Hey, if you're gonna be a queen, I wanna be a king!" Onti said. "I want a red cape with lion fur at the end."

"That's so cool!"

Aida pretended that she wasn't as interested in dresses as she was with historical accuracy, but if Chrissie found her spark in dresses and wanting to be a queen, Aida let it be.

In all honesty, she loved dresses as much as any other little girl.

—◇—

"Can we make them into shapes?" Chrissie asked as she played with her dough. "I wanna make mine into stars."

"Have you ever had star-shaped bread?" Aida asked.

"We can try," Onti said. "I wanna make mine into blue birds. They're my favorite kind of bird."

"I wanna make mine into a palace!" Chrissie said, and each child crafted their bread into their dreams.

Aida watched them to make sure they didn't hurt themselves. When they had it under control, she turned to Lorian. "I found a new painting of Eve. Those things are few and far between. It's in the Catacombs near the Roman Palace."

"Why did they think to hang up art in such a place?" Lorian folded her piece of dough and transported it into a wooden bowl. Chrissie, too excited for the next step, dumped too much sugar into her bowl and began pounding it with two hands.

"I'm not afraid of it," Aida said. "I know their history. I just want to find more..." She squeezed the air in front of her. "Shit."

"*Hey*!" Onti said.

"Stuff," Aida corrected, then addressed Lorian specifically because this wasn't a conversation for a ten- and seven-year-old. "My jump gave me more information on Eve than the dozens of books I've read on her. I feel like if I follow more in her footsteps, I'll be able to find out this secret history the crown is keeping from us. And who knows, maybe this's what our stupid future selves wanted us to do. It makes the most sense, don't it?"

"You're so passionate about this woman."

"What about it?"

"Nothing. I just wish I had more to offer you. I wasn't interested in knowing my family's history. I wanted to get away from it."

"I can't get over how you have *no* juicy gossip for me."

"There's honestly not a lot of secrets about the royal—"

Aida eye-rolled at her.

"—that I *know of*," she said. "That I know of, and ones that aren't overt to the public."

"You're *part* of the family, you dumbass. Think about what we could dismantle with your information. I still don't believe you. I'll break you. I'll find everything out."

"I really don't know of any. I can tell you most officers have spouses even though it's forbidden, and that my mother's interested in pastry decorating even though it's uncouth for her to enter the kitchens."

"It makes sense. She's always been interested in humble lives."

"And that my sister is disinterested when it comes to family matters."

"Again, it makes sense. I don't think I've ever seen her smile in portraits. I can only assume you were close."

"Well, we were twins. *Are*." She set their bread in a cabinet to let it prove. "She wasn't one to smile or be engaging with anyone outside of the family. Or inside the family."

"I can relate," Aida said. "Sisters are the worst."

"Hey, Chrissie's a good sister!" Onti exclaimed.

Aida disregarded them with a hand wave.

"But," Lorian said with a finger to her chin, "before I left, I stole my fair share of inheritance money, jewels, and keys from my bank account."

"What?" Aida asked.

"Along with my signet ring and skeleton key, I also broke out all the lyria from my bank account."

"No, forget about the money. *Keys*." She pressed Lorian up against the wall. "What keys do you have?"

Lorian looked away from her. "Uh, well, it's...one key."

"*Lorian*," she said exasperatedly.

"It's a skeleton key our parents gave us. It doesn't open all the doors in the palace, but it's—" She stole a glance at Aida's lips, then gulped. "I-it can't open my parents' room or the war rooms, but the chapels, galleries, the entrances to the Colosseum and the Catacombs, it can open them."

Aida almost screamed. "You have a key to the *Catacombs*!" she said. "Damn you, well played, Lorian! If I knew you could unlock all the secrets about Eve, I would've stolen the thing days ago! Where is it?"

She timidly undid the top button of her blouse and took out her long necklace. It had that horse whistle on it, along with her signet ring and skeleton key.

Aida reached for it. "Let's go, then! Now! Tonight!"

"Wait a moment." Lorian hid it close to her chest.

"What? Lorian, there's probably hundreds of secret art pieces down there that'll give us more information on Eve. Don't you wanna follow in our future selves' footsteps? Don't you wanna figure out their mission? What if this's it?"

"Aida."

She began shaking, she was so excited. "We can do this, Lorian. We can find out the truth. Together."

"But we can't." With Chrissie and Onti listening in on them, Lorian took Aida into their Nest and sat her down. "We can't jump into this too soon."

"I agree. We can start planning for this week."

"That's still too—"

"Lorian, we've been here for almost a week. We'll go at night. You know officers don't make their rounds after dark."

"But Alessio said they've been looking everywhere for us. We can't be reckless like we were near the—"

"Lorian," she interrupted, "I don't know how to explain this to you, but I *need* to go down there. There's just something in my brain telling me to, and something about seeing that picture in the Catacombs is making my brain itch like crazy. I won't go without you, but I need to see this piece for myself. Please."

Lorian pursed her lips, reading Aida's unblinking, determined stare.

Aida tapped out her nerves. So many ideas and plans were forming, all she needed was Lorian's agreement. She couldn't do what she was planning to do alone, and she didn't know why, but she felt like she needed Lorian by her side. It made sense that way.

Her eyes went wide. "I'll kiss you."

Lorian let go a breath. "Pardon me?"

"If you come to the Catacombs with me, I'll kiss you. I'll take your concerns to heart and plan this out thoroughly, but if you come with me, I'll kiss you. On the lips," she teased. "Once we get there, of course."

Lorian pressed her lips in a hesitant line, then looked off to the side, seriously considering this new offer.

Aida took Lorian's warm, sweaty hand and let it touch her cheek. "Please," she begged, "for me."

Lorian stared down at her. Her fingers cupped the fullness of her cheek like she couldn't help herself and fondled the baby hairs around her ear. "O-okay," she said. "I'll go with you. We'll find the answers to your questions." She pulled out her key and gave it to her. "Together."

"Together," Aida agreed, and got to work planning their adventure.

Chapter 19:
A Decision between Royals

Beatrice's time in Roma had been, as she knew it would be, dull. Incredibly boorish, and sluggish, and utterly, utterly dull.

It wasn't as if she was unprepared for this. In Bělico, her husband took authority over most things. This included every meeting. They were for him, "not for women," and she'd given up arguing that. After threatening divorce and earning a black eye for it, she'd found it pointless to fight back.

They were in such a meeting now. Her husband, her parents, and the royal sect from Aldaí had been bickering about what to do about Lorian and her new girlfriend, and Beatrice hadn't spoken up once. They were on the third hour of getting nowhere. She'd almost fallen asleep.

"I believe we should bring more of Constable Carmine's officers into the city," one advisor argued. "We should elongate their shifts into the night and double the number of men in the morning."

Beatrice breathed out through her nose. As soon as he said, "double," the room exploded with disagreement.

She pet the top of Nina's head with her shoeless foot. She'd broken one of the rules and invited her daughter into the meeting. She was currently underneath the table, sleeping in the folds of Beatrice's dress and using her foot as a pillow. Beatrice's leg had gone numb an hour ago.

"We should give more of an incentive for the common-wealth to find these two hooligans," Dmitri said. "I can bring in a platoon of my most famous spies and this matter will be over."

"We shouldn't impose work upon the commonwealth," Zaahir said. Poor lad had big shoes to fill. His mother was ill and nearing seventy; she couldn't make the voyage overseas. "We should find them swiftly with a condensed version of Her Majesty's officers and sweep the countryside for them. They couldn't have gone far, and we can only assume they're still in the country."

Her father's advisors dismissed him by not even address-ing his concerns. He was a prince, not a king.

"It's been a week since this woman harassed our officers," said one advisor, and turned to Carmine, who was drinking his fourth cup of coffee. He was trying so hard not to slump in his chair. "Carmine has been run ragged trying to deal with this woman."

"She seems attached to him," another advisor said. "Could it be that her arrival has something to do with him?"

"She hasn't given me anything to suspect that," Carmine said. "From what we've gathered, it seems that her and her accomplice's goal is to play as many pranks on the city as pos-sible."

"Calling them pranks is a little demeaning to the real threat she poses on us, don't you think?"

"And what threat is that?" Zaahir asked.

"The threat of trespassing onto royal grounds."

"And invading Her Majesty's quarters."

"And stealing away our men!"

"By placing them on chandeliers!"

Beatrice nearly laughed.

"Regardless of that," Carmine said. "I'd like to turn our attention away from the woman we know little about and turn it back to Lucia's disappearance."

The room's atmosphere shifted.

"I know our focuses have been pulled in many directions this year, but I know we're all concerned about the whereabouts of Lucia. If we can find her, that might bring morale to our workforce. The people might be more inclined to help us detain these future Visatorre if they know our princess has been found."

The advisors, instead of arguing, mumbled to one another, covering their mouths and thinking over the possibility of putting a person's life before persecution.

The king placed his fists on the table.

The room went deadly silent. Carmine dropped his cup of coffee. Zaahir pressed his back into his seat. Beatrice, who was thinking about dropping her cheek into her hand, sat up to act respectful.

"The detainment of these future selves," he said, "are of utmost priority. I don't care what needs to be done. I don't care if you capture them alive or dead. Until I have that woman in chains, I will not hear of any other matter."

Beatrice looked up to her mother, who was silent against the word of her husband.

She was holding back tears. The king refused to look at either of them, only at the men who'd follow his every order.

Carmine was slowly rising from his chair like he didn't have control over his actions against the king. His mouth was parted to speak. He was shaking, but in what? Beatrice's mother was a moment away from taking his hand and sitting him down before he got in trouble.

The king turned to him. "Do you have something you wish to say?"

Carmine didn't speak. His face was so focused on an emotion he was trying to bury. He looked ready to hit him, which resonated with all the advisors. Some scooted out their chairs in case to run.

Beatrice sat up quicker than all of them. "That's dumb."

Her mother gasped. Zaahir and his advisors looked up in alarm. Dmitri nearly hit her for speaking out of turn, but he was on King Durante's land. He couldn't be too outspoken with his wife and the king's daughter.

The king stared Beatrice down murderously.

She controlled herself so she didn't look as scared as she was. Carmine could've been killed for what he was about to say or do. At least with Beatrice, the king couldn't seriously hurt her.

She spoke her truth. "That plan won't fix anything. This woman's a time traveller and you want her in handcuffs? She'd slip out of them. You can't contain her. You need to think of something else."

Her father leaned in, his look sharpening. She'd said the wrong thing.

Good. Finally put some spice into this godforsaken stalemate of an argument.

Dmitri cleared his throat. "I apologize for my wife's *disagreeable* attitude she's had for the past few days. She's tired, you see, from the journey here."

"She isn't tired," her father said, telling people what she felt instead of letting her speak for herself. "Tomorrow morning, I will come up with a plan for these two Visatorre. We will put them in their place, once in for all. Meeting adjourned."

At that, the forty or so advisors shuffled their papers, thanked or ignored the advisors to their lefts and rights, and got up to leave. Her father's top advisors and liegemen talked with him before they left, but from that deep-set scowl, he wasn't in the mood to talk. They caught on and left him to his thoughts.

Beatrice eased her daughter into her arms. One of her guards offered his assistance. The exchange barely awoke Nina as she drooled onto the man's fur.

Dmitri went for Beatrice's arm. His grip hurt. "What were you *thinking*?" he whispered. "Do you have *any* idea what that kind of remark made on me?"

"I spoke at him honestly, and honestly, I don't wish to continue this conversation in the presence of so many ears." She regarded a small man who was pretending not to eavesdrop. He ducked his head out of the room.

"You said that you'd behave on this trip," Dmitri said. "Just because they're your parents doesn't mean you can act like a child anymore."

Beatrice blew out her cheeks. *Nina* was a child, she who had a bedtime and loved sweets more than vegetables. Beatrice was only twenty-three and yet she was both barred from speaking out of turn while also expected to cater to everyone's expectations.

Before anyone scolded her any more, Carmine and her mother broke away from her father and rounded the table to meet her.

Whenever her father was in one of his moods, Carmine often played the role of her father. After one of his outbursts, he'd take them on trips or go flower-picking with them. Beatrice caught a glimpse of what used to be.

"Good evening, Your Majesty," Carmine said with a bow. "I apologize for disrupting you tonight."

"Is something the matter?" her mother asked, code for, *"Why on Earth did you give such a reckless answer to your father?"*

"I apologize. I'm quite tired from my journey here."

Her mother's worried frown grew creases on her forehead. She hadn't had those before. "Darling, if anything's bothering you..."

The king walked by, swarmed by men writing down notes on scrolls.

Her mother looked away, hands folded in front. Carmine bit his cheek before averting his gaze in a bow.

Beatrice and her father exchanged a wordless look with one another. Their eyes weren't even the same; his dark eyes hadn't infected her emerald green. She inherited them from her mother, as well as her compassion and humanity.

The king scoffed and turned away, and Beatrice almost smiled at her triumph. She'd won.

Her mother looked back up, almost ashamed for speaking with her own daughter. "If there's anything troubling you, please, come talk to me in my study. We can talk more there."

"In her study." Code for, *"Away from your father, the only place we can speak openly without fear of disturbing his Royal Majesty."*

Trusting that she was being genuine, Beatrice nodded. "Thank you."

"Thank you. You're well otherwise, aren't you? I'm sorry we haven't spoken much this past week. It's been such a relief to see you again."

"I've been as well as ever," she lied. "How have you been?"

"Well as ever," she said.

"And you, Constable Carmine?"

He smiled at the formal phrasing. "I'm quite well, Your Majesty, thank you for asking."

"You don't seem it," Beatrice wanted to say, but both adults seemed a thousand kilometers away, overthinking more important issues Carmine had tried to raise during the conference.

"Your Majesty," he said to her mother, "would you like me to escort you to your room now?"

"Yes, please," she said urgently. "I've been beginning to feel rather faint."

"Then let's not dally. Your Majesty." He gave Beatrice another bow, which Beatrice replicated, before he took off with her mother down the hall.

Beatrice watched them go, wondering if she'd take her mother up on her offer, when she saw her father down the opposite hall, staring at her. He mouthed two words: *"Come here."*

She wouldn't have gone if not for her husband. If she insulted him, it would reflect badly on the country of Bělico. And Roma, since they shared the same blood. And it would be a mockery to the king himself, and she knew he wouldn't take kindly to that. She feared what would happen to Nina if she continued this bout of betrayal.

So, lifting up her dress, she obeyed and went to her father.

Later that evening, Beatrice, exhausted, escaped to her bedroom's balcony to star watch.

A strip of trees separated her from the royal gates, but still, five stories high, she saw enough. She saw the hills rising and dipping with the curve of the Earth, carrying with them hundreds of houses and municipality buildings. She saw the Colosseum, so close she saw the individual fires flicker between passing guards. She saw everything she could've been ruling.

She tried to flex her bandaged fingers. Ten slashes, five on each palm. The skin had sliced open upon the second strike. She was told to keep her gloves on for the remainder of her stay. Nobody would think twice about a queen wearing gloves, but those savvy on Roman customs would know that she'd been punished for acting out.

Carmine had knocked on her door earlier that night and asked if everything was alright.

"Everything is as it should," she'd said, and Carmine looked guiltily at her gloved hands.

She hid them. "They're fine."

"Do you need any medicine, or new bandages?"

"No," Beatrice said, "but thank you."

Even though she'd said that to make him happy, it struck a chord in his heart. "I'm sorry," he said. "You shouldn't have spoken up at the meeting for my sake. I was... being irrational."

"No, you weren't. You were justifiably angry."

"How could he not..." He sighed. "I'm sorry. I shouldn't say anything. Do you wish for me to leave?"

"Yeah. Get some rest. You look awful."

He smiled. "Please do the same. I'll come check on you in the morning," he said, and left.

She closed the door. She didn't feel like sleeping tonight. She'd rather read out on the balcony. Her husband was asleep in a separate room as requested, and Nina had finally fallen asleep in her princess room. Beatrice was reminded of how uncomfortable the Roman beds were, with their fluffy beds of feathers and not fur. It was cold outside, but she liked the chill.

Someone new knocked on her door. She grated her chin and cheek against the wood. "Yeah?" she called out.

"My apologies, Your Highness," her guard behind the door said. "Prince Zaahir Lahlou of Aldaí is here. Do you wish for him to enter?"

She hid her hands behind her back. "He may."

Zaahir came in cautiously like he wasn't supposed to be here. And he wasn't. If either of their parents had caught them, they'd receive more than a few slashes to their palms. How sensational for two royal heirs to be found together at night. No, their officers knew, as did Zaahir's knights, or knight. Instead of waiting outside with Beatrice's stationed officer, Kadar came right in with Zaahir.

The officer made a face and checked that Beatrice was okay with this.

She assured him with a raised hand, and he shut the door.

"How're your hands?" Zaahir asked, skipping formalities.

Beatrice took off her gloves with her teeth and showed them the damage.

Kadar looked away. Zaahir frowned. "I apologize. Here." He pulled out a glass vial from one of his tunic's inner pockets. Its label read the Aldaían word for "Nectar." "I'm sorry it took so long to get this to you. I had a lengthy conversation with your father tonight. He had me positively fuming."

"*Just* fuming?" She popped the cork and downed the honey-like substance greedily. She handed back the last half to Zaahir, who took a sip before passing it to Kadar. He finished it underneath his headscarf.

"This fucking sucks," Beatrice said, finally able to vent. "I fucking hate him."

"I know." Zaahir slouched with her. "Not that you need to be made aware of this, but your father's becoming more aggressive. His decision-making isn't clear. He's becoming unstable."

"He wasn't always like this. Or rather, less like this. Fuck, what're we to do?"

"They're looking for Lorian and Lucia when they're both the same person. Not to mention this Aida person who came out of nowhere from Bělico."

"And here I thought I was the only one to make the connection," Beatrice said. "When did you figure it out?"

"When I saw her future self a few days ago. They look identical."

"Glad to know you have a brain cell. Not many people here do."

"Has your mother said anything?"

She shook her head. Maybe her mother *had* recognized her own child and hadn't said anything. Maybe they both knew that mentioning anything would've caused more trouble for everyone.

"She'd also told me her preferred name once," Zaahir added. "Lorian, though I don't suppose she remembers. She was high when it happened."

"That's how she told me." She tried outstretching her hands. "I don't get it. They're acting like children. They're not making progress."

"That we know of. I'm sorry. Do they hurt that badly?"

She cast a nasty look at the wall, narrowing in on where she thought her husband was sleeping. "You better make a better king than both of these men combined."

"I'm trying my best. Here." He offered her his hand. "Do you want to take a walk, take your mind off things?"

"That would be incredibly unwise, given that the king is at his wit's end with me." She put back on her gloves. "Let's get the fuck out of here."

Chapter 20: A Welcome in Ruins

Lorian couldn't help it: She was positively whipped by Aida.

She'd worn her key for a reason. Instead of keeping it hidden in her bag, she'd worn it around her neck, knowing Aida would one day learn that it could open every door she needed open. And Aida had been right. They couldn't hide at Missus Sharma's forever. Trickster gods didn't stop their antics. They'd keep pushing the envelope until something ripped.

"So, does this mean you're going on a *date*?"

Lorian covered up Onti's mouth. "*Shh.*"

"Do you like her?" Chrissie asked.

The two children had Lorian cornered into receiving an answer.

She looked over to Aida reading something only meant to be understood by old scholars. She bit the end of her quill as she reread the pages. Lorian could've spent hours watching her like this, dreaming for the day she'd tell her about her love.

Aida had finally touched her. Had she ever held hands with another person before? She said she'd tried falling in love before. Did looks matter more to her, or was it more so about the heart, the brain?

Chrissie pulled on Lorian's sleeve. "So? You like her, don't you?"

"You held her face," Onti said. "Only moms and dads do that."

"She's a very nice girl," Lorian said, knowing Aida was too wrapped up in her notes to hear them. "Don't you like her?"

"Yeah, but you like her in a different way, don't you?" Onti asked. "You look at her like how Mama and Mo'mma look at each other. That's totally different."

"That's a special kind of love," Chrissie explained.

Lorian looked into the kitchen at the two mothers. They were helping each other with the dishes. Mi'Sharma bopped a dollop of bubbles onto Missus Sharma's nose, making her giggle.

Lorian clasped her hands together to keep them warm.

"Okay." Aida folded the map she'd taped together from three books and stuffed it into her jacket. The art styles varied, but they each gave distinct paths in and out of the Catacombs. "It'd be wise not to take our horses, one of which is a royal horse."

"She can just be a horse now," Lorian whispered. It was nearing midnight in the Sharma cottage.

"Whatever. Are you ready? I won't leave unless you're one-hundred percent with me."

"Yes, but I'm nervous. I feel like the world is very unstable right now."

"You can feel the world?"

"No, but..." She tried finding the words. "Back in the palace, whenever my parents were gone for extended periods of time, I got this pit in my stomach. Their absence meant they were having an important meeting that'd decide the fate of countries. I don't know how to describe it, but I have that sinking feeling now."

Aida began tying up her boots. "I have the same feeling, but it's the opposite. I feel like if we don't go now, something bad might *happen*. I think—" She lowered her voice even more. "I think it might have something to do with Circa. All of this can't be a coincidence, right?"

"If you come to the Catacombs with me, I'll kiss you."

She got hot all over again. Had she meant that? Would she kiss her tonight in exchange for this dangerous favor? And if she'd meant it, would it mean as much to her as it'd mean to Lorian? Did she like her at all? Lorian hadn't dressed in her best pants, blouse, and overcoat for nothing. It was the good one that reached her knees in gold lace.

Aida snapped in front of her. "Hello?"

Lorian nodded. "Hello."

"Are you good?"

"Yes." She focused on helping Aida and tied on her boots. This was important not only to Aida and herself, but for the future. Somewhere in the depths of Roma's Catacombs, they'd surely find their answers.

"Are you okay with walking?" Lorian asked. "It's about a forty-minute walk from here."

"I'll manage. Have you been through a lot of the Catacombs?"

"Some, yes, but I was very small when Bea and I explored them."

"Unsupervised? You and Bea?"

"She never enjoyed it as much as I did. Most of the time, I dragged her along."

"What a criminal." She tied a small pack to her bag. "Alright, you ready?"

"Let me carry that," Lorian insisted.

"I got it. Trust me, I'll hand it off when it starts to hurt, but even then, I ain't gonna let it bother me now." She pointed at her bad leg. "You hear that, you piece of shit damaged nerve? You're not fucking this up for me."

What was she expecting them to find? At best, they'd find an empty corridor, at worst, the bones of slaughtered Visatorre. When she'd first discovered them with Beatrice, she was laughing and poking out the eyes of the skulls, testing to see if worms would crawl out. She hadn't believed they were real.

Aida stood up confidently in the moonlight. "Ready?"

Lorian nodded and left for the front door.

"Your Highness."

The two froze. From Lorian's time on the run, she expected an officer or even, God forbid, her family. Her emotions had been so over the place that her brain expected the worst.

Missus Sharma was at the bottom of the staircase wearing nothing but her nightgown and sleeping cap. She held out a chamberstick to witness their departure. Onti and Chrissie were watching from behind.

Lorian bowed to them conditionally. "I apologize. Did we wake you?"

"Where are you going?" she asked. "It's dangerous to go out now, especially when so many of those officers are looking for you."

A lie was already forming in her head, something about sleeping outside because Aida was more comfortable around farm animals. "We were—"

"We're going to investigate the truth about Eve," Aida said. "We might've found something out pertaining to our mission that we need to go see."

"Where is it that you're going?"

"The Catacombs. Near the Colosseum," she added when it looked like Missus Sharma was about to protest, "so it's not far."

"But that's still near the palace."

"We'll be walking on the eastern side of the palace, closer to the Colosseum. We'll be covered and hidden, and we'll be back before morning."

Missus Sharma's frown deepened. She must've known that they didn't take well to authority. She could only warn them about the dangers of their impulsivity.

"I don't know about this," Missus Sharma said. "I've seen so many officers around the market. I don't want them to hurt either of you."

"There won't be many at night," Lorian confirmed.

"Trust me," Aida said. "King Durante rarely assigns officers this late into the night."

"And most of their shifts end at midnight," Lorian said, "and it's usually officers in training so the higher-ups don't have to cover them themselves."

"We'll be fine," Aida stressed, "and I appreciate your kindness, Missus Sharma, but I think time is only going to be against us the longer we waste it. I just have that feeling about it. I think Circa is with us tonight."

Missus Sharma lowered her candlestick. "I fear so greatly about you two and all these choices you and your adult lives are making," she said. "It keeps me up at night how much I worry about you. But..." She gulped. "I don't think I can stop you from leaving. I think Circa has many plans for you, and it's not right for me to stop you when she's giving you such forward hints."

Lorian, who was ready to continue fighting for their right to leave, closed her mouth. She knew her nursemaid was a spiritual person, but she hadn't thought she respected Circa as Aida did.

"Thank you," Aida said. "We won't be long, for your sake."

"Thank you. I'll keep a lantern lit on the porch for when you come back." She gave Lorian a big hug. Lorian smelled a hint of something flowery. She nestled her face into her.

"Be safe," she whispered.

"I will."

She turned to Aida. "Do you take hugs?"

"I don't." She held out her hand, and the two of them gave a firm handshake before she and Lorian left on their journey.

Autumn chilled the night air and turned their breath into puffy, white clouds. After shutting the gates, Aida lit a cigarette to keep herself warm, their only artificial light down the dirt road. She offered one to Lorian, but her nerves didn't need the added nicotine.

What a shitty first date, if breaking and entering could be considered a date. She'd tried practicing courting techniques in her palace bedroom, but as they walked, she couldn't find her tongue. Not even a joke was coming to her. She had the same problem when she'd first met Aida at the Academy. Maybe she should've taken her up on her offer and smoked resolve into her lungs as possible.

They walked towards the beginning of a stone wall, and Aida pivoted and started walking on top of it. She held out her cane for balance.

"Careful." Lorian reached for her hand, and she took it. They were growing distant the higher she went.

"I always am," Aida said. "Now, I'm not one to read the room, but from the vibe you're giving off, it feels like you want to say something to me."

When their hands were about to break apart, the stone wall leveled out, and Aida returned to her side.

They continued walking. Neither of them let go of the other's hand.

"Well?" Aida asked.

"I don't want to say anything in fear of messing up what we have."

"Have you always been such a romantic?"

"I suppose. I read a lot of poems growing up. Some of the etiquette must've stuck."

"That, and you've been bred to be a princess one day, dressed like a doll and set to marry a man you'd never love. If that were me, I would've run a long time ago."

"Because you marrying a man to bear children is all you ever dreamed of, huh?"

Aida gagged. Lorian chuckled. Both of their hearts returned to semi-normal.

They entered the heart of Roma City on dirt roads and through alleyways, trying to stay as inconspicuous as possible. Lorian only counted three houses with their lights on, and they were up on the hills near the palace.

Her old home was coming into view at a staggering pace. She'd rarely left its cage as a princess, and when she did—when she wasn't escaping like a criminal—it was in a golden carriage with the windows blacked out or on a ship where she saw nothing but endless ocean.

They walked through the marketplace. The bakeries still smelled of fresh dough. A hair parlor advertised discounted haircuts. So much of her people's lives came from these shops, from the poorest haggler to the richest noble. Lorian had tried keeping away from such crowded places, but with Aida, she felt the purpose of the city and its potential for change.

Someone who could run a country would take great care of it.

Their road dipped into a slope of ruins. Giant pillars of white stone grew around them, some turning into arches, others crumbling into the air. Guardrails helped keep delinquents like them from climbing to their deaths, and wooden signs had been placed around the corners to warn passerbys of the fragility of the structures. The Colosseum was in front of them now, hiding the Moon behind its hundreds of arches.

"These were around during Eve's time," Aida said, grazing the stone as they stepped down. "They say her palace was built around here. All this architecture is thought to belong to Roma, but really, this's all Siina."

Lorian looked behind her. That small moment of pride she had for her country was once again drowned by its bloody history. "Why was her palace so close to the Roman one?" Lorian asked.

"The true Roman Palace was built ten kilometers to the west. After Julia's murder and the eradication of the Visatorre population, they rebuilt their palace in Siina and took it over. That marketplace we just went through used to be a part of Siina." She walked over to a sign reminding people that officers would be in the vicinity from dawn until dusk. She read it, huffed, then took out a dark piece of charcoal and began scribbling over it.

"*Aida*," Lorian said in a mocking tone. "How dare you? That's private property."

"Well, it wasn't theirs to begin with." She signed her work with a circle, then paused before drawing another circle in it.

"That's your future self's marking."

"I know."

"I thought you disliked her."

"I do, but try meeting someone who doesn't hate themselves." She ashed her cigarette into the wall. "Well, where's the entrance?"

"Do you hate yourself?"

"No, I said it to be funny. Look, we're wasting daylight. Or moonlight. Here."

The door was unmanned and dipped even deeper into the Earth with a flight of stone stairs. When Aida unlocked it, a breath of cold air tickled the hairs on the nape of Lorian's neck.

"We can finally use this." Aida pulled out a lantern from her bag and lit it with her lighter. "You ready?"

"Not really," Lorian said, and followed her in.

The air smelled of a cave system home to bats and monsters. The temperature dropped at each turn and their footsteps echoed into the dark. Their lantern barely helped; it was like walking into the underworld with your eyes shut.

Aida stopped walking. Lorian reached for her rapier. "What's wrong?"

She shivered, and the walls closed in around them. Something was watching them. She checked for a ghost following them into this dead end.

Her parents had sugarcoated this place to her in her youth, telling her she wouldn't find any decaying bodies or hung-up corpses, that it was just a place meant to bury the dead.

Hundreds of skulls had been thrust into the wall. They looked like bricks packed heavily on top of one another. The fillings between each skull: bone fragments and long human femurs lined up like doorways to nowhere.

And deep inside every single skull, as if burned into them with a cattle prod, was the thin halo of a Visatorre marking.

Aida had gone on about how Lorian wasn't her father's daughter, but how could she think that now? This was *her* history. Visatorre couldn't hold down jobs, go to school, or attend operas. She could've stood up against her father or at least questioned his ruling, but she'd taken the coward's way out and ran away. All she thought about was herself, a selfish heir to a selfish kingdom.

Aida kept her face locked as she took in skull after skull. Some were chipped or missing teeth. The shadows caught on the grooves of their jawlines. It looked like they were whispering.

"We're gonna change this," she whispered, but in the passage, her voice carried.

"How?" Lorian asked.

"We'll go back in time and fix this."

"How? You can't control your jumps."

"I'll find a way. Even if it means..." She swallowed. "Even if the threads of time and fate get so knotted that I don't come out of this on the other side, I'll change this godforsaken timeline. I swear it."

Behind her glasses, her eyes, which were fixed in the path in front of her, burned with as much hatred as Lorian's for change. She wasn't just declaring a new goal, she was manifesting one into reality. She was going to change the rules of time or die trying.

Towards the end of the hall, they entered a large foyer that reminded Lorian of the palace's ballrooms. It had the fewest number of skulls in its walls, and instead had pillars holding up nothing but empty space. The bats Lorian had been waiting for hung upside down from the ceiling. They neighbored the spider webs that colored the domed ceiling grey.

Aida stepped forth into the room, her boots echoing like thunder. On the wall were the pieces of artwork she'd been researching: a palace, people being carried away by birds.

Centered on the front wall was a six-meter tall painting marred beyond recognition. The only traits of a painting being there at all were the scratches of paint in the stone. Lorian saw two people holding hands, the top of a crowned head, and the gold border the artist had must've spent days working on.

Aida went up to touch the painting, then tipped back like a non-existent breeze was whisking her away.

"Aida?"

She stumbled back. She held her forehead.

"Aida!" Lorian went to her side. "What's wrong?"

"I-I'm gonna jump soon."

Lorian's heart fell. The last jump had nearly killed her. "Okay. Where should we go? Should you lay down?"

"Take my glasses. They always fall." She tried to take them off herself, but with her fingers trembling, Lorian took them off for her.

"Here, sit down. I have you."

"I-if I don't come back in an hour—"

"Stop it. I'm not leaving you. How long do you have?"

"Just take my glasses."

"I already did."

That spark of electricity sliced through the air, announcing a Visatorre jump, but Aida was still in Lorian's arms. It came from above.

Two figures were perched upon the highest pillar, one sitting, one standing. So far away from their light, it was hard to guess who they were, but Lorian wasn't daft. She saw the flowing hair, the dress, her very own hair tied into a longer ponytail: Future Aida and Future Lorian.

Aida's shoulder hit the stone wall. "S-something's different," she panted. "It's different."

"Is it more painful?" Lorian tried watching both her and their future selves. What were they doing? What were they planning?

The air shifted. It scattered the dust and howled like a dying wolf.

The next crackle came in slowly, building itself up from nothing. Lorian saw and felt its energy like static electricity. It was alive, birthing itself into the world.

Dust bubbled out in front of them. The Earth shook. Shadows cast in different directions and splattered the ruins with excited light. Something fell in front of them, but Lorian had to close her eyes. The light was too bright.

A hurt voice choked for air, and Lorian looked up to blood.

A woman was hunched over, staring at her bloody hands. Her stomach was bleeding out profusely over her burlap dress. It ran down her legs and feet as she walked in circles before collapsing. "Circa?" she called out. "Circa, God's Death, where have you gone? Where have you taken her?"

Lorian stepped back with Aida in her arms.

She clawed her way towards them. "Circa! Circa, why...?" She held her spilling stomach. "Where have you brought me?"

Aida fell to her knees with the woman. Lorian tried helping everyone. "You're in the Roman Catacombs."

"Where? How?" She coughed. "*When* am I?"

"The year is 1159. Miss, you mustn't move." Lorian took off her jacket and patted her down of her own blood. What did one do for an injury this severe? She feared pressing down too hard. She saw the inside of her stomach pulsate.

The woman finally looked up at her, then at the Catacombs around them, the ruins, the art. She had no head injury that Lorian could see, but her face looked beaten. Her brownish-red hair was short and unevenly cropped, her sclerae were yellow due to lack of nutrients.

Her pupils were solid white, the same as Aida's left one.

And her Visatorre marking was twice ringed, the same as Aida's future self.

Lorian reexamined the woman's accent and manner of speaking. "Are you from the past?" she asked. "Have you travelled forwards?"

The woman coughed wetly and palmed where her heart was. "A-aye. From the past, I..." She suppressed a scream. "Oh, Julia, my jewel, my love, I'm sorry."

"Don't talk," Lorian begged. "You're hurt."

"Oh, my dear, forgive me. I tried, and I failed. I admit my wrongdoings now. I do, I do."

Lorian wiped her now sweating forehead. "Let me call for someone. Aida—"

Aida was staring at the dying woman, but she wasn't staring at the blood or injury. She was staring into her eyes, and she was crying.

"Eve?" she asked, whispering the royal name.

Eve arched her neck to see who'd addressed her. Her jaw dropped. "*You.*"

Lorian went to warn her that moving would make the blood flow quicker, but she expected that this woman—this queen—already knew her fate.

Circa, with all her power and wisdom, was truly a heinous god to these people.

"You," Eve breathed again. "How?"

Aida, grimacing through her delayed jump, reached out for her.

And Eve, queen of the Visatorre, caressed her. "*Aida.*"

A stray tear fell from Aida's face. Lorian saw a thousand questions flicker through her eyes, trying to pick what question to ask the person who meant the world to her.

Aida opened her mouth to speak. As soon as the question formed, her body jerked, her lantern tipped over and, in a flash of light, she was gone.

Chapter 21: A New Side to Eve

Before Aida ate shit in whatever bullshit timeline she was meant to be in, she was crying. Not sobbing—who'd embarrass themselves enough to audibly sob—but after losing Queen Eve of Siina from a death she could've prevented, she figured she'd lost all dignity at that point. What were a few hateful tears to remind you that you were a failure?

Her jump brought her into a dark corridor lit by sconces. She fell onto an expensive-looking red rug next to a marble statue of some dead man's head, but who cared? Who the fuck cared about anything anymore?

She curled up against the statue. Eve had been murdered by the crown, but she was alive, barely, struck in the gut like an animal and in need of Aida's help. And she had her powers, or her future self's powers, able to travel forwards. Had she been injured from the jump? Had something gone wrong?

What did it matter? No one could survive injuries like that for ten minutes, let alone the hours Aida would spend in this fucking jump. She would die, in the present, beside Lorian, and Aida had done nothing to stop it from happening.

"Fuck," she cursed, then louder, slamming her fist into the rug. If she hadn't been so awestruck by her queen, she could've asked her what'd happened, who'd done this, and where she'd been the moment it happened. She could've been helpful. She could've fixed history.

But beyond all that, beyond her fuck-ups, Eve had known her. *"Aida."* Her voice, so frail and close to death, had called out to her. What had her future self done to make Eve know her? It almost made the pain bearable, to hear her say her name.

Aida got up with the help of the statue and squinted to read its name. His date read 2–52 AUC. The numbers were written in Roman numerals, not numbers, a custom primarily used in Eve's time.

"Fuck off." Aida paced, then went back to the statue and read it again. "No. Fuck off, Circa. Not again."

She couldn't have travelled back more than a millennium twice in one year, or one lifetime. Circa was cruel, but she wasn't a sadist.

The main hall opened up into a corridor filled with more pieces of art. Murals of the country landscape and portraits of more well-off gentlemen who were both Visatorre and not Visatorre.

"Oh, go fuck yourself." Aida held her arms tight to herself. She felt sick and unclean, lost in a place not meant for her. She was so stupid for wanting to learn more. Learning only led to death.

Someone laughed down the hall. It was lighthearted and a bit childish. Someone made a joke about the weather.

Eve, accompanied by three gladiators, came around the corner looking as radiant as a god. She was healthy and youthful like Aida had first seen her, with no hole in her stomach. In fact, she was notably pregnant in her maroon dress, her baby due any day.

"She is *such* a delight," Eve mused. "A forward state of progress for this mundane city. Put in a request that I meet with her tonight before the feast. I'd like to have a private affair with her."

"Of course, Your Majesty," one of the sterner-looking gladiators said.

"You best be on your best behavior, Your Majesty," said another. He had orange, spiky hair and freckles dotting his angular face. "I don't want to see you misbehaving."

"I'll be sure to be the outstanding queen you know me to be, Frederico," Eve joked.

Aida ran after Eve and kept with her pace. Her Visatorre marking was only one circle as opposed to two, and her eyes were their normal shade of deep brown.

Aida touched the back of her bicep. In the Catacombs, she'd reached out for Aida. She'd known her name. Did she know her now? If she were visible, would Eve recognize her?

"Here's his room, Your Majesty," one of the gladiators said. He was a little more standoffish than the other two. He was the only one with a metallic etching of a lion on his shoulder: A Roman gladiator.

"I'm familiar, thank you," Eve said with a smile. "You can wait out here. You—" She looked the Roman gladiator up and down. "Well, I don't know where to place you. Would you like to follow me in?"

"I…" He looked away, annoyed yet bashful.

Frederico laughed.

"Nothing like Siina, 'ey, Frederico?" Eve giggled and knocked for herself. "Julius? I have arrived."

Aida's first impression of King Julius at the festival was that he was a powerful, standard king of Roma: domineering, regal, composed. He looked like a true king in his chariot meeting with another equally regal monarch.

Now, he was short and had a bit of a beer belly, wearing a plain shirt and socks. No boots, just ugly socks. How *dare* he insult Eve like this in his own palace, and how dare he go against Aida's expectations of him?

He bowed to Eve. "Good morning, Your Majesty. I hope my accommodations were to your liking."

"Very much so, Your Majesty."

"I do hope you know that 'Julius' is more than enough when we're like this."

"Oh, it is? Forgive me." She let herself in. "I recall you preferring a different name when we were alone."

Aida took her chance and ran in with Eve. If she was hearing them right, this talk had a double meaning to it. Not only was it inappropriate, they were supposed to be rivals. Right now, Roma City should've been overseeing the ocean, while Siina had settlements along the main rivers to grow grapes, Roma's most profitable export. In a few months, Siina and Roma would be at war, and Eve would be...

This room was no doubt King Julius' personal bedchamber. His canopy bed looked too expensive to sit on, and the art on the walls looked fit for a museum. Outside was a courtyard of flowers and pathways she'd only heard about in novels. This flower garden had been kept for generations. A vase on the writing desk held two of them: purple and yellow, the colors of Roma.

"I hope finding me wasn't too difficult," King Julius said, locking the door behind him. "You'd said you spent twenty minutes wandering my halls last time."

"To keep you waiting, yes, for I never get lost, though I do admit your palace is grand." She ran her hand down the length of his desk. "Almost as grand as mine."

King Julius prowled over to her, his saunter slow and calculating.

Aida's mouth contorted in disgust. They couldn't. They wouldn't.

Eve licked her lips as her hands wriggled into his hair. She pet him like a dog before grabbing a fistful of it and yanking his head up.

He gasped into a smile. "Good God, woman."

"I'm present." She flung him onto the desk. She thrust her pregnant belly into him.

Aida covered her eyes. "Eve, no."

"Tell me what you want," Eve ordered.

"I want *you*," he said, completely submitting to her. "I want to mark you, claim you. I want your everything inside of me, Eve. I love you."

Eve smiled, then pinned the king's hands behind his head and kissed him.

"What the *fuck*," Aida said. "Eve, stop! What're you doing?"

She continued kissing him like Aida wasn't there. And she wasn't. She was a ghost in this timeline, trapped in a room with two disgusting monarchs with no manners or class.

She covered her ears, but the slurping and jerking sounds came through her fingers. Wasn't Eve married? Wasn't King Julius married to Julia? And didn't *Eve* have something with Julia, too? That was what she'd thought, with Julia blushing at her touch and that painting in the Catacombs.

Was Eve just *like* this, immoral and crazed by lust and greed?

Banging her head against the window helped block out the noise. Eve had undone Julius' pants and began stroking him. His ugly moans and the satisfaction Eve gained from it sickened Aida. Centuries of history and she *had* to have landed here without a chance to escape?

She hated human beings. Why were they like this? She could barely establish meaningful friendships with people, so when they acted this intimate, moaning and grinding against each other to get off, it horrified her. It felt like everyone had been built with this special piece in their heart, and she was missing hers, or she'd destroyed it along the way and couldn't get it back. She knew it must've felt nice, and sometimes she found herself dreaming about it, but reality soured the whole fantasy.

She pictured Lorian when she thought about this, and she didn't know if that was a good thing or not.

After getting the king off, Eve stood up, proud of herself, and wiped her lips with her sticky thumb. "Good boy."

King Julius lifted himself up on his elbows with a drunk smile. His cheeks burned red with lust. "I love you," he slurred. "I *want* you."

"As your letter foretold," she said.

"Aye. Your being encapsulates my every waking moment. I adore you sincerely, Eve. You're everything."

"I know." She traced circles over his now unbuttoned shirt. "But, alas, you can't take up as much refuge in my mind, for that border disagreement has my people so worried. They take up all of my time, they do."

"I must do what's best for my people, Eve. Surely you of all people understand that. I need the Tiber."

228

"As do I. Now, if you were to cease building that little dam that will shorten a fifth of my people's agricultural resources, think of how much time I'd be able to spend with you."

"The flow of the river is damaging the water beds near my plaza."

Then we can redirect the flow into a new river. We have the funds to do that." She stroked his head into his beard. "What do you say, my love? Will you satisfy me?"

He hung back his head. "My advisors will not take this well."

"Aw, is my puppy afraid of the men he rules? Do you need a reminder of how it's done? How to govern men with one hand?"

Julius wrapped one leg around her. "Alright. I'll talk with them tomorrow."

"Good boy." To reward him, she kissed him again. "Now, what about your wife?"

"What about her?"

She sat back up. "You're an adulterer. Surely you feel shameful for what you're doing. How do you treat her, knowing what we do?"

He scoffed. "You need not worry about that woman. She gives me no pleasure compared to your grace. You are all that's in my heart, as I hope I am with you." He settled down his fervor. "I'm sure you know that I'm better than anything Meyeso had given you."

Eve cocked her head. "That so," she said cooly.

"Aye," he said. "Tell me. Tell me that I'm better, and the river is yours."

Eve looked over the king of Roma, twirling his exposed chest hair with her finger. Then she got up and went for the bathroom.

"Where're you going?" he asked.

"To freshen up for round two."

When King Julius began unbuttoning his shirt, Aida decided that her time was better spent with Eve and followed her into the bathroom.

Eve quietly shut the door, almost politely, and walked to the mirror to look at herself. Aida did the same and only saw Eve staring back at her.

Furiously. Biting her inner cheeks, Eve was pissed off and jumping her leg in total frustration.

"*What?*" Aida demanded. "What're you thinking? Tell me."

Eve pushed back her bangs to better reveal her Visatorre marking, and Aida saw her youth aging away. Despite being in her twenties, there was the weight of a country in her eyes. She was tired, in need of a rest from politics and men.

She forced out an exhale. "Bastard," she whispered.

"He is, so why did you do that? He's a horrible man. He's going to kill you, so why are you like this with him?"

She fixed up her hair and checked her face from all angles. She was a very beautiful woman. Flecks of gold in her eyes with makeup complementing her tan skin.

She ruined it by slapping herself in the face. The strike took Aida off guard as well as the second, much harder slap. She pinched the death out of her cheeks until they were redder than her blush. To finish it off, she stared at her reflection without blinking until tears dripped from her eyes. She hiccupped, fanning her face like she was in distress. "Oh, I cannot bear it!" she said dramatically, and flung herself out of the room.

"Fuck." Aida slipped out before the door slammed.

The king was up, trying to battle to fix his pants on. "What's wrong?"

"I...Oh, I can't do this right now. It's too soon." She cried into her wrist, but when Julius went to hold her, she aggressively shoved him back and ran out of the bedroom.

"Eve—" He jumped back behind his dresser so the gladiators didn't see him. "Are you mad?"

"I need to leave. Farewell."

"God damn it." Aida ran before she lost Eve again, but the king's stupid, elegant rug tripped her up, now as solid as stone, and those few seconds cost her everything. Eve ran, shut the door, and Aida was left alone with a sweaty, horny King Julius.

"Fuck!" She hit the floor again. "Damn you, Eve!"

"Curse her," Julius agreed. "Cursed courtesan. The things I do for her."

"Do *what*?" Aida spat. If she was going to be trapped in this damn room with him, the least she could do was vent out her grievances. "Your actions are what cursed the Romano family tree. You're a selfish, stupid, horny disgrace to all Roman customs! Fuck you. I don't ever want to see you again."

Her woozy feeling came back, and she braced herself for the pain. Would she survive this trip back? She hadn't thought about it.

Very much like her to worry more about dead monarchs than her own self.

The air around her swirled in her ears, and she fell forwards into darkness.

—◇—

She fell wrong in several ways.

One, she dropped on her bad knee, and while it didn't hurt directly, her brain acted like it did.

Two, she wasn't hurting badly. Her head was normal, her thoughts clear.

Three, she was still in the Roman Palace. It even looked like the same day, with the Sun cooling the hall in a comfortable blue.

She felt her Visatorre marking. One ring.

Hurried high heels ran down the hall Aida had fallen into, and she turned to see Eve running with her gladiators. She'd lost her tears as well as her meek demeanor as she ran with her dress lifted. Her cheeks were still red from forcing the tears out. "Jules."

Jules—Queen Julia—poked her head out from a corridor. "Eta."

The two embraced and hid in the dead end. Aida dusted off her confusion and followed them. The gladiators stayed back to give them privacy.

Julia grasped onto Eve's sleeves. They were wearing those matching bracelets from before. From this close up, Aida could tell that the stone in Eve's bracelet had the letter *J* carved into it. Julia's had the letter *E*.

"Oh, Eta, please be merciful," Julia begged. "What did he do? What did he say?"

"I regret to say that he reaffirmed your fears. He did come on to me. I'm sorry."

Julia cried into Eve's shoulder. Despite being so short, Eve held her tenderly, massaging her back in comfort.

"I knew it," Julia cried. "I didn't want to, but I knew it, I did. What did he do?"

"He confirmed that what he wrote to me was genuine and confessed his love. It was a short-sighted love, Jules. He said nothing about my inner beauty."

"Oh, Circa almighty. I knew it. I heard the rumors but wanted to know myself. Did he do anything else?"

Eve wiped away her good friend's tears. "No, love. I left before he did anything." She kissed her temple. "He's too good for you, my love. Don't plague yourself over his misdoings. You're a beautiful gemstone in this city of greedy fools. Do not let their sins overcome your sense of truth."

Julia nodded along with everything she said. "I-I won't. I'll stay strong, for Roma, for you."

"Good girl." She tilted up Julia's head and left a gentle kiss on her chin, then on her lips, a feather touching a still pond.

Aida replicated their hands over her own body. Their energy was so much different than Eve's encounter with Julius. These two were, from what she knew, love itself, pure and experimental and fortified by understanding.

"Wait," she said aloud. "You're lying to her. You did much more than talk with him. You're as much a cheater as he is."

She kept watching them, these confusing women embracing in secret, and felt that sinking feeling again. No matter how much history she crammed into her brain, everyone was dancing to a song she didn't know.

Her body swayed, dancing its own dance, and she was swept back into time.

Before she lost sight of the girls, her body burned up in blistering, mind-numbing pain.

Chapter 22: Royal Affairs

Lorian didn't take well to stress. Whenever something went wrong in her life, be it minute or monumental, she panicked. It was an animalistic reaction she hadn't evolved from, and it was becoming more impossible to deal with those feelings without Aida.

Eve groaned and fingered her open wound.

"Please, stop doing that," Lorian urged. "It'll only make it worse."

"Oh, will it, young one?" She coughed. Her breath was barely there anymore. "I wasn't aware."

"Just keep still. You'll be alright." Holding on to her fake smile, Lorian glared up at the pillar their future selves were still perched on. They were like onlookers awaiting death at the Colosseum.

"Do something," she whispered to them. "Please."

"Child," Eve said. "Tell me. Your beautiful locks, your fair complexion. Are you of King Julius' line?"

Sensing she had no reason to lie, Lorian said, "I am, Your Majesty. He's one of my grandfathers. I'm second in line for the throne."

"So his reign continued on. How fortunate. And... And Aida..." She reached over her head like Aida was still there. "Where did she go?"

"She travelled, Your Majesty. She's a Visatorre like you." She gulped, not ready to hear the answer to her next question. "Y-Your Majesty, how do you know her name? Did you know her future self, older self? Have you met her before?"

"Aida." Her eyes closed. "I need to speak to her...again."

"No—no." Lorian shook her. "Please, stay with me."

It was pointless. Lorian knew that. It wasn't as if a few stitches or a hasty surgery could save her now.

A tear hit Eve's cheek. She opened one eye.

"I'm sorry." Lorian sniffled. "I'm sorry I can't do anything to save you. Aida, she loved you. She's studied every history book with your name in it. She would've loved to meet you. But you'll be with Circa soon. You'll be with your God."

A blissful smile fell over Eve's face. "She loved me?"

"*Loves*. She *loves* you. She always has."

If she could've, she would've laughed. Lorian saw it in the corners of her mouth. Instead, she took Lorian's hand like a newborn baby.

"I have you," Lorian said. "You're going to be okay."

"You're lying."

She nodded, face scrunching to keep from crying. "I am."

Eve closed her eyes. "As a royal does."

The next few moments passed slowly and too fast all at once. Lorian thought that if she ran fast enough and found a doctor, she could've saved her. If she'd allotted more time with her nurses, if she'd studied suturing or tourniquets, she could've helped.

Lorian hadn't known her, but with how often Aida spoke about her, losing Eve felt like losing a close family member.

When she stopped breathing, Lorian, suddenly alone, cried for her. She didn't know how long: ten minutes, a half-hour. The Catacomb air froze her tears to her face as she wiped them dry. It wasn't fair, or right. She didn't want this memory in her.

She looked back up to the pillar. Her and Aida's future selves had vanished.

Overcome by true loneliness, Lorian sobbed into her hands. It'd been months since she'd been so alone. All her life she had her family, maids, nurses, officers, everyone heeding to every beck and call. After leaving the palace, she'd cried like this in the woods, overwhelmed by the feeling of not having anyone to talk to. If only she had Aida back.

"Lucia?"

Her eyes went up to the pillar, but it was still empty.

"Lorian."

It should've been unmistakable, that voice. It was hers, pitched an octave higher, her emotions held back.

Behind her, standing in one of the open archways with two lanterns, were Beatrice, Zaahir, and Zaahir's lover, Kadar.

Lorian tried to move away, but Eve had become dead weight.

Beatrice walked down a short staircase. Her hands were gloved, that's what Lorian saw first. She'd been caned recently. "What happened here?" she asked, then, clearer, "What did you do?"

Months without seeing each other. Lorian could've been murdered or held hostage, and all she got was chastisement.

Reading the atmosphere, Zaahir asked, "Are you alright?"

She didn't know why, but hearing that question broke her. Her senses overcame her and she began to tremble. Breaking fully to pieces, she lowered her head and sobbed in front of the world's two monarchs-to-be.

How humiliating. They'd inspired her to be better in every way, not as a royal, but as a person. Her sister was that of a second parent, so level-headed and sensible, and Zaahir. When Lorian was first introduced to him, she thought he was already a king with how he carried himself.

She wasn't meant to be like them. She'd been born wrong, left to act out while these true leaders held up the world.

Zaahir let Lorian cry on him. His shoulder was warm and his breath smelled of Nectar.

Kadar eyed the clearly dead body with revulsion.

"What happened to her?" Zaahir asked in a soft voice.

"I-I don't know. She jumped right in front of us. She was already bleeding. I couldn't do anything to save her."

"What do you mean? Was she visible when she jumped?"

She nodded. "She's Eve. Eve Costa. She was the queen of Siina a millennium ago."

Eve's mysterious eyes were still open, the tranquil look becoming more unnerving than anything. Zaahir touched her wet bangs to reveal her unique Visatorre marking, then checked her pulse by placing two fingers against her throat.

"I didn't do it," Lorian told them. "It wasn't my fault."

Zaahir wiped his fingers on a spare handkerchief. "I believe you. Her haircut is reminiscent of that of the Roman style in the Classical Era, and her skin, aside from..." He analyzed her wound. "She smells like Roman roses, and you can see it on her skin." He pointed to the side of her neck that was stained not from blood but from a powdery substance. "This was very common during that time period. I believe you, so do not worry."

"I-I wouldn't hurt anyone," she said, cursing the stutter now present in her voice. "She just fell into us."

"Us?"

"Aida and me. The girl I've been with."

"That future self."

"Yes. But she isn't like that. Gods, it's so hard to explain without her here. We don't know anything about what's going on."

"Easy," Zaahir said. "How long has it been since she passed?"

"Just now. Aida jumped somewhere. It'll take hours for her to come back. I don't know what to do."

She dug up a fistful of cold dirt. She wanted Aida back. She needed her for this.

Zaahir pushed up his sleeves. "She needs a proper burial. Officers will be skeptical about her body. She won't have any records of being a Roman citizen."

"You can lie," Lorian offered. "She's a Visatorre, we can say she was homeless. It wouldn't be unbelievable."

Zaahir nodded. "I will see to it that she is buried here, with her people, but we can't stay here. We need to get help."

"I can't leave," Lorian said. "I need to wait for Aida to come back. She'll be in the dark, and to see Eve's body—" She caught her breath. What would Aida say if she knew Lorian had let her die?

"We can't stay here," Beatrice argued. "It's not safe. These walls are ancient. The ceiling can come crashing down on us."

Lorian turned to her. She couldn't believe that after months of not seeing her, Beatrice was still turned off by everything Lorian did that wasn't up to her standards. Even when she was crying in a cemetery their ancestors had created. "I'm not going back to the palace."

Beatrice held firm. "If you come back to the palace now—"

"I'm not."

"*Listen* to me," she said. "If you come back, we can set aside these rumors about these...people." She made a face. "What is this, these future selves everyone's been going on about? What are you doing with them?"

"Beatrice, might we—?"

"What does it matter, I'm not going back!" Lorian argued. "That's the whole reason I left, to be rid of this. I have no idea what those two are doing." She pointed upwards at the empty pillar they'd been sitting on. "They're our future selves, *ergo*, I have no say over what they do. They've only spoken to us twice, telling us there's some grand plan we need to accomplish, but whatever we try to do ends up blowing up in our faces. We get chased by Carmine, we think coming down here will help us find answers, but we keep fucking up, so stop yelling at me for the right answers, because clearly, I have none!"

She knew her voice was rising, so she huffed and ran her hand through her hair. "I don't know what's happening, but I know I'm not going back home. I can't."

Zaahir nodded understandingly. "Alright. We won't bring you back."

Beatrice shot him a look.

"But we should take refuge while you calm down. Your sister is right, it's not safe for all three of us to be here, and this scene is unsettling. Is there anything we can do to help right now?"

Lorian began collecting Aida's clothes. "I need to wait for Aida to return. Something's been wrong with her jumps and I don't know what's happening. I don't know how to help her." The tears came back. She blotted them with her sleeve. "I have to be here when she comes back. I have to protect her."

"That's completely understandable." Zaahir took off his winter robe and draped it over Eve's body. Then he took Lorian's hand, and the four of them went towards the wall, behind a pillar. "Why were you down here in the first place?"

Lorian crouched behind the pillar. "We were searching for clues. Aida said she had a hunch to come down here tonight. Looks like that hunch was right, but..." She dug the balls of her hands into her eyes.

"Lu..." Zaahir knelt beside her. "Is it Lorian now?"

She nodded.

"Okay, Lorian, I know you don't wish to go back to the palace, and we will not force you to go back. But can you tell us what your plan is for the time being? What do you need? What are you planning to do next?"

"Do you think someone like me thinks ahead of her actions?"

While Zaahir smiled politely at Lorian's attempt to be humorous, Beatrice just clicked her tongue.

Lorian had so many mixed feelings about her. One moment, they'd be playing games on the palace grounds, the next, Beatrice would be yelling at Lorian for being a nuisance. She got into as much trouble as Lorian, yet she'd wiggle her way out of scoldings. As the years progressed, Beatrice became closer and closer to their parents and their ideals, leaving Lorian by herself.

She hadn't even hugged her. Was that asking too much, for a hug and a, "How are you?" and not a, "Why are you like this?"

She knew it was, for her.

"What happened?"

Lorian tried not looking at her.

"When we were coming down, we heard a crash," Beatrice continued. "Was that from the Visatorre jumping, or..."

Lorian looked down at her hands. The blood was still there. She didn't know if wiping it off would help her forget. "Why were you three down here to hear it? Surely, your guards wouldn't have allowed you to have a fling in the Catacombs."

"We were taking a stroll to clear our heads," Zaahir said. "Your father has been very adamant about finding these two future selves to calm the city down. Then we heard what sounded like loud firecrackers coming from the open door of the Catacomb, and we decided to come investigate."

"Who's being impulsive now?"

Beatrice scoffed.

"Frog in your throat?" Lorian asked.

"The air down here is not right for our lungs."

"Well, I'm not leaving without Aida, so, by all means, leave if you so desire. Nobody's forcing you to make choices you vehemently disagree with."

"Lorian." Zaahir sighed. "I don't want to see us fighting again. Now is not the time. Where have you been living?"

"You won't rat on me to my father, will you?" She looked to Kadar. "Not him, right?"

Kadar placed a pointer finger to his lips.

"He'll take any secret with him to his grave," Zaahir promised. "As will I."

"Then I've been with my nursemaid, Missus Sharma."

"*She's* keeping you?" Beatrice asked.

"Yes," she said, and gave them a condensed version of everything that happened since the wedding.

They didn't interrupt her. It wasn't like in council meetings where everyone was yelling for a chance to speak. She appreciated their silence, but it was odd talking for so long and not being interrupted with facts she wasn't aware of.

When she finished nearly two hours later, their lanterns had dimmed to a deep amber. Zaahir was holding the back of his head with his hands. Beatrice was leaning against a fallen column. Kadar hadn't moved.

"That sounds very exciting, don't you think?" Zaahir asked.

"Not really. I've been shaking since I left. All this hiding and running about in the dark. My future self scares me the most. She's dressed like a queen, or king."

"Maybe she is," Zaahir said. "You have royal blood in your veins. Maybe you'll become a great ruler."

Lorian didn't entertain the fact. "We were thinking they might be from an alternate universe. I've heard about those in fictional stories. A world where it's almost the same as ours, but certain things are different. Instead of riding horses, we ride things like wild pigs or birds, or something entirely different, something we can't fathom. And maybe, in this world, Aida and I turned into reckless beasts."

"Why do you think that? Being that they sound like you, talk like you, act like you—"

"Because I can't imagine putting a crown back on my head."

That snap, the electrifying pulse that shaped the air whenever a Visatorre travelled, now terrified Lorian. Her heart jumped at the fear of secondhand pain.

To Lorian's relief, Aida wasn't coughing or convulsing like she'd done the last time she'd jumped. She looked asleep, knocked out from a regular jump.

"Aida." Lorian ran over to her.

She was staring up at the ceiling, her eyes unfocused, mouth agape.

Lorian's heart thudded in her ears. She shook her shoulder. "Aida?"

She didn't react.

She shook her much rougher than she should've, but she needed to see her move, breathe, something. Aida wasn't the type to keep quiet, and she wasn't that heavy a sleeper.

Her head thrashed back and forth. Her unfocused eyes stared off into nothing.

Lorian searched her body for another way to test it. She wouldn't believe it. It didn't make sense. She had a future self, she had so many plans set to come true. Surely, this wasn't two timelines. She knew she'd considered the alternate timeline, but she knew it was wrong. She knew that boisterous, fun-loving woman was a part of Aida that couldn't end here.

"What's wrong?" Zaahir asked

"S-she's not breathing. What do we do? She's not breathing."

"Let me try." He checked for a pulse. When he found nothing, he opened up her airways, laced his fingers together, and began pressing down hard into the middle of her chest.

Lorian scooted out of the way. The amount of pressure he was putting on her was sure to splinter ribs. She almost told him to be gentler, but he seemed to know what he was doing. He counted under his breath the number of seconds he needed to keep going to bring her back.

A minute ticked by. Zaahir kept stopping, checking for breathing, listening to her heart, and continuing his rhythm. That lifeless look in Aida's eyes was beginning to resemble Eve's.

"Come on," Zaahir panted. "Come back to us."

"Please," Lorian begged the Gods. "Aida, you have so much more to do. You can't leave me now. I won't allow it."

Zaahir, tired from chest compressions, breathed life back into her mouth.

Aida gasped into him, hoarse and broken but back from the dead. She reached for Zaahir, but he kept her down.

"Easy, *easy*," he said. "You're alright, just relax."

Aida had her back arched, contorting herself in agony. She sounded like she was gargling water, but nothing was coming up other than her own air.

Beatrice stayed back in the shadows without saying a word.

Kadar helped adjust her. She was scratching her neck like she couldn't breathe, but she was gasping properly, or improperly. Lorian didn't know. How lost she felt, seeing someone she loved in pain and being unable to help them.

Giving room for Zaahir and Kadar to work, Lorian crept up to Aida and held her hand.

Aida seized it like she was still on death's door. Her nails cut into her skin and made her bleed.

"We need to take her to a doctor," Zaahir said. "I've never seen this type of attack in a Visatorre before."

"We can't," Lorian said. "They're still looking for us. If they find out we're here, they'll have her detained or hanged, and

I'll…" She stopped herself short. Who cared about her feelings when Aida was this badly hurt?

Then she figured what Aida would've wanted, or hated, rather. "We can't," she finalized. "We'll take her back home."

"Where?" Beatrice asked.

Lorian helped lift Aida up. She pretended that Eve's body wasn't a few meters away. "To Missus Sharma's cottage."

Chapter 23: Royal Fray

It didn't take much to convince the trio to follow Lorian to Missus Sharma's. Seeing Aida convulse sent Zaahir into his protective nature, and Kadar did anything his prince asked.

Lorian felt Beatrice's eyes on her for the whole venture back, judging her, hating her. She'd only agreed to come along per Zaahir's request. It wasn't like she could go back home without him.

Lorian kept her eyes ahead, ignoring her. She'd learned to brush aside her poignant glaring from past family outings.

She was failing.

Before they opened the gates, Missus Sharma slammed open the front door with chamberstick in hand. She'd heard them, or she'd been waiting by the window all night. "Lorian!"

Lorian hopped off her horse before it fully stopped. They'd taken Zaahir's and Beatrice's horses back. "Aida's hurt."

Missus Sharma looked between Aida's weathered state and Beatrice and Zaahir. "Is she—?"

"She's alive," she said, but it wasn't convincing. Aida had stopped choking on her own breath, but she still wasn't "there." She kept moaning whenever she moved.

Zaahir and Kadar helped Aida off of their horse. They were tall horses meant to see over savannah grasses, so when she fell, she fell hard. It took both of their combined strengths to keep her from twisting an ankle. Beatrice picked up her dress so she didn't dirty it.

They helped her into their Nest of blankets and pillows. Zaahir had to walk over fallen books Aida had been reading for her research.

"Oh, no, dear, please." Missus Sharma motioned for the stairs. "Let her stay in a proper bed. It's what she needs right now."

"But you haven't any spare beds," Lorian said.

"She can have ours. Oh, darling, what has become of you?"

Lorian didn't know if she was talking to her or Aida. She didn't have an answer for either.

They brought Aida up the stairs. She'd found her feet, but her knees were bent at odd angles and her head sagged and twitched at every step. It was like she was partly there, partly somewhere else, like she didn't know why she was walking but knew that she had to keep going. Lorian couldn't fathom what she was going through.

At the top of the stairs, a door creaked open to Chrissie and Onti. They were looking past each other to see what all the commotion was about. At the sight of Zaahir, Chrissie blushed and ran back into the shadows. Her hands shot out and dragged Onti back to bed.

"Wait!" he protested. "They're important, ain't they? They're royal, right?"

Mi'Sharma took their entrance very well. She looked up, dropped her jaw, closed it, closed her book, and flapped open the covers for Aida. "Sit her here."

"I'm sorry," Lorian said.

"Look at her." She went to Missus Sharma. "How awful."

Lorian didn't realize she was falling until she dropped to the bedside with Aida. Her chest was pounding and she was breathing as heavily as Aida was. Aida herself fell asleep in a wink. Her twitches receded to head tics and eye flutters.

"Is there anything we can do?" Zaahir asked. "Say the word and we'll be here with doctors, medicine. We can be as discreet as possible."

"I think we've done all that we can do," Beatrice said. "They don't have treatments for what she's going through. All we can do is wait."

Even though she spoke the truth, it still pissed Lorian off that she said it so nonchalantly, like she couldn't care less about helping anyone so long as she could get back home before sunrise.

The night wind shifted the walls of the cottage into place. The low fire they had going crackled with heat.

Mi'Sharma cleared her throat. "Shall I make everyone some tea? Your Highness, are you hungry?"

"That's quite alright, Missus," Zaahir said. "We should be on our way. The two of us shouldn't be out like this in the first place. We appreciate you inviting us into your home. It looks like you have a wonderful family."

"Thank you, Your Majesty. Your Highness. Oh." Mi'Sharma covered her mouth. "How did you do this for almost two decades, darling?"

"It comes with practice and expectations," Missus Sharma said, "neither of which I can muster up at this moment." She pet back Aida's hair. "Poor dearie. She's gone through so much."

"I'll keep an eye on her," Lorian promised. "I'll stay with her all night to make sure..." She gulped. "Make sure she doesn't..."

"She'll be alright," Zaahir said. "If something were to happen, you know where to reach us. We'll be here for you."

"Thank you. And thank you," she said to Kadar, "for helping her."

He bowed.

Missus Sharma looked over to Beatrice, the only one not addressed.

"Oh, I can't stand this!" Mi'Sharma said. "I need to offer you something, anything at all. If word gets back to my family that I neglected to serve tea to the future king of Aldaí, I'll never hear the end of it."

Zaahir smiled charmingly. "A spot of herbal tea will be lovely, then, thank you."

"I'll help as well," Missus Sharma said. "If any of you need anything else, please, don't be shy, I'll be happy to get it." She walked close to Beatrice and bowed. Beatrice bowed back. She almost smiled.

And almost went to leave with the two women. Went to but didn't. A conversation hung in the air, begging to be said.

"What?" Lorian asked her.

Her perfect hair whipped around her perfectly angled face. She'd inherited neither their father's aggression nor their mother's meekness. When anything bad happened, she became a corpse without a heart. "I'm glad you're okay."

Lorian's brows shot up.

"But I want you to come back home."

Her face fell, as well as her expectations for her sister yet again. So close. Why was she so hard to love?

"I know you left for...reasons that I understand, but you can't live your life evading what needs to be talked about. You're still engaged to Zaahir and you have a country and *world* wondering what you're going to do next. You should speak out about what you're planning. You should come up with a *plan*."

"I *do* have a plan, and it's staying as far away from Father as possible."

"That's not logical. You need to go back at some point."

"I won't."

"Think about Mother."

"I'm not going back!"

Kadar, someone Lorian remembered as always being in the shadows, jerked forwards with a sudden hand over his temple. Zaahir held him by the shoulders.

"*Amar?*" Zaahir whispered.

"I'm sorry," Kadar grunted. "I need to..."

"That's alright." He led his servant to the center of the room. "I'm here."

"But you're alone. It's not safe."

"I'll stay here. I'll send a message to the king. I'll be fine, okay?" He whispered more to him in Aldaían, then kissed the top of his brow before a bright light took Kadar from Zaahir's arms.

Lorian jumped back, not expecting the disappearance. "He's a Visatorre?"

Zaahir began folding Kadar's clothes like he was picking up the morning newspaper. "He is, yes."

"And he's allowed to be a knight? Wouldn't that cause liabilities?"

Zaahir went to the open window and whistled with his fingers to his mouth, and a pair of heavy wings flew to the sill. An Aldaían hawk, brown and sleek with a black head, came to him. It wore a woven pack around its chest.

Zaahir took out a small piece of paper and a writing pen from his pocket. "He's not a liability because of the way he was born, but for safety reasons, I'm always followed by a carrier hawk in case I need to send out an emergency letter."

Lorian lowered her head, ashamed for how she'd been programmed to think. "I didn't mean to offend you. I'm used to how Roma works. Roman Visatorre can't become officers."

"I know." He folded the letter into the hawk's pack and sent it into the night. "It's one of the changes I want to see in Roma. When we were married, I had plans to reform your schools, help the Visatorre jobless crisis. We have so many models in Aldaí that we could've incorporated here."

Lorian looked away, as did Beatrice and even Zaahir himself.

"Well," Beatrice said, "since we're going to be here longer than initially planned, let me go speak with Missus Sharma about our untimely visit."

"Wait a moment," Zaahir said. "Now that we're finally together—"

"My say is whatever you agree with," Beatrice said with a wave of her hand. "We won't get anywhere with our emotions so high-strung."

"Aida almost *died*," Lorian snapped at her. "She *did* die. Can't you be a little more considerate of that?"

"I *am* being considerate. I'm saying that we won't come to a sound resolution with you acting this way and Zaahir's mind on Kadar. Don't try and deny it, Zaahir. I know you too well."

Zaahir tried. "I still think we should talk about—"

"Bea's clearly not going to voice her opinion on the matter," Lorian said. "She gave it one try, no use in trying anymore."

Beatrice flared her nostrils. It got Lorian going. Her chest burned. "And you won't get a logical answer from me, right, Bea, so there's no point in counting me in to the discussion."

"Please," Beatrice said. "Spare us."

Lorian jumped to her feet. "What is your *problem* with me? You haven't seen me in months. I run away without giving a reason why. I've been tormented by these future selves who only want to poke fun at our misdoings, and I've been...I—" She felt herself tearing up at trying to come up with an excuse for this anger, but all she saw was Beatrice. The person who was supposed to be there for her. Her sister. Her twin.

"What the fuck happened to you?" she demanded. "Why did you become like this?"

Beatrice stood up taller with the scowl Lorian had been waiting for. "I took care of what needed to be done. We have duties, Lorian, and if you hate the idea of coming back so much, then *don't*. *Don't* come back. *Don't* abide by the rules. But *state* what you need. Abdicate properly. Annul the marriage. Let the world continue on so we don't have to wait for you to stop acting like a brat."

Lorian gaped at her. She was used to her lectures, but this was something new.

Lorian pushed her. "You make it sound like I don't care for my country. It's not like I want Roma to burn. I just don't want to be an heir. You knew, you *always* knew I didn't want to be a princess."

"You two, stop it."

"Of *course* I knew," Beatrice said, "and I didn't want to be married, either. What are you getting at? Do you think Zaahir wants this? Do you think *I* want this? Our blood isn't ours, Lorian. Zaahir has a lover and knew that marrying you would appease our parents. I knew that the alliance with Bĕlico during a harsh winter was needed for the family, for our country. It was what *needed* to be done."

"You were six!"

"Yes, I was! Are you trying to say that it's unfair, that being a royal heir means that you're thrown about to appease others without your consent, because yes, that's what it means. That's what our lives will always be. So yes, Zaahir will marry a person he doesn't love, I'm stuck with a man who I couldn't care less for, and you"—she pointed at Lorian—"will marry Zaahir, unless you abdicate and fail your country, like you should've done this summer. If you're mad at me for saying that, tough shit. It's the truth, but you've been doing a damn good job at fucking over your life without my input, so why do I bother at this point!"

Lorian didn't know what happened next. One moment she was by Aida's bedside. The next, Aida didn't exist. All that was in her sights was Beatrice, then Beatrice's shocked face, then Lorian reaching for her neck and squeezing.

Lorian slammed her sister into a wall painting. "You've never been there for me!" she screamed at her. "What the fuck did it cost you to love me? Why couldn't you be there for me, for once, the *one* time I needed it?"

"Get off!"

Lorian hit her. Life was *so* easy for her. Do everything Father says, don't fight, be complacent. She'd been molded to be perfect, and Lorian had been the spare. And instead of helping Lorian—fuck, *talking* to Lorian—she'd ignored her like a virus she wouldn't dare touch.

"Lorian, enough!" Zaahir yelled.

Lorian battled Beatrice into the hallway. She punched her, kicked her. She sought out blood.

"Get off!" Beatrice ducked out of her embrace and shoved her away. Lorian, anticipating her escape, grabbed her puffy sleeve before she reached the stairwell.

She turned too quickly, looking over her shoulder to anticipate Lorian's fist, but all she must've seen was Lorian gritting her teeth in pure rage.

The stairwell, it wasn't long, but the sudden drop, their bodies slamming into the railing and feet disconnecting from the steps, recontextualized Lorian's feelings.

One, she didn't want to die in such heated anger.

Two, she couldn't let Beatrice die in such an anticlimactic way.

Three, she hated herself more than ever for stooping so low.

Lorian pulled Beatrice back and took the full embrace of the fall. Her elbow cracked. Her head went fuzzy. Beatrice's hair came undone from her braids and spilled out over them. Maybe that was what Lorian wanted, to see her come undone the same way she'd felt herself becoming that year.

Lorian heaved herself up. The fight's energy dripped off of her like rain on a waxy leave.

Missus and Mi'Sharma ran in, holding back Chrissie and Onti. Zaahir jumped the last three steps. "Now, see here!"

Beatrice's nails cut into Lorian's cheek and drew blood. She yanked her down and smacked her chin into the floor.

"Bea!" Zaahir grabbed her by the arms. "That is *enough*! Stop it!"

"How *dare* you?" She pinned her to the ground. "I've done *everything* for you. I defended you from Father, I've talked him out of caning you so many times, and yet—" She ripped off one glove with her teeth and showed Lorian her caned hand. "I *always* received the pain he'd meant for you!"

Zaahir used all of his strength to pull Beatrice off. "That is *enough*."

It wasn't, not for either of them. "I spent night after night with Mother," Beatrice said, "calming her down, telling her she hadn't failed as a mother in raising us. What a great liar I'd become."

Lorian touched the spot where Beatrice had got her on the cheek. Her fingers came back bloody, and wet.

Beatrice sniffled. "The night you left," she said, "you left out the windows, didn't you? With a ladder made of bedsheets? Everything was so cleverly packaged for you to leave and gather your thoughts, to leave and never return?"

Lorian blinked back her sister's tears.

"Who did you think did that for you?" she asked. "Who went out of her way to give you your escape?"

Zaahir, sensing the fight was over, pulled Beatrice off of Lorian.

"I thought I was doing you a *favor*," Beatrice continued, "so why is everything still so wrong? Why is Mother still crying herself to sleep? Why do you look more unhappy than ever? Why am I still failing you?"

Missus Sharma helped Lorian stand. "Lu—Lorian," she whispered. "Come now. Sit up."

Zaahir bowed a ninety-degree angle to both Sharma's. "I sincerely apologize for this inexcusable behavior. This was in no way how we'd meant to thank you for your kindness in allowing us into your home unannounced, and we deeply apologize for any damages we might've caused you and your family."

Beatrice, after fixing her hair, copied Zaahir's bow. "I apologize as well."

Lorian knew she should've done the same, but it wasn't as if anyone in this room would forgive her for behavior they expected.

Still, in a whisper, she said, "I'm sorry."

"I think we should leave," Beatrice said.

"I'm sorry, but I cannot leave without my knight," Zaahir said. "He should be back in a few hours. We'll take our leave then. Again, please forgive us, Missus and Mi'Sharma."

"You needn't be sorry," Missus Sharma said. "Lorian, come with me. Iris, please make something for Her Majesty and His Highness. Chrissie and Onti, upstairs. Now."

Lorian had little say when it came to what Missus Sharma wanted after a fight. It'd always been this way, her swooping in to pick up the pieces Lorian left scattered across their feet.

Locking them inside the bedroom, Missus Sharma clutched Lorian's shoulder. "For the Gods' sakes, Lucia, what on Earth were you thinking? Your sister is a monarch now, you can't start petty fights like that anymore and think there won't be repercussions."

The first tear fell too quickly. She tried to stifle them to preserve her honor, but did she have any left? Hadn't she lost it all after her wedding ceremony? Her sister had helped her escape, but it was only as a last-ditch effort. She was a lost cause that was better off dead.

"Oh, Lorian." Missus Sharma hugged her.

"I'm sorry," Lorian cried. "I couldn't...I didn't..."

"I know, dear. Sit down. Relax."

"I just didn't want to hear what she was saying. But I know I shouldn't have resorted to violence. I know I know better." She dug her hands back into her eyes, not wanting to have this conversation she'd had a million times. "I'm sorry I'm such a lost cause."

"You're not a lost cause, Lorian. Sometimes we act out when we're feeling scared or helpless, or cornered, and I know that's how you've been feeling all this time."

"I don't wanna be a princess," she said into her shoulder. "I don't want to marry a man and bear his children. I can't."

"I know, dear, I know. Now, listen to me. I want you to stay up here and rest, okay? You've had a long day, and I don't want you doing anything you might regret in the morning."

Lorian bitterly laughed. As if her whole life wasn't something she regretted every morning.

"Well, I should make up beds for Zaahir and Bea," Missus Sharma said to herself. "You should think about apologizing to your sister properly in the morning, once the waters clear."

Lorian promised her that she'd try.

—◇—

Beatrice left early that morning with Zaahir and Kadar, who'd returned mostly unscathed, just a migraine that made him dizzy.

Allegedly. Lorian had heard that from Mi'Sharma.

Beatrice hadn't come up to say goodbye.

Chapter 24: Two Turtle Doves

As a child, Aida didn't dream. She *had* dreams, had them piled up on her desk and written out in journals, but she didn't sleep-dream. She'd tried different methods, but nothing stuck. She'd toss and turn from leg pain and wake up five hours later when it felt like two minutes and a song had gone by.

This sleep was different. This sleep was a dozen blankets smothering her in weight and heat. And she dreamed. She dreamed of crossing forest islands and searching for Red Dragon through a thicket of roses and thorns. She found Eve and her daughter locked in a tower with help from a magical key.

What made this sleep a nightmare was that she didn't want to wake up. She smelled the forest and felt the gritty texture of the medieval palace walls. She was having fun, why would anyone want to come back to the real world? In the real world, she had sisters who taunted her and a mother who struck her. Here, she was her own Goddess.

And lonely. As she dreamt up new worlds, she discovered a loneliness she wasn't used to. There was someone missing.

"*Aida.*"

Her head throbbed.

"Aida, please wake up."

She looked behind her.

A bloody body lay behind her in her past, intestines spilling out into the dirt.

They looked at her with hollowed-out eyes.

"Run, my Aida!"

———✧———

Her body fell into bed sheets, bobbing in their waves. The blankets weren't as suffocating as before, but she didn't have the strength to push them off.

A headache welcomed her to the world, and she expected nothing less. Her body was a bruise that ached with every thought. She couldn't remember why and she also didn't want to open her eyes and face it head-on.

But her hand was stuck. Trudging through her brain fog, she cracked open one eye.

Lorian was asleep on the floor, holding her hand. She had a bandage over her left cheek, a bruised eye, and spit forming in the corner of her mouth. Aida wondered if she herself looked any better, given the state of her headache.

She called out Lorian's name and coughed. Her voice tasted like gravel.

Lorian lifted her head before opening her eyes. She looked more dead than alive. She needed more sleep. "H-hey." She took both of her hands. "Hey, you're awake."

What did that mean? What'd happened to her pre-sleep?

Why was Lorian crying about it? She tried playing it off like they were sleepy tears, but she hid her face in the crook of her arm to sob. "I'm so happy you woke up."

"Was I not supposed to?" She fell back into her pillow. If she were to close her eyes, she didn't think she'd wake back up. "Wha' happened to you?"

"Don't move around too much. Just relax."

"My head hurts."

She fixed Aida's hair from her eyes, and she was too weak to resist, or she didn't want to. Hadn't she touched someone like this before?

Lorian placed the back of her hand across Aida's forehead. "Your fever's down, that's good. And your eye's different again."

"What's wrong with my eyes?" She blindly reached for the bedside table for her glasses.

"Aida."

Her vision doubled. That name, and how she'd said it. That woman...

Unexpected tears pooled in her eyes.

"Aida?"

She passed out seconds later.

The next two times she awoke, either her brain wanted her dead, or she was that tired, falling back asleep after a few turns.

She was more aware of her surroundings. She heard the creaks of the floorboards from downstairs, two kids playing in the room across the hall. By the smell of freshly cooked sugar bread and spices, she figured she was back at Missus Sharma's. When she saw a painting of Missus and Mi'Sharma on the wall, she realized that much more than her head was aching.

Like her first trip into the past, her brain had been affected.

The memories resurfaced behind her eyelids and dripped down into her conscience. Lorian and their date to the Catacombs. Eve, dying in Lorian's arms. Eve with Julia, with King Julius II and her affair amongst affairs with them. She'd been right there, and Aida had lost her again.

The tears rolled down her warm pillow. What an idiot she was. If only she'd acted quicker, she could've saved her. The timeline could've changed.

"Lorian," she called out. *"Lorian!"*

Her voice broke in her throat. What was she expecting? That Eve might've survived? Half of her stomach had been torn out, begging for Aida's help. She'd killed her. She was a murderer.

Eve had known her, and Aida had let her die.

Her mother had been right. She was a failure. Her brain, body, and heart were wrong and bad and she was a bad person for existing.

Someone held her. Lorian's voice delivered her back into a dreamless sleep.

——◇——

The following day, Aida was able to sit up. Missus and Mi'Sharma had come in with a wet cloth for her forehead, a change of undergarments, and a bowl of homemade soup filled with chunky pieces of carrot and celery.

"Is there anything else we can do for you, baby?" Mi'Sharma asked.

Aida shook her head but gave them her thanks.

She lay in bed for most of the morning, sinking into her body heat. It got considerably cold that week and even snowed for a few hours. Missus Sharma had come in multiple times with a bag of warm rice for Aida's feet.

Chrissie and Onti went up and down the hall as kids did, sometimes stopping by her door and whispering before scampering away. At around noon, a piece of paper slipped underneath the door, and Aida wiggled out from her cocoon to find a drawing of herself and Lorian and their family. They were ringed by flowers and happy rays of sunshine. On the bottom read *GET BETTER SOON!!*

Aida returned to sulking. Then, after wavering in the middle of the room, she picked up the get-well-soon card and balanced it against her candlestick, studying what the children thought a happy family was. They must've spent a long time on it.

Lorian didn't come back up to see her. Missus and Mi'Sharma did, and she received another card from Chrissie and Onti through the door.

Fuck her. Fuck her and her humility. Aida didn't need space any longer. What she needed was to hold her hand and feel her near and talk to her about nothing because she needed *her* and she wasn't embarrassed by that.

As she went to nap away her thoughts, a chirp drilled into her ears. Even though winter was starting, these animals were stubborn enough to keep by the branches near her windowsill.

She glared through the pane. Two turtle doves, of all things, were sitting in the lemon tree: Old World birds meant to symbolize love.

She threw her feet off the bed.

The birds didn't move.

She stood, swayed from the sudden vertigo, and threw up on the floor. It wasn't a lot, but it was enough to make her feel sicker than she thought she was. Stumbling over the mess, she donned her blanket and went to the window.

"Get out." She knocked on the glass, then blew on it as if her breath could reach them. "Stop it."

One nuzzled up closer to its mate.

"That's it." Aida left the bedroom with her blanket. "You earned your death sentence."

Someone was cooking downstairs, maybe a soup, and Lorian was questioning the right number of potatoes to add to the broth.

"I'm sure she'll be happy with anything you make her," Missus Sharma said. "I've never seen you so restive over a task before."

"I want to make sure it's right."

"What a noble thing to do for a sick girl," Mi'Sharma said.

"A sick *friend*," Missus Sharma corrected.

"That's it, isn't it? Just a friend?"

Lorian chuckled. "Is it two potatoes or three?"

"Preferably three," Aida muttered to herself, and snuck out through the back.

She plowed through the frosty grass. The birds were looking down at her mockingly.

"Oh, *shut* up. You're out here at whatever time of the day it is chirping like you give a damn about people hearing you. You're *birds*. You're flying rats. I've survived through so much and don't need to hear you squawking like you think you're chickens—You're *worse* than chickens, you know that?" She pointed at them. "You are nothing but noise and easy meals for hungrier birds. Remember that. I mean...I mean..." She began walking around the tree. "Here I am. I put so much energy into the world. Some of it's good, a lot of it's shit. But I'm trying, you know?"

"Aida?"

"And yes, I mess up. I know I'm rude and a know-it-all, and I can be selfish when it comes to what I want. Do I wanna be better? Yeah, but to do that, I need my sleep, so shut up and let me rest for a minute!"

"Aida."

"And stop preening each other. You're in public."

"Aida."

"What?" She fell against the tree.

Lorian caught her. "Hey."

"Hey. I'm falling, so..."

She walked her to the hammock. "I got you."

As she fell back horizontally, feet dangling, her eyes began to close. She was back in bed, she needed sleep.

Lorian came around the hammock and pushed back her hair. "Who were you talking to?"

"The birds. They kept chirping. I had some complaints."

"Oh." She smiled in the fake way. "That's fine. They say the smartest people talk to themselves. Back at the palace, I'd pace in the clock tower to the beat of the seconds."

Her head cleared a bit. "You can pace in the palace clock tower? There's enough room to do that?"

"There is. I'd bring blankets up and sleep on the curve of the clock. I loved looking out the glass and seeing my country. *The* country," she corrected herself. "It's not mine."

"I didn't know that. I'll have to redesign the palace in my head."

"Do you have it in your head or your journals? I can draw out the hidden rooms for you."

"You *must*. Let's do it now. I'll find some paper." She went to sit up, then remembered she was dizzy and fell backwards into Lorian's arms.

"Easy."

She tried and closed her eyes. "What happened to her?"

"Zaahir had her body buried. When you jumped, I met with him and my sister in the Catacombs. I told you all about it when you were somewhat conscious. I don't know if you heard me."

"I didn't. Don't you hate your sister?"

To answer, she pointed to her busted face. "We got into a little spat."

"A little spat? It looks like she went for your throat."

"That's what I did to her. Anyway, after that, Zaahir did most of the work. He'd lied to the queen's men and said she was a homeless Visatorre who had family in the Catacombs. They buried her in her own niche, surrounded by others. I'm sorry. I tried to help, but..."

Aida looked up at Lorian so hurt for something that wasn't her fault. *Aida* was the time traveller, *she* should've been the one to prevent this from happening. "I can't believe you kept that fucking necklace away from me." She tried digging her hand into Lorian's vest.

Lorian's face went red and she scooted back. "Uh, maybe a different time. My emotions are mixed up right now."

Even being upside down, Lorian looked so much like Julia, with her blond, curly bangs framing her face, long nose, tiny freckles. She wondered if Eve also thought they looked pretty on the person she liked.

Her brain finally connected the pieces. "Ah."

Lorian hid her head in her shoulders. "Sorry."

Her head tingled, and it wasn't from her brain being how it was. This feeling was something different, a self-discovery coming at the absolute worst time. Through everything wrong happening in her life, this was both a blessing and a curse in terms of timing. Circa *loved* to fuck with her, didn't she?

"Before all of this happened," Aida said, "before I travelled, before Eve, I promised you a thing."

"You can forget about that. Your health is more important."

"And you don't think kisses are connected to my health? My well-being?"

Lorian ran her hand through her own bangs, covering her eyes. "I don't know."

"Well, I do." She touched her thigh, bringing her in closer. "I want to experience it. It's not fair that Circa decided to skip over my development. Hugging, kissing, everything that comes after. I think frolicking in fields is a part of it."

"You're still injured."

"Yeah, and I feel like I'm high on Nectar."

"I gave you some when you were sleeping. You were thrashing."

"Okay, then. So, you're not going to get this chance again, I'm asking for it, and it seems like you want to kiss me, don't you? What's stopping you now?"

She swallowed. "Not that I disagree with any of those points, but I don't want to ruin what we might have."

"Lorian, you just caught me talking to birds and you didn't call me weird."

"I'd never. Aida, you accept and listen to me. I'm a problem child and you still like being with me. Do you know how much that means to me?"

She didn't. And she couldn't place why. She couldn't understand why people liked being around *her* when she hated everything about herself. But knowing Lorian liked her in the same way Julia liked Eve, that must've meant something.

"You won't ruin anything," Aida said. "If anything, I'll ruin it like I ruin our lives, so you don't have to worry."

"But you don't—"

"Quit making me wait." Wrapping two arms around her neck, she pulled Lorian in. "Take my mind off of this, will you?"

Lorian's breath, which smelled like cake batter and something nice, hit her nose. Aida saw the faintest green of her eyes before she moved in, tilting her head in closer and closer until their lips touched.

She probably should've called it a kiss, but her mind was racing over other nonsensical bits. The way Lorian's hand curled around her ear, for instance, and how she moved herself onto the hammock to get a better angle for this...interaction. An interaction that made Aida's heart race, something Lorian must've been dreaming of for weeks or even months.

Her hands. Her soft lips. Nobody had ever touched her like this before.

All the poetry and novels she'd read about were wrong.

This was so, so much nicer.

Taking a breath, Lorian went in for a second kiss, then a third. Sensing she wanted to keep going, Aida brought up her legs, toes curling around the edge of the hammock, and something between her inner thighs pulsed. She pulled down the blanket so she wasn't flashing the cottage.

Lorian pulled back. "Hi."

"Hey."

"I think I love you."

Huh. She thought that was only said in the dead of night or in a lover's melodramatic embrace. She expected that from her future self, but then again, she felt it appropriate that her firsts came to her half-naked, half-dead, yelling at birds outside a grandmother's home.

Aida felt a new warmth flood her veins with the knowledge she now knew.

"Hey, there she is." Lorian gently pinched her cheeks. "I've been waiting to see that again."

"See what?"

"Your smile. It looks good on you. And your eyes, too. Did you see that?"

"Not unless I look in a mirror." Feeling daring and less like herself, she kissed somewhere on Lorian's face. Between her lips and cheek, in an awkward place. She was feeling it today; she wanted to take her mind off of terrible truths.

Lorian covered her mouth in embarrassment. "My goodness."

"What a baby."

"What do you want from me? I'm sensitive."

How long have you been wanting that? A kiss?"

Carefully, Lorian sat with her on the hammock. Her weight pulled Aida into her lap. Her long legs stretched out around her thighs. "You really want to put me through a swell of emotions today, huh?"

"I can see my future self being like that to you, so I guess I should start early."

"You now think she's you, huh?"

"Enough. Give me a timeline."

"Honestly, it was in the library."

"Ah, the *one* time I was in the library."

She chuckled. "It was the week school started. I was making my rounds, surveying the campus, when I saw you at the end of one of the aisles. You had about fifty books stacked around you. I was going to ask what you were doing when you smiled down at whatever you were writing. Let me tell you, it was one of the cutest little smiles I'd ever seen, and it stayed on you even when you turned the page. That's when I tried grabbing your attention, waiting to see that smile again."

To tease her, Aida made a point to not smile and instead pouted like she was angry. It had little success and made Lorian blush. "I was probably reading about Eve, I'm not going to lie. The first month I was there, I tried learning everything I could from that damn library. I must've read every history book there."

"Twice."

"About as much."

Lorian went to touch her face again, but before she did, Aida snatched her fingers back. "You're going to give me more acne than I already have."

"Sorry. With you giving me permission, I feel like I need to try everything I've ever wanted with you. You're a very beautiful girl, Aida."

"And I suppose you, too, are quite a pretty girl."

Lorian opened her eyes a bit wider, processing that, then smiled and dropped her forehead onto hers.

And this time, Aida didn't think about running away.

Chapter 25: Talk with Yourself

Aside from bringing in groceries and exercising their horses so they didn't go stir-crazy, for the next month, they stayed indoors. They didn't plan heists, they didn't go back to Eve. Zaahir had sent a letter via his hawk detailing the events of Eve's burial. He'd gotten permission from Carmine to bury her and hosted a private vigil in her honor. Lorian thought about responding to thank him, but it felt unwise. The letter she wrote burned in the fireplace.

Aida's sickness rolled over into winter. After their hammock kiss, her fever returned and she became bedridden for most of November. They switched back to their Nest in the living room, giving Missus and Mi'Sharma their bed back. During meal times, Lorian helped Aida eat and wore a face mask so the sickness didn't spread.

"I always get sick during the winter months," Aida said, sniffling. "It's not because of my jump."

"I believe you." Lorian wrung out a wet rag and placed it over her forehead. "How're you feeling?"

"Better than ever. Can we go back to the Catacombs now?"

"How about you learn to keep your food down before we illegally trespass again?"

"I won't eat, then. Problem solved."

Lorian licked her lips before kissing the rag over Aida's head. "No one in this house will let you go to bed hungry. Come now." She blew on her spoonful of porridge before hand-feeding it to her.

"Am I a baby bird?" Aida asked, but took the bite regardless. "It's good."

Lorian beamed with approval. Missus Sharma had taught her well.

"I'm still surprised you know how to cook, being born a princess and all."

Lorian lowered the serving tray until it almost tipped over the couch. Then she faked a smile and prepped her eating station. "I picked it up easily."

—✧—

The next day, Lorian woke up early and cleaned the first floor before Missus and Mi'Sharma came down. When they slogged down the steps in their nightgowns, they jumped to see someone already in the kitchen.

"Good morning." Missus Sharma fixed her glasses to see Lorian's handiwork: eggs in different varieties, crispy toast, orange juice with sugar settling at the bottom of the jug. "What a lovely spread."

"I hope I made it to your liking." She pushed out a seat for her. "Would you like any milk? Coffee?"

"No, dear. Thank you."

"Did something happen to make you so jolly?" Mi'Sharma asked.

Lorian rolled on her heels. While taking care of Aida was everything she dreamed of...

"And I suppose you, too, are quite a pretty girl."

She washed her hands in the sink.

"Being born a princess and all."

"I'm just happy to see Aida recovering," Lorian said.

"You said she went back into the past with that Eve person," Missus Sharma said.

"How is she doing it?" Mi'Sharma peered into the living room. "Poor soul. And to catch a cold as well. I hope she'll be okay."

"I'm sure she will." Lorian dried off her hands. "I wanted to ask if it's alright if I took a walk."

"A walk?" Missus Sharma asked, already worried.

"Just in the woods. I wanted to clear my head. You know I'm not one to stay inside for very long."

"Well, I can't stop you from doing so, but do be careful, Lorian. Please promise me that?"

"I promise." Lorian was already putting on her coat and boots. She'd tailored the hood to better conceal her identity. "I'll be the most careful."

She hated to lie, especially to Missus Sharma, but she'd needed to learn the skill to save herself. To not be hit by her father, to save her mother, to keep her sister away. She had to hide her true feelings and identity from everyone, because if she added one more thing to her list of failures, nobody would ever be on her side.

She most certainly didn't have to lie about her gender to Aida, but as she passed by Missus Sharma's garden and hurried for the forest with no intention of just "taking a walk," Lorian felt guilty.

She was born a girl, a *princess* meant to give birth and look pretty. Surely, she felt a bit feminine. She liked girls, both romantically and the idea of them, and she didn't hate her body when she wore baggier clothes. And dresses were fine. They were pretty. Cute.

It was just that there was something *more* inside of her, something more than just a girl that she didn't have the words for. She knew some ancient gods were genderless or had multiple genders. Their names changed with the culture. She wished Aida didn't know about her past, that she could reinvent herself based on her own terms.

Lorian had noticed something the day she met her future self. Future Aida, while holding Lorian's hand, had called them a "they." Not a she. Not a he. They.

Lorian didn't hate being a girl. She didn't despise it.

She was just something more.

She snuck down the busier street to the bookstore by the sea. It was emptier than before; not even the clerk was readily available, but she didn't need him quite yet. With her pouch of lyria, she had all she needed by the windows.

The one good thing about being a royal heir: When you quietly abdicated, you had a wealth of coins to spend on your loved ones.

She searched for the *En Tempore Rose* box set. Aida deserved to own the series. Her copy of the first book was weathered, the spine cracked in several places.

Someone knocked on the window.

She looked up at her own reflection. She was staring at herself, her older self, the one who was taller than her even though they should've been the same height.

Lorian jumped back with the box set acting as her shield.

Future Lorian gave her a "sorry" smile and motioned for her to come outside.

Lorian looked between them and the box set, then groaned and went to the front desk.

A minute later, she came out with her new purchase and a pit in her stomach. She'd only spoken to this person once, but their presence usually signaled chaos and bad news, and she'd had enough of that for a lifetime.

Future Lorian was waiting by the side of the bookshop, near a discarded barrel filled halfway with snow.

Lorian approached them gingerly. It was so odd, seeing someone with your face living out their own lives. She thought it was bad enough with Beatrice, but after the hours she'd take to do her makeup, the two looked as different as night and day.

"Hi," Future Lorian greeted.

"...Hello," Lorian said.

"I apologize. This must be very awkward for you."

"You're a wanted criminal."

"That goes away with time. It's good seeing you like this."

"Wouldn't you remember this happening if you're me? Or are you a trickster god toying with us?"

Future Lorian gave her an incredulous look, then chuckled. "Ah. I forgot this was a debate you had about us."

"Where is she?" Lorian asked. "Future Aida?"

Future Lorian looked down the alleyway. Somewhere down the road, a man yelled for someone to stop running, and a woman laughed at his attempts to stop her.

Future Aida and Carmine came out dashing through the streets. They were far enough away that neither Lorian had to fret about being seen. In fact, it gave them a front row seat to Future Aida's antics.

She was ahead of Carmine but barely. Carmine had his arms out to capture her, but just as he grabbed her dress, Future Aida jumped behind him and gave him a shove. As he fell, she caught him, stole his hat, and jumped down the road.

"Stop stealing my hat!" Carmine shouted, and continued their game of cat and mouse in the opposite direction.

"What's her goal by wasting time like this?" Lorian asked.

"She likes seeing him mad."

"No, I mean, why can't she tell us what we need to do? We're cooped inside the cottage with no way of knowing what move to make next."

"Then perhaps you need to keep leaving the cottage despite the rules forbidding you from doing so. It's something you two have experience with, is it not?"

Lorian didn't disagree but said, "We saw Eve die. She died in my arms. What is there left to find? What else do we need to be searching for?"

"I can't tell you that. It'll ruin the surprise."

"Ruin the—?" That anger Lorian had been suppressing since meeting with her sister resurfaced. "What can *possibly* make this *more* entertaining? Don't you remember her dying in our arms?"

Their face fell. "I do. Aida made sure to be there when it happened."

"You're insane."

"We're really not."

"Then *help* us!"

"I *am*. Listen, I know you're stressed out. I know the future seems all sorts of frightful to you right now. But understand this: It. Will. Be. Okay. You're going to figure out what you need to do. And you have Aida, so you already know that you're going to be alright, don't you?"

"I don't know anymore," she said. "She hasn't been doing very well."

"Are any of us? You bought her that box set, so you're trying to find a way to tell her that you're more than a woman, right?"

Was lying to her future self even an option at this point?

"Tell her, Lorian. What's there to be afraid of? Do you think she'll be angry? You know she's a good person, so don't be afraid. Don't let your anxiety dictate how you live. Just be smart about your choices," they said. "Sometimes, Aida gets a little in over her head. It's hard to rein her in."

At least that was one thing they could agree on. "How'd you tell her? Does it go well?"

"What do you think, Lorian? You know how travel works."

"Not really, no. It seems like a crazed fool is playing with the timeline to suit their needs."

"See? You know more than you think."

A distant jump crackled the air, and Future Lorian turned to meet it. "I hope you don't hate me too much for that," they said as they left. "If I could, I'd tell you how this story ends."

"You'd 'spoil the fun', wouldn't you?" Lorian mocked with hand quotes.

"Too right, I would." Before leaving the shadows, Future Lorian turned the corner.

There, as if waiting for them, was a Visatorre child of barely six, dressed in rags.

"Hello there," Future Lorian said. "Were you spying on us?"

"No, Sir," the child said.

"There's no good in lying to your elders, little one." Future Lorian knelt to their level and fished out something from their pocket.

The child's eyes shone with the gold lyria being presented to them. There must've been twenty pieces in Future Lorian's hands that could've afforded the child *and* their family food for a month.

"It's a secret that you saw us, okay?" Future Lorian said. "Now, take this and be off."

The child, not wasting time in letting the offer go, thanked Future Lorian and ran off.

Lorian weighed her own coin purse. How full it felt even after buying the box set. How many lives could she have saved like that between now and her future self? If she hadn't left the palace, what could she've done for all Visatorre people?

The voices of two officers carried down the alley. Lorian went to warn her future self.

But they were already gone.

Missus and Mi'Sharma were still in the kitchen, cleaning up their plates and talking about going shopping. Lorian hid her present bag behind her back as she closed the door.

"There you are," Missus Sharma said. "Where did you go off to? I looked outside and couldn't find you."

"I was in the forest, like I said. I'm sorry I worried you." She walked backwards into the living room. "I'll stay closer to the house next time!"

"You better!" Mi'Sharma said. "You had Missus Sharma close to death!"

Lorian found Aida resting in their Nest, lounging backwards with a book to her chest. She gave Lorian a wave without looking up. "Hi. Where'd you go?"

"Out into the forest."

"And where after that?"

Lorian held up her tote.

That got her to look up. "I hope that was for a good reason. Please tell me you bought a book retelling the history of Visatorre slavery at the end of the Classical Era, because I'm trying to figure it out and it's not making sense. This book says thirty-seventy, which I thought was low-balling, but when I travelled back, it seems like a lot of us were average serfs. It's like we're living in two different timelines."

Lorian squatted beside the couch and handed her the bag.

"What is it?" Aida asked suspiciously.

"Close your eyes and smell it."

She gave her a strange look but trusted her game and sniffed.

Her hands moved quicker than her eyes. "Did you really? Is this about the history of Roman monarchical—"

The box set dropped into her lap.

"You've been sick for so long, I wanted to surprise you with something that's not about death."

Aida opened up the second book and fanned the pages close to her nose, taking in its scent. "How'd you pay for this? Did you steal it?"

"I used my own gold to buy it, but I did steal it from my vault at the palace, so in a sense, I did steal it."

"How'd you know?"

"Know what?"

She closed the future volume. "That it was my birthday yesterday."

"What?" Lorian asked. "Yesterday? Why didn't you say anything?"

"Because I despise it. My mother wouldn't celebrate it as grandly as she did with my two sisters. After a while, it was too painful to deal with, so I asked her to stop celebrating it, which she'd said yes to without question. Over time, they stopped congratulating me on being born."

Lorian sat in bed with her. "*I* appreciate that you were born. I appreciate that I found you, that we found each other, and I thank Circa every day for having you in my life."

Aida smiled up at her with hurt in her eyes. Hurt and love and comfort knowing that she now had someone who cared for her life.

Lorian poked her side. "Just don't breeze through those books in one night."

"I won't. I'll finish it in two." She flipped through the first chapter. "Do you mind if I talk about it with you?"

"I'd be honored."

Aida adjusted her bad leg to give her more space in the bed. Her idle fingers then rapped over the blankets she'd been living in that month.

She patted the empty space next to her. "Hop in, then."

Lorian waited to hear more of an explanation for such a request from Aida of all people. It was true that they'd technically slept together before they'd even kissed, but she didn't know that this was an option.

She got in, making herself tiny so Aida didn't have to move from her warm spot. Aida brought the blanket around them and snuggled up close. She almost spooned Lorian, for Circa's sake, but held her book above the pillows, like this was normal.

"So, where was I?" Aida said, not looking Lorian in the eye. "Ah. So, Pinnacle had a best friend named Ivory from his home island, did you know that? They cut her from the opera so you probably don't, but I was mad when I learned that. They could've at least cast someone to play her as a nod to the book fans. We're the reason that opera does so well. Oh! Can I tell you my hypothesis on Red Dragon's eye shape? You can see it drawn here on this book cover. Trust me, it'll make sense once you hear it."

"Excuse me." Missus Sharma waddled into the room. "Before anything happens, may I intrude?"

Aida and Lorian looked up.

"Did I hear that it was someone's birthday this week?"

They didn't have any readily available presents, but both Missus and Mi'Sharma promised Aida ten years' worth of presents come next year. In exchange, they made her a strawberry cake with frozen strawberries and icing. Chrissie and Onti woke up to the best breakfast ever and wished Aida a happy belated birthday with their mouths stuffed with 9 a.m. cake.

Lorian spent the next two hours listening to the worldbuilding lore of *Pinnacle Isle*. Aida read most of it from her journals so she had the facts straight, a series bible she'd created since being at Missus Sharma's. Back before, she was able to tell Lorian all of this from memory. Lorian didn't mention that; Aida was having too much fun.

"What do you think?" Aida asked, biting into a juicy strawberry. "Do you think Pinnacle has dark hair or blond hair?"

"Isn't it blond? It's blond in the play."

"Wrong! The author specifically..." She double-checked her notes. "In book one, he has dark hair that appears cobalt near the sea, but the stage adaptation gave Pinnacle's role to Finneus Craw, an actor with sandy brown hair. *So*, between book three and four, the author retconned Pinnacle's hair to blond to appease the new readers."

"*Ugh*," Lorian said sarcastically. "How dare he."

"I *know*!" Aida said seriously. "I spent three years reading Pinnacle with black hair! He said it wasn't important to the story, but *fuck* that. I need visuals. If you're not going to write out your character's hair color, eye color, and skin tone, what's the point of writing a book?"

"I completely agree with you. You should write your own version of the book."

"I have! Thirty pages of it." She blew out her cheeks. "I love these books. I love this boy so much."

"I know you do."

"Thank you for buying this for me. You didn't have to, but I appreciate it more than you know."

"I figured you'd enjoy it a tad." Lorian laced her fingers in her lap. Throughout Aida's explanations, she'd been trying to figure out when and how to ask that important question.

"And I suppose you, too, are quite a pretty girl."

Aida stopped talking to find a specific page in her journal to cite. Taking the chance she knew wouldn't come for another hour, Lorian said, "Hey, Aida."

"Yeah?"

"Can you call me a boy for a little while?"

She cringed. That wasn't at all how she wanted to ask that. *"Call me a boy?"* Who said it like that? She'd been trained to give speeches to enunciate past her lisp. What had happened?

"Yeah," Aida said casually. "Did something happen?"

"Oh. No. I just wanted to try it out."

"Anything else you want me to do?"

"I don't believe so."

"Alright, then." She reopened the first page of her book, then slammed it shut. "Did I tell you about the leaks we found out between books three and four that the Goddess has a mortal brother, because it seriously keeps me up at night and I've been dying to tell somebody about it."

Lorian laughed and readied himself for another tangent.

Chapter 26: Good Deeds

When Aida awoke that morning, it was as if the whole fall season had been a dream. Life flowed back into her bones and she kept down her food like an adult. The fog fucking up her brain was still there. It helped that she had more books to read.

Nobody had ever given her such a thoughtful gift before. During harvest festivals and New Years, her mother would buy her one or two random contemporaries she had no interest in reading. Lorian, who she'd only known for a season, had given her something she needed at her worst. And he hadn't even asked.

She touched her lips as she read. She'd wanted to get in a few chapters to sharpen her brain before breakfast, but he kept coming to mind. What Lorian had asked of her—how he wanted to go by he/him for the time being—and the way he'd kissed her. This trust had serious implications, didn't it? It made them more than partners in time-travelling crime. She'd been unknowingly swaying her hips, hearing the beat yet not knowing how to join the dance.

She did like him, she just didn't know if her heart was big enough to take on his. Lorian loved so earnestly with his body and words. She wasn't equipped to handle that.

They'd date, right? She'd kissed him and tasted that vanilla scent that clung to his skin. She remembered his hands caressing the sides of her face, like he was afraid she might break, and how he'd cared for her in their Nest.

She closed *Pinnacle Isle*. Her mother's marriage had been dismal. Marriages around her growing up were dismal and ended dismally. She didn't want to put her everything into someone knowing she was going to fuck them up. Lorian didn't deserve that.

"Lorian loves you," a voice in her head said.

"Shut up," Aida said to herself, and got ready for the day.

"What was that?" Lorian, who'd been sitting across the room from her, put down his book. He was halfway through the second book of the series, right when Pinnacle should've lost Yellow and Blue in a snowstorm. He looked more than stressed. He was definitely at the right part.

"Nothing," she said.

"Alright. Also, Aida, does Red Dragon die?"

Was she evil enough to spoil him? Red Dragon was only on five of the six book covers.

She left for the bathroom smiling to herself, and took in her new matching eyes. Two white pupils. She'd been avoiding mirrors because of them, but ever since Lorian made her feel more wanted, she'd been spending more time looking at herself.

They weren't that bad, she supposed.

"Aida, you get back here. She just survived this onslaught of horned wolves—she'll be okay, right?"

After cleaning up and playing keep-away from Lorian, Aida made herself a bowl of porridge. Onti was sitting by himself at the kitchen table with his own breakfast. It was rare to see one child without the other.

Onti sniffled into his piece of burnt toast.

Aida set down her cup of coffee. "Did Chrissie jump?"

Lorian came in with his book bookmarked. "She left a few hours ago. I'm sure she'll be back soon. We'll have to bake her something delicious when she comes back."

Onti nudged his food away. Bundled up in-between his fingers was a red ribbon Chrissie often wore in her hair. "It's not fair," he mumbled into the nook of his elbow. "It's not fair this only happens to us. I hate being Visatorre."

"Don't say that," Lorian said. "It's what makes you *you*."

"And I hate it. I wanna be reborn so I can be normal like you."

"Well, I'll be the first to tell you that I'm not anywhere close to normal."

"*Yes*, you are. You're pretty and you're smart. You're royalty, too, so that makes you rich, right? You get to travel the world and do really cool things with other people that look just like you. Visatorre don't get to do that. So, that makes you normal. That makes you *super* normal. We're *not* normal. We're freaks."

Lorian looked away, ashamed for suggesting that his differences could be comparable to theirs.

Aida took the seat across from Onti. Up until college, she'd believed that the circle on their foreheads only marked misery. That they were a mistake in humanity, a plaything for the Gods to torture.

But now, things were changing. She had this future to look forward to, this woman who could laugh with someone she loved and jump without pain. Her existence excited Aida for an unseen future.

It kind of sickened her how optimistic it made her feel. Since when had she ever been hopeful? Since her Durante Academy acceptance letter? Had she even smiled when she'd received it, or was it a reminder of how much harder she needed to now work?

"Onti," she said, "sometimes, being a Visatorre sucks super hard. Look at me. I was bedridden because of it. I have to use a cane to walk around, all because we go back in time for an hour or two."

He frowned harder.

"But do you know why it happens?"

"Because we're—"

"Because we're made of Gods. Circa created us in her image. She and the rest of her friends created the stars and planets and all the pretty colors we see in sunsets. To have an ounce of their powers inside us, there has to be a trade-off."

"But why?"

"Because Circa allows us to travel back in time so we don't repeat the past. We hurt, but it's to better the world we've been given."

"But why is it only us?"

"Because we're special. We're special people able to do special things. We get to see lives our parents have never seen. We get to experience a world growing into ours. That's a really special thing to be able to witness."

"But I don't want to hurt anymore," Onti said. "I don't want my headaches."

"I know. I don't want my inner pain, either, and if I could, I'd take on the burdens you bear in a heartbeat. But my future self, have you heard about her? The girl parading around in the streets, causing a fuss in the villages and making the Constable crazy?"

He nodded. "It's the person that scary man was looking for. I don't really get it, but she's like you, isn't she, but grown up?"

"Yes. She's learned how to jump without getting hurt. She looks like a rabbit, hopping around from moment to moment. I swear, when I get to be her age and figure out how to do it, I'll tell you how to jump without getting hurt. I'll tell everyone, and I'll...I'll make a better world for you. I promise."

Onti's eyes swam with nervous hope.

Aida was panting, her own brain rationalizing the promise she'd just made. In her future, she saw herself opening up a bookstore with her historian license. She'd wanted a space for people to learn more about a history scrubbed from textbooks. Now, she wondered if that was too small of a goal. She was Aida Mirko, destined to fuck over the world by the time she was thirty. If she wanted to, she could've become a queen if she desired.

She looked at Lorian. If the two of them came out of this together, if he finally talked to his family...

Onti ate a bite of his porridge. "If this girl's you," he said, "and she can travel backwards and forwards, how come she hasn't told you how to do it yet? If she has clues you're trying to figure out, shouldn't she have told you them already?"

"I guess she's a—" She stopped before the curse left her lips. "Complex woman," she finished with.

"We'll figure this out," Lorian said. "I'm sure of it."

A spark of energy zapped in the upstairs bathroom, and Onti gasped and jumped out of his seat to reunite with his best friend. "Chrissie!"

"Onti!" Chrissie was upright and in one piece, holding her arm but otherwise okay. Onti hugged her, hiding his tears with laughter.

"Oh, that's good." Missus Sharma came in and read the grandfather clock. "Only forty-five minutes, Chrissie. That's good."

Aida checked the clock herself. Lorian had told her that, when she'd jumped during Eve's death, she'd been gone three hours, almost double her standard jump time. And even then, two hours in the past, while not uncommon, have been her normal for nearly ten years. Her past chided her in that way, reminding her that her life would be hard.

No. What had she just told Onti, and what did she believe? That being a Visatorre was painful, but it showed you something nobody else could see, and that you shouldn't hate how you were born.

And that self-reflection needed to start from the ground up.

"Mi'Sharma?" Aida asked. "Are there any community shelters nearby we can visit?"

"What kind of shelters?" she asked.

"Shelters for the homeless, specifically ones that don't shun away Visatorre. This year's harvest will be plentiful. We should take advantage of that."

"Did you want to do volunteer work?"

"Of sorts." She nudged Lorian. "You still have your lyria, right? All 12 billion coins of it?"

"A little less than that, but yes."

"Good, 'cause we're gonna drain your bank account dry."

—◇—

Aida nixed the meats and eggs that might've spoiled during the carriage-ride into town. She figured half a kilogram of meat versus a kilogram of rice would've done a family better. She kept that thinking in mind during her shopping trips.

Discreet shopping trips. Hooded cloak and everything. Some people stared, but with her hidden marking, limp, and cane, nobody called the nearest officer on an old lady that smelled like books and moth balls.

Lorian didn't object to helping the needy, but Aida was surprised to see him so cautiously enthused about it. He didn't argue with her or remind her how dangerous this was. It wasn't like the Constable had paused his search for them for the holidays, but their wanted posters had faded on the bulletin boards, replaced by ads for sheep.

Missus' and Mi'Sharma's carriage was able to fit all of them. Chrissie and Onti were as excited to help as Aida was, so their food was secured on a wagon Lorian helped attach to the back. Onti insisted that he ride in the wagon to keep safe the food, which prompted Chrissie to tag along. Lorian sat with them on bags of rice, bread, beans, and jams. Aida stayed inside the carriage. Lorian said she was more of a target than he was.

"This's a very noble thing for you to do," Missus Sharma said as they rode into town.

"Aye, it's very nice," Mi'Sharma said, "though we shouldn't stay very long. I don't want anyone giving us trouble."

"They're not monsters," Aida reminded her.

"Oh, I'm not talking about the people in the shelter, dear, I'm talking about the people running it. They traditionally have an officer or two around, making sure no fights or arguments come about. And when they get large donations like what you've put together, some people might get...riled. I've seen it back when we adopted little Chrissie and Onti. Most of the people there are nice. Just watch for anyone looking at you like a meal and not a person offering them something."

That soured her mood. She wasn't naive about pinching lyria to stay afloat, but she hadn't been truly homeless. She *had* run away from home, but it was to Durante Academy, then to Missus Sharma's cottage. She had fought in her life, just not for a plate of food.

The shelter was located in the eastern corner of Roma City, far away from the palace. When the owners saw that everything in the carriage was for them, the woman almost fainted into her husband's arms.

"All of this, for us?" she asked. "Your letter didn't say nothing about all this. Are you sure?"

"Our children would like to help in any way they can," Missus Sharma said.

"Are you sure?" the woman asked. "We wouldn't want to impose."

"You're not imposing at all," Lorian said, and held open the door for them.

The woman, who was almost as short as Aida, blushed. "My, what a polite, young man."

Lorian beamed brightly at the compliment.

The fires they had going were more than enough to keep the place warm, but the dozens of people sitting at the tables kept the shelter boiling. They sat as families or as companions. Children and mothers, lovers cuddling one another with a shared plate of buttered bread. Many of them were too skinny for the winter and didn't have enough clothes on to be safe.

Aida, Lorian, Chrissie, and Onti stayed back as volunteers organized their wagon of non-perishables. They should've better hidden themselves, but Aida kept stealing glances into the main floor. There were Visatorre who couldn't walk, children who ate alone. Mi'Sharma had to excuse herself to weep in the back room.

She wanted to do more to help. What good was she in hiding? She was a little head-fuzzy and a "criminal," but something inside of her told her to do more for these people. She felt it in her bones, her broken, hurting bones.

She leaned over the counter. Out of everyone here, one person kept catching her eye. A woman was on the floor near the fireplace to keep warm. She was dressed in a thin, white sheet that covered her head.

Aida squinted at her. She looked familiar though she couldn't place it.

"Aida?" Lorian asked.

She beelined for the cloaked woman. She *knew* she knew her. Somewhere in time...

The woman didn't move. She had flawless, dark skin and long, healthy limbs. She looked glowing. Aida couldn't turn away.

Physically, she couldn't. She'd been drawn to this woman like she'd been drawn to Eve or knowledge, and now, she was frozen in time. Her eyes began watering. She couldn't close them.

She started breathing heavily. She'd never *not* been in control of her body. Had she been drugged? Had someone placed a curse on her? Why was she scared stiff, and why was she trembling?

The woman stood up. The cloth fell from her head, revealing long, white braids that were hidden down her back. She towered over two meters tall and had a face that was at once youthful and wise in age, round and long, human and something not-so-human. She was divine like that, someone who shouldn't have existed in this realm.

She was smiling. Wildly, wickedly, reaching from ear to ear but not her eyes. They were as blue as the sky, with white pupils like her future self, like Eve.

Aida's body seized as her vision exploded into stars. Her world burst into colors she hadn't experienced before, like she was discovering a new medium of art. She heard a buzzing and then a loud explosion of white noise. Her head felt a hundred times heavier with an influx of thought.

She blinked awake. The room had been completely undone. Chairs had been tossed against the wall, the candles snuffed out. Lorian was in the middle of the room with a ladle in hand, confused. Chrissie and Onti were staring at her in horror.

A black circle of ash surrounded her like a booby trap.

"Aida?"

The tingling staggered her around in the circle. When Lorian rushed to her, she did what came naturally and grabbed his sleeve. She fell back as he fell forwards, her vision blotted out, and she travelled somewhere into time with his hand in hers.

Chapter 27: Second Chances

Aida fell into somebody's arms, keeping her from eating shit for the first time.

She and Lorian tumbled onto a vacant, dirt road. They were somewhere outside of Roma City—it was dark, but she saw the Colosseum not too far up ahead.

"Aida—Aida." Lorian hurried to find her hand. His eyes were as wide as the full Moon behind them.

Aida sat up with his help. They were fully clothed but definitely in the past. The roads leading out of the city were dirt, not cobblestone, and none of the buildings other than the distant palace and Colosseum reached past three stories.

"D-did you jump into the past?" Lorian asked. "Are we in the past?"

"I think so."

"And I'm here, too? I'm—" He touched his face. "*I'm* here?"

"Yeah." She tried sitting up. Her hand was stopped by the grass like usual, but as she tried again, the blades caught on her fingertips. She was there, but barely. "I'm about tangible, are you?"

Lorian was rubbing down his knuckles as he searched the empty grasses, a deer in wait of hidden dogs.

"Lorian?"

"We're in the past."

"Are you okay?"

He shook his head, and with that sincere admission, Aida took in the true scope of his fear. She remembered her first jump, how lost and afraid she'd been. She'd wanted someone to help her through unnamed streets and tell her that everything would be alright. But she'd gotten used to it. She knew what to expect.

She took Lorian's hand. "It'll be okay."

"I don't feel good."

"Everyone's first trip is bad. You'll get used to it."

"Is this how it usually feels? This...emptiness, and shock?"

"I think it's different for each person. Just focus on you and you'll be okay."

"But what if we can't go back? I-I've never done this before, Aida."

"Hey, Lorian, look at me." She smushed his face with both hands. "You're going to be okay. I won't let anything bad happen to you."

"I'm scared," he confessed.

"I am, too. We're both going into this blind and scared out of our fucking wits. But we're going into this together, right? I need you for this."

After looking deep into Aida's eyes, Lorian nodded to himself, shook it out, and breathed. "Okay."

"Okay. You good?"

"No, but you said I'll be fine. I'm holding you to that."

"Good. Let's go."

They travelled into the city, keeping their heads low so as not to draw any attention to their semi-physical forms. Aida felt herself being watched, knowing she could make contact with this world if she tried. Ordinarily, she would've been more adventurous and bolder. With Lorian, she needed to be extra careful.

"What happened back there?" Lorian asked. "That woman you met, who was she?"

"I'm not sure."

"She had the same eyes as your future self. And Eve before she died. *And* she had the same double-ringed Visatorre marking as them."

"Really? I don't remember seeing that."

"Aida, do you think she might've been...a god?"

"From *Pinnacle*—Oh." She played with her braid still intact from the jump. "I don't know. I didn't picture her like that."

"She was tall."

"She was scary." She recalled that look in her eyes akin to her future self's. "Let's keep going. If we bring deities into this, I'm really gonna lose my mind."

"Are you afraid?"

"No," she lied.

Something was wrong tonight. These Roman/Siinan streets weren't decorated with flowers and music to celebrate creation. Signs were hanging by broken chains. Windows had been smashed open. Aida swore she saw bodies lying in the alley and didn't say anything. Both of them wouldn't take well to seeing death again so soon.

"Do you know what year this is?" Lorian asked. "Is this a war zone?"

"I don't know. I need more information."

They neared the Colosseum, Aida's focal point. It was aglow with lanterns and torches, and a dull roar told that hundreds, perhaps thousands of people were seated for a show.

An ear-piercing scream split through the night. It howled like a dying wolf to its pack of stadium cheers.

Aida heeded its call. "Eve. That was Eve."

"What was?"

She took off, cane burying into the mud.

"Aida, wait!"

She didn't listen. Screw her failing memories, she'd memorized *everything* about Eve, including her screams the moment she lost her.

She ran faster, ignoring her increasing leg pain. She wasn't going to let it happen. She didn't care how time worked. Nobody was dying tonight. Not Eve, not whichever royal she may or may not have killed. She wasn't losing Eve a second time.

Manic onlookers crowded the Colosseum entrance like ants to their crushed anthill. Guards were stationed at the main and side doors so they couldn't see beyond the walls.

"Aida."

"Don't worry, we can get in. They won't see us."

"No, Aida."

"What?"

Lorian was walking backwards. His face had turned sallow. "I can't go in there."

"Why not? Here, I'll hold your hand so we won't get separated."

"It's not that. Whatever horrible atrocity is occurring in there, it's being done on my family's command. Every drop of blood that's been spilled behind these walls is on my hands."

"You never ordered these people to die."

"I might as well have!"

Aida took a step back.

Lorian took one forwards. "*Everything* in history is a result of my family's lineage. We're at the epicenter of every war and genocide. Even today, my family fucks over the world with their selfish choices to be better than those we kill, yet we've become the very entity of death itself. So I shall not go into the place where it all started, I cannot do that. I won't."

To historians, that list of accomplishments would've been something to take pride in. But if one had a heart as fragile as Lorian's, you'd find that the throne you romanticized smelled of innocent blood.

"Lorian," Aida said slowly. "If I'm right, then Eve is in there right now awaiting her execution. If we find her, we might be able to alter her fate. We might erase the horrible future your forefathers and my stupid future self are going to bring about. We can save everything."

Lorian looked worriedly at the multiple levels of the Colosseum. His lower lip began to bleed with how much he was biting it.

Aida took both of his hands and forced him to look at her. With their height difference, it was difficult to reach his face, so she tugged him down so their lips were a breath apart.

She touched her warm forehead with his cool one. It was all she could offer him at that moment. She hoped it was enough. "Trust me," she said. "We'll be okay. We'll save Eve tonight and change history. We'll fix everything, you and me."

Lorian's hands found their way to Aida's hips. A few months ago, she would've detested the touch. Now, she needed it to keep up this fake confidence.

"Come on," Aida said. "Let's save Eve."

The first three doors they tried were blocked by gladiators with non-Visatorre demanding to be let in.

"It's full," the gladiators kept repeating. "You'll be able to bear witness to her body the morning after."

"We have to see her now!" one person cried out. "Let the public see her before her death!"

Aida jogged halfway around the Colosseum. On the right-hand side was a wooden door not being guarded by any nearby gladiators, but it was padlocked shut.

She tested her finger strength. "Okay. Let's try this door. One, two..."

They both pulled on the latch. Her hands materialized through the metal. Lorian tried using the strength of his shoulder to pry it open. The foundation was sturdier than it looked.

"Shit," Aida cursed.

"We should keep looking."

"We're wasting time like this. Can we climb it? What's fifteen meters to the next row of arches?"

A tree branch snapped in the tree line.

A gladiator masked by a cloak ran in-between them and fiddled with the lock.

"God," he cursed, and took out a medieval hammer. With a grunt, he slammed it against the lock and broke it in two.

He looked up to the Moon. "My God, Circa, protect us, protect her," he said under his breath, and flung open the door.

Aida caught the door before it swung close. It was like stopping a wave from crashing into her.

They followed the man down the passage. The halls were pitch black save for an occasional torch at the start of each four-way. The lights flickered as they passed.

"If we can do this," Lorian said, "if we're able to change the past, the entirety of history as we know it will be altered."

"I know." Aida turned the corner. She couldn't match speeds with a trained gladiator.

"Doesn't that frighten you?"

"I have bigger issues on my mind."

"Aida, if we do this, we might not be born. We might never see each other again."

Aida was ready to snap at him to stop distracting her with worry, but it dawned on her, why he was freaking out over the what-ifs.

She looked up at him and smiled confidently. "There won't be a timeline where we won't meet each other. We're too stubborn to let that happen."

Lorian's eyebrows shot up with how boldly she proclaimed that. They knew they'd be together in a hazy timeline set in the future, but in another life, another story, another play?

Whichever the case may be, she knew that they'd always be together because that's what she wanted. She'd allowed herself to fall in love with him and wasn't going to give him up that easily.

Lorian smiled for the first time since they jumped into the past. "I suppose that's true."

"I know it is. And, for what it's worth, I think you'd make a great ruler."

"What?"

"If you were to take the throne after your mother, with me by your side, you could probably reshape the world within a day, maybe a few hours if we worked harder than we already do now."

Lorian watched his boots as they ran, mouth parted to form disapproval of Aida's suggestion. "Now's not the time to think of fantasy."

An arrow flung past Aida's head and clattered against the stone. The gladiator cursed and drew a hidden blade from his cloak. Behind them, two Roman gladiators drew their swords while another nocked another arrow.

"Halt!"

The gladiator was more skilled at running from authorities than Aida and Lorian were. He ran in a straight line and knew how to cut corners to keep himself ahead. As he ran, his hood fell and revealed his red hair.

Frederick, or Fausto. Something with an "'F," Aida couldn't remember: the man who'd been with Eve the day she'd seduced King Julius II.

"Unhand me!"

A dim light was beginning to grow in front of them, but instead of hiding, the gladiator ran headfirst into the threat.

Two gladiators had Eve up against the wall. She was wearing the raggedy smock she'd died in and was bruised and bleeding. Her braided hair was free and tangled down her neck like a rat's nest. Her eyes, Aida noted, were like hers with two white pupils, but her Visatorre marking had only one circle.

"Unhand me!" Eve thrashed against her captors and freed herself. Her wrists were shackled, and the gladiator to her right, momentarily off-guard by Frederick—Frederico?—grabbed at them to keep her from escaping.

"Let her go!" Frederico struck the gladiator and nicked his shoulder plate. The gladiator returned the jab and stabbed him in the arm. Outnumbered, the third gladiator kicked at Frederico's knees and caused him to fall in front of his ally like he was about to be knighted.

"No!" Eve kicked at the gladiator raising his sword upon Frederico, but because of her height, she could only reach so high. She got him off balance, but it wasn't enough to stop the swing from falling. "Stop!"

Lorian looked away, but Aida didn't. She didn't know if she'd tried to, to save herself from seeing it: the sword striking down and sticking halfway out of Frederico's skull. His mouth hung open, already dead, and when the gladiator yanked out his sword, he fell backwards in a pool of stagnant water and flowing blood.

Eve screamed, both in lament and in anger. She battled for the sword that'd taken away her friend, cursing all the men left in the room.

"Curse you! Curse you behemoths! You monsters!"

The remaining gladiators forced Eve back against the wall, securing her into submission before leading her away.

Aida looked down at Frederico's corpse before following her queen. She carried Lorian with her. His hand was cold.

"Why does the king want her alive?" one of the gladiators asked. "Why not end this sorrowful life?"

Aida pulled on one of the gladiator's vambraces. Her fingers couldn't make contact. "Let her go!"

"He wants to make an example of her," the leading gladiator said.

"Curse you!" Eve spat. "Tell me where she is. By my God, I swear, when I survive this hellish act of defiance, I'll see you hanged for your crimes against the capital of Siina."

"That's far too kind of you, Your Majesty, given what King Julius has in store for you."

Aida began hitting the gladiator with her cane. "Why isn't it working? Why can't they see us?"

The gladiators stopped at a metal door. Behind it roared the cheers of thousands of spectators. Their voices rattled the sconces nailed into the wall.

"Eve, come on. Look at me." Aida set herself in front of the queen and waved. Their eyes didn't meet.

Lorian backed up.

"Lorian, help me." She struggled to pull on Eve's arm.

He shook his head.

"Lorian, please. None of this is your fault."

"Then why does it feel so painful?"

A gladiator unlatched the door's metal lock and turned a gear embedded in the wall.

The stadium was aglow with lanterns, torches, and moonlight, bathing everything in gold. The tiers went up four, five stories high and were packed with spectators. Armed gladiators lined the walls like statues. Some stood in front of caged lions that were snarling for a meal.

In the center, standing on a raised platform, was King Julius II and a little girl. She was about four or five, with curly, brown hair. Her eyes were bloodshot.

"Mama!" she cried out.

"No!" Eve struggled for her, but the gladiators ignored her and carried her into the stadium. When the crowds caught sight of her, an uproarious booing mixed with general shouts of unhappiness. They threw food at her, men screamed at her for what she'd done, but what? What had she done to make so many people despise her? Had they not been overjoyed by her pregnancy a few years ago?

Aida ran up to Eve and touched her shoulder.

Her hand floated through her.

"No." She tried again. "Why? It worked in the field. Eve!"

Eve was positioned in front of the king's platform, thrown on her knees, head yanked up to meet his eyes.

King Julius II looked down at her like an animal he'd hunted, proud and smug, with a murderous hint to his cold eyes. The caged lions growled in impatience.

"Give my daughter back," Eve pleaded. "Please, she's done nothing wrong. Do not involve an innocent child in these discrepancies!"

"'The sins of a father shall be passed to his son'," King Julius quoted. "Such is written into Roman law." He took a scroll given to him by one of his advisers. He unfurled it. "Queen Eve Hyuang Costa, you have been brought here today on August 11th in the year 209 AUC before the eyes of Roma to pay for your unjust treason done upon by the Roman State."

"No!"

The king continued. "You were offered sanctuary in the peaceful city of Roma as an act of good faith done so by I, King Julius II, with the promises of joint and amicable agreements, yet you have abandoned my trust and name for the sake of committing adultery with my own wife, Queen Julia Ferro."

The crowd upheaved into batshit wailing. Eve kept her fiery eyes on the king. "Yet you keep women of the night in your bed and no one questions it! The roles are reversed for women who need to claw their way to the top to be seen in the presence of those who society places above us!"

"And this act of adultery," the king continued, "as it's written in our laws, is punishable by death."

Aida couldn't stand it. Even if she had done something wrong, she didn't deserve this level of pain and humiliation.

A hand grabbed her wrist.

"Lorian, let me go," she said. "We need to stop this!"

"Wait, look." He pointed at the armed gladiators around them. One had his eyes locked on to them, drawing near.

Aida backed up into Lorian. "Can they see us or not?"

"I think they see us partly."

The king rolled up his scroll. "For the acts of adultery against the king, withholding truths from the king—"

"Julius, stop it!" Eve screamed.

"—and breaking the oaths of which you swore to defend the peace agreements between Siina and Roma, I hereby sentence you, your kin, and your Visatorre people to death."

The crowd grew louder until his final words sent them into hysteria. Men too eager to see Eve pay poured into the Colosseum. Visatorre began getting up, confused at the decree and trying to find a way out. The entrances were being blocked.

"No!" Eve screamed. "Don't you dare touch her, you vile hypocrite in sheep's clothes! Don't touch her! Don't touch my people!"

King Julius ignored her wants and dragged Eve's daughter to a slab of stone. He laid her down, one knee against the small of her back. Nobody heard her crying.

"W-we have to do something," Aida said, convincing herself to act.

"I can't move," Lorian said. "I'm scared."

But the little girl. Whatever these two monarchs were dealing with, she must've been feeling it tenfold, trapped between the argument of lust-filled adults.

Eve broke free from the gladiators holding her back, but she didn't break into a run. Her body was flung forwards, then she righted herself only to fall backwards like an invisible force was hitting her. The gladiators tried to grab her, but when one touched her, Eve, with a spark of light, disappeared.

The crowd gasped as they looked around the stadium for the defiled queen. Some ran from incoming gladiators. They were being taken away.

The king yelped. The little girl had found her chance and bitten his hand. Freed like her mother, she leapt off the stage.

"No!" He flung out his hand for two gladiators to subdue her. "Get her, and find her! End this fucking lineage of hers! End—!"

The ground where Eve had once stood cracked and gave way like a crater. The nearest gladiators got knocked off of their feet. A black, sooty circle encircled it. The energy tumbled out in excess.

Eve stood awkwardly in the center, holding her mind. Her shackles had been broken. She swayed by the sudden jump.

Aida held her own head. It was like her jump here, dizzying without reasonable explanation. That ashy circle...

The gladiators paused, waiting to see what would happen next.

"*Grab* her!" the king bellowed. "Take her!"

One tried. He ran at her with his sword raised.

"Eve, watch out!" Aida yelled.

Eve twitched hard and disappeared with a crack. She reappeared seconds later three meters in front of the crater. She looked down at her hands. She clenched and unclenched them, cracked her neck.

The gladiators ran in, first bumping into Aida and Lorian, then phasing through them. One went to grab Eve, but she was prepared. Jumping, she disappeared and reappeared left, then right. She jumped around them, toying with them, until she got too close to a gladiator with a dagger.

She smiled, consciousness dawning over her double-ringed Visatorre marking bleeding down her forehead.

"How?" King Julius yelled. "How're you doing that?"

"Eve!" Aida went to run, but another gladiator bumped into her and sent her to the ground. Her braids came undone. Her dress ripped.

"Aida!"

Eve grabbed the gladiator's arm and brought it down. Before it cut her, she used his own weight to steal his weapon and end his life with a slash across his neck.

He fell so easily, as if knocked unconscious instead of murdered.

The men bent on killing her now gave her the widest berth. The blood from their comrade splattered onto their boots.

Eve, without mourning the life she'd just taken, disappeared and reappeared on the steps of the raised platform. She fell, but that didn't matter to someone like her now. She jumped forwards and landed next to the podium on which her daughter had almost lost her head.

The king had one man left to defend him. The rest had abided by his orders to do whatever they could to capture Eve. They hadn't expected her to be blessed—or cursed—with Circa's powers.

Eve ducked low and aimed her dagger at his heart.

She missed.

She buried the dagger into his stomach instead.

Julius bent forwards over her, blood spilling from his open mouth. They shared a look of disgust and anger, as Eve then jumped into him, arched her shoulder, and cut straight through his neck.

Julius' head thudded to the floor, and the stadium wailed like a siren, growing louder as more people took in the sight of their dead king. A sea of bodies stormed the Colosseum floor. Gladiators and servants, Visatorre and slaves, the roars of lions uncaged, they all bombarded the space. Aida had lost Lorian somewhere. All she saw was chaos and Eve, standing tall at the podium to oversee her doing.

She picked up the head of the Roman king by his hair. She stared into his glazed eyes, then raised it high above her. "For Siina!" she screamed.

Enraged gladiators ran in to defend their king in death.

Eve threw Julius' head at them and vanished.

Aida looked around. People were running. Screaming. Half of them clipped into her.

She locked on to a congregation of people screaming the loudest and ran for them. Those with a keen eye double-took her as she made her way through the crowd.

She wiped her wet eyes. She'd never wanted to believe the history of Eve. She was the Visatorres' most beloved queen. She was bold and smart and had built Siina into a prosperous young kingdom, but now, Aida was a part of her history. She knew the truth.

Eve hadn't murdered the queen of Roma.

She'd murdered its king.

Aida caught a blond ponytail through the crowds. "Lorian!" she shouted. If she wasn't touching him by the time she jumped back...

The person with the blond ponytail, Queen Julia, turned around. She had Eve's daughter tucked safely against her dress, protecting her from the belligerent crowds. She was still wearing the bracelet Eve had tied around her wrist. After so much hurt and betrayal, she still kept that piece of Eve with her. "Eta!" she cried out. "*Eta*!?"

"I'm here!"

Eve was battling her way towards them. She had more blood on her. "Jules, where is she? Do you have her?"

"I'm right here," Aida whispered.

"I have her, she's right here!" Julia answered.

Eve flipped her blade to the hilt and butted innocent people from her path. Some of the Visatorre in the crowd were helping her, even though she'd just murdered the world's most powerful monarch. They scuffled and fought with non-Visatorre, birthing a battlefield.

Aida tripped and fell atop a dead body. They'd been stabbed and trampled from the crowd.

Eve passed right by her, a meter away.

"Eve!" she shouted. "Eve, I'm here! I'm right here!"

She knew her voice wouldn't reach her. The world was on fire and Eve couldn't waste her time on a voice in her head. But she needed to have tried.

Eve stopped in her tracks and met Aida's eyes.

The world stilled. Eve's magical eyes hooked on Aida's. She panted, unable to speak out to this half-visible girl before her.

The spear that plunged into her abdomen silenced whatever she was going to say.

Aida cried out. The piece of wood lodged straight through Eve's side and made her top-heavy.

Julia screamed with Eve. The little girl watched her mother drop, too traumatized to express the right emotion.

A body hit Aida's back. "Aida," Lorian said. "Aida, we need to leave. It's not safe here."

Aida kept her hand out. She'd been meant to save her. For what reason had she dedicated so much of herself to her if not to save her, like an officer to their monarch?

The ground melted underneath her hands. The sinking, swaying feeling crept up her body like a virus. Her vision blurred, her arms gave out.

Eve, gagging on her own blood, reached for her daughter. The little girl tried keeping the blood inside of her.

"It'll be okay," the little girl cried. "You're going to be okay."

Eve might've disappeared with the little girl. It was what looked like happened, the two of them disappearing in one final burst of light.

Aida didn't know. She and Lorian flashed back to the future at the same time Eve did, their doomed timeline remaining unchanged.

Chapter 28: Getting Bored

"Fuck!"

They came back to the homeless shelter, dark and cold without the lit fireplaces. The chairs were on the tables and the floors had been scrubbed of that soot circle Aida had created when they'd jumped.

"Fuck!"

Aida was on her hands and knees, screaming through her curses. She slammed her fists against the floorboards, then used her head to increase the pain.

"Aida, stop."

Pushing Lorian away, Aida ran into a communal bathroom and shut herself away from him yet again.

Lorian felt disconnected, like he wasn't all there yet, but he wasn't dying. He didn't have a headache, he had all four limbs and five senses. He still felt the wet blood splatter the stadium stone and heard Eve screaming for her daughter before they teleported somewhere.

They could've saved her again, but once again, Lorian Ashwell fucked everything up by putting his feelings first. How could he face Aida knowing he'd let Eve die a second time?

He pulled himself up to the counter. Sitting on the edge was a key, a plate of cookies, and a letter written by Missus Sharma. Even in the dark, Lorian recognized her handwriting. She always wrote Lorian's name, new and old, with a heart dotting the "i."

Dearest Lorian and Aida—

I'm so sorry I'm not there with you. We stayed until closing, hoping you'd both return. The owners promised that the building will be locked and secured for the night, but you can use this key to leave out the back should you return before morning.

I hope you are safe, my loves, and are not in any pain. I don't have the answers for how or why this's happening, but I pray that you come back safe and unharmed. Please, please be vigilant, and Lorian, protect Aida. I worry so much about her. I don't want to see either of you getting hurt.

If I don't hear back from you, I'll be back first thing tomorrow morning to pick you up. I can't wait to see you again, my loves.

P.S. The cookies are a gift from the owners.

Be safe,
—Missus Sharma

Lorian reread her letter, hearing her caring voice in his head, and nibbled on one of the sugar cookies. He would do better. He couldn't stay wrapped up in his own head while the world continued to ask more of him. For her sake, and Aida's, he'd work on being his best possible self.

"For what it's worth, I think you'd make a great ruler."

He knocked on the bathroom door. It was locked.

"Aida," he whispered. "Please, open the door. You said we'll always find each other. So don't keep putting up barriers for me to break down. I don't want to do it anymore. I'm tired."

The floorboards in the bathroom creaked.

"Please, let me be there for you. Don't handle this all on your own. Being alone..." He dropped his head on the wood. "Being alone is as suffocating as it is lonely. Please, let me in so we don't have to feel that way anymore."

The door remained closed. He didn't hear another sound come from the bathroom.

Then the door wrenched open.

Tears drenched Aida's red cheeks. Her hair was a mess and her glasses were thrown near the sink, cracked near the top rim.

"I can't jump back," she said. "I tried and I tried and I can't do it. I-I tried hitting my head, I bit my hand, thinking it was mental. I tried imagining how far away we are from the Colosseum and tried to physically, I don't know, *propel* myself in there, but I-I—"

Lorian took her into his arms.

"She's dead."

He hugged her tighter.

"She's dead and I couldn't fix it. I'm useless."

"You're not useless."

"Look me in the eyes and tell me that, Lorian. I let her die *twice*. I could've moved. I could've done something, but I couldn't." She fully embraced him now in sobs, no longer trying to hide it. "History's not changing, Lorian. She's never coming back."

Lorian steeled himself for her. "History cannot be made without losing the people we love."

"Fuck that. But I still don't understand. One moment she's a normal Visatorre, the next, she's crisscrossing through time. I did it once and I can't control it for shit." She peeled her wet face off of him to look in the mirror. "Why didn't I get my second Visatorre circle? You would've thought that after seeing that, I would've, I don't know, earned it."

"We should find Circa again."

Aida peeked out to the empty shelter.

"That was her, I know it was. All of this must be her doing."

Aida looked like she'd throw up. He couldn't imagine the pain of loving a God only to find out that they truly did not care how much you suffered because of them.

She put the balls of her hands into her eye sockets and stretched backwards. "*Fuuuuck,*" she drawled.

"I know. You'll figure this out."

"No, *both* of us better figure this out, because I don't know what the fuck we're gonna do next." She started re-braiding her hair. "Eve's gone, I have fucked eyes, and I don't know about you, but I can't focus on any thought for more than a fraction of a second."

"Hey, at least you're not writhing on the floor this time."

She went to argue with him, then closed her mouth. "Yeah. Yeah? I don't know if that's a good thing or not."

"Count your blessings. We don't get them very often."

"No," a voice said, "we don't."

Lorian went for the absent rapier at his side. With the number of times his life was in danger, he should've had it sewn into his jacket.

Future Aida, with her hands behind her back, grinned devilishly at them from the doorway.

"Oh, go fuck yourself," Aida blurted out.

"Hey, no," Future Aida said. "Language. And don't fuck me yet. *I* am here to help. Gods, I never know how to greet you two. You're always so mopey."

"We don't want your help," Aida said. "You're the reason we're getting fucked over like this. Why did you let Eve die twice?"

"Hey, whoa, who says I'm not helpful? I've given you *so* many clues."

"Bullshit."

"*Language.* Now, come on, in, in." She shut the door behind her. Lorian kept his distance. It was like she was a poisonous snake ready to lunge for her next meal. "Look, I know I don't give you a lot of information. It kind of comes with the territory. But from what I remember, neither of you have good brains right now."

"What does *that* mean?" Aida asked.

Future Aida held up her hands. "Hey, I'm not the best at picking up social cues. You know that. Gimme a break."

"Why should I? We're criminals because of you. I lost my scholarship because of you. Eve's dead because of you." The look in Aida's eyes changed. "How do we even know you're me?"

Future Aida blinked. "I mean, does the face not give it away?"

"How should I know? You could be a demon disguised as me."

"Uh, yeah, demons don't actually exist."

"Then tell me something," Aida demanded, "something only I would know. Right now. Don't jump away with some cryptic, lyrical bullshit you pull out of your ass. Tell me or else we're leaving and you don't get to have your fun anymore."

"I *always* have my fun, Little Aida." She lifted her chin, staring her younger self down. While Lorian had confessed that the white pupils did make her prettier, this woman's eyes stirred something else inside of him, something sinister. He'd do anything for her if she asked, even murder.

"Fine," she said. "You think all of this will be easier if Lorian went back to the palace and reconciled with their family."

Aida didn't respond.

"You think that if they went back home, it'd give you an easier path to saving the Visatorre people and telling the king and queen everything you've learned. But you won't do that to them, so you haven't asked them yet."

Aida was staring dead-eyed at her future self. Did she really think that? If Lorian went back, things *would* be easier. The hunt would end, Carmine wouldn't be run ragged every day, his mother would be happier, and Beatrice wouldn't act like his leaving was somehow her fault. His father would be calmer, too, something everyone in Roma wanted, and they likely *would* get closer to finding out these answers they needed without the nonsense of their future selves.

But to not even ask him because she knew it'd hurt them, if she'd done that, he wouldn't know what to say. He'd only kiss her and thank Circa that he'd found his person.

Aida crossed her arms. "What do you want from us?"

"Oh, you believe me now? I could tell you more, like how you're terrified of cows or that you like the way Lorian touches your—"

"*Enough*," Aida said. "Answers. Now. Why're you here?"

"Currently? I'm bringing you to the palace, tonight." She clapped her hands as if she were beckoning for a servant. "Let's go. Pack your bags. It's difficult to jump with one person, let alone two."

"What?" Aida asked. "Did you not just—We'll be thrown in jail, or killed."

"We won't use the main entrance, silly, please. You're talking to someone who's trespassed into many homes and many constable quarters. Have more faith in yourself." She fished out a key from her dress pocket. It was silver and worn, with an emblem of a lion engraved on the top.

"A Roman skeleton key," Lorian said, touching the middle of his chest where his own key was. "Where'd you get that?"

"I have my ways," she said. "How easy it is to break the law when the laws of the universe don't apply to you."

"She stole it," Aida paraphrased.

"I did not, it was gifted to me, though you'd be surprised how few times they change the palace locks. Some are still the same from Eve's time."

Lorian nodded in agreement.

"Lorian, stop nodding," Aida said. "Okay, what's your plan, then, other than to get us killed?"

"Look, if you don't already get it, you ain't dying yet. You're *me*. And let's be honest here, this's boring."

"Oh, watching Eve die, feeding the homeless, that's boring to you?"

"Yes! Well, not the last part, but come on! We're wasting too many pages of our lives wondering when or if or how when you should be *doing*. I want to pick up the pace, so I am nudging you to the place you're meant to be."

"But what if—"

"Aida, I am not gonna hurt you, I'm not a masochist," she said in a rush. "Stop being so distrustful of yourself. I am on your side. That's a promise." She held out her hand, waiting for her to take it. "You've always wanted to change the world. Do you trust me to achieve that?"

Aida didn't take her eyes off of herself, glaring with a thousand questions on her sharp tongue. The two of them seemed to be having a conversation without words. She did that at times, mentally organizing and rearranging her thoughts around the person so she could create a new, well-thought-out opinion.

Then she struck out her hand to Future Aida.

"There we are!"

Aida quickly retracted it before Future Aida touched her.

Future Aida's mouth dropped open. "Oh, you're a *brat*!" She grabbed at their collars. "Hang on!" she said, and the three of them jumped into brightness.

—◇—

Lorian mentally praised himself for not landing on his face twice in two jumps. Future Aida brought them to a cobblestone road, but the unevenness of the ground actually worked in his favor. His boots caught on the stone and, while he fell with the elegance of a newborn foal, he landed somewhat gracefully.

Aida didn't. Even with her cane, she stumbled into her future self and brought the two of them down.

"Whoa!" Future Aida swung the two of them around, keeping both of them up. "Watch it. Your leg doesn't get better with age."

They were at the front of the palace, right outside the iron-clad fence. It must've been the same night. The crescent Moon was at level with the tallest spires.

He hadn't been this close to the palace since his wedding day. It was an ugly thing, blocky and made of sandy stone, with too many merlons for a city that hadn't fought a war in close to a hundred years. The only elements that stood out were the hidden flower garden in the center of the palace and the clock tower. With a face nearly ten meters across, it was surrounded by stained glass that sparkled both inside and out: his clock tower, his safe haven.

He saw himself there, as a child: He'd be dancing on the wooden floor behind that clock, skipping over the colors reflected on the boards while Carmine watched. It'd be past his bedtime, but Carmine would only put a finger to his lips to keep it a secret between them.

One night, the two of them had snuck off after a rather hard day. Lorian's father had scolded him for breaking a window with one of his toys. He'd hit him across the cheek and sent him into a screaming, kicking rage.

While he was locked in his room, crying about how unfair life was, Carmine had come in.

"Get out!" Lorian screamed. "Leave me alone!"

He had stubble back then that he called a mustache and wore his hair in a long ponytail. It wasn't suitable for officers, but he got away with these things, even today. Such were the perks of being the queen's childhood friend.

"Hey, there, little spitfire," Carmine said.

"What do you want?" Lorian asked. "Leave me be."

"I found this lying around in the kitchen." He pulled out a plate from behind his back with a fork, a folded napkin, and a perfect piece of strawberry shortcake drizzled with sugar. "I wouldn't want it to go to waste, would you?"

Lorian remembered his face brightening up despite the pain still infecting his cheek. He gobbled up the cake and shared the topping strawberry with Carmine.

"I hate daddy," Lorian told him. "All the kings in my history books are cool and strong, but he's mean. You know he's not a nice person, don't you, Carmie? How come you can't be king?"

"Because you either have to be born into nobility, like how your mother was and your sister and yourself, or marry into it."

"Then how come you can't marry Mama?"

"Your Highness." Startled by the forwardness of a young child, Carmine patted Lorian's head. "Why don't we change the subject?"

He pouted. "I don't wanna."

"Fine. Come with me."

"Where're we going?"

He smiled. "To break a few rules."

They snuck up all the way to the sixth story, to the clock tower. It rang by itself, so no one ever found them. The dust was practically baked into the wooden floors, it was so unused, but it was a room Lorian called his own. No expensive dresses. No gold jewelry he was pressured to wear. This was a place for him to be his authentic self.

He giggled as he twirled in his white nightgown. "Dance with me, Carmie!"

"I shouldn't, Your Highness."

"I command you to! I'm gonna be king one day, so you have to do what I say!"

"You're going to be a queen, *Your Highness, not a king."*

"Says who?" He grabbed his large hand and brought him into the center of the room, the moonlight their spotlight, the giant clock ticking to the song in Lorian's head.

Carmine laughed as he succumbed to his request, and the two of them danced for hours, singing and laughing about nothing. When Lorian got tired, he'd stand on Carmine's boots, until Carmine would carry him to bed like a baby.

"Lorian."

Both Aidas had made it down the path and were waiting for him. His Aida was closer to him, refusing to move until he followed her.

"Are you okay?" she asked.

He nodded once.

"Let's go, lovebirds," Future Aida said. "You both know what the officers will do to us if they find us this close to the palace."

Lorian knew, but the problem was that he didn't see any officers on patrol. Not even the lights of the main hall were lit.

"Why didn't you jump us into the palace?" Aida asked.

"Have you ever tried jumping with two people before? Not as easy as it seems. And you two are shaking in your boots about meeting the king, so I didn't wanna scare you even more."

"I'm not scared," Aida was quick to point out.

"You—"

"Anyway," she said, "before we get in, I need more answers from you. One: How can you jump forwards and backwards? How can you control it?"

"It comes with age."

"But how do you do it? And why are my eyes different? Why haven't I received my second circle?"

"It comes with age."

She threw up her free hand. "Come *on*."

"A little information would help us figure out this task you want us to complete," Lorian said, "whatever it may be."

Future Aida opened the unlocked gate and allowed them entry like she was their butler.

"They never leave this open," Lorian said.

"I opened it prior. I try to keep twelve steps ahead of the program."

"You're avoiding my question," Aida continued. "What am I missing?"

"Okay, Little Aida, imagine, if you will, that when I came into your house, I told you that this blond-haired cutie pie you had reservations about was going to be your lover."

"You didn't come into my house, you came into my dorm."

"Same difference. Anyway, if I told you that ya'll were gonna break into the Catacombs to unearth the true history of a dead queen you hadn't truly known until this month while also trying to evade the queen's right-hand man, would you have believed me, or would you've thought I was crazy?"

Aida continued staring at her.

"*And* what if I told you that Eve was not a great person like you'd built her up in your head to be and had more flaws than both our stepmom and Lorian's father combined? If I told you that she was a power-hungry adulterer, would you have believed me?"

"If you would've explained yourself, I would've."

"No, you wouldn't have. And if I didn't get you in trouble with the law, you wouldn't have found, uh, what's her name..." She tapped her head. "Missus...Miss—"

"Missus Sharma," Lorian said. How could one forget her?

"Right, right, Missus Sharma. You wouldn't have found her nor would you have found that little book illustrating Eve and Julia holding hands, and then you wouldn't have found Eve herself because you wouldn't have had Lorian's key to get into the Catacombs because you never fell in love with them because you never trusted them." She read something written on her hand. "So, by leaving you without answers in your dorm room the first night we met, Lorian stayed with you, fell more in love with you, protected you, got you to Missus Sharma, got you to the Catacombs, got you to Eve, and got you here.

"Do you see where this's going? Time, it's all annoyingly connected and the more you explain how it works, the more it makes your brain fuzzy. The best thing you can do is roll the dice the Gods have given you and try not to die in the process. You know, I've always wanted you to work on your memorization skills, but evidently, you haven't."

Lorian waited to hear an earful from Aida. She hated people who questioned her intelligence without giving her the chance to find her own answer.

Aida's grip on Lorian doubled. "Evidently, I haven't."

"Don't take it too hard," Lorian whispered, but Aida was slowing down and distancing herself from Future Aida.

"Come on, you two," Future Aida said over her shoulder. "We're almost there."

"You said 'evidently'," Aida said. "Why did you say that?"

"Do you want another adverb? That's what they're called, right? Adjectives, adverbs. Ugh, they get so confused in the old noggin."

"You're trying to help us so we don't fuck over the past, but I'm you, so why does it matter?"

"Uh, duh, I like sticking my head into other people's business." She started humming to herself, tossing her head back and forth. Her swaying hair mesmerized Lorian until he realized what Aida was getting at. Neither of them knew how this time travelling business worked, but what Aida was laying out was like a puzzle, and the pieces were beginning to fit.

"You're my future self, but you're more scatterbrained than I am," Aida said. "You keep forgetting things and losing track of time. You don't *know* what's going to happen next, do you?"

Future Aida said nothing.

Aida stopped walking. "I thought we weren't using the main doors."

Future Aida reached for the handle. She checked her hand again. It had notes written on it. "Huh. Seems like I forgot about that bit."

Dozens of officers barged out of the double doors. They were armed like their forefathers were in the Colosseum, with rapiers and archaic bows and arrows to kill them.

Future Aida laughed and jumped to a third-story balcony overlooking the front doors. "Whoa! I guess *that* was gonna happen, huh?"

"What is *wrong* with you!?" Aida snapped. "What were you *thinking*?"

"I'm thinking many things at any given—"

"*Silence!*"

Lorian's royal blood ran cold. He thought he'd never be subjugated to that horrifying voice again. He'd run away for several reasons, all of which he tried to justify in his mind, but every reason—his fear of marriage, his fear of becoming a ruler, his fear of disappointing everyone—stemmed from him.

Out from the front doors, guarded by Carmine and more armed officers, were his mother, his sister, Zaahir and Kadar, and his father.

Beatrice gasped and went to run out to see Lorian, but their father struck out his hand, corralling her back.

"It seems your plan backfired on you, you accursed woman," his father said, looking up to Future Aida. "I overheard your conversation with this boy's alleged 'future self'."

Future Aida peeked over her balcony, hair flopping over her face.

"I knew about your plans to infiltrate my home and bring these two deviants to my throne room. You thought you could so easily break into one of the most secure palaces without my knowing."

She tried holding back her laughter. "Oh, *never*," she giggled. "Do you know how hard it would be for me to steal your keys and have access to every bathtub and parlor in this stinky place? Also, when were you listening to me? I was, like, being so discreet in the gardens. Maybe that's why Lorian was so tense when I was talking to them about this."

Carmine tried to usher the queen back inside, but the king held up his hand.

Lorian shuddered. He was about to give the order. To have them detained, whipped, tortured, executed, and he couldn't do anything about it. They were dead because they couldn't go against his father, so they'd have to...

They'd have to...

"Run."

He looked down at Aida.

"Run," Aida whispered. "Get a head start. They're angrier with me, so the quicker you leave—"

"I won't leave you."

"You're going to be taken away and married off because of her, of me." Her grip tightened, her feelings betraying the words leaving her brain. "I'm sorry. I should've known not to trust her. It all seems so obvious now."

"I'm not leaving you, Aida. I'm never leaving you."

She looked up at him, a fight on her tongue. Then she squeezed his hand back. "You stubborn asshole."

The officers surrounded them. Carmine wasn't angry like his father. He held the same look as his mother, darting between them and the officers and the weapons trained on them.

"Please wait a moment, Your Majesty." Zaahir stepped between them. "Is this not what you wanted? Did you not want to speak with both women about their plans?"

"Hey, you did?" Future Aida said. "Aw, that's so sweet of you, *Your Majesty*."

"These two have been a disgrace to my kingdom and my men," the king said. "I shall see to it that neither have the chance to escape my custody again. Remember that you are a guest in my kingdom, Prince Zaahir, so I suggest that you hold your tongue and stay in line."

"Uh-oh, this's getting good," Future Aida said, as if watching an opera's third act. "Hit him, Zaahir! You know you wanna! Bea, speak up!"

"I—"

"Be *quiet*, Beatrice," the king said. "I am tired of you. I'm tired of both of you."

"But why not listen to them?" Beatrice asked. "Hear them out."

"I shall not hold a conversation with these people any longer. I want them dead."

Zaahir stepped up to the king, beside Beatrice. "Your Majesty, I have been on Roma's side since the moment I was betrothed to your child as a toddler, when I had no choice in any chapter of my life except to serve the world. Beatrice only wants what's best for you and your kingdom. I want what's best for both countries, and you seem to be holding your own pride above us."

As he raised his voice, the officers protecting Durante unsheathed their swords, all but Carmine.

"My!" Future Aida said. She jumped through a jump and landed in front of Aida and Lorian, clapping. "Well said, King and Queen! Brava! Brava!"

"*Silence!*" King Durante yelled. "Officers, capture her and these two. I don't want to see them leaving my soil. Carmine, take Zaahir and Beatrice away. I'm tired of seeing their faces in my—"

"You're to capture *us*?" Future Aida asked. "*Me*? Now, how on Earth are you to do that?"

An officer let the first arrow fly.

Future Aida jumped out of the way and jumped straight at the king. Grabbing the back of his head, she then slammed his face into her knee as hard as she could.

The nearest officers jumped back. Carmine dove not to protect the king, but to run Lorian's mother into the safety of the palace.

"*That's* for hurting Lorian, you *prick*." Future Aida spun into another jump, and when she came back, she was with another.

Future Lorian came onto the scene with Carmine's rapier held firmly in his hand. He lost his footing for a moment as he took in the scene around him. "You just *had* to make him mad, didn't you?" Future Lorian asked. "Why knee him?"

"You know I had to," she said, and the two of them charged.

Pandemonium broke out on the main lawn. Future Lorian parried swords, Aida took on officers half her size. She'd found a dagger between now and her jump and was disarming men with it. She jumped every other second, confusing her assailants for her to knock them out with shoves and kicks. Lorian's family and Zaahir were brought back into the palace. Amidst the fray, Carmine was battling to either join the fight or protect his loved ones.

"Listen to me, Lorian," Future Aida called out while fighting. "Go to your secret spot in the woods, the place you haven't been in years. You know the place, don't you?"

Lorian didn't know what she was talking about. He was too focused on the stunned Carmine. He had his sword drawn now and was ready to attack Future Aida, but the girl paid him no mind. Instead of fighting him, she pulled something out of her dress pocket. It was an orb as small and black as a marble.

When Carmine saw it, he scrambled back and hid behind the door. "Damn it, not again—!"

She flicked the marble into the air, snatched it back into her clutches, then threw it at the palace walls.

The grounds exploded with black smoke, thickly and swiftly like a storm of hungry locusts. Officers coughed and tried swatting the smoke away. It stained the air and left them aimless.

Future Aida jumped high into the air. She pointed at the dark forest behind the palace. "Go, Lorian, and let the hunt begin!"

The *woods*. The *hunt*. Little clues, like breadcrumbs leading him to the right answer. It was the second-best place for them to be at the moment, excluding Missus Sharma's cottage, and perhaps the middle of the ocean.

Keeping hold of his Aida's hand, Lorian followed his lover's advice and ran for the dark tree line.

Chapter 29: Log Cabin

An arrow almost struck its target, but a hand pulled Aida back and saved her. She had a five-second delay on everything happening. All she saw were swords and smoke and her future self destroying any chance she had of talking to the Roman king. She registered officers and a constable or two, but she wasn't sure. She kept her eyes on Lorian until they passed the tree line.

"Go to your secret spot in the woods."

Was that another lie concocted by her future self? Another ruse to get them into more danger? She'd given them to King Durante for what? A good laugh?

She could *not* believe she'd fucked up yet again. Why did anyone put their faith in her when she burned everything she touched? She trusted her future self, she walked into the hands of King Durante. Truthfully, she'd been burning down her chances ever since she left Bělico, thinking she could make it in Roma when everyone, especially the man in charge, thought she wasn't good enough to live.

The noises from the fight died out through the snowy branches. There had been a path Lorian had taken, but he ditched it a few minutes ago, opting for a less traceable route through the snow.

After twenty minutes of aimless trekking, Aida found the thickest tree on which she could catch her breath. Her leg now had a steady heartbeat beating down to her numb toes, begging that she lay down and alleviate the pressure from it. Lorian stripped off his jacket as puffs of cold smoke left his lips.

She didn't know what to say to him. What could be said? An apology? A deadpan delivery about their situation? A question? A demand? She kept panting to gain back some strength.

Lorian gave her a nod and motioned for her to keep following. "We're almost there."

There he was. "Where? Some treehouse in the pine?"

"There's a place my family used to vacation at. The last time we used it was about ten years ago, so I doubt they'll search for us there. First."

After another ten minutes of walking and stopping to breathe, Lorian slowed down and drew back to Aida's side. "We're here."

The trees parted to a crystal lake reflecting the night above. Across the way, a homey cabin with a short dock made its home on the water's edge.

"Ah," Aida said. "I've been here before."

"Have you?"

"In a jump. I think it was the jump I made when we first met. Back at the entrance to Durante Academy. You helped me to my dorm."

"Is this where you went? This used to be my mother's and father's cabin when we went on hunting trips. We took them a lot when I was a child. It looks like they abandoned it."

"Is it safe?"

"For the time being, until you can walk better, it has to be."

"I can keep going."

"You're limping. You've been limping since we crossed that stream."

"I don't remember crossing a stream."

"We crossed two." He gave her his arm. "Come now."

As soon as she entered the threshold, Aida felt a sense of peace. It was a heavily furnished cabin with couches, paintings of the Roman landscape, and flatware that must've cost hundreds of lyria lining the glass cabinets. It gave off the impression of being rustic with tinges of royalty sprinkled in.

Lorian lit a spare lantern from the kitchen and explored childhood memories. Aida fell into an armchair in the living room. Someone had carved out a crude lion head on the arm with a knife. The workmanship resembled Lorian's tattoo.

She looked down at her tired, muddy feet, at the dress Missus Sharma had bought for her that she'd ruined from the run. As Lorian inspected each room of the cabin, Aida sniffled away real tears that she couldn't keep back. She was to become Future Aida, a loud and stupid and hurtful person to all who came near her. Whatever she had in store for them, it would be because of Aida and her stupid, broken brain.

She pulled herself free from her dress. She shrugged out of her bodice and petticoat like they were a disgusting second skin and kicked off her heels. When Lorian came back, Aida was in nothing but her tank top, bloomers, and stockings.

"Did you happen to jump whilst I was away?" he asked jokingly.

Without looking at him, Aida held out her hand. "Take this for me."

"What is it?"

She dropped her hand in his, a weak attempt at a hand shake. "My dignity, and any responsibility I have moving forwards when it comes to our relationship."

He looked over his empty hand. "I don't understand."

"I shouldn't be the one who has the final say in anything anymore. Just take over for me. Change the timeline. Make things better."

He must've had some semblance of authority in his blood, being royal and all. He probably wanted to take control of things, after everything Aida had done.

He knelt beside her and clamshelled her hand. "And you think *I* want that kind of responsibility?" he asked her. "Why do you think I left the luxuries of being royal? I want absolutely nothing to do with any power that I hadn't asked for directly. You handle it so well, why would I take that from you? I can, surely, but Aida, I won't be able to do it as well as you can."

She scoffed. "What do you mean? I'm going to be *her*, Lorian. I'm going to be stupid a-and more loud and annoying than I already am. I thought I had a clear understanding about what I wanted from my life, but knowing I'm gonna turn into her is..." She wiped her eyes. "I have no idea what I'm doing anymore, Lorian. I'm scared of the future."

Lorian took her into his arms. "That makes both of us, Aida. I too have had reservations about getting you caught up in my life. What I've been doing is selfish and cruel to my people, but I'm too bull-headed to accept that I *should* go back and right my wrongs. You're the one who has kept me grounded in a world where I feel like I have no power. You talk to me not as a royal heir but as Lorian Ashwell, a person who sometimes doesn't know what to say, who tries to pretend everything's alright when it clearly, *clearly* isn't."

He touched his forehead to hers. "You're an amazing woman, Aida, and I'm sure, through whatever crazy plot your future self is concocting, that everything you do is for the best."

She sniffed. She didn't know how, but the way he talked, the sound of his voice, made her trust everything he was saying, even though most of it he couldn't prove.

He took her hand. "Let's go somewhere a bit more hidden, in case they try to find us again."

"If they're meant to find us, our future selves already know."

"At least we know we aren't going to die anytime soon."

"That doesn't make me feel any better."

"Darn it. And I try so hard."

They climbed up to the second and third floor of the cabin. Lorian waited patiently for Aida to make it. She'd lied; her legs had given out from their run. Her bad leg was now quivering.

"Sorry. Just one more flight." He pulled a string from the ceiling to reveal the attic door. "This's where I used to sleep sometimes."

"You have a strange fixation with sleeping in unusual places."

"I guess I was an unusual child."

"You guess?"

Despite being another attic space, Aida didn't hate the room. It was furnished with a king-sized bed, a couch one could use as another bed, and its very own furnace to keep the space warm. A map of the world was tacked behind the bed frame, and there were two writing desks against the wall with books and papers on them. It looked like someone had been using the space the night before.

Pushing up his sleeves, Lorian dragged one of the writing desks up against the door and fastened the curtains closed. Aida went for the books on the writing desks. Whoever had last used this room had good taste. *The History of Roma: Their Lives Untold. The Classical Era Reimagined. The Sanitation System of Roma.*

She fanned through the pages. "Were these yours?"

He looked over his shoulder. "I don't believe so. I wasn't much into reading as a child. Perhaps my parents left them here for storage." He left to light the furnace.

"We can't," Aida said. "The smoke will give us away."

"Right." He opened one of the closet doors and fished out heavy, knitted quilts and plump pillows. "My sister and I used to make pillow forts with these."

"Is that something normal siblings do?"

"Back before we started regularly fighting, I suppose, though I'd hardly call your sisters 'normal'." He palmed the bulkier pillows. "There's something..."

It came out before he finished the sentence. The case slipped off the heavy pillow and a fountain of red rose petals fell out across the bed. Some caught in the air like snow before resting over the covers.

Lorian, gaping, checked the innards of his now empty pillow case. It had no pillow in it at all.

Aida snorted. "Are you joking?"

"I-I don't remember putting those in there."

"Maybe it was from your sister pranking you or something." Aida closed the book she was about to start and

337

waltzed over to the bed. Her weight jumped the petals. "What're we going to do now?"

"About the roses?"

"About our incoming execution."

He sat beside her. "What's there to do?"

"Hide out in the Catacombs?"

He went to say something, then closed his mouth.

"Too soon," she answered for herself. "I don't know, Lorian. I really don't."

He gestured to the quilts. "Are these warm enough?"

She wrapped herself up in one. Lorian helped get it over her exposed shoulder.

"Want me to redress?"

"...You don't have to," he said in delay.

"Wow, ten minutes at your old family cabin and you've completely reverted to a blushing babe." She showed off her ankle, then knee. "Is *this* too much for you?"

"You know it is. When I was a child, I was such an ass about it. I'd be so vulgar at the dinner table, testing how much I could say before getting reprimanded. It's hard to completely undo what's been instilled in you since childhood."

"I know." Aida's roaming fingers found a rose petal. She played with it between her thumb and forefinger. "Wanna talk about it?"

His hand found hers between the roses. "Yeah."

—◆—

Lorian told her secrets not even his mother knew. Pranks he and Beatrice would play on the Constable, the time they'd stolen a handful of newly hatched sea turtles from the coastline. He told her of his times in this cabin, spending summer after summer hunting, foraging, getting caught in trees like a cat. He talked with a forlorn smile; these memories hurt, but they held moments of happiness he felt comfortable sharing with Aida.

Aida tried to find a piece of her history that was worth building on, but every time she uprooted her past, she remembered being beat or grounded and kept quiet.

After she remembered a particular memory that'd left her arm sore for two weeks, Lorian stopped talking and cuddled in closer with her. They'd taken to sharing one pillow under a quilt, their knees knocking, feet touching.

"Everything okay?" he asked.

"Just compartmentalizing."

"That doesn't sound good."

"Go on with your stories."

"I don't think I have much else to tell you." He looked up. "I'm afraid of you being too close to the window."

"Well, you're closer to the door."

"I should've brought my rapier."

"To a homeless shelter?"

In the end, Aida rummaged through the kitchen using the low-lit lantern and found a decently-sized kitchen knife. It felt nice keeping it underneath her pillow, but it reminded her of Eve.

"Most trained officers aren't used to working at night," Lorian said. "It's left for officers in training like Alessio and Matteo."

"The king and queen will probably extend their hours into the night to find us," Aida said, "but did you see the Constable? He hesitated to attack."

"Well, I think he was trying to protect my mother."

"He went against the king's orders."

"My mother's the true sovereign, and they've been friends since childhood."

"You think there's something there?"

"Gods, I hope not, but who knows, given what we know about monarchs?"

"Gross."

Lorian yawned and moved up a bit closer to her.

"Thinking about sleeping?"

"Not yet."

The ambiguity lingered between them.

"Aida, may I ask you something?"

She braced for the worst. She knew where this was going and didn't know if she should've been leading him on like this. *If* this was leading him on. Should she've been sleeping on the floor? She hadn't yet redressed.

He wrapped an arm around her waist. "I know you aren't one for romance or feelings of any kind. I know it's selfish for me to place those feelings onto you."

Her stomach fluttered. "That's not selfish."

"When I saw those officers honing in on us, I was terrified. I want to see you succeed with everything you want to fix in the world, and I don't want to see you hurt or fearful anymore. I want to be with you and take care of you, forever."

His nose brushed against the back of her neck. "I love you, Aida."

She exhaled, though she didn't know if it was in relief or not. "That so."

"It is. It's always been." His hand travelled upwards, almost touching her breast. She wondered if he could hear how fast her heart was beating. "Before anything else happens to us, I want to know if I have a chance to act on these feelings bubbling inside of me."

"Feelings." Whenever someone talked about feelings of love, they used poetic language and metaphors to get their message across. With anything else, with anger or jealousy or happiness, everyone knew what that meant and didn't need long explanations to convey their meaning. People couldn't do that with love. It was something so abstract that Aida thought most people didn't understand it.

Just like her.

She kissed the rose petal. "Try."

He lifted his head. "Excuse me?"

"I don't know how far I can go, but my adrenaline is atypically high right now. With you, I'd like to try."

The breath on her neck faded. The bed creaked.

After an unreasonable amount of silence, Aida, red-faced, looked at him.

His eyes were brimming with tears. He laughed as he let one go.

"What's wrong?"

"I'm just so happy. I'd be honored."

"That sounds like a marriage..."

Lorian brushed back her stray hairs before leaning in and kissing her.

How brazen of them, she thought, to kiss in his childhood cabin under the vigilant watch of the entire city's law enforcement. But she understood, the motives of most people: No matter how bleak life was, it was lovely to feel loved.

Lorian dipped down and kissed her neck.

She gasped. His lips heated up parts of herself she never knew were cold.

"Oh, Aida."

Their thighs touched. Their socks grazed one another until Lorian lost one over the edge. He kept pressing into her like he wanted her to fall. She pressed back into him, touching him more.

He freed her chest out of her loose undershirt and fondled her breasts. It was like he was touching the wetness of her heart.

"May I?" he asked, a deep hunger dropping his voice and hand lower. He tickled her thighs.

She bit her tongue. That was going too far, wasn't it? At least she knew where he'd be touching when it came to her chest. This other hand could've gone anywhere it liked and she couldn't see it. "Y-you may. Not promising you anything, though."

"You don't have to promise me anything." He tried for it, slowly. "It's a bit awkward at this angle."

His fingers curled underneath her bloomer elastic, through the curly hair she now felt extremely self-conscious about. Did virginity have to be exclusive to penises, or could it be overcome by inexperienced hands? Did he *have* one? She couldn't think.

He left a wet kiss on her collarbone as he reached down, down. Aida copied what she'd read in books. She tilted her head back and spread open her legs. She let go a moan to show that she was enjoying it because she thought she was. She was hot. Her brain wasn't working.

His fingers curled up inside of her.

And her overworked heart stopped. She grabbed his arm. "Stop."

Immediately, his hand shot away. He almost knocked himself out. "Sorry."

She squeezed her thighs together to make the tingling go away. Kissing, she got. Touching, that was fine. Anything more was dangerous, foreign territory. "You don't have to apologize. I just don't want to do that again."

"I'm sorry. Fuck, I knew that was going too far. I should've waited. I'm sorry."

She claimed his lips. "Don't apologize. I command you."

"Oh, you're commanding me now?" He left a lighter kiss on her cheek. "Don't think I'd mind that."

"Is that what you're into? Should I change positions?" She lifted one leg over his knee. "That better?"

"A little bit." He sighed into her neck again. "I'm a little worked up right now."

"I mean, I can try and do something for you, if you'd like, if the threat of being found out doesn't trample your boner."

"Aida, please."

"I'm serious. Is that okay, by the way? I don't want to use words that might make you uncomfortable."

"I'm not sure." He kissed her chin, then left his lips there. "I was thinking," he said, "instead of she or he, how about we use what your future self keeps calling me?"

"She calls you 'they'."

He nodded. "Why don't we give that a try?"

"Okay."

"I know it sounds weird."

"It's not."

"It just sort of sticks right now."

"That's fine." She pressed into them. "It'll always be fine."

She awoke not on her own, but from something hitting her. A jolt, a stirring of darkness spilling from her head, and she had a hand over Lorian to protect them.

A bright light flooded the room. It took a few seconds for her to remember where they were and what they'd done instead of remembering all the places Lorian's hands had burned into her the previous night.

Lorian was sitting upright. It looked like they were about to escape but were waiting for Aida to wake.

A sword unsheathed itself from across the room. The Constable was standing at the top of the hidden staircase. The table had been thrown against the wall.

"There you are," he said, and took out a whistle from around his neck.

Aida covered her sensitive ears at its shrill tone. It must've reached all corners of Roma.

"Aida, go out the window!" Lorian warned. "Now!"

She tried, but she was more or less naked from her night with Lorian, and she was tangled in the blankets, and her head wasn't yet screwed on.

"Oh no, not after the months of trials you've put me through. I know you aren't those wretched future selves of yours. You can't escape me."

Aida grabbed her hidden knife and went to lash out at him, but from startling awake with the need to cover herself, her movements lagged, and the Constable easily knocked the knife out of her hands.

"Get off of her!" Lorian rammed their weight into him and disarmed him. "Aida, go!"

The Constable dove backwards and picked up his rapier. "Don't move!"

He got into a sparring stance, ready to kill two naked, un-armed people in bed, when he saw Lorian's naked chest. Once they realized what they'd done, Lorian clawed their way back to bed and covered their upper half.

The Constable dropped the sword he'd fought so hard to keep in his hands. It clattered to the floor like a saucepan until it stopped and the room was quiet.

He was staring slack-jawed at Lorian's tattoo.

"Lucia?" he breathed. "Is that you?"

Chapter 30: Forest Scuffle

She hadn't meant to fall asleep with Lorian. She'd wanted to stay up and guard them, but when they'd fallen asleep in her arms, crying and at the happiest she'd seen them, she couldn't help herself. She'd wanted to forget that their hateful world existed for one night.

She'd been right: Love was a monstrous choice to lose yourself in.

Lorian covered up their chest, but the Constable had finally caught on. After months of hunting down his time-traveller fugitive and beloved heir, he'd found both of them in the same place.

He tried to form the words. He kept backing away from them until he hit the desk he'd thrown to get to them. "I don't...understand," he finally said. "Why're you here?"

"I haven't done anything wrong," Lorian said.

"I thought..." His throat closed up at the last word. "We thought you were dead."

"Funny what a haircut and a corset can do to someone."

Someone shouted outside. A flurry of boots flooded into the cabin.

The Constable looked between the attic door and Lorian. He held out his hand. "Wait—"

Four officers came up with their rapiers drawn. Two went for the bed while two stood back and gasped at Lorian.

"Wait. *Wait*." The Constable picked up his rapier. "Tell me what's going on right now. Why're you...How did this happen?"

"What's going on?" one of the officers asked.

"Should we call for backup?"

"No. For the Gods' sakes, stand down." He pinched the bridge of his nose. "Do you have any idea what your mother has gone through because of this?"

"There hasn't been a day she hasn't crossed my mind," Lorian said.

The rest of the daft officers finally understood and lowered their weapons.

"This...must be dealt with by their Majesties," the Constable said. "We need to tell Rosalia—Her Majesty—and His Majesty, of course..." He closed his eyes for a three count, then came back to his true self. The emotions died in his glazed-over eyes. "The king asked me to take care of the girl." He jabbed a finger at Aida, bringing her into the picture. "You are returning back to your village in Bělico."

"*Excuse* me?" Aida asked.

"Her Royal Majesty The Queen put forth a decree saying she will not see you dead on her orders. His Majesty, on the other hand, said there was no use detaining a person who might have the ability to teleport freely."

Both Aida and Lorian held their tongue. She guessed that she had some power over her jumps—she went to Eve every time, the only timeline that mattered—but she couldn't jump willy nilly. She couldn't time how long she was in the past or where exactly she ended up. She kept that to herself.

"You...can't," Lorian said for her. "Her mother's—"

"Meanwhile, we'll bring Lucia back to the palace. Her mother needs to know that we found her alive."

"No!"

"We'll take my carriage," he told his officers. "We can't have this getting out to the public too soon."

"Understood," they said.

"I won't go," Lorian said. "I'll scream."

"Then they'll gag you."

"I'll fight."

"Then they'll bind you. You're returning home whether you like it or not, Your Highness. This game is over. You are a princess and you are meant to obey."

Aida slipped out of bed and went for her knife. As if either of them were going back home. She'd scream and fight for Lorian until they broke both of her legs and blinded her.

As she wielded her knife, an officer slammed her into the headboard and handcuffed her wrists.

"Get off of her!" Lorian kicked the man away, but the officers flipped them over and restrained them.

"Wait!" Lorian begged. "Please, at least let us change first. Give us some dignity."

The Constable considered this, like there was some humanity in those soulless eyes. "You have two minutes."

Aida didn't move. She felt like she'd landed on her hip wrong. It pulsed in pain, but she was far too proud and pissed off to say anything. She could *not* go back home. She would rather die.

She looked to the floor, holding herself up with her cane. Before Lorian, she *would've* rather died. She'd done everything to escape that household, she'd spent all of her earnings on that boat to Roma for a chance to restart.

But now, she *had* Lorian. And Missus and Mi'Sharma. Onti and Chrissie, people who liked her and protected her and gave her a home and real, familial love. And she needed to find out the last pieces of Eve's life, and she needed to kick Future Aida's ass for letting all this happen to her. This wasn't her ending.

As Lorian shamelessly got dressed in front of the men meant to serve them, Aida focused on the swirling patterns in the floorboards. They either stretched out to the walls or ended in dark knots like how scientists thought the universe looked. With how many knots were in this room, she envisioned hundreds of universes interconnected.

The Constable walked up to her. She felt a hand come close. "Are you alright?"

Aida gave him the finger. "Get fucked," she said, and jumped into time.

She dropped into snow by the lake. Two officer carriages were parked nearby. The royal horses nibbled on what grass they could find.

She looked behind her to the log cabin still in sight. She could outline Lorian's blond hair from the attic window. They were staring at where Aida had been not a moment prior.

She'd done it. She'd willed a jump to occur. Back at the palace, she'd tried a hundred times to jump. It was why she hadn't let go of Lorian's hand in case she was able to jump them back ten minutes in the future, or the past, but she would've seen herself if that'd happened.

How had she done it? She'd been thinking of universes.

She touched her face, making sure she'd made the jump in one piece, before staggering to her feet and dusting off her undergarments. Book it or not. Get a head start into the woods or go back for Lorian.

Lorian spotted her. It alerted the other officers to the window, then the Constable. He dismissed them downstairs on a mute order.

Lorian shoved him aside and threw open the window. "Run, Aida! Go!"

Her feet started moving before her brain told them to stop. She didn't want to abandon them, but she couldn't get caught. Lorian wouldn't forgive themselves.

She heard the Constable order her to stop. She knew it was a fruitless endeavor to run, but it felt good knowing she was giving the man grief. Retribution for ruining her life, the ass.

His boots came in closer, faster, two steps for every one of Aida's. She wondered if her cane was making a difference, then remembered its potential.

Stopping mid-run, she swept the Constable's feet with her cane, and the two of them went down in the snow.

They struggled for better leverage, Aida kicking, the Constable grabbing. He refused to pull on her hair or punch her, but Aida wasn't as kind. She hit, scratched, bit. She'd continue to fight until her cane snapped in two.

"Stop it!" The Constable tried sitting on her so she'd quit squirming. "Stop fighting me!"

"Fuck you! Fuck you and the crown!" She took the end of her cane and whacked the Constable in the face. The impact hit harder than she expected and flung his head backwards.

"Oh, shit—"

Without looking, the Constable flipped Aida to her stomach, and a ready officer handcuffed her wrists behind her back. The metal pinched her skin and made her squeak in pain.

"We're done," the Constable panted, and stole away her cane. "We're done."

"Where're we going?" she asked.

To her surprise, they didn't escort her back to the cabin. The Constable brought her into a clearing where his carriage was parked. He'd washed the side she'd egged without remorse.

Two officers opened the side doors for her and the Constable. The horses shuffled in place, ready for travel. Aida did the same but kicked at the door and wheels.

"Knock it off!" the Constable shouted, and shoved her into the back seat, bracing himself for the next hour they'd be blessed with each other's company.

Aida glared him down as the carriage rode over the snow. Their fight had ripped up his elbows and golden aiguillettes. Her cane whack had left a bruise above his temple, but he didn't care for it. He took out a quill and pad of parchment and began writing something down.

Aida willed herself to jump again, but her mind was too full. She needed a way to escape not only this carriage but the Constable and his goons for a third time while her hands were bound.

The Constable flipped a page of his parchment. "I see you've acquired that hideous glare from Lucia. I thought she'd outgrown it by now."

"That's not their name."

He looked up.

"They go by Lorian now, and they ain't gonna be a princess. No matter how many crowns or gowns you make them wear after this, they're going to tear all of it off because they don't want that life anymore." She clicked her tongue. "One of the many reasons they left was to get that through your heads. Can't believe it didn't stick."

The Constable's upper lip curled. "How was I supposed to know that?"

"Was the name change, wardrobe change, and haircut not dead giveaways?" She squinted out the window. "Are you seriously taking me back to Bělico? Now?"

"His Majesty commanded it. He said that taking you back home and stripping away your rights to enter Roma again would suffice for now."

"Take away my—?" She laughed bitterly. "As if you don't do that every damn day! You work for a man who's thrown away everything I've worked for to be recognized. A scholarship, gone! My residency, gone! For what? Because of a circle on my forehead? How pathetic."

"I don't have the power to change that."

"But you enforce it. You have the chance to change the fate of people like me but you don't. You're as bad as he is."

"If it were up to me..." He sighed. "Forget it."

"There! See? If you want to help us, fucking *do* something about it. Don't be a watchdog for a man who doesn't respect you or your opinions."

"My opinions don't matter in the course of my job. I have been with the crown for more than twenty-five years. I try my damndest to keep Roma safe while keeping my oaths to Their Majesties."

"Fuck the king and queen."

The Constable's jaw dropped. "How dare you?"

"Oh, shut up. The queen has no spine and the king hits his children. Lorian's told me everything, so don't try to deny it."

The Constable set down his paperwork. "Don't talk to me about the hardships Lucia and Beatrice have faced in their childhood. I was there. I watched them grow up and I was there to comfort them when they were struck. Do you think I enjoy children suffering? Don't you think that if I had the slightest bit of power in those walls, I wouldn't be fighting day and night for their protection? I had to *sit* there and watch, knowing that if I ever stood up for them, I would be sentenced to the gallows for speaking out of turn."

He squared out his shoulders. "I love those children with all my heart. Don't you dare insinuate anything else."

"I didn't insinuate that you didn't love them, I said the way the king treats them is the same way my stepmother treats me. They're abusive and cruel, and delivering us back to them is allowing the cruelty to continue."

Keeping her gaze for as long as possible, the Constable reached for his reports and thumbed through his notes. "I have no records of abuse in your family."

"Nobody cared enough to check up on me. I was adopted off the streets and treated like a slave until I got accepted into my dream school. You have no idea how happy I was the day I got that letter. Then you came along and took it all away based on a prejudiced ruling that wasn't even fair to begin with."

He tried reading through his papers again, then threw back his head and began unbuttoning his jacket.

Aida pushed back. "What're you doing?"

"I can't hold a conversation with you looking like this." He got up and placed it around her shoulders.

She went to kick him in the balls when she saw the tenderness in his mannish hands, the way his mustache looked this close up. He smelled of coffee and evergreen pine. Throw a bit of manure underneath his fingernails and he would've reminded her of what a father was supposed to be.

She let him place it around her shoulders and sit back down without hurting him, hating herself for this moment of weakness. From her night with Lorian to running for her life to thinking about the very real threat of going home to making her first controlled jump. Her mind was scrambled.

But it wasn't. It was just working in overdrive every minute of every day. She hadn't known that the sense to control a jump was always inside of her. She assumed she'd have to unlock a hidden path and decode an unsolvable riddle, but that's not how the world worked. Things happened gradually like how one fell in love: You didn't know it was happening until suddenly a person became *your* person and everything they did tasted like effortless magic on your tongue.

The Constable asked her something, but her ears were clogged. Doing the only thing she could do, she struck out her good leg, hitting him in the shin and making the needed connection to take him away with her.

Where, she had no idea. She could only control *if* she jumped, not where or when. Yet.

The two of them disappeared a second later into a timeline unknown.

Chapter 31: Home

Lorian had given one officer a black eye and broke another's pinkie before they had the sense to blind and gag them.

"Where's Aida?" they demanded. "Please, I need to see— Let me see her!"

They transported Lorian out of the cabin into a nearby carriage. They thought two officers in the backseats would be enough to contain them. Lorian relished in proving them wrong.

"Restrain her!" called the driver.

"We did!"

"Give her back!" Lorian yelled through the gag, and their head was shoved down.

When their carriage ride ended, Lorian's neck was sore from desperately fighting against the officer's hand on their neck.

Ducks quacked upon their arrival. It was the first clue that they'd been dragged back to the palace. In the back of the palace near the servants' entrance was where they kept the palace ducks, geese, chickens, and roosters. Without the means to walk on their own, Lorian announced they were back home by shattering a vase with their foot.

"So much for the art of surprise," one pissed officer said, and Lorian responded by degrading their mothers.

The officers led Lorian into a spacious room. Once the door was locked and Lorian pulled off their blindfold, they were struck with god-awful familiarity.

Their bedroom. The paintings they'd torn had been replaced with bolder, gaudier artwork. The bed had been shifted and the locks had been changed. The windows now had bars incarcerating them like they were a criminal.

Nothing smelled like them. Nothing smelled like home.

"Fuck!" they shouted, and kicked the door handle. The door had been replaced multiple times throughout their childhood. This one hardly dented. "Let me out! You can't keep me here!"

Nobody answered them.

"Please!" they begged. "You can't—I can't be here! I can't!"

Nothing but the silence in this godforsaken palace responded.

They pulled at their hair. It was over. In a few minutes or hours, their father would come in and tear out the chapters they'd written with Aida. He'd chain them up—literally or figuratively, it didn't matter—and their signature would be forged to marry Prince Zaahir. They'd be sent on a boat and locked in another room that wouldn't smell like them, and then...

They kept kicking.

"Enough!" the officer on Lorian Watch said through the door.

"Let me out! I can't breathe!" And they couldn't. This world wasn't ready for them and they couldn't father children because if they did, if they couldn't be with Aida...

"Your mother and father are in a meeting. They'll be in to see you shortly."

Too busy. Too busy to care for their child screaming in need. It wasn't unexpected, just something they longed to be different: the definition of "insanity."

Lorian held back their tears as they paced in circles. They wondered if their parents would even see them as their child anymore. Maybe their mother, but a look from their father would've changed her mind. Their father likely only saw them as a pawn to be wed off, not a daughter, or son, or whatever they were now.

In his eyes, they'd always be nothing.

The rays of Sun that managed to stream through the barred windows counted down Lorian's last hours of freedom. The meeting must've been running long. Aida would've been on the last boat to Bělico by now, if she hadn't done anything too illegal to land her in the gallows.

Whoever had reset their bedroom to better appease their father hadn't found Lorian's hidden stash of Nectar bottles. They kept them hidden underneath their closet floorboards. They'd hidden notes here when they were a child, secret presents of animal bones wrapped in leaves to give Missus Sharma. Next was knives they'd steal from downstairs, and then cigarettes and Nectar onwards.

They emptied their stash once night came.

They took a greedy swig from their last bottle. The thick ambrosia burned going down. Their parents must've known the truth by now, that Lorian was Lucia and their runaway princess had become a time-traveller's assistant in crime. They wondered what Beatrice had said to them, if she'd said anything at all. Had she kept their identity a secret this whole time?

They took another swig. The officer outside their room was mysteriously quiet this evening. They didn't speak to anyone in the hall and didn't answer Lorian's questions pertaining to Aida. Was she safe? Had she fought harder than Lorian to escape?

Lorian fell out of bed and crawled to the door. "I wanna go to the clock tower," they slurred. "I can't think straight."

The officer said nothing.

"You can't keep me here! I've broken out before, I'll break out again. I'll—" They faced the windows. "I'll slam my head in so hard—"

"Your Highness, you mustn't say such things."

"Don't call me that!" they shouted. "That's not me."

Their head swayed. Wasn't it, though? If they were to marry Zaahir, becoming the princess of Aldaí *and* princess of...

They returned to bed. They didn't want the responsibility of ruling a kingdom right now. They didn't want *any* of this. What they *wanted* was Aida and what they *needed* was her guidance to get them the fuck out of here.

They were nothing without Aida. She inspired them to be better and without her, Lorian was a selfish, bratty princess who couldn't do what they were told. They needed to give in to the fact that they wouldn't see Aida again, or if they did, it would be her future self that'd likely destroy more of their future.

A knock rapped on their door. Lorian cursed them out.

The door unlocked with a key.

Zaahir nodded to the officer outside Lorian's bedroom and entered with Kadar tailing behind his robes.

Lorian lifted their legs onto their bed. "What, is this beautiful wedding finally on? Are you here to ravage me?"

Zaahir pressed a finger to his lips until he and Kadar were out of earshot from the door. He walked around Lorian's discarded bottles. He set one on their nightstand. "Are you alright?"

"Positively suicidal."

"You shouldn't be drinking. Your father wishes to speak with you tonight."

"Oh, really? I had no idea."

"Lorian, please, stay with me a moment."

"According to our parents, we're to stay together for the rest of our lives."

Zaahir picked up another bottle of Nectar. "You must sober up. I cannot stress this enough. I know you're panicking. This past month with your father has been horrendous and I do not know how you survived a quarter of a century with him." He looked nervously at the door as if he was listening in. He drew closer to Lorian. Lorian scooted back.

Zaahir looked up, confused by everything Lorian was, then cursed in Aldaían. "Lorian—Let me be clear: I have absolutely no interest in pursuing you in any romantic or nuptial way, and despite what you may think of me and what I'm going to suggest, I am not interested in this fifteen-year-long engagement our parents have molded around us, okay?"

Lorian went cross-eyed at his long speech, then came back when he stopped talking. "You don't wanna marry me?"

"I never have, and I believe you've shown your distaste in the idea in more ways than one."

"My Liege." Kadar leaned in to their conversation. "We need to hurry."

"How come you don't wanna marry me?" Lorian asked. "I thought you wanted to."

"Was it not clear that I'm already committed to someone? Haven't I told you?"

"You're in *love*?"

"Lorian—"

"But are you? Are you?"

"Yes, Lorian, I'm in love with Kadar here. You've met him before, he's a wonderful man."

Lorian looked to his quiet knight. They waved. Kadar waved back.

Then Lorian jolted. "Wait! If *you're* in love with him and *I'm* in love with Aida, then why in the Gods' names are we still engaged? What's the point if we don't want each other?"

"Because we have obligations."

"To whom? To the people who will soon be under *our* ruling?"

"There're rules, Lorian, but listen to me."

They did, now knowing that this secret midnight meeting didn't have a nefarious undertone to it.

"If we can make this meeting with the king work, you and I can gain some advantage against him and end this."

"What's your plan?"

"Your father just got out of talking with his council and he's *very* cross. All this time, I've been trying to please him and make him respect me as a young heir, but he only sees me as a child trying on my mother's shoes. Your sister has been helping me, but we need you to not rustle any more feathers to get some sense into him."

"I have rustled no feathers."

"You—"

"I'm joking. I'll be good."

"Good, because your father sent me up here to get you. He wants to speak with you now."

Two officers, along with Kadar, escorted them to their father's meeting room. Given that the country had just recaptured their lost heir, the halls were exceptionally barren. The lights were lit low. The officers said nothing. Lorian wondered if they'd been ordered not to pry. Their father controlled everything, even the people's thoughts.

"Now, once you meet with your mother and father and they begin asking you questions," Zaahir said, "I'll take over most of the talking. Your mother values my viewpoints and your father might understand our situation through a sober thought."

"I'll sober up. I was just upset. Mother and Father haven't even visited me."

"I'm sure they're busy tracking down those future selves. You haven't a clue what their next ploy is, do you?"

"No. That's the thing with future selves, we're always gonna be ten paces behind them."

"I figured."

"Do you know anything about Aida?" they asked hopefully. "Do you know where she is?"

"Did you hear about their carriage?"

The implication of that question was a cold bucket of water over their head. "What happened to her?"

"They don't know. The driver heard a jump from inside the carriage and found both Aida and the Constable missing. It seems they both travelled together."

Lorian sighed in relief. She'd bought herself some time *and* had gotten Carmine off of their back. Truly a wonder, that girl.

"We'll get through this," Zaahir said, "you and I, and Kadar and your sister. Despite everything that's happened, she still loves you dearly."

Lorian went to argue that last point. For every reconciliation they had, two fights were birthed from it. Hair pulling, screaming matches. They'd once injured a maid who'd tried to pull them apart. That was back when they could still punch each other and not send waves of unrest throughout multiple kingdoms.

They peered over to Kadar, who'd been holding his tongue like a true Aldaían knight. "When did this happen? You and Kadar?"

Zaahir smiled. "Do you remember when we first met? We were still too young to understand what was going on with our arranged marriage, but I was told to be courteous and chivalrous to you, to act like the prince I read about in fairy tales. When I memorized what I needed to say and asked for your hand, your little, six-year-old hand, I believe you told me, 'Why in your right mind would I ever want to marry you, you...' I believe you called me a 'pompous shithead'."

The officers gave in and turned their heads to such outlandish talk between royals.

Lorian laughed. "Did I really say that to you?"

"Yes. Our parents were furious, especially your father."

"I'd believe it. I was so against the thought of marrying someone I didn't know, I'd make myself throw up before meeting you. I tried everything to get out of it. It doesn't seem I've matured past that."

"Nothing of the sort. Despite only meeting you a handful of times, you inspired me."

"I *inspired* you?"

"Greatly. You were the first girl—" He looked to Lorian.

"'They' is good for me right now."

"Of course. My apologies. So, when I met you, I hadn't known children could deviate from the norm like that. In Aldaí, while same-sex couples aren't discouraged, royal heirs are expected to continue the royal line to keep the family tree pure. We were expected to conceive a child with a favorable suitor already picked out for us. But then I met you and heard the way you acted as either a boy or a girl."

"Sometimes neither."

"That as well. I hadn't been raised with such nuanced interpretations of gender and sexuality. After that, I began exploring my...options." He took Kadar's hand, which Kadar shyly reciprocated. "While I'm still expected to have heirs, I'm fully allowed to keep Kadar in my heart. And right now, I *only* want him in my heart."

All the hesitation Lorian had with Zaahir completely vanished. Before tonight, Lorian saw him as this pristine rule-follower from Aldaí. Now, he felt more like a true friend, an ally.

They turned the corner to a short hallway Lorian knew well. It had only one room next to a row of windows that overlooked the private gardens. Whenever Lorian acted out, their father would bring them here and cane them. Even now, hearing a man yell made them flinch.

Lorian felt like vomiting again. Three officers were outside the door, signaling how many people of importance were in that room.

"It'll be okay," Zaahir whispered, and the officers knocked on the door for them.

Someone talking in the room stopped.

"You may enter."

Lorian locked onto their mother first, for when they came in, she bolted upright, hair and dress bouncing, a hand over her chest.

Lorian grabbed her arms to keep her from falling. She was crying, something that hurt no matter what led to it. Her hair looked greyer, her features more pronounced like a detailed portrait.

"Oh, my love," she cried. "I'm so happy you're here."

Lorian massaged her back. *She* smelled like home. Her long face, her long, beautiful hair that reached the floor, it was comforting, despite the harsh memories connected to her.

Their father was still sitting with two of his advisors. Their sister was on a couch by herself, hands folded on her lap. She did sit up when Lorian entered but didn't speak.

Their father did instead. "Rosalia."

Their mother pulled back from Lorian and bowed.

Zaahir and Kadar bowed to the room. "Thank you for having us so late in the evening," Zaahir said.

Their father motioned at the empty couch in front of him.

Lorian refused at first, then remembered the plan and sat.

They all sat in a circle, yet nobody made eye contact with each other. The quietness settled over them like a poisonous gas waiting to be inhaled.

Lorian tried keeping still like their mother. They knew this silence before the storm. They knew this side of their father.

Zaahir cleared his throat. "As we promised," he started, "I've spoken with Lucia in detail about the events—"

"What will it take?"

They all looked up to Lorian's father, who was now leaning forwards, his fingers interlocked in thought.

"What will it take," he repeated, "to put this behind us?" He gestured to Lorian's outfit like he was pointing out something tangible. "These...outfits, and the names you're choosing to go by. If that's what you want, you can have it. If it means keeping you here with us, I'll allow this 'Lorian' in my palace."

The tiniest hope flickered in Lorian's heart. It sounded ridiculous, that name on his lips.

She needed to find his ulterior motive. That's how it worked in these meetings. He hunted for something to gain from every conversation. From asking for his mother's hand in marriage to his constant questions about Aldaí's resources and their own prince. He just *wanted*, like a sink hole in a field of loose sand.

"That's what you want, is it not?" their father repeated. "That's why you left. That's why you've been acting out ever since you were born. Well, now you have it."

Zaahir faked a smile that Lorian was convinced young heirs needed to master to stay afloat. "What...fantastic news, Your Majesty. That's incredibly thoughtful of you."

Lorian reevaluated the room. Their mother had taken out a fan and was hiding her mouth. Beatrice was holding something back. Their father's eyes were as cold as the Bělican mountains.

Lorian gulped. "In exchange?"

Their father continued holding their gaze. They didn't know how Aida could do this and not feel intimidated by the other person.

"In exchange for what you promised us when the Gods bequeathed us with two girls."

That sick feeling churned again in Lorian's stomach.

"No matter how many tantrums you throw, you are still engaged to Prince Zaahir, and I expect you to bear the children expected of you."

Zaahir's composure cracked. "Your Majesty, perhaps we should—"

"Silence," he snapped, and Zaahir went still.

"You two are to abide by the rules of our world. What you're called by doesn't matter in the case of formal union. You are the royal successor to Roma. In three days' time, you will marry Prince Zaahir, after which you will consummate and make the marriage official. Until then, you'll be kept under watch in your room until the ceremony begins."

The simplicity of this fake family reunion fractured and bled out into the room.

"Dear," their mother said. "This isn't what you—"

"I told you that there's nothing more to discuss."

"But I—"

"Listen to me!" their father roared, and their mother sobbed into her fan. "This is over. Pretend to be anything you desire, Lorian, but you are a royal child, first and foremost,

366

and in three days, you will be married to Prince Zaahir and you will fulfill what is expected of you."

"Wait!" Lorian stood up for themselves, their knees knocking into the coffee table. "Father, please, give me a chance to speak. I know you expect a lot from me."

"Do I, after every single time I've given you what you want? I gave you your own clothes, I let you do so much that my father would've killed me for, and every day you insist on making a fool out of our family."

Their confidence wavered. "I-I know, but believe me when I say that this isn't about me. Aida, the real one, the younger one, knows things. About the past," they pressed, trying to make themselves sound urgent and intelligent and failing at both. Gods, why had they drunk so much? "She's been to the past. She's met Eve."

Their father motioned for his wife's men.

"No!" They backed away from the approaching threat. "Please, we've seen her. Beatrice and Zaahir, they've both seen her."

Beatrice and Zaahir tensed, unsure of when or if to speak up on the burial of a 1,200-year-old queen.

"There's so much Aida needs to tell you," they continued. "It's why we came yesterday to talk, but you attacked us without so much as asking why we were there."

"Your future selves—"

"Fuck our future selves!" Lorian shouted. "They aren't us! Not now! I'm here, and I need you to hear me out for once."

"Wait until you're sober. I can smell the honey on your breath from here."

"Father, I think you should listen to them," Beatrice said, but their father held up a hand, silencing everyone in the room.

"Keep her in her room for the time being," he ordered. "I need to begin organizing the guest list and cooks. Do not let her out until the eve of the ceremony. I don't need her causing another mess like last time."

"Father!"

The officers grabbed at them, at their one chance to persuade their father to listen to them not as an heir or even his child, but as a person who needed their voice heard.

The double doors shut before they got another word in.

Chapter 32: En Tempore Rose

Thank the Gods she brought the Constable into the past with her. He made a great cushion to soften her fall.

She rolled off of him. Her brain was pounding against her eyes. Usually, the jump hurt when she came *back*, not when she first landed. This pain wasn't anything compared to what she'd dealt with that year, but her brain hurt, and it wasn't because she'd travelled without her glasses. She sunk her shoulder into the cobblestone until she could focus on something in front of her: the Colosseum.

They were in its monolithic shadow, hidden from the summer Sun and in the Colosseum Plaza. Street performers juggled for passerbys while stores sold their wares. There were as many people out today as there had been when she'd been here with Lorian, but there weren't nearly as many officers. People had laid out rugs and set up tents in makeshift aisles to sell everything from cheese to swords.

"It's a street market," Aida said.

"What?" The Constable started refolding his white buttondown and collar. He, like Aida, had made the jump fully clothed. "Where are we? *When* are we? Where did you take us?"

"I don't know. I just felt a jump coming on and happened to touch you when I did it."

"You *kicked* at me, you did it entirely on purpose!"

"Look, I can sometimes control it. It's complicated. I'm learning as fast as you are."

"Well, this was a poorly thought-out decision on your part. You should learn to be more thoughtful when it comes to your powers. You don't know what effect it has on people who don't normally do this."

"Well, I don't *normally* do this, so I don't know unless it happens. And don't call me stupid."

"I didn't."

"You implied it. I might be a Visatorre, but that doesn't mean I'm stupid off the bat."

"I didn't—Look, I know you're in a precarious situation at the moment, but that doesn't give you the right to talk to me like this. I am a constable, the right-hand man to the queen."

"Oh, wow. That totally changes my opinion of you."

"Look—"

"I *am*." She tried sitting up. Her hands were still handcuffed behind her. "I *have* been for twenty-four goddamn years. That king you love so much hasn't done shit for either me *or* Lorian, nor has the queen. You attacked us and separated us when we have nothing to do with our future selves. You called Lorian by their old name, you tackled me to the ground and handcuffed me. So excuse me if I don't think highly of you, because from where I stand, you're just a reminder of all the people in my life who've hurt me for the sole reason that I have this fucking mark on my head."

Her headache panged so hard that she doubled over. All she wanted to do was yell at this stupid man for everything that angered her. His stupid rhetoric, his stupid mustache. She had half a mind to step on his foot just because she could.

The Constable reached out to her.

"Don't touch me," she snapped.

"Stop it. I'm taking off your handcuffs."

Aida grinded her cheek against the hot pavement.

The Constable had his key out and quickly detached the metal cuffs from her wrists. "Are you alright?"

"Stop asking me that. If I were as shitty as you, I'd leave you here for the rest of time. Luckily, I'm a Goddess, the best person in the world." She headed towards the Colosseum. Maybe she could catch an opera and ride out this unfortunate timeline in peace.

"Wait." He jogged up behind her. He looked so vulnerable without his jacket. No way was Aida returning it. That and his rapier were hers and Lorian's.

"I apologize for my previous actions against you. I was only working underneath His Majesty's orders, so it wasn't as though I could go against—"

"Oh, fuck off. Don't try sucking up to me now just because I'm your ticket outta here. Eat dirt."

He stayed quiet but continued following her.

Nobody looked their way, and when Aida tried waving at someone to get their attention, they looked right through her. Great how her time powers continued to make no sense. She relaxed, though, knowing that she could safely ride out her frustrations with only the Constable as her witness.

She walked up the Colosseum steps. The front doors were closed, but the advertisement board detailed an upcoming show. The posters were painted dark with the motifs of roses and clocks and bordered by a red, scaly tail.

Aida read the title of the opera and bit her lip. *En Tempore Rose.*

Finally, the one good thing to happen to her during a jump. Even with the Constable stuck here, at least she could be backstage in the opera of her dreams.

A crowd of highly dignified people took their time coming up the steps. One woman carried a parasol. Every man was dressed in their formal reds and blacks.

A little Visatorre girl of eight or nine was with them. She was dressed in a plain, brown dress and had her hair done in two outrageous braids she must've done herself. Her glasses were too big for her face and kept falling off of her little button nose, and she had a bandage over her skinned elbow.

Aida's heart skipped a beat, but not in a gentle, giddy sort of way. She was looking into a mirror nearly two decades old, her little self.

She, with wiser hindsight, searched the crowds for her mother. This must've been when she and her family had come to Roma City to sell their meat and hides. If her mother found Little Aida getting into trouble...

Little Aida was smart. She'd been waiting for a family of wealth to come by. When she had her targets, she ran up against their dresses. She even maneuvered around the ladies' dresses so she wasn't seen by officers. She had a plan.

The officers preemptively opened the doors for such a large group. As they exchanged tickets, Little Aida tiptoed her way into the Colosseum.

Aida lost her voice. She couldn't warn the little one about how much trouble she'd be in for this. She didn't remember when, but she remembered the beatings that followed. The opera, was it ever worth it?

"That girl looked like you," the Constable said. "Are we meant to follow her? Is this how time travel works?"

She needed to run away. Now. Her mother. She needed to save herself before it was too late.

The Constable got bumped into the crowd and was taken in like a bobber against the current. "Wait. I-I can't stop myself—Hey!"

She was so stupid. She was a child lost in dreams, but she should've known better.

The officers began closing the double doors. The Constable tried fighting his way back out. He called for Aida.

She knew the consequences.

The doors locked shut, separating them.

The direness of her actions hit seconds too late. She could barely control her jumps. If she were to accidentally jump back into the present, the Constable would be trapped here forever and, despite her hatred for him, she couldn't leave him here to die.

"Wait." She tried for the door. "Hey, Carmine!"

He didn't answer. The doors were too thick, she couldn't even hear the sound of the possible hundreds of people gathering for the performance.

Panicking, she ran down the steps and around the perimeter of the Colosseum, déjà vu guiding her. She came up to the side entrance where Frederico had once entered a millennium ago. A carriage was parked by the tree line, and bored officers were playing cards on the steps. Their swords were unfastened from their belts. One even had his boots off, much to the dismay of his other comrades. They were poking fun at him for the smell.

"Should be over soon," one of them said. "Intermission's coming."

"They see the opera so often, I'm surprised they don't have a personal performance at the palace."

Aida eavesdropped from behind a column.

"Wouldn't be the theatre if there wasn't an audience."

"Maybe you should play the princess, then!" one officer jeered, and tossed his shoes at the officer.

Aida ducked her head through the open door into the Colosseum.

A bleakness gnawed into her bones as she travelled deeper into the building. It was so empty, and the hallways were cleaner than they had been during Eve's time. Paintings were hung up on the stone walls, and she followed a red carpet instead of puddles of condensation and blood. Thousands of people had been carted down these halls to their deaths, and there were paintings of the royal family at each intersection.

She stopped in one. Sconces were lit for her, but she felt darkness crawling up her legs towards her heart. Beneath her feet lay the bones of families she could've saved, of Eve, decaying, her potential being eaten by worms.

Someone ran down the dark hall for her. An officer, her mother, Eve, a corpse ready to exact revenge.

The Constable almost knocked her down. "Good Gods, where've you been?" he asked, exasperated. "No one in this damn building can see me. It's like I'm invisible to them."

Aida washed her face of emotion. The dust down here was making her eyes water. "That's because you *are* invisible. Aren't you used to this from my future self?"

"She never brought me back in time. She always brought me around in the present." He shivered. "Is this how it is when you travel back? This...cold? I feel like a ghost."

"Consider yourself lucky that you're not stark naked and going to jump back with a bloody nose or broken spine."

"Gods, you make me out like a monster. It's not like I take pleasure in the fact that Visatorre suffer from their jumps."

"Sure." She started walking.

He followed. "Are you alright?"

"Splendid."

"Because you seemed afraid of coming here. Do you have memories of this place?"

"You'd be afraid too if you were a Visatorre."

"What does that mean?"

"Uh, it means that hundreds of thousands of Visatorre are buried underneath our feet due to your boss' kin. Are you that daft about the history of your own country?"

They continued walking in silence towards what she believed to be the main arena. The walls vibrated from the sound outside. They were getting close to the center.

"I'm not daft," he finally said.

She was too upset to speak with him. She was too close to tears.

"Will you stop walking so fast? We shouldn't stay so far apart."

Aida continued ahead.

"If I can do anything to make things—"

"Gods, shut up!" she shouted. "You're not gonna make things better, so stop trying! You fucked up with me and you fucked up with Lorian, and no amount of sorries are gonna fix what you ruined."

He opened his mouth to protest her, then closed it and chewed on his inner cheek. He actually looked regretful. She didn't know if that was a gain for her.

Why was she so nervous about hurting his feelings? She should've left him in the past for a few years before even thinking about saving him. He was the enemy.

The Constable stopped following her. He went for his rapier as he looked behind and above him. His eyes were wide.

"What?" Aida asked.

"What day is it?" He ran up ahead and peered around the corner, then checked the next. "The date, what's the date?"

"Uh, like, fifteen years ago? I don't know. What's with you?"

"Shit," he cursed. "Is there any way to change time?" he asked urgently. "Can you do it? Can you change things that happen now so they don't happen in the future?"

"Uh, I don't think so any—"

And he left.

"'Ey!" She gave chase. "I was talking to you!"

He didn't stop. It looked like he somewhat knew where he was going, double-taking each intersection before choosing the right or wrong path. Wherever he was going, they were moving farther away from the thrumming of the theatre.

"What's wrong?" Aida called out.

She first heard a girl, then a girl crying, or pretending not to, covering her mouth so as not to be so blatant about her pain. Aida first thought it was her little self, but this person sounded more mature with her sorrow.

Turning their last corner, Aida bumped into her frozen Constable. They were at a dead end. Two young people sat on a bench beneath a painting of a Roman field, holding each other close.

Young Carmine looked better without his full mustache. He seemed to be growing it out, but it wasn't doing him any favors to look older than what he was. His hair was longer, too, tied in a ponytail that ran down his back, and he wore an officer uniform without any honorary medals.

The girl he was with had the longest hair Aida had ever seen. It hit the bench and flowed down to her high heels. It—she—looked like royalty.

Aida's Constable touched his heart in reverence.

"Oh, shit," Aida said, realizing a second too late what they'd stumbled into.

Young Carmine took out a handkerchief and patted Young Queen Rosalia's cheek. She had a bruise forming on her delicate wrist. It swelled purple and blue from injury.

"It's nothing, really," Young Rosalia whispered. "We should get back."

"You needn't worry about Durante right now. I'll take care of him." Young Carmine wrapped the handkerchief around her wrist. "Does that feel any better?"

"It does, yes. You're too kind to me, Carmello. I can't ever repay you for how much you care for me."

"When have I ever stopped, Your Highness?"

She chuckled. "That title no longer applies to me."

"It does when I'm with you."

Real Carmine, Aida's Carmine, broke from his spell. "W-we need to leave, now."

"Uh, no?" Aida said. "What's going on here?"

He only shook his head, breathless from this secret being exposed. He still hadn't looked away from the queen.

Young Rosalia flinched from a pulse of pain. Both Real Carmine and Young Carmine flinched as well, but his younger self came to her rescue. He placed the gentlest kiss against her wrist, then, adding to his crimes against the crown, left a sensual trail of kisses up and down her fingers. Around her palm, the underside of her wrist. It made everyone in the room blush.

"I don't know why he was so angry with me," Young Rosalia said, not addressing his affection. "I tried so hard to keep everyone happy this morning, but the moment I take a second for myself is when he grabs at me and says I'm a neglectful mother."

"I should've been there to intervene."

"You were busy with Bea and Lucia. I don't fault you for not being in two places at once."

Turning over Rosalia's hand, Young Carmine licked the center of her wrist.

"Carmello." Young Rosalia looked around the hall. "We can't. This isn't like back in my study."

"Rosie, I can't see you getting hurt by him any longer."

"It's not that bad."

"Oh, no more of that, please." He stroked the underside of her chin. "Have you sought the option of divorce? I've done the research. If he's abusing you and you are the leading monarch—"

She was already shaking her head. "The public's already polarized from my fragility. If I go through with a divorce, they'll see me as weak. My advisors warned me about this. And I can't do that to poor Lucia and Beatrice, they're already going through so much right now. This is fine." She held him with her good hand. "*This* is all I need."

Young Carmine played with the hair behind her ear. He brought her in closer. She fluttered her eyes closed.

Aida's Constable physically pushed her and himself away. "Hey!"

"I can't do this," he muttered to himself. "We need to leave."

Aida tried to stop, but he was stronger than her. Turning her head, she caught the couple hand in hand, their faces close enough to kiss.

She sped up to walk side by side with the Constable. She'd never seen a love displayed so softly before. Not even Eve held Queen Julia with as much care. Figuring this was the best she could give him, she said, "I ain't gonna squeal about what I just saw."

He lowered his head in shame.

"I won't," she promised. "What you do behind closed doors is not my business."

"I...I can't find a way to justify what we saw."

"She's your queen," she said with a shrug, "and she's gorgeous. I get it. But, Gods, if the king found out you were fadoodling his wife, he'd hang you so fast."

"Please, stop," he begged. "I know. Just...don't tell Lorian. I want her—them—to trust me, and if they find out about this, it'll damage our relationship more."

Aida studied his pleading, embarrassed face. His love life, no matter how messy, was at the bottom of the fucking list of things she needed to care about.

"Please, don't see me in a bad light," he then said. "I'm truly trying to do what's best for my country, and I don't want to doom it like some people because everyone I love is in that palace."

"Hold on a second, do you think *I'm* trying to doom Roma?" Aida asked.

"If I'm to go off of what your future self's been planning, how could I not? She's given me no hints to her plans, just that she revels in making a fool out of me. And that she's planning big things for you, and that she's excited about what's to come, whatever that means. I try to ignore her when she speaks.

"I saw your grades at Durante Academy," he continued, "and all the hard work you're putting into this mission of yours. You would make a fantastic historian."

Another piece of dust flew into Aida's eye, making her blink too hard. "Then why did you take it away from me?"

"I had my orders."

"So I was right. I was only taken off of the scholarship because of who I was, not because my grades were lacking or my determination was misplaced."

"I can't speak on what His Majesty thinks is right."

"You can certainly tell what your girlfriend thinks about it. She's against it as much as you are, isn't she? Even more so? But you're so afraid of Durante abusing you that you comply with his every demand."

"You don't know him."

"I'm not saying I do, I'm saying that I feel sorry for you and want to see things change. I want Lorian to be happy and it all starts with you and her and Durante. You..." She readied herself. "You're a good person, aren't you, Carmine? Deep down, you don't want this."

"I'm saying that I want to see the royal family happy. I've never seen Lorian so protective over anyone but you. And knowing they're becoming that future self, I can't describe it, but they're filled with purpose. Back in the palace, they'd stay in their room for days, eating alone and lashing out. I believe you fixed them for the better, and I don't know how much you'll believe me, but I'm grateful that you've given them a future."

When had that happened? It'd come naturally, like their first interaction at Durante Academy. She'd talked *at* them, spilling forth all she knew because no one had ever listened to her.

What was the Constable talking about? *She* hadn't done anything. It was *Lorian*. Lorian had permanently broken her barriers and allowed her to enjoy being alive.

They made it to the loudest region of the halls. She heard the individual string instruments and drums playing. They were ramping up. Someone was giving a speech.

"This door wasn't open before," the Constable said. They'd come to two double doors that led into the main auditorium.

Romans were known for their hedonism. Their parties were wild, their sex lives sporadic. And the art they made had to live up to their high standards.

So, for grand theatrical productions, the monarchy reconstructed the Colosseum into a theatre. They hung up special tiling to allow performances to play in any weather. The stadium was transformed into a half-circle stage draped with curtains and levels for the performers to invent worlds at their will. The royal seating, seats for the wealthiest spectators, were in boxes constructed high above. Five stories high, these seats, furnished with sofas and red curtains, let the rich enjoy art like true gods.

The theatre was filled to capacity, hundreds of eyes drawn to the stage. The ballerinas were poised around a crystal lake. Neither Pinnacle nor Red Dragon nor even the Goddess were on stage. Black smoke was settling around the ferns and hanging crescent moon. This must've been somewhere during intermission, when the Goddess had been struck by Red Dragon's tail and all of nature weeps. The ballerinas were meant to be flower dewdrops, dressed in delicate whites and pearls.

The stage drew Aida in. All she saw, all she heard, came from it, from these characters she loved to get lost in. The world could've been ending tomorrow and it wouldn't have mattered. At this moment, all she had was her Pinnacle and his Isle.

The curtains fell, and a short murmur spread through the crowd about what they'd just seen.

Aida sat down in the aisle next to the first row of seats. She smoothed down her undergarments, taking in the front row seat she'd never have again. The orchestra wasn't as loud as she'd imagined. The seats felt firmer than they looked.

"Wow."

Aida hadn't seen the two figures hiding next to her. They'd made themselves small so they *wouldn't* be seen, but the audience nearest them had. They were whispering to their company about the two lost children.

Little Aida was holding the hand of a blond-haired child. Together, they watched the stage with stars in their eyes. Their childlike joy—the dropped jaws, them leaning in to watch at a better angle—was everything the theatre stood for.

"That was *incredible*," the blond-haired one whispered. They wore their long hair down with a white dress laced in gold. They had a lisp.

"That boy was fantastic," Little Lorian continued, "I've seen Pinnacle be played by many men in the past, but that one was the best. He looked like a real gladiator."

"He looked like you," Little Aida whispered back. "Was he your brother?"

"I haven't a brother, but the Goddess looked just like you. You have the same braids." They picked up one of Little Aida's braids and played with the end between their fingers. "They're pretty."

"Don't lie. Mo'mma calls it a rat's nest."

"I'm not lying. You're really pretty. Really, super pretty."

Aida covered the smile forming on her face. To think she'd forgotten this first meeting with her favorite person, *her* person. Lorian had been her first. They'd always been her first.

"Thanks," Little Aida said, "but where'd they go? Where is everyone?"

"I believe it's intermission. Do you wish to give chase?"

"Yeah! But..." Little Aida looked up at the balcony boxes. "You said your family's up there."

"They are, but they don't care about me, so it's fine."

Little Lorian said that too matter-of-factly and without a hint of sorrow in their little voice. To think a child thought their family didn't care for them at such a young age.

"Mine don't, either," Little Aida said easily. "I snuck in here without them knowing."

Little Lorian's smile doubled. They were missing a front tooth. "That's so cool."

"Thanks. "What's your name, by the way?"

"It's a long name, but you can call me—"

"No," Little Aida interrupted. "I like hearing people's full names. You can tell a lot about a person by their last name. It's also called a 'surname'. Did you know that?"

Little Lorian placed an exaggerated hand over their heart. "My name is Lucia Maria Carolus Durante di Romano."

Little Aida pieced the name together in her mind. "Maria Carolus...Wait, Romano? Like the royal family?"

"Well, my name is actually Lorian."

"Oh. So, are you a princess?"

They shook their head. They lied as easily as they breathed, even at this age. "No, but I'm gonna be an officer. No, a prince. Like Pinnacle."

"Pinnacle isn't a prince, he's an orphan who lost his father to sea, and if you read the books, you find out that he's a God who lost all of his powers and needs to get them back. Have you read the books?"

"Alas, I have not."

"Oopsies."

"Oopsies, indeed. You'll have to show me sometime."

"I will." She held out her pinkie, and Lorian locked theirs around hers, their fates interwoven.

"I'm sorry, I forgot to ask for your name," Little Lorian said.

Little Aida sat up proudly. "*I'm* actually a princess from a faraway island. I can control the wind and read people's minds. I also own a dragon, just like Pinnacle."

"That's impressive. What island do you govern?"

"I don't know. My memories got all fuzzy when I was adopted, but my pet dragon's sleeping underneath this place, so don't make me mad, or I'll make her eat you."

384

"I'd love to meet this dragon one day. My sister says dragons aren't real, but there're too many stories about them across the world for them not to exist."

"Your sister sounds like a dummy like mine. Where is she? Up there?"

Little Aida turned back to the play, and Little Lorian, staring lovingly at her, pulled out their skeleton key from around their neck. It was comically large in their small hands. "Do you want to go backstage? This key can open almost any door in the world."

"The whole world?"

"Yeah! Let's go now, though, before—"

"Lucia!"

The Constable, the younger one, came down the stairwell. He was still red-faced from his time with Young Rosalia.

The Constable she'd come with, who'd been watching them from the shadows, turned at his younger self's voice.

"Lucia Romano, you come here right now!" He brought Little Lorian to their feet. "Your father said not to leave his side."

"No!" They gave Aida a pitiful look and reached out for her. Little Aida did the same, desperate to keep hold of her first and only friend.

"Aida!"

The anger burning in that near voice stifled both Aidas. Young Carmine sounded no more than a young adult trying hard to command authority.

Aida's mother, who was bounding into the auditorium with two officers, knew how to wring out a young child's heart.

Young Carmine gave Aida's mother a short bow before hauling Lorian back up the stairs to their family.

"No!" They screamed, causing a scene that would've surely gotten them in trouble.

Aida, as well as Little Aida, stared in horror as their mother came for them.

"You come here!"

"She must've snuck in," one of the officers said.

"She does that, always getting into places she doesn't belong. *Come here.*"

The whispered threat sent both Aidas up. She could almost defend herself for getting into trouble now, but as a child, without knowing that such punishments weren't meant to happen...

She followed her mother and little self out of the Colosseum. She was a different type of Visatorre. Perhaps, if she willed herself, she could finally change the timeline.

She grabbed hold of her mother's tense shoulder, trying to get her to stop. "Stop it."

Her voice was as small as Little Aida.

The Constable followed them. "Is this your mother?"

"Stop it," Aida repeated, louder.

Her mother brought Little Aida outside near the fences, away from curious Roman eyes.

"Ow!" Little Aida tried prying herself away. "Mo'mma, that hurts!"

Aida tried for her. Her fingers threaded in and out of theirs, her ghostly presence just that. She wasn't smart enough to master how to be visible during the times it mattered.

"You could've gotten me fined for that," her mother said. "Why don't you ever listen to me?"

Little Aida wailed at being tied to such a mother.

"When I tell you to stay by the carriage, you stay by the—Listen to me!"

"Stop it!" Aida shouted, but her mother raised her hand.

She knew how to give her beatings quietly. She hit Aida's cheeks and temple, her back and arm. Slaps gave away the abuse, so she resorted to punching. It was her signature.

Little Aida knew not to cry out. Crying made the punishments more severe, behind closed doors so neither of them had to worry about being loud.

Aida turned away and covered her ears.

"What is..." The Constable looked at the real Aida. "Why is she doing that?"

She didn't know. She never, *ever* knew what warranted a mother to hit her own child, even if they were the loudest, brattiest child. It wasn't right. It didn't make sense.

The Constable turned back to Aida's mother. "Stop it."

Her mother continued her beatings.

"I command you!" He forced his hands upon her, trying to break them apart. "Stop it! She's but a child!"

Aida couldn't find the voice to tell him it was in vain. If only he could've stabbed her mother through the heart, then she could've felt a fraction of the pain she'd caused Aida for so many years.

When her mother was done, Little Aida was on the ground, sobbing as she covered her head. Her cheeks were swollen and her nose was bleeding. Her legs wouldn't stop shaking.

Her mother huffed and wiped her hands on her smock. "Come with me," she ordered, "and stop acting so stupid."

Little Aida hid her entire face in her arms as she was led back to the family that didn't want her.

For the first time in her life, Aida thanked Circa for tampering with her memory. It'd helped mask the pain she tried to forget, but now, reliving it secondhand, she would've preferred bleeding in the brain. Anything more than these resurfacing feelings. Anything more than the truth about her past.

Someone touched her shoulders. She flinched again, hands up to defend herself.

The Constable stepped back.

"Please," Aida said, "I'll do anything. I'll take jail time, I'll take time in the Colosseum, old-fashioned style."

"Aida—"

"I'd rather die." A hundred hurtful thoughts hit her at once. She sobbed. "I'd rather die than be part of this timeline. Without Lorian, I can't do anything by myself. I'm nothing. Without them…"

The Constable touched her again. An older person's hands didn't feel right on her body.

"I want Lorian back," she cried. "I want them back by my side. Please, I don't want to be alone again."

The declaration hurt as painfully as her memories, but it was true. She was a lonely girl and had been lonely for so many years. She had to cram her young life with pages of someone else's story, but Lorian had come in, and together, the two had co-written series. Adventures and romance and horror and mystery, presenting the most real version of herself.

She couldn't let all those words disappear. It was their story to give to the world.

The Constable looked down in thought, his hands still on Aida's shoulders.

"You want to see the good in Roma," Aida said. "Do you seriously think bringing Lorian back to the palace is going to fix anything? Do you honestly think we'd stay separated? Our future selves are married, Carmine, fighting to keep history the way it's supposed to be in their own chaotic ways. It's true that I don't know the ins and outs of it, and maybe I don't understand everything that my future self is planning, but I know where I need to be and what I need to do. Help me help Roma, Carmine. Help the people you love, and above all else, if not me, help Lorian, because I know you care for them like their own father."

The last word broke through to him. It sparked his true intention to see Lorian safe, and happy.

He fixed the cuffs of his undershirt that were still dirty from their scuffle in the woods.

He gave her his hand to take. "You and that future self of yours are going to be the death of me, aren't you?"

She smiled. "You know it."

Chapter 33: The Clock Tower

Lorian threw another glass at the wall. They'd lost their voice hours ago from screaming. Breaking bottles was the next best thing.

They felt violated by their own family's hands. On Circa's name, they wouldn't go through with it. They'd run away again. Somehow, they'd leave this accursed palace and reunite with Aida, wherever she was in the world.

They tripped on their stupid rug and fell. It'd been hours. Aida wouldn't be coming back for them. She was back in Bělico with her abusive mother and they'd never see each other again because the world was that cruel.

The officer outside their bedroom hit the door. "Your Highness," they said to someone in the hall. "His Majesty ordered that nobody enter this room."

"I'm sorry," a voice said, "did you hear that from Her Majesty The Queen, because last time I knew, the leading monarch has the final word on such matters. Please move."

Lorian backed up from the door. She sounded so put-together, like her own sibling's life hadn't been ruined for a second time that year.

Beatrice entered their destroyed room with poise, the officer keeling over to her natural charm. Lorian had always been jealous of that power.

She was dressed down more so than usual. She'd changed into a nightgown. She wasn't wearing heels. Coupled with a throw-over cardigan, she looked ready for bed.

Lorian couldn't meet her eyes. *She'd* married her husband and had a child without protest. She did what was told, didn't speak out of turn. She was the perfect daughter and monarch. They weren't ready for her talk.

Her shadow froze Lorian in their submissive crouch.

"We never wanted this."

They squeezed their eyes shut.

"You and I never asked for this. We grew up rich and wild and lost like spoiled animals, and we were beat for acting as such. I tried my hardest to keep Mother and Father happy, but you had a different agenda.

"I talked with them, Mother and Father. Each time you fought them, when all the doors were slammed and you wouldn't speak to anyone, I'd run to Mother and Father and defend you. From the moment I knew how to speak, I was defending you."

Lorian didn't deny it because they didn't know if it was true. It didn't sound like her.

"And I now know that wasn't enough."

Wasn't it?

"I should've helped you and been there for you more...presently, instead of helping from the sidelines. It's what you needed growing up and I wasn't there to provide that to you, and for that, I apologize.

"But I can't defend you from Father now. I've tried. He's become unhinged on gaining this alliance with Aldaí that Aldaí doesn't even want anymore, and we know Mother isn't strong enough to stop him. Zaahir nearly broke into Father's study with how he spoke to you, and Mother hasn't stopped crying. Nobody other than Father wants this, and that includes me as well."

Her recovering hands found their way to Lorian's cheek, forcing them to finally see her.

Her eyes were cloudy with tears. "I love you, Lorian, in however you choose to live your life. I'll have your side. I know I don't show it. I know I have trouble showing my emotions, but I favor you, and if you truly cannot see yourself marrying Zaahir, then I swear, I won't let it happen to you. I'll do better this time. I'll be there for you."

Perhaps, if they dug deep enough, there was some semblance of Beatrice left in Lorian's heart. It was the tiniest flame that reminded them that they had a sister. Not a perfect one, but one that *had* been there. Their upbringings had just divided them into two rooms with a near impenetrable wall.

And she'd bruised her hands to break down that wall.

Lorian bolted upright and hugged her. They cradled the back of her hair, digging their fingers in, in case this was the last chance to hold her like someone they truly loved and needed.

Beatrice returned their embrace.

"I'm sorry," Lorian said. "I'm sorry for everything."

"I'm sorry, too."

And they broke down harder. They cried into her shoulder. She was so warm. Had she always felt like this?

She held them for as long as they needed, which, unbeknownst to them, could've lasted the whole night. They didn't want to let her go. They wanted her back in their life.

But things were getting awkward and Lorian pulled back to clear their face.

"You're an ugly crier," Beatrice pointed out.

"Shut up."

"I'm sorry I wasn't there for you. I'll do better now. Twenty-three years too late, but I'm here."

"Almost twenty-four."

"Almost half of half of a century."

"You mean a fourth."

She blew out air from her nose, which must've been her adult laugh. Lorian remembered her babyish laugh. They hadn't forgotten those snorts.

Not much sound came through these near-impenetrable walls. You had to knock hard to be heard, and the flight of maids and cleaners receded from view like background props in an opera.

But above them, through the ceiling, they heard the crackle of a Visatorre jump.

The two looked at one another, a silent question and answer passing between them.

Beatrice lifted up her gown, Lorian lit a chamberstick, and the two of them bounded out of the room.

"Hey!" The officer failed to stop them in time. "Wait!"

They broke the rules and bounded for the stairwell unattended.

"Who is it?" Beatrice asked. "Aida or the future one?"

"I don't know, I can't read her mind."

"With how close you two are, I wouldn't doubt it."

"Shut up, I just got to forgiving you." They unlocked the door and flooded the room with light.

Carmine was on the floor, legs over his head, hat gone. He was moaning from the sporadic jump.

Aida, wobbling on unstable legs, had fallen beside him, but she'd dropped to her knees and was trying to get up with his help.

"Aida!"

The two of them found each other, arms wrapping around backs and shoulders. She was so cold. "Where were you?" they asked her.

She held them tighter, burying her face into their chest until they worried she was suffocating. Her nails were digging through her corset.

The giant clock ticked in time with their synced breathing. Little nutcrackers paraded around the numbers each time it struck the hour. Back when Lorian was a child, Missus Sharma would hum songs to the melody. It put them to sleep, the anthem of their country.

With Aida still unresponsive, Lorian turned to Carmine. "What happened?"

"I was on my way to bring Miss Mirko to the harbor, but she jumped into the past and took me with her."

"Really?" Lorian asked the top of Aida's head. They kissed it. "You're getting better at controlling it."

She pressed her face deeper into their chest, making them blush at how much she trusted them to protect her.

They moved her away from Carmine. "She's not leaving me."

"I know."

The tension of another fight left as quickly as it came. "What?"

"I know," he repeated. "I...understand now. This might be bigger than what I'd initially thought. You two might be on the right path for Roma's future, and I don't believe it's right for me to object to your efforts any longer."

Without his hat and the hatred for disorder in his face, Lorian saw Carmine, for the first time in years, as the family friend who only wanted the best for them and their sister.

Lorian said, "May I speak with Aida alone for a moment? I promise I won't run away. Not when I have her again."

Carmine and Beatrice exchanged looks, then Beatrice nodded once and left for the stairs, just like that, completely entrusting them. Carmine left after a moment of hesitation, seemingly tied to both twins.

When the door closed, Aida sighed tearily into Lorian's chest.

"Hey." They wiped her eyes. "What's wrong?"

"I saw it," she said, "*En Tempore Rose*. Back when I was a kid and my family was visiting Roma. I saw it. And I saw you."

"What?"

"You and your family were seeing the same opera. Both of us had wandered off like we weren't supposed to and met." She sniffled. "We knew each other as kids, Lorian. Years before we met at Durante Academy, we still found each other."

They pet the back of Aida's head. They didn't have many solid memories from childhood—the ones they did have were painful and blurred and rushed together—but they knew the theatre. They enjoyed it, but like their hunting trips, they'd become less frequent the older Lorian and Beatrice got.

"Our parents separated us back then, and it left me feeling so...empty. I was such a stupid kid and you still accepted me."

"You're not stupid. You're a brilliant girl that I was smart enough to fall in love with, twice. Did you tease me back then, too?"

"Is that what I do?" She wiped her boogers on their shirt, then looked up at them, eyes red.

She frowned. "What's wrong? There's something wrong with you. What happened with your parents?"

A dark cloud crossed over the palace. "My father's going along with the wedding. It's happening in three days."

Aida laughed breathlessly. "Yeah, right."

"No, we had a talk tonight. He told me I had no choice."

"No, I believe you, but if he thinks they're marrying you off when I'm still in the picture, he must be as stupid as he is bigoted." She patted their now wet vest. "You're not getting married to someone you don't wanna marry. Get that through your skull now. You're with me, and you'll always be with me. Unless you don't wanna be with me, which is fine, might make your parents happier, but until then, Lorian, no one is ever, *ever* taking you away from me."

Lorian watched the whole world swirl in her eyes, her white pupils like full moons. What Aida wanted, Aida fought for and got, no matter the cost.

Lorian couldn't help themselves and kissed her. They missed all that she was, her reliance in a world that hated them, her smile when nothing was going right. They missed holding her, and it'd only been a day.

Aida kissed back, gentle despite the outrageous claims that'd passed through her lips.

"What're we going to do?" they asked into her. "How're we going to stop the wedding? If my father sees you, I don't know what he'll do."

"I got some pretty damning blackmail on Carmine that'll keep him on our side, and I'm getting the hang of timing my jumps, though they're not as precise as my future self's. The first few jumps back here dumped us in the Aldaían deserts."

"Can you jump anywhere, at any time?"

"Not yet. My brain's mush. Give me a day to get back to normal and I'll concoct a plan to sneak you out of here."

"You're incredible, Aida."

"I told you. On Circa's name, nobody's taking you away from me."

The clock struck midnight.

"Just a few more days until we ruin your wedding."

"For the second time."

"How chaotic," Aida said. "Let's go."

Chapter 34: Wedding Pep Talk

If Lorian liked anything about being royal, it was the parties.

They wanted no business with them as a child. The way the old men and women fawned over them made them uncomfortable, and the *dresses*. Ballroom-cut that made walking an athletic sport. Later into their rebellious age, they'd discovered their appeal. The drinking helped. Ale spiked with Nectar and suddenly, everything was a joke and Lorian was the butt of it.

Their first wedding ceremony had flipped their opinion on such parties, and this second ceremony would've sent them over the balcony without a blanket ladder, but tonight, they were okay. Okay because somewhere in the palace, Aida was with them.

They kept in touch via Carmine. Lorian was still quarantined in their room, doors and windows padlocked shut, but Carmine was given access. Supposedly, he'd spun a tale about Aida travelling him into the palace library and her jumping into the night. He lied well; their father believed him enough to drop the subject and increase the number of men to find the mysterious Aida Mirko.

200 people had been invited to the wedding. A cut from the 600 that summer. Honestly, who'd want to show support for such an unstable relationship? Only the assholes who salivated over the feet of the royal family no matter what they did.

On the second night of prep, they bullied Carmine into letting them out on the floor's balcony for fresh air. They heard carriages come up to the main entrance while maids and officers scurried through the halls like mice.

"Your Highness."

Carmine was dressed extra special for tonight, wearing his full military regalia. He'd even gelled back his hair, leaving his silly hat somewhere in his quarters.

"Don't call me that," Lorian said. "Why are you dressed like that?"

"It was ordered by the king. He wants everyone looking their best for this weekend."

"Act like everything's not falling to shit, huh?"

"Language." He joined them at the edge of the balcony, taking in the winter night.

"How's Aida?" Lorian asked.

"She's still up in the clock tower. I've brought her blankets and pillows as well as some food, but she hasn't slept or eaten. She's been practicing her jumps in case anything were to go wrong. She's planning on speaking to your father."

"Is she well?"

"She's dead-set."

"That's not news to anyone."

He nodded, annoyed yet not really. "I became aware of that when she threw her cane at me. She is quite...committed."

"That's the best part about her. I think she'll do great things for Roma if this damn country will give her a break."

"Let's pray she doesn't break Roma first."

Lorian smiled. Either way, to them. "Thank you for helping us."

"She didn't give me much choice in the matter." He sighed. "Lorian, I sincerely apologize for the pain you've been through."

"Aida was there to help me through it."

"I'm talking about before then. Back when you were growing up, I tried doing all that I could for you and Beatrice, but that wasn't enough. I...knew you were struggling with everything. With your father and the whole wedding and your gender. When we'd have music practice or when I'd bring you up to the clock tower, I never asked about what you were going through. I thought it would lighten your mood, doing these things for you, but then I was chastised for being unassertive."

"I was a bastard, Carmine. I don't blame you for not prying into my personal life. Not like I wasn't used to it with Father."

"But I should've. You should've felt comfortable opening up to me."

They already found themselves drawing back emotionally. They felt like they couldn't burden Carmine with their life problems. They knew they should've felt comfortable opening up to the only man who had their side in the palace, but they couldn't. Hopefully, more time with Aida would help them with that.

They faked a smile. "You're not my dad, so you shouldn't take on that responsibility."

Their answer had meant to brighten him up, but his face drooped even lower, a wet blanket over his golden shoulders.

They tried again. "Carmine, I don't blame you for anything that happened in my childhood. You and Missus Sharma made it bearable."

"I pointed my sword at you," he said, "back at Durante Academy."

"But you hesitated."

"Only because you called me by my first name, and only you, Beatrice, and Rosie—M-members of the royal family use it."

"*Rosie*?" they teased. "Do you possibly mean my mother, Carmine? Calling Her Royal Majesty by her first name, and by a nickname, no less."

"I-it's from our childhood. This wasn't where I wanted the conversation to go."

Lorian crossed their ankles and got better comfortable over the railing. They'd known Carmine was smitten by their mother. He didn't hide it well, nor had their mother when she'd assigned him as her personal right-hand man. Such gossip was banned from the palace walls, but that didn't stop the servants. Little information was known about their family, anyway. It was fun making up stories that may or may not have been true.

"Just tell me," Lorian said, "that you aren't going to screw us over like our future selves have been doing."

"Of course not. I'll do whatever I can to make sure you're safe. I failed the first time—first several times—but I swear to you, I'll stay by your side."

"Okay, okay, easy, Constable. If Aida trusts you, then I trust you. Just don't go screwing up our plans again."

"Oh, goodness, Lorian. You need to use better etiquette. What happened to all of your lessons?"

"Right, I'll just ask Aida how to act like a royal."

Carmine rolled his eyes. "Oh, by the way, she mentioned that you go by, uh, a different way of presenting yourself. You use different pronouns now."

"I use they/them."

"Right."

"That okay?"

"Of course, but, uhm, if I mess up or get anything wrong, please correct me. I don't want to do anything that might drive you away again."

"I won't run away again," they promised. "This time, I have someone to fight for."

"Do you ever think," he said, "if your father were a different man, you could try to stay in the royal line?"

Lorian blew out a cold breath of air. "What do you think? I mean it," they clarified. "What do you think I should do? I'm not planning on going through with the wedding—if anything, I'd like to marry Aida."

"Really?"

They smiled into their hand. "I haven't known her for very long, but I know I don't want to live without her. She's smart and kind, straightforward when I need it, and she lifts me up when I think I don't deserve it. She introduced me to this book series she loves, and we think the same way, even if her way usually winds up going ten more paces than I would've gone. And, being modest like you like, she has one of the prettiest faces I've ever seen."

"You're that taken by her?" Carmine asked.

Their smile turned devilish. "Just as you're taken by my mother."

Carmine's face fell like a brick into mud.

"What? I'm not stupid, Carmie. I'm a hopeless romantic, I know love when I see it. I've seen the way you reach for her, how you're always near her and comforting her when my father acts out."

Carmine didn't lose the fear in his eyes and backed up.

Lorian stood up straighter. "*Is* there something—?"

"No," he said. "No. Just. Don't bring that up again. I mean it." He left for the doors. "Come. You need to get ready."

"Do I need to get primped up for this days in advance?"

"If you don't want your father to throw an even bigger temper tantrum than he threw last night."

Lorian shrugged and gave in. They knew this wouldn't go through, not with whatever Aida was cooking up, but if they were going to dress up for the only wedding their parents would attend for them, they should've made a decent effort.

They checked the time, craning their neck over the balcony railing to see the clock tower.

Sitting in the curve of the clock, near one of the swinging doors used for maintenance, was Aida. She was far enough away to be out of sight of someone looking for intruders, but Lorian knew those braids and the casualness of her lounge.

She was watching them, a cigarette bitten between her teeth. She gave them a single wave.

Lorian returned it and mouthed their love for her.

Chapter 35: Trying on the Dress

She practiced travelling in the present first. Three meters to the right, across the clock tower room. She wanted to prepare in case her plan of crashing a royal wedding backfired.

She hadn't managed a single jump in the past ten hours.

"Oh, come on!"

She focused on the jump itself, then on her body and where it was in the universe. When that didn't work, she tried to jump physically, twirling around like her future self, but it only left her stomping about like a caveperson. She had Carmine's word that no one would hear her up here, but she trusted that man as far as she could jump.

So, unable to aptly control her jumps, Aida spent the rest of the morning working up her plot to fuck over the royal family.

She scribbled out the page she was working on and tossed it near the clock face. Carmine had brought her up a comforter and pillows to sleep on, as well as an oil-lit lantern and some paper and quills. He also delivered food, but she wasn't hungry.

"*Carmie*," she whined, "on a scale of one to ten, how cool will the king be with me after my future self kneed him in the face?"

"Don't call me that." He offered her another slice of short-cake. This was the second one he'd brought up from the kitch-ens. "And why do you want to speak with him? I thought you were going to do something to stop the wedding."

"They're all tied together, Carmie. I need to tell him the truth about his history. His wife's great-great-great-whatever not only murdered Queen Eve under two-timing pretenses, he also murdered the entire race of Visatorre for her sleeping with the queen."

"I don't want to hear this," he said, ears hot.

"But you have to. It's discrimination. The king was fucking Eve, too, yet he's not dethroned for sleeping with her. It's all so convoluted and stupid, and that fucker needs to hear it. I also have to convince him about the very real person that is Circa."

"I still don't believe you saw her."

"And I still don't have to convince you." She gathered her notes. "I've narrowed down some options: One, demand a hearing with the king in the middle of the wedding; two, kid-nap Lorian in exchange for a hearing; or three, burn the palace to the ground." She stared him straight in the face, then threw her papers in the air. "So I got nothing."

"I heard that Queen Beatrice and Prince Zaahir have been asking for a hearing with him, but he's denied all of their re-quests, and he said he doesn't want to see Lorian until they walk down the aisle."

"What an asshole." She started a fresh page. "I can't imag-ine him hearing me out, and the queen won't be helpful in that regard."

"She's trying her best," he said under his breath.

"I know she is. Can you imagine being married to that man? My self-esteem would be more of a wreck than it already is."

"Alright, do you need anything else from me, or am I allowed to continue prepping the palace?"

"If you can get me more cigarettes, that'd be great. I'm down to my last pack and I'll need another one before I come up with a good enough solution to this nightmare."

"Here." He offered her a pack from his back pocket.

She took it. "I didn't know you smoked."

"I don't. Lorian said you might want them."

She hated herself for how big she smiled. "Before you leave, Carmie, I need you to buy me something."

"*What*? No, absolutely not. I said I'd protect you, not be your personal chauffeur. And stop calling me that."

She pouted at him, crossing her arms with her quill in her mouth.

His eye twitched. "What do you even need from me?"

"A dress," she said. "The fanciest, most beautiful dress you can find."

Bullying Carmine shouldn't have been as fun as it was.

The morning of the wedding, Aida awoke with too many ideas in her head and a long, white box sitting at her blanketside.

"*Hey*, what is this?" she asked Carmine. He was tending to her with a glass of water and plate of crackers. He said nothing.

"Did you really get me one? With *your* taste in fashion?"

"I don't know. I went to the store where Her Majesty commissions her dresses. *La Madame's Boutique*. You gave me little to no direction with what you wanted, so I thought going there would suffice, given the short time frame you allotted me."

Aida popped open the box, and layer upon layer of pure white poofed out. She couldn't find the dimensions with how thick and full it was, but the texture felt nice, nothing she'd hate wearing for a few hours.

"I didn't know what color you needed," Carmine said, "so I picked the first one I saw."

"I didn't say to get a *white* dress, Carmie."

"For the occasion, I thought it'd be appropriate."

"Appropriately antagonistic. Who wears white to a wedding other than the bride? My future self's rubbing off on you, Carmine. You're becoming a maverick."

"I'd say the same thing's happening to you."

"Don't insult me." She placed the dress against her chest, then saw that at the bottom of the box was a pair of matching white slippers.

"Ha." She tried stepping into one. "That's cute you think I'm a size six."

"I based it on Beatrice and Lorian's sizes."

"Lorian has massive feet." She showed the size difference between her augmented shoes and the ones he'd bought for her. She tried them on for his sake. They did look, and feel, pretty.

She brought the whole outfit over to the stained glass of the clock. She did fancy pretty dresses, but growing up, her mother gave her ones akin to rags. And nothing was ever her size, so they were either too small or too loose around the edges that made her feel more insecure.

This dress gave off the opposite effect.

"So," Carmine said, "uh, since I have no idea how fashion works, and I suppose you want to show up to Lorian's wedding whether I tell you it's a bad idea or not—"

"Correct."

"I have someone here who might be of help." He went to the door and peeked it open, then nodded and allowed her to enter.

It was the first time Aida had met Beatrice face to face. She'd seen paintings of her in Bělico and knew she'd helped her out of the Catacombs, but she'd become a real person. She was tall and had thick, blond hair braided around her head.

She looked a lot like Lorian.

She bowed to Aida. Aida bowed back.

"It's nice to finally meet you," Beatrice said. "My apologies for taking so long to introduce myself to you. My family, as you may be aware, is falling apart at the moment."

"I hear you," Aida said. "Uh, just so you know, you don't have to get involved with this if you don't want to. Your Majesty." She had no idea how to tread these waters. They were the same age and came from the same country, more or less, but this was like confronting Lorian's mother, a true queen.

"On the contrary," Beatrice said. "I've heard many things about you from various sources but haven't had the chance to get to know you. Carmine said you might've needed help getting ready. You can imagine how I haven't had a chance to give another girl a proper makeover." She took out a small case of hair supplies and makeup. "If you'd let me, I'd love to help you get ready for my twin's disastrous wedding."

Aida's eyebrows shot up to her Visatorre marking. "Fuck yeah," she said, and Beatrice smiled.

Chapter 36: Ballroom Whirl

Lorian thanked who they could. They thanked their seamstresses who tailored them into a three-piece suit, they apologized to their hairdressers who mourned over their cut hair. They kept asking Lorian which pairs of earrings and heels they wanted to wear tonight, intoxicated by the chance of true love. Lorian didn't have the heart to crush their dreams.

As the Sun set, Lorian got a tingle in their side that wouldn't go away. All the party planners and maids and chefs warmed up the palace with buzzing energy. Their mother and father were nowhere to be seen, which should've made Lorian calmer, but knowing they could come out from anywhere— their mother crying and their father shouting—consumed them.

At eight-thirty, two maids and an officer entered their room.

"They're ready for you," the officer said.

Hundreds of individual chandelier candles had been lit. The palace smelled of gravy and sweet puddings. Maids Lorian had seen working extraneous hours were now taking it in on the sides of the halls, leaning on their brooms and swaying to the orchestra.

As per Roman tradition, the two to be wed partied in separate rooms. Guests could come and go as they pleased, giving each group their blessings, but the two weren't to meet until the twelfth song ended, usually two or three hours into the night. The guests would whisper how beautiful the bride was in her gown and how lucky the groom was for his lucky woman. Lorian had spent the better half of their first time getting drunk in their room, aching to be saved from this wretched night.

Now, they stood on their heels, searching for their true soulmate in a sea of dull magnates. None were Visatorre, they noticed. They should've noticed that more as a child.

The pressure of the night doubled with every dress and feathered hat they passed. They tried being on their best behavior and bowed to those who came. Bold men commented on Lorian's outfit and asked where the mysterious time traveller was, but the officers and maids stationed with Lorian politely guided the conversation. They must've been handpicked by their mother and father to make sure Lorian didn't terminate any treaties.

Getting what seemed like only halfway through the meet-and-greet, Lorian was guided towards the ballroom windows, where a crowd was forming around Beatrice.

The overly polite dipped their heads, allowing Lorian a private yet public moment with their sister. She was wearing a high-neck ball gown with flowers melting down the tulle like paint. Her daughter, Nina, was matching her in a pink dress. Her husband was thankfully MIA.

Beatrice cocked her head to one side, showing them her neck, their signal since childhood that they needed to talk.

Lorian gave her their arm, and the three of them roamed into the emptier part of the ballroom.

"What's the plan?" Beatrice whispered.

"No idea."

"Wonderful. Aida hasn't one, either."

"You talked with her?"

"I was hoping to help you two. Do you do everything off the cuff of your sleeve?"

"Hey, if you have any ideas, I'm all ears."

Nina crept out from around her mother's dress.

"Hi there," Lorian said. "It's nice to finally see you."

"You're really pretty," she said. "You look like Mo'mma."

"We're twins."

"But you don't look identical."

"That's because we're fraternal, though I *am* prettier than she is, aren't I?"

"Don't answer that," Beatrice said.

"Have you seen Carmine?" Lorian asked Beatrice. "He's supposed to be giving me updates on Aida, but I haven't heard from him all day."

"Not sure. I met up with her a few hours ago. She'd needed help putting on her ball gown."

"Where'd she get one?"

"Carmine. It's quite a beautiful piece."

It wasn't as if they hadn't seen her in a dress—they hadn't seen her wear anything else—but with Aida, they knew she was planning something dastardly with it.

A hush fell over the main ballroom. People looked up from their conversations. Champagne glasses fell to waists as whispers broke out about what they were seeing.

Lorian followed each of their gazes to the top of the stairwell.

Aida stood at the top. She had a hand on her hip and one over her eyes as she used the high grounds to survey the ballroom. Carmine stood faithfully beside her. He'd dressed up in his most regal attire, but there was a reason everyone had stopped their mindless talk, and it wasn't because they'd seen the infamous Aida Mirko.

Her dress was that of a dream. It was a white ball gown that hugged her curves, an off-the-shoulders, sweetheart cut that dipped down her chest that would've made the most indelicate woman faint. The lights caught on whatever diamonds had been sewn into the fabric. She was wearing earrings, rings, jewelry they thought they'd never see on her. Her hair had been styled in a way that must've taken hours to complete. Like a true princess of Roma, she wore it down in perfect curls.

Lorian didn't know how someone could fall for the same person twice, three times. They'd lost track, but curse her, she had that power over them. By just existing, she had reworked every cell and atom in their body to fall ever more effortlessly for her.

Their eyes met. Carmine said something to her. The crowds, keen for anything out of the ordinary, came over in droves, whispering about the girl from wanted posters.

With her eyes piercing Lorian, Aida lifted up her dress, revealing silver matching slippers.

And she disappeared in a perfectly controlled jump.

The crowd gasped, turning every which way to catch sight of the mysterious time traveller. One woman screamed and alerted officers into the space.

Aida touched down before Lorian. Something tripped her up—her slippers, perhaps—and she fell into Lorian's body, claiming their lips as hers.

Lorian felt themselves falling, so they locked their arms around her.

She glared intently at them. "You're mine tonight, and tonight, I want to dance with you."

They were so lost from her entrance, her dress, the lasting, tingling sensation on their lips, that all they could say was, "Pardon me?"

"I wanna dance with you. Right now."

They looked at the crowd. "Right now?"

"Yes." She took their hand and readied a dancing stance.

The penultimate song before Lorian met their spouse began.

"Lead me," she commanded.

And Lorian, for the first time in these palace walls, did what was asked of them.

Aida only knew to keep her dress raised to one side as she danced, so Lorian helped her the rest of the way. Neither of them knew what dance they were dancing to; they made it up as they went. It fit, them dancing with her, because all the while, they weren't watching for their parents or sister. They didn't care how their form was off. It was simply fun, lovely and romantic in their own way.

Lorian twirled Aida around in a swing. "What're we doing?" they asked her.

"Figured this was the best way to weasel your father out of hiding."

"You don't think your presence will take care of that?"

"Because I'm not one to push anyone to their limit. How're you feeling?"

"Unresponsive?"

"Why?"

"Well, right now, you look the most stunning I've ever seen you, and you're leaving me quite breathless."

"Oh, come now. You've seen me naked multiple times, I remind you."

"Do you want me to faint? Is that your goal for tonight?"

She didn't disagree. "Carmine suggested it, you know. He said it'd look good with the darkness of my hair or eyes or something. Man has more fashion sense than I do."

"You're beautiful."

She shrugged, though her cheeks burned red. "Same to you, I suppose. Your parents haven't clocked you yet for wearing a man's suit?"

"Haven't met them to find out." They rubbed her arms. "You okay?"

"Yeah. Just feel sort of funny, like my brain's in two different places."

"Do you want to stop?"

"Absolutely not, are you kidding me? We haven't even gotten to the best part." Taking Lorian tightly by the arm, she stood up on her tiptoes and went for their lips again. Lorian licked them—they were so dry from her—but she didn't kiss them. Touching foreheads with them, Aida connected with them and whisked them away in a jump.

They landed across the room, spooking a man off his feet and into a server. Then again, off to the right and into a gaggle of women.

Lorian laughed, laughed at the impossible becoming possible at the worst possible time. She was utterly amazing, this girl they'd found themselves with.

Aida teleported them back twenty paces and literally jumped a man back in fright.

Aida laughed so hard she snorted, and from that, it was all over. Lorian dropped their head onto hers and laughed hard and uncontrolled. "You can control teleporting other people now?"

"More or less. Did you see his hop? How embarrassing."

"But Aida, Aida, can you control it now? What's there left for you to do?"

As their song ended and the two of them kept holding one another, guessing at what was to happen next, the crowds parted once more. The people bowed or left the room entirely when they saw the king, the queen, Zaahir, and three officers run in.

"Lorian!" the king shouted. "What are you doing?"

Aida stepped back with Lorian in tow. She puffed out her chest. "Good evening, Your Majesty."

He looked over at Carmine, who was halfway down the ballroom steps and not apprehending Roma's most dangerous criminal. "I need you to come with me."

"I have done nothing wrong other than exist."

"You'd been withholding my daughter from us, you've been toying with my men, you attacked them without just cause—"

"The *queen's* men attacked me unlawfully, your *child* ran away from you, and my *future* self attacked you. None of that falls onto me."

"Constable Carmine, arrest her."

"What do you think he's gonna..." Aida closed her cheeky mouth. Her eyes caught on something in the crowd, someone, and all the willpower she was willing into her body left in a slow exhale.

"Aida?" Lorian whispered.

It was that woman, that tall, silent, smiling woman draped in white cloth who stood like a statue. She was on the other side of the room and blended in with the columns holding up the ceiling.

She disappeared in a jump. Those around her acted as if she was never there in the first place.

"Carmine, I said seize her," the king repeated, but Carmine stayed still, and all the officers in the room stayed still, and all the guests stayed still in wait.

The hesitance in power gave Aida enough time to pick up her dress and dart backwards into the royal palace.

"Aida!"

Her run snapped off something from her slipper and sent it clattering to the tiles. She turned to go back for it, then thought better of herself and kicked off the second shoe, too. She continued around a group of taken-aback men, hooked the corner, and then she was gone, leaving all but her shoes in her wake.

Chapter 37:
Back into the Catacombs

"Fuck me."

Circa disappeared around hall corners and skipped entire stairwells. Aida, shoeless, did her best to keep up with her, but the officers running behind her made her rethink her chase after a Goddess.

"Fuck me."

The feeling of dancing with Lorian in a place not meant for either of them had felt daring and fun. The way they'd looked at her filled her heart with longing, and she hated leaving them for it.

It made her chase all the more clumsy.

"Fuck *me*."

The clocks around the palace chimed for midnight, repeating her failed time limit of saving Lorian from their own wedding.

"Aida!"

One of Zaahir's knights ran up to her. She forgot his name. He had his hand on the hilt of his scimitar.

"Are you trying to stop me?" she called out to him.

"No, though I feel like I should." He easily caught up with her and met her pace. "Prince Zaahir told me to defend you. Where exactly are you going?"

She pointed at Circa, who was waiting for her on a chandelier. She was upside down. "Do you see her?"

He looked up, but before he could denounce her hallucinations, two officers called for them to give up.

"Ugh, why're they following me, anyway?" Aida asked.

"Might it be because you just publically and verbally humiliated the king in front of the most important people in the country?"

Aida blew out her cheeks. "He ain't the king of my country," she said. They were deep into the palace now, towards the gardens near the northern side. Circa kept teleporting, leading them deeper.

"What was your name again?" Aida asked.

"Kadar Basan," he said. "I'm Prince Zaahir's consort."

"Consort? Are we fighting for the same fucking team?"

"It appears we are."

"We're idiots, is what we are."

"I'd gladly be an idiot for him."

Aida shrugged, unable to deny that she herself had done some pretty stupid things for Lorian in the past few months, save for calling herself their consort.

"Can you please enlighten me on the whereabouts of where you're going," Kadar asked, "before I die making sure you get there safely?"

"I have absolutely no idea, all I know—"

Circa turned down a dead end and disappeared, their chase abruptly ending.

The only thing down this hall was a painting of the Roman skyline and a locked, chained door. It'd been glazed over by paint and barely had a silhouette. Aida would've run past it in search of other, more important doors.

"There," Aida said.

"The Catacomb entrance?" Kadar asked.

"You can enter the Catacombs by way of the palace? How morbid."

The officers turned the corner, their rapiers drawn.

Kadar backed Aida up against the door. "I don't know much about being criminals, but if I were you, I'd think about heading for that door."

"I'm not sure I want you to kill yourself for me getting a ten-second lead on armed officers."

"I've been given the task of keeping my *amar* safe in this country and mine for more than ten years. Do you think Aldaían standards are so low that my skills are comparable to that of three *alqatat*?"

She didn't know what that word meant, but before he had time to translate, the officers unsheathed their swords.

Kadar sidestepped, took the arm of the nearest officer, and shoved him into the curtains across the hall. He brought the momentum of the two others and heaved them against the wall. He easily switched his sword's grip and readied for the offense. Each slash cut through the clothes and skin as the officers tried and failed to land a hit on him.

Panting with a bit of blood on his tunic, Kadar doubletook Aida still standing there and sliced the air behind her ear. The locks on the door clattered to the floor. He kicked the metal open with his foot. "Go, please," he said impatiently, and pushed up his headscarf to reveal his Visatorre marking, "before your time runs out."

Aida gave him a nod of appreciation and wedged herself through the tight entrance. Kadar held it open for only a moment before he started closing it.

In the darkness, she heard the heavy footsteps of officers running down the hall: backup.

She almost turned back. It felt wrong leaving Kadar by himself, but she trusted his promise at being better than her expectations and helped him close the door.

Sudden emptiness welcomed her back into the Catacombs. The floor transformed from glossed marble to cement that chafed her feet. The only wealth on the walls came from a sign telling those to be wary in the Catacombs and a lit torch.

She freed the torch from its hook, unsure of whether to thank Circa for the generous light.

She avoided the wetter puddles forming on the uneven steps leading down into the Earth. Her stockings had been destroyed from her run. She felt a bit bare, walking down here barefoot, and unbidden.

Down, down, the ground carving cuts into her unstable feet. Her cane did little to help as a stabilizer. She nearly lost it on the rougher rock.

The skulls came in slowly like a plague. They curved around her, pointing outright and watching her from the ceiling. She'd already seen their ancestors before, but seeing the smaller, cracked skulls shoved into the dirt made her sick all over again.

"Down here!"

She took in a sharp breath. She hadn't expected them to come looking for her down here, where a wrong turn could've sentenced you to death.

She dropped to one knee and slammed her torch into a puddle, trying to snuff it out. The officers' voices echoed down a myriad of paths she couldn't trace, making them either a kilometer away or around the next turn.

"Circa, if you're really on my side," she whispered in prayer.

The splashing grew closer.

"Then show me where to go, *please*. Give me a hint, for *once*. You brought me down here, now finish the job. Stop playing with my life."

The fabric of one of the officer's uniforms kissed the hall she was hiding in, and their voices and footsteps disappeared down a frivolous path.

Giving it a ten-count, then another, Aida lifted up her dress and finally exhaled. "Thanks. For now."

She took more wrong turns. She second-guessed herself whenever she thought she was going the right way. "Right way," as if a gut feeling could be anything more than a wild shot in the dark.

After passing the same outcropping of stone twice, Aida stopped walking and covered her eyes. The officers were gone. Nothing but spiders and Visatorre bones were here. She didn't even know what direction she was going now. She didn't know how deep she'd gotten.

"*Aida.*"

She hurt her neck turning around. It was a feminine voice, but who and where, why and how, she couldn't place.

Her heart beat loudly in her ears, masking the noises she knew she had to be focusing on.

Against all of her better judgements, she followed her own voice. What was her future self doing? Why was she calling out to her?

She stopped like quicksand had swallowed her feet. To her right was the first door she'd come across. It had no bars, no locks or chains to keep people out. It was an average door at a dead end.

There were no bones in its small room. There was hardly anything at all.

Nothing, except for a statue, a two-meter-tall recreation of Circa on a platform. She wore a Pre-Classical Era white gown that flowed beautifully around her curvy body. The artist had taken some liberties and sculpted her with bird wings and a halo, but Aida knew. This Aldaían woman was her Goddess.

The door, too heavy for a non-existent wind to close, began scraping the dirt and shutting on its own.

"Wait—wait, no!" She fought against it, tried shoving her arm between it and the doorway, but she couldn't risk losing her arm down here. It shut and trapped her in absolute darkness, hundreds of feet below the surface.

Chapter 38: Lost Found Family

"Kadar, protect her!" Zaahir yelled.

Kadar tensed at being named outright. His foot stepped towards where Aida went. The other stayed pointing at his prince.

"*Now*," Zaahir urged.

After a second warning, Kadar bowed and outmaneuvered the Roman officers to run after Aida.

The crowds crashed together in waves of a violent sea. Aida's untimely departure had sent in every guest to see what'd made King Durante yell. Lorian, lost amidst the chaos, clung to Aida's slipper, a child to their stuffed toy.

The king beckoned for Carmine. "What on Earth are you waiting for? Was this not your mission for months, to find these two and keep them from effacing all that Roma stands for? Go!"

"A-a moment, please," their mother said. "Lorian—"

"*Silence*," their father said. "Constable, go!"

The pressure built on Carmine's shoulders. It took the king striking him for him to act, staggering forwards, hand reaching for his rapier.

"Father!" Beatrice gave the king a disgusted look. Zaahir, untroubled by showing his contempt for Roma, went for something sharp hidden in his royal tunic.

The king suspected his watchful people, his lingering family, his distrustful guards. "I will not stand for this," he said at Lorian, directing all his anger at them. "I am your *father*, I am your *king*. Whatever you think you are, you are mine, and you will do as you're told."

Carmine's rapier, the one Lorian had stolen from him all those months ago, was unsheathed. Its long slice of metal-on-metal *shinged* from its scabbard.

He turned and aimed it at the only threat he saw to Roma.

The crowd gasped. Lorian's mother covered her mouth in horror.

The king gawked at the blade being pointed at him, the realness of this mutiny finally settling on his baffled face.

"I won't...I won't let you strike fear into their heart any longer," Carmine promised. "This *will* end, tonight."

Lorian stood in stunned silence. They'd watched Carmine rise in rank and power for years. They celebrated whenever a new medal was pinned to his uniform, not knowing they were hardening him into a heartless constable.

To throw that away, to risk his own neck at the blade of a guillotine, for them...

Despite the circumstances, the king sneered at the threat against his life. "I knew you were on her side. You always treated her as if she were your own."

Carmine nervously turned the blade over in his hand. "That's because they are."

Their mother, who could no longer hold herself up, fell to her knees, hands over her face like petrified spider legs.

425

Lorian agreed. Comparatively, Carmine had been more of a father than their own father had been. He'd braided their hair and gifted them toys and sweets from overseas. He made time for them. It hadn't been his place—he'd been an officer in training, a family friend—but when Lorian pictured a father...

All they saw was Carmine.

Carmine's hand trembled with the weight of his words. "That's why I won't let you harm them any longer. Your paranoia's driven you and your men to hysteria. It's affecting your people. I pledged my loyalty not only to your family but to the future of Roma, and I do not see it in your eyes. Not anymore. I see it in Lorian's and Beatrice's. I see it in my children's future."

The crowd had tried to stay silent. They wanted to hear every detail so they could talk about it later with their friends and family.

They broke all formalities of a duel and began talking over one another. Bold, whispering rumors that would've imprisoned them. But nobody stopped them, and the volume grew. Officers joined in. Delegates from Aldaí turned to their translators to follow the noise. The tides of this sea were eroding the brittle coastline.

In Lorian's periphery, Beatrice wavered. That strong sense of logic she was known for was dying in her eyes.

The king's face was heating up in white. "Be quiet," he said. "You're...This's preposterous. *I* am their father."

"You're infertile," Carmine said. "Your doctors—"

"Quiet!"

"—did everything they could, but nothing could come from it."

"Shut *up!*"

"So you tried different methods and failed. You tormented Rosalia with doubt that *she* was the one who couldn't bear children. To appease your ruthless hands upon her, she asked me..." He smiled. "She asked me the greatest honor I could bestow to my queen, and I did so happily."

Durante exploded. Growling like a true animal, he stole a sword from a nearby officer and lunged for his second-in-command.

The crowds still with them fled the scene. Zaahir jumped back, protected by his additional knights. Beatrice hid her daughter in the crowd. Two officers carried Lorian's mother to safer grounds.

"Carmello!" she yelled. "Carmello, stop it!"

Carmine parried the first attack, then blocked the second by ducking. The two rivaled one another in endurance and speed. Each one dealt out swings meant to kill.

Lorian's hand opened and closed by their side, their grip lost without a future tethering them down. Their identity, their motivation, all of it was washing away from them.

Were they considered royalty anymore? Did any of this formality matter when, in the eyes of the state, they and their sister were now considered bastard children of the crown?

Carmine was their father.

An officer knocked into Lorian and dropped them to the floor. Zaahir was being hauled away despite his protests to help. People were running now, and the most loyal officers were surrounding their king in yielding support.

One got behind Carmine with their sword raised.

"Carmine!" Lorian shouted.

Carmine turned in time and parried it. Durante, finding an advantage, attacked him from behind.

He missed and got his belt instead. Officers who'd once followed Carmine's commands tackled him to the ground. They held up his head to look up at his king.

Durante raised his sword. "No matter who you think you are, you are *nothing* to your king."

Carmine spat at his feet. "But I am—and have always been—*everything* to your wife."

Durante kicked Carmine in the face, arching his neck for a perfect hit. As he examined him like a piece of meat, his eyes, so cold and distant, locked on to Lorian from across the room.

He lowered his sword, not to bury it into Carmine's neck, but to angle it so that he could run.

Five wide steps and he was above Lorian. His sword arched like a crescent moon to cut into Lorian's head.

"No!" their mother screamed.

And Lorian, so foolishly, closed their eyes.

The blade struck so quickly, so loosely, Lorian thought they were already dead. They imagined death as a slow process, their last thoughts drifting into the sky.

They opened up their eyes to a brilliant flow of blond hair standing between them and their father.

Lorian's heart pulsed in their neck. "Bea."

Beatrice had her blade crossed with Durante. It was an officer's rapier, likely stolen. "Like I'm gonna let you fuck up their life a second time," she said, and slashed upwards at their fake father.

Durante stumbled back. Beatrice didn't. She parried and blocked each careworn swing he dared to throw at her. Lorian had never known she was privy with swordplay. She was better than they were.

"Stop her!" Durante screamed. "Kill her!"

The officers lowered their weapons. Durante against Carmine was an easier side for them to choose. Durante against both Lorian and more so Beatrice...

Beatrice pivoted her body and moved Durante away from Carmine. He was thrashing like a fish to get free. The officers, now undecided on whose side they were on, were becoming more lenient with him. Hitting one hard in the mouth, Carmine scrambled out and ran, only pausing to look between a sobbing Rosalia, a defenseless Lorian, and Beatrice aiming to spill the king's blood.

"You've never behaved," Durante said at Beatrice. "You're just like your sister."

"We're *twins*, you fucking idiot. What do you expect?" She parried another blow that sliced too close to her head. It knocked the crown off of his head. "I am *done* listening to you sputter out commands and destroy our lives for your own gain. Lorian and I are our own people, and you cannot fuck over the world's prosperity to advance over a country you hate."

"Shut up! Just—!" Without any warning or forms of strategy, Durante fell forwards and thrust his sword out.

Blood spilled down the front of Beatrice's burgundy dress. She stepped back, not yet processing the pain she should've been feeling.

The sword plunged deep into her right arm. It bent her forearm in a way it shouldn't have gone.

Her severed arm fell to the floor like dead weight, and the room erupted into screams.

Chapter 39: Circa's Decision

As if she hadn't just thanked her Goddess for endowing her with the tiniest bit of luck in her unfortunate life, as the stone door closed behind her, her torch snuffed itself out.

"Oh, come on." She struggled to push it back open, but it was shut by whatever—whoever—had moved it.

The darkness enveloped her. Her ears picked up white noise that wasn't there before, and the walls, even though they were still as gravestones, closed in around her.

Maybe being found by officers wasn't such a bad thing anymore.

"What the fuck did I do wrong by you?" Aida asked no one. "I did everything right, didn't I? I opened up, I fought to get into school. I made friends, I fucking fell in love. I survived through time and back, I watched the woman I worship die without being able to save her. Now, after all that, I die in a crypt by following *you*? Nothing gets solved and Lorian gets married off to a man they don't even like? That's it? Again?"

Without a reasonable answer to follow, Aida picked off a piece of stone from the wall and chucked it behind her. "Fuck you!"

The stone she expected to hit rock instead hit something solid and warm, like a hand grabbing hold of it, and didn't fall.

She froze. All that was in this crypt was her and the statue, nothing more.

She pressed her back against the door. "Hello?"

Nothing moved. Aida heard herself wheezing.

The torches around the crypt lit without matches. One by one they came alive, until the room was aglow in orange.

The statue of Circa was staring down at her, fully formed into the real person, real Goddess.

Aida dropped to her knees, showing her submission to a being that could end her life a thousand times over. "Uh, sorry," she said, "about that."

Circa cocked her head, a curious owl sighting a plump mouse.

"I didn't, you know, mean all that stuff I said so confidently a second ago. You know how it is, thinking you're...about to die."

She stepped off of her statue's podium and reached out her hand, and Aida, on instinct, flinched. Dominant women, whenever cross with her, had the habit of striking her instead of warning her about her disobedience.

When she peeked one eye open to see the damage, Circa still had her hand out, palm out: an offering, or waiting for an exchange.

Aida let the room settle before taking her hand.

Her body floated her to her feet. Weightless, like being underwater without the fear of sinking. She didn't move or breathe. She allowed Circa's magic to lift her.

Circa held Aida's hand. Her flesh was neither warm nor cold, neither soft nor calloused. It was like touching something inanimate yet filled with magic.

She brought Aida towards the locked door.

"Wait—"

Circa materialized through the wall. Good for her. Unable to change the will of a God, Aida recoiled at the thought of being pushed through the cracks of something tangible.

Merciful Circa willed Aida through the wall with her.

"*Fuck*," Aida breathed out.

Exploring the Catacombs was far less terrifying as a ghost. With the ability to walk through walls, Circa toured Aida through locked tombs into tight corridors. Torches lit and died out as the Goddess passed them. She made no noise as she walked, no footprints, either. She only existed, and carried Aida with her.

The sound of officers came down their hall, too soon for Circa to hide them through a wall. Aida braced for another fight.

They came. And went. They breezed right through them, fluttering Aida's dress and the tiny wisps of hair clinging to her sweaty forehead.

Circa continued on like nothing had tried to stop them.

Aida tried reading anything from her expression. With that unbreaking smile, she appeared doll-like, despite looking very much like a real person.

Circa glided down a hall that ended at a handle-less door. Keeping her hand light on Aida's, she allowed them inside.

It was half the size of the first crypt dedicated to Circa. It couldn't have fit a life-sized statue of a God, much less a child. All it had was a small platform raised in the center. The walls curved in around them, and at the center of the ceiling, rings like a tree stump radiated out and down around the room in dark, sooty lines.

Circa led Aida into the center.

Aida waited. She heard herself breathing again but not Circa. She didn't need to breathe.

"Should I—"

"Be doing anything" was the end of that sentence, but as she tried to form the words, she plunged down into the Earth and back into darkness.

All she had was Circa's hand to hold. Her feet left the stable ground. The air or whatever was around them whistled through her ears, thrumming her head in a migraine and shaking up her brain. She felt herself getting sucked into a tight space and tried to stop herself from falling any farther. Invisibility and time travel made sense, at this stage. Her life was fucked enough to believe that absurdity.

Living *through* the steps to get there altered her world too much.

Aida kicked her feet until she dropped onto something. Her eyes came into focus like a dirty mirror.

She and Circa had travelled into a grand bedroom. The walls were gold and embellished from floor to ceiling in artwork. The ceiling was carved with constellations and phases of the Moon, and the floor's carpet was illustrated with roses and thorns.

Eve was lounging on a settee, bare feet kicked up while wearing one of those beautiful maroon dresses she loved. She was eating sweets dipped in golden Nectar.

"No," Aida whispered.

Her husband, Meyeso, was sitting by her side. He was in a rocking chair, head drooped, a hand dug into his black, curly hair.

Eve bit into her pastry. The filling came out and leaked down her jaw. "Meyeso." She snorted. "Meyeso, look. Look at me." She arched her neck over the settee's armrest. "Look. Imagine Julius' face if he—"

Meyeso doubled over and coughed up a mouthful of blood.

Eve sprang up and wiped the cream off of her face. Her bedroom doors opened. A gladiator—Frederico—came in. "Your Highness—"

Eve held up her hand. "Leave us."

Aida almost left on her command. Being in her queen's *bedroom*, seeing her in these intimate moments, it wasn't right. She looked up at Circa for guidance.

Circa was bouncing on her heels.

Eve knelt beside her husband and ran her hand down his cheek. "Hey—hey, *amar*. You're alright. This's nothing."

Meyeso continued coughing into his hand. Each cough seemed to take all of his strength away, until he was bent over in his armchair and sniffling. "I'm sorry," he said. "The medicine you gave me...doesn't seem to be working."

"We'll find something new."

"I'm sorry."

"No. Do *not* say that." She lifted his chin. "We *will* get through this. You *will* get better. You have a little one to meet." She brought his hand to her stomach. "I know she can't wait to meet you."

Meyeso rested his weight on her. "You don't think it'll be a boy?"

"No. She has my spirit in her, and your love. I sense it."

Meyeso smiled weakly and touched his Visatorre marking with hers. "Whoever she becomes," he said, "I'm sure she'll be wonderful."

As they cuddled up closer together, sharing this one moment Aida knew wouldn't last, Aida stepped back and pulled

434

on Circa's arm. "Why're you showing me this? I know how this ends. I saw—" She choked up. "I *saw* it end. She dies because of me."

Circa's smile, somehow, widened even more, the thought of Aida's failures filling her with delight.

Aida tried to walk backwards towards the windows. "I don't want to see her anymore," she confessed. "Bring me back."

Circa didn't let go.

"*Please.*"

They sunk back into the ground. Tethered to Circa, Aida had no choice but to land beside her in a hallway quite familiar to her now.

It was months later. Eve's belly bump was growing against her tight corset, but her usual smile was replaced by mourning. Her eyes were heavy—she hadn't slept in days. Her maroon dress had been dyed black.

King Julius II and Queen Julia were standing before her in a hall Aida had once run through. Julia had her hands folded and was standing behind her husband with his gladiators. All of them were wearing black.

Each of them bowed. Eve barely moved her head down in acknowledgement.

"Allow me to speak for both of us," King Julius said, "when we say we give our sincerest condolences to you. He was a good king and a great man to have led Siina. He will be missed sincerely."

Eve said nothing back.

Aida tugged on Circa. "Couldn't you have fixed this? You could've saved him. All of this would've been different if you'd intervened, so why didn't you?"

Circa continued bouncing on her heels, watching the opera play out before her, waiting for the climax.

Julia broke from her husband's side in a sob. She captured Eve in a hug and cried on her shoulder. "I'm so sorry, Eve. I'm so, so sorry."

Eve looked past her into the chandeliers.

"I'm so sorry you're being put through this by the Gods. Oh, Gods, you don't deserve this, Eta. You don't deserve this fate."

From this angle, Aida saw Eve's tears. She blinked once and they were gone, but in their place, the release she'd been waiting for: sadness, a chink in her armor.

The scene faded. They were now in a room lit only by a fireplace. Eve was in bed, clutching the sheets and screaming in pain. Gladiators and nursemaids were there for her with burning sage and bowls of water.

Julia brushed back Eve's sweaty bangs. "You're doing amazing, Eta. Just breathe. She's almost out."

Eve screamed and banged her fist hard into the bedpost. It cracked in multiple places. "*Curse* this process."

"It's almost out—Frederico, hold her leg now, please."

"Yes, Your Majesty." He helped spread them open.

Julia placed a damp rag to her cheek. "One more push, Eve. You're so close."

Upon her command, Eve's body seized, she screamed, and one last push birthed the infant, or heir to Siina.

It was a lot different than what Aida imagined. The baby was *not* cute and was covered with white film that made it more grey than pink. Everyone in the room cried with it, relieved for this bald, wrinkly almost-human with a grandfather's scowl.

"Look," Julia told Eve. "Eta, my love, look down. Look at your baby." She placed it against Eve's bare chest.

The weight of her baby nestled against her heart. She tried stroking its head, then cheek. Her softness contrasted with the baby's wailing and the rashness Eve was known for.

Aida touched her own cheek.

"She looks like you," Julia said.

The next few scenes passed by too rapidly for Aida to make sense of them. Jumps between Eve's palace and the Roman one, an argument with Julia in tears, Eve having sex with her and then Julius, them feeding into her gluttony.

In the last scene, Eve was sitting at a desk in a child's playroom. She was reading something in an old book.

"Mama, how come it's so hard to read?"

Hiding underneath Eve's dress was her little girl. She'd been reading her own book of fairy tales and placed it in her lap. "My eyes keep getting blurry when I focus on the letters."

Eve set aside her work. "They say you inherited your father's poor eyesight, my love. There's nothing that can be done with eyes such as yours."

"How come? You're the bestest queen. Surely you can make something to fix it. I was thinking..." She reached her tiny arms across Eve's desk and picked up a glass paperweight. "You see how this glass, once you place it across the words"—she demonstrated it—"enlarges them and makes things easier to see? Well, I was thinking, Mama, what if you put a thinner glass near both of your eyes? You could hold it up with sticks or something around your head or behind your ears, and allow the weight in the front to be balanced on your nose. That way, someone who can't see would be able to. What do you think? Do you think that'd work?"

Eve examined the paperweight. "That...does seem like it could help, yes." She scooped her up and left heavy, wet kisses all over her face. "How did you grow up to be so smart? Every day you amaze me."

"It's because you're already so amazing, Mama!"

Aida took off her glasses and rubbed down the frames. How long until this little one was able to see the world for what it was?

The scene faded once more, and Circa brought Aida back into darkness. There was no sound, no light, but she saw Circa and herself, and she saw stars twinkling above her.

She was lost to time, trapped in a dream.

Aida fell into Circa's robes. "Please, don't show me any-more," she asked. "I can't take it."

Circa looked down, watching and listening.

"I get it, okay? I fuck up every decision with my own selfish ones. I'm stupid. I studied history and writing for years, I learned about wars and the people who survived them. I knew everything I thought I needed to know, but I don't. I'm a Visatorre. I know nothing and will die knowing nothing. So please, just take me back to Lorian so I can fuck up their life, too. It's all I'm good for."

"Stop that, my love."

Aida jerked her head up to her Goddess, but she was gone, ten meters back, always at a distance.

Across the way, standing alone, was the woman Aida had poured her everything into. She was wearing her beautiful maroon dress. No hole in her stomach, no baby in her womb. She was simply there, and alive.

"Come now," Eve said to her. "There's no need for self-pity. It's ill-suited for you."

Aida wiped away her tears to better see her. Would there ever be a time where she met Eve with dignity? "I've gone mad, haven't I? I lost my mind wandering the Catacombs."

"You have not. Whether you want to admit it or not, you have a sound mind, Aida. I presume, at least. I heard that your parents were exceptionally wise."

"You know my parents?"

She smiled warmly.

"My birth parents?"

The smile tightened. "One of them, yes."

"No." She didn't believe her. *She* didn't even know her own parents.

She thought. Oh, how she thought it, thought around it, against it. The paths leading her here sounded inane, and good things didn't happen to her. It was Circa's way, making her life harder than she could handle.

She held her head. It was pounding. From her brain or heart. They were too connected in her body. Too affected.

Eve walked up to Aida. "Stand up, my love."

She did. She hung her head so she didn't meet her eyes.

"You didn't let me die, so don't even let that thought pass you," Eve said. "You were experiencing a painful jump. Nobody would've expected nor asked you to save someone already in death's arms. People die, Aida. No matter how much we scream and beg and pray, we need to welcome death that comes for all. And yet, the world continues on. It allows us the room to grieve and, in time, allows the pain to subside, and you will be able to let new love into your very full heart."

Aida shook her head. Her eyes were beginning to sting from new hurt.

Eve hugged her. "We cannot think about what we should've done. All we're able to do is spend what few, precious moments we have in becoming our best self, which you have been doing since the moment of your birth. And between you and me," she said, "it ain't *our* choice." She motioned to Circa, who had yet to move. "It's been a millennium and I haven't gotten a peep outta her."

Aida sniffled. "Tell me," she said, "your baby, where is she now?"

Eve kept massaging her back. "You know the answer, don't you? You've known for a while."

"No." Her tears left a wet spot on her embroidered sleeve.

"Aida."

"No."

"My Aida."

A sob left her throat as she held on tighter. She couldn't let her go, not again. She wanted to savor these feelings. A mother's touch, one whose world revolved not around their child's devotion to them, but to their child's growth into a newer, better person.

Eve let her cry as a true mother would. "I'm so happy to see you again."

"How?" Aida cried. "How're you my...?" She barely got out the final word. It sounded like a curse, like bringing it up would shatter the reality being formed.

"You were born such a curious little child," Eve reminisced. "Always looking for answers, reading everything you could get your hands on. I had you just after your father passed. I was distraught, unable to keep my own people in harmony, but then I found Julia."

"Did you love her?" Aida asked, because she needed to know. "Did you really love her, or was she a means to an end, like King Julius was?"

"I loved her almost as much as I love you. I had to do many things as queen that I regret, many entailing rather unfavorable favors to that wretched man Julius in order to see Siina prosper. But I did—I do—love her. Julia helped raise you while I advanced Siina. We gained land and wealth, and I gained two lovely, beautiful, strong girls whom I cherish with all my heart."

A thousand more questions came to Aida: her time as a child, how she'd been brought to the future, how her father had been. What was Siina like? What did their palace look like? Was it grand? What were the pillows made out of?

But she needed more important questions answered before she broke. "How were you able to travel into the future? What does the second Visatorre marking mean? How come my future self can do it so well?"

"Circa has the same marking, you know."

"Are you a Goddess?"

"I don't believe so. I think I've been made a saint a few times, but I only had a handful of Circa's powers before I died."

Aida's heart fell. She crossed "immortality" off the list.

"Back in my time, Visatorre were able to travel without the pain they feel today. We were blessed to bring back information from our past that allowed us to progress. We were treated respectfully.

"When Julius told me he was going to murder my people for me being with Julia, I'd planned on dying for every single one of them. I was going to fight until my dying breath to keep

441

them safe. Circa had seen that. Before I lost my life, she took me here."

A flash of lightning lit up the dark space, and off to their side, about as far away as an actor was from their audience, were another Circa and Eve. Past Eve was on her knees, dressed in her tattered rags with her hands unshackled.

When she saw Circa standing in front of her, she bowed. "My Goddess, please, lend me your mercy. 100,000 of your people are about to be slaughtered for my sins. I beseech you, I'll do anything you ask, just let me save them."

Circa's robes fluttered against the non-existent ground. A wind Aida couldn't feel lifted Past Eve off the ground. Energy congregated around her Visatorre marking.

Circa's finger touched the middle of the circle.

Past Eve's head was thrown back with the force of an arrow piercing it. It should've snapped her neck, but the Gods delayed her death. Her body burst ablaze in white fire, and the two of them disappeared with a harmonious *crack*.

"She gave me the tiniest bit of power of a Goddess," Current Eve said, bringing Aida back. "She saw what was going to happen and gave me part of her powers to save them. You saw, didn't you? How I jumped to and fro with complete control? I did it quite well. I could've done wonders for our people."

"So why did she let you die seconds afterwards? Why let them be murdered anyway?"

"Do not look so afraid, my love. The Gods do not seek constant suffering. They give us choices to better ourselves every day."

"But she didn't. She watched you suffer and did nothing—"

Eve placed the gentlest of fingers against Aida's lips.

"You were born with so many thoughts in your head that the only way to let them go was by discussion," Eve told her. "Let me tell you everything about the Gods before you form your opinions about them, because believe me: They have good in them.

"From the moment I was born, I was an atrocious girl. I lied and cheated and fought my way to the top so that my people could thrive. I took so much, so when she gifted me these powers, I thought she was going to take my life in exchange, which I accepted with fervor."

Pain emanated from her face as she faced her end. "To be granted these gifts, you must give up a part of yourself that you treasure most."

"So she took away your *life*?" Aida replayed the timeline in her head. She'd lost so much in one day, and for what? "That's manic. What does that teach you?"

"She didn't take away my life. What she took away—" She sighed, brokenly. "On that day, I lost my composure. I lost my titles and you. I lost my *pride*," she finished with. "*That* is what she took from me, and that became my undoing."

The scene came back, but now, Past Eve and Circa were with Little Aida. Past Eve had earned her stomach injury. Little Aida tried to keep her alive.

"Mama!" she yelled. "Mama, breathe! Mama!"

Past Eve's eyes now held a trace of anger at the Goddess who she thought had betrayed her. "Circa!" She coughed. "Why?" She rolled to her knees, holding back her innards and child.

Aida was thankful she had no memories of this happening.

"Circa, please. Forgive me. Forgive me for the sins I so knowingly committed in your name. I know my wrongdoings now. But please, Goddess, don't punish my daughter for this. She is all I have left to my name. I know I am not a good person. I know I have my faults. But my Aida." She placed Little Aida in front of Circa. "Do not let my mistakes ruin her timeline any more than they already have. If I cannot be saved, please, save my daughter. Save my Aida."

Circa cocked her head at the little girl being given to her. She must've been a giantess to her. She cowered in fear of her mother dying behind her and the God weighing her life before her.

Circa stretched out her long arm, and before Little Aida could react, the Goddess touched her forehead, and Little Aida fell limp into her arms.

Circa picked her up, cradling her so her head didn't sag.

Past Eve bowed her head. "Thank you, Circa. Oh, thank you."

Circa started walking away.

"Circa?"

She didn't look back.

"Circa, where are you taking her?" She groaned as a new wave of blood emptied from her stomach. Her shoulder fell. "*Circa!*"

Without receiving her answer, both Circa, Little Aida, and Past Eve disappeared in a flash, off towards the far future.

"She delivered you 1,200 years into the future, away from the aftermath of my mistakes, and delivered me into your arms, within the Catacombs I helped build, not a second later."

Aida covered her mouth. Not only had she been cared for by a mother who'd risked her life for her, but she'd been the cause of so much misery for generations to come.

"I shouldn't have called out to you," Aida said. "Back at the Colosseum, if I hadn't called out to you, you'd still be—"

"You wouldn't have been able to stop it. Can you imagine a life where I kept my powers and continued ruling? By that time, Julia had found out about my relationship with Julius. We were having a falling out, arguing constantly, and I would've run both Siina and Roma to the ground. You know this. I was able to have you in my life for six years, and those were the happiest years I'd ever lived." She wiped away Aida's tears. "You've grown into such a beautiful princess, Aida Alba Meyeso Costa."

Aida held Eve again. It was the only place she felt safe.

Eve pet her head. "Circa had taken a chance on me, and I'd abused my powers yet again. Because of my selfish choices, Circa cursed the Visatorre people with indescribable pain, and hasn't chosen another person to wield these powers since."

Aida felt a presence against her back, and she turned to see Circa standing statue-still over her.

She hid close to Eve.

"Circa has been watching you, as have I. We've seen you grow into this compassionate woman who lets people into her heart even though it's not yet ready for them. You want to save people not because it'll benefit you, but because it's the right thing to do. You're kind, you listen. You're the perfect person to inherit the gift of the Gods."

Circa leisurely reached out her hand.

"But," Eve added, "you know that the Gods do not give us anything we don't think we can handle. Circa has shown you part of these gifts this year. If you do not want this path, you do not have to walk it. You have a choice in your decision, as do all of us in life."

445

But if she were to become part-Goddess, what did she love most?

Well, Lorian. That was all that was coming to her. Lorian's happiness and their future. She couldn't hurt them from this decision, even if it cost her being closer to Circa.

But Future Aida had Lorian, and they looked in good health. It had to be something internal, then. Would she steal away her mobility? Her wit? What did she have that Future Aida didn't? She still had Lorian, she was still smart, at times.

The thought, the unthinkable thought racing through her mind, made her shiver. The one thing Future Aida didn't have...

Aida folded her hands in front of her. All her life she'd wanted to speak to both of these goddesses, but now, she just wanted to crawl into somebody's arms and stay quiet for a moment.

So, that's what she did. She held Eve and breathed in, breathed out. She thought about how free her future self looked when she jumped. She thought about what Lorian meant to her. A few months ago, she hated both herself and her future self, herself because she didn't see an easy future, and her future self because that's what she had, with Lorian, with herself.

When she was ready, Aida asked, "Since my future self is me, hasn't this decision already been made? Aren't I going to inherit the powers?"

"You will," Eve confessed. "Circa knows everything that has, is, and will ever happen. It's charted in her eyes. She knew I'd be born ruthless and die the same way, and that you'd be sent to a little village in Bělico and fall in love with Julia's kin.

She already has the story written out, Aida. She is our author, and she's connecting the final chapters together."

Aida dared another look at Circa. That wicked smile was becoming less malicious and more proud, proud of the story she'd been able to watch grow over the course of centuries.

Aida laughed. "Ya'll are a bunch of bored, egotistical loons. Who writes stories just to see people suffer?"

"That's what makes life worth living." Eve took something out of her pocket and wrapped it around Aida's wrist.

It was a bracelet, made from the same twine hers and Julia's were made out of.

"Your roads will cross and tangle and appear uninstructive at times, but you will make it through. You will return to your past and find the roads to lead you back here. Remember to be kind to yourself, Aida." She secured on the bracelet, then winked playfully. "If you can help yourself."

"That's..." She laughed at nothing. How could she *not* tease herself now? This time last year, she was working overtime with essay-writing to pay for her application to Durante Academy. In under five months, she'd become a princess— a queen—to a dead country. How could she not tease herself, just a little?

Eve touched foreheads with her. "You're so strong, just like your father."

"Just like you." She took a breath. "I'm scared," she whispered. "Don't tell that creepy person behind me I said that."

"I'm pretty sure she knows. I have that feeling. Omniscience, you see."

Aida embraced her one last time, a being that may or may not have been real. It didn't matter to her. Fact or fiction, she knew what this woman meant to her.

And what she needed to finish for her, for their future.

She turned back to Circa and mashed the Goddess' finger into her marking. "Do your worst," she said.

And her heart stopped beating.

Chapter 40: Aftermath

Beatrice's arm hit the ground with an unnatural *thud*. Bones were poking out of her wet skin and severed tendons. Nothing splattered dramatically. Her arm was just gone, unusable.

Lorian didn't know they were holding their breath until Carmine screamed and jump-started the whole foyer.

Carmine dove atop his king and crushed his skull in with his fist. All the feelings Lorian was suppressing came through him. Rage boiled over in his eyes, an animalistic urge to tear a living thing apart. Durante was helpless against his primitive state. He was still waiting for someone to save him.

"Stop him!" he called to his officers.

"You're a monster!" Carmine screamed. "What the *fuck* did you do!?"

The officers who'd dropped their swords picked them back up. A few broke formation to help Beatrice. Through sudden exhilaration, she was still standing.

"You—I am your *king*," Durante panted. "You—"

"*Fuck* you!" Carmine punched him in the face. "She's my daughter, you—!" He went for the throat. Durante went for the eyes.

Beatrice tipped.

"Bea!" Lorian and nearby officers grabbed her. Her dead weight almost brought Lorian down, but they stayed strong for her.

They gently lowered her to the ground. She didn't scream out once. They wished she did.

Carmine punched Durante good in the mouth before three of his own officers dragged him off.

The room stilled. Frightened guests hid around staircases and doorways in wait. Maids whispered about what to do next.

"—and get her to the infirmary."

Lorian hadn't realized they were talking until the officers were nodding at them. "Make a tourniquet for her arm and get her to the doctors immediately. Help her stand. Don't let her fall."

"Yes, Your Highness," one said, and led her away.

Beatrice's good hand reached for Lorian's. Their fingers grazed before she was taken away.

"Lorian."

Lorian watched Beatrice go.

"Your Highness."

They turned to two faces they thought they'd never see again. They were dressed in formalwear with their swords locked at their sides. Matteo had been crying.

"What're you doing here?" Lorian asked their friends.

"We need to get you somewhere safe," Alessio said. He looked older with his hair styled down.

"We can guide you to the infirmary, Your Highness," Matteo said, "if you can follow us."

They weren't ready to reintroduce themselves like this. It was supposed to be their last secret, their two worlds forever separate.

Casting one last glance at Carmine being taken away, Lorian followed their friends to the infirmary.

—◇—

The public was politely kicked off royal grounds as the palace dealt with this medical and historic emergency. Lorian felt it in the air, the change. Everyone from officers to doctors had their sister's name in their mouth. They didn't care that their words made the queen weep. Nothing Lorian was hearing was hopeful.

And so, they fled. It was all they knew how to do. Leaving their mother and sister behind, Lorian found their chance and ran until they hit the garden courtyard.

It was quieter here, and colder, enough to wake Lorian up from the stupor they'd found themselves in. They felt like they should've been crying or screaming, but all they felt was nothingness. A numbness had drained them of everything, even their tears. They couldn't show this side of themselves to their mother. She'd think them apathetic.

Alessio and Matteo dutifully stayed by Lorian's side. Maids and other officers asked if they were okay, but Lorian left them unanswered. They couldn't speak.

Alessio walked up to Lorian. They were slumped on the railing, spitting off its edge and watching it disappear in the leaves.

Alessio spat with them. "Never had a clue, you know," he said, "about you. You played it off real well. You're a valiant girl. Or person. Don't know which one to use."

"Regardless of that, you're really brave," Matteo said. "I don't get much of what's going on with this future self talk, but I really look up to you. Well, I always have."

"Because you're so short?" Alessio teased.

"Hey, I'm not short!"

Lorian sniffled.

"However you decide to move on from here," Alessio said, "know that we'll support you. You can stick with being royal or abdicate fully. Whatever happens, we'll have your back. You piece of shit."

Lorian hid their face in their arms.

Alessio's and Matteo's hands found their back. One of them ruffled their hair.

"You'll be okay," Matteo said in his calm voice, and Lorian mentally thanked them both, for being there.

"Come on." Alessio tugged them up. "Let's clean up your face."

Lorian jolted awake. They, Alessio, and Matteo had brought out a couch from one of the sitting rooms into the hallway by the hospital door. Lorian couldn't be in the hospital with Beatrice, so they kept as close as they could and fell asleep with nightmares chasing them. Alessio and Matteo were cuddled up at the edge, keeping guard.

A light grew brighter from around the hallway corner.

By the look of their mother's smudged eye makeup, she looked like she, too, had had trouble sleeping.

Carmine walked arm in arm with her as lovers would. He had a bandage underneath his bruised eye and walked with a limp. He must've been free of all charges, off scot-free for defending his royal family.

Their mother's arms were like vice grips around Lorian. Despite the day she must've had, when they fell into her, her strength was there for them.

"She's recovering," their mother said. "They don't know if...She hasn't woken up yet, but they're trying to reattach it. They said she might be able to use it again."

She didn't cry. Neither did Carmine. By the looks on their faces, so emotionally and physically tired, they must've run out of tears hours ago.

"I'm sorry," their mother said. "We should've told you sooner about us. It wasn't fair that we kept it a secret."

Carmine tried to bow to them, but the pain in his side made him whimper. "I'm sorry as well. Your mother and I wanted to tell you for so long, but..."

Lorian broke from their mother. They had nothing to apologize for.

They could see the similarities between them now. They had the same nose. Tall like their mother, with the same face structure. They hadn't noticed that before. Must've picked up that keen eye from him.

Lorian's heart cracked. "Can I...can I have a hug?"

One nod, and Lorian was in their father's embrace. They inhaled his scent. It smelled nothing like themselves, but no wonder they yearned for his affection.

Lorian let go twenty-three years of built-up anguish against him. They sobbed like they'd never shed a tear before. They let themselves wake the palace with the tears they'd been too shy to reveal. Carmine's hand cupped the back of their head and they cried harder.

"I have you," he said, voice wavering. "I have you."

What a blessing it was to be able to cry and be held.

"Your father, he wasn't able to have children," their mother said in a rush. "He was threatening to take my life if I didn't give him what he wanted. We were out of options, but then he went on a hunting trip in Bělico for a week. We thought what we did was best."

"But we should've told you," Carmine said. "You were old enough to know. It was just, with everything you were going through, we thought telling you would've angered you."

"Which we should've paid more attention to, as your parents," their mother said. "I cannot begin to apologize for that, Lorian, but I'm truly sorry."

"But...this had nothing to do with me," Lorian said. "You shouldn't have worried about what I would've..." They trailed off. They had no idea what they were saying, they just couldn't bear to hear their parents be upset any longer.

"No," their mother said. "You were hurting and in pain. You and your sister both, and we should've helped you, but instead, I was too fearful to speak up. I shouldn't have done that to you, and I'm sorry."

"We played into King Durante's fear tactics," Carmine said.

"We never went against him."

"Even when he hurt you."

"But things will be different now. Your...King Durante will have to face the consequences of his actions. After he's seen to, he will be confined to a cell until further notice."

"In the dungeon?"

"After what he did to Bea..." She breathed deeply, her eyes closed. "I won't allow such abuse to continue on in my palace. After tonight, he will no longer be in our lives."

"Statuses will change because of this," Carmine said, "and once your father is out of the infirmary, we'll have to speak with him about the next step."

Lorian shrank at the thought. To be promised a life without Durante in it only to know they'd have to meet with him for the next several months.

"Hey." Carmine took their shoulder. "We'll get through this. We've been through hardships and your father's temper all before, and we're still here."

Lorian nodded along with Carmine's newfound optimism. Their sister wasn't here with them, the whole palace was a wreck with nerves and uncertainty, and Aida...

A tear fell off their nose. "Aida. Aida—Has anyone found her?"

"I haven't heard anything," their mother said.

"Nor have I," said Carmine. "I know a few of my men pursued her through the Catacombs, but they never found her. But she *will* be found," he added. "She can never leave me alone for more than an hour."

"Right," they said. It'd been hours, though. She should've come back.

Their mother tried on a smile. "Let's go see your sister."

—◆—

The doctors warned them not to come in. They told them that Beatrice was in unstable condition and that they needed to monitor her.

Then they saw the queen, and they let all three of them in without a word.

Wherever the king was, he wasn't in the infirmary. It wasn't a large space—ten cots against the walls. It was mostly in place for the officers and kitchen staff who got cut up while working in the palace. Lorian made regular trips here as a child. It'd been years since they'd come back. It looked smaller.

Their sister was asleep, propped up by pillows and bandaged with gauze. The room smelled of blood but Lorian saw no traces of it. Beside her, in the only other occupied bed, must've been Kadar. His curtains were drawn, meaning that he had his headscarves off. Zaahir was slouched in a waiting chair beside him. Lorian couldn't tell he was asleep until they closed the door and he didn't stir.

Lorian took out one of the chairs for their mother. She whispered sweet encouragement to her, holding back her tears even though she didn't have to. Carmine tried to fix her hair, but he ended up keeping his hands on the covers. Lorian timed her breathing.

"She's so strong," their mother whispered.

Lorian couldn't agree more.

"You should go," Lorian told their mother after they left the infirmary. "You look exhausted."

"We should all head back and get some rest. It's been too long of a day to stay awake with the night."

"Let me take you back." Carmine winced and pulled back. Their mother touched his lower back, reading his injuries.

Lorian bowed for him, a custom they thought they'd fully scraped from their memories. It seemed that being royal would always be rooted in them, even if their status might've been revoked once the Sun rose.

"I need to find Aida," Lorian said. "It's been hours. I'm worried that she might be..." They didn't finish the thought. "I need her."

"I'll stay with you," their mother said. "I won't leave you when you need me most."

"And I can send out a search party for her," Carmine suggested. "We can send dogs through the Catacombs to find where she was last. And I'm sure she'll come back, Lorian. You don't have to worry."

"...Okay," they said, but worrying was all they could do.

They waited until they returned to Alessio and Matteo on the couch. They were playing cards together to pass the time and greeted the royal family kindly.

After losing the smell of their sister's blood, Lorian pressed their back into the wall and covered their face with both hands.

"Are you alright?" Carmine asked. "Do you need to sit down?"

"I-I can't be alone right now," they confessed, "but I didn't want you all to keep doting on me. You've been through enough."

"Okay, stop that." Carmine took them back into his arms. "I won't leave you."

"Nor will I," their mother promised.

"I'll stay with you until you slam the door on me," Alessio said, "which you've done multiple times, might I remind you. And I know this's horrible timing, but I still need my horse back."

Lorian chuckled. "Then can we take a walk? I won't leave the palace."

"Or go through the window?"

They hit Alessio's arm as the five of them walked the unusually quiet halls.

There was a full Moon tonight, a wakeful presence that reminded Lorian of Aida. Lorian should've gone down to the Catacombs themselves to find her, but they were still a coward of the past. And if Aida had been gone for this long with the full ability to travel wherever she could, that probably meant she didn't want to be found, or she'd found herself in the past again.

Their feet brought them up to the clock tower. The ticking signaled it was three in the morning. The nutcrackers were fast asleep on the sides of the clock.

The bed Aida had made for herself was unmade. Neither of them cared to make theirs when at Missus Sharma's, so it wasn't unusual to see, but the pillows were thrown about. The blanket had been launched into the wall. A box with a red ribbon around it was crumpled from being stepped on.

A dark figure was silhouetted by the cool night. They had their back to them as they watched time tick by.

"Aida!" They couldn't contain themselves and ran in after her. They knew her silhouette by heart. It shaped theirs. "Aida, what happened? Where'd you run off to?"

She turned to them. She had her glasses off and quickly put them back on in a squint. Her Visatorre marking had gained its second ring.

"Oh, my goodness." They touched her forehead. "You got your second mark."

She stepped away from them. "Uh, hi?"

"...Hi? What's wrong? Are you hurt?"

"Uh, I don't think so. I just woke up here trying to find out where I was."

"You're in the palace's clock tower."

She gave the room another once-over, then examined Lorian's friends and family like unwelcomed roaches. "Uh, okay."

Lorian took another step back. "Aida?"

More and more of that hateful apprehension created a rift between them. She gripped her cane more as a weapon. "What is this room," she asked, "and who are you?"

Chapter 41: Rediscovery

They called themselves Lorian and she Aida.

That was all she knew about this world.

Her brain, by her account, had been utterly fucked. She knew how to breathe and why night turned into day. She knew how to clothe and bathe herself, and she knew this "house" she thought she was in was actually a palace.

But her age and her background, her surname and her parents. Her likes, dislikes, what she wanted for breakfast that morning, nothing came to her. It was a dark void trying to be lit by these strangers.

The person called Lorian seemed the most affected by her loss of memories. When they found out she didn't know a thing about them, they began to cry, and Mustache Man helped them ride out their feelings. The two gladiator-looking friends were in a panic, and so was Long-Haired Lady. She was trying to calm everyone down.

Honestly, Aida felt bad, knowing she was the cause of their worry. She wished she knew them and what'd happened ten minutes ago. Then she could've placed her heart in the right emotional box.

They brought her downstairs. Incredibly upscale, this place. They all were. She came to wearing this white dress that felt much too expensive for the night, but someone had dirtied it.

She had, from a time she couldn't recall.

They brought her into a sitting room filled with books. Walls of books, books on the table, elaborately-placed novels framing paintings and statues. For the craziest moment, she wanted to read all that she could. She had a feeling it wasn't all fantasy—there'd be history here, pages to recount the years she was missing.

Then she read the room and guessed it wouldn't be appropriate. The Lorian one hadn't stopped crying.

"What're we to do?" Mustache Man asked.

"Has she truly lost everything?" Long-Haired Lady asked.

"For the moment," Lorian said. "Something always happens when she jumps. She must've jumped far enough that she can't..."

They looked at her again. Something about those doting, green eyes did something to her brain. She wondered if they were friends.

They asked her questions about things she should've known. Circa and Eve, two names that meant nothing to her. She got Mustache Man's name—Carmine—and he asked her about her time at Missus Sharma's. Long-Haired Lady—the queen, she got through context clues—asked where she'd gone after Lorian's wedding. Lorian asked how she was feeling.

"Numb," she said honestly, because everything they were saying sounded like an unfunny joke. Carmine had one account of her life while the queen seemed out of the loop. Lorian kept chiming in with parts of their lives together, trying to make the timeline linear, but all she could say was, "I feel numb and tired."

The queen sighed. They all looked tired from the night. "We should retire and come back to this with leveled heads."

"I agree," Carmine said. "You two, especially." He addressed the queen and Lorian.

"Aida can stay overnight, can't she?" Lorian asked. "She can sleep with me. Or she can sleep alone." They checked in with Aida on what she wanted.

Aida stretched out her right leg. They must've been more than friends if they were so ready to share a bed with her. In, what she assumed to be, their home.

They were more than fancy: Lorian was royalty.

"Sure," she said with a shrug. She couldn't imagine being of royal blood. It must've sucked.

They ushered her through the palace. Their hand hovered by hers, but it didn't feel right to be close with them. After everything she'd heard, they could only surmount to a friend she'd lost contact with years ago. She couldn't relate to them. She didn't even know their last name. That was important to her.

She walked ahead to see their face. "Hey, what's your last name?"

She caught them spacing out. "Oh. Well, I've had two. Romano's my family name. Ashwell's my chosen name."

"Do you get to choose your name if you're part of the royal family?"

"No. I was told to marry someone I didn't want to marry, so I changed my name and made a new life for myself."

"So is Lorian your chosen name?"

They nodded, and Aida was content with that. It was a pretty name.

Lorian rubbed the back of their neck as they looked into the rug. "My real name is Lucia Maria Carolus Durante di Romano."

"Oh." Even though her memories were gone, she did know the naming conventions of this world. Names that ended in "a" were meant for girls.

Strange that she hadn't seen them as a girl since meeting them. She'd automatically seen them as something more. "Got you," she said.

"I know it's off-putting."

"It's not."

They faked a smile. She knew that, and hated it, how they hid their true feelings behind a facade. "I apologize. This's...Well, it's odder for you, of course. Of course it is."

She admired the architecture. "How old's this place?"

"It was built around 1,200 years ago. After Queen Eve's time. Do you remember her?"

"How would I remember someone who died 1,200 years ago?"

"Long story, I guess."

Aida eyed them suspiciously. "How long have we known each other?"

"Since the fall."

"Then how is that a long story?" She took their hand and led them through their own home. "It's snowing, so it couldn't have been more than a few months, right? How much could've happened in a few months?"

"More than you can imagine."

"Well, my imagination's fried, so I'm sure nothing will surprise me."

Lorian's bedroom was nothing like a bedroom. The walls were gold and the four-poster bed had six differently-sized pillows on it. The fireplace meant for fires held not a trace of soot and everything smelled of perfume.

"The maids must've come in here before the wedding," Lorian said. "You should've seen the looks of it twenty-four hours ago."

"What happened twenty-four hours ago?"

"Oh, nothing too grand."

"Really?"

They laughed. "No, I'm sorry. I forgot I need to be more direct with you. I was married off to a prince named Zaahir, but then I ran away. Then many things happened in succession. I met you, and your future self, and my future self. We kissed," they added in, like that wasn't important, "and then Carmine found us and separated us, and then I was forced to re-marry Prince Zaahir again. I thought I'd never see you again and raged."

"Good."

"Huh?"

"Good," she repeated. "You shouldn't have to marry someone you don't want to be with, and you shouldn't have to be a princess if you don't want to be. Good on you for leaving. Should we leave again?"

They smiled a little more genuinely. "You came back for me right before I was meant to remarry. You met Eve, a wonderfully complex human being from a thousand years ago. You were able to control your jumps. I assume you met Circa and that's why you're like this now."

Aida looked them over. "And this all happened in the span of a few months?"

"It didn't feel that chaotic. Mostly."

"Huh. And who's Circa?"

"Who knows anymore."

Aida wanted to keep the conversation going, but she couldn't do that to Lorian. They were falling into bed as they spoke, their feet unable to support them.

"I apologize for being so dreary. I don't think I've slept in the past two days. Oh, excuse me." They pulled out a nightgown from one of their drawers. "While you look lovely in that, I assume it's difficult to sleep in."

"Why was I wearing it?"

"To crash my wedding."

"That how I was, huh?"

"You have no idea."

"I don't." She excused herself into the bathroom connected to their bedroom to change. When she returned, Lorian had dressed into a white button-down and silk bottoms. They were under the covers. Her side of the blankets had been folded for her.

Aida climbed in awkwardly and settled down on her back, the easiest on her sore leg that hadn't yet healed. She hoped she hadn't lived with this dull ache all her life.

The quiet hurt. She felt like she needed to fill the space with words of affirmation and help Lorian with whatever they were going through.

"Maybe your memories will come back when you wake up."

"I doubt my luck is that great," Aida said. "Is it?"

"I'm not sure how to answer that. A lot of unlucky things have happened to you, but you've gotten out of many deadly situations with your head held high. I think that counts for something." They got into position, their back to hers. "I can't keep my eyes open."

"Go to sleep if you're tired."

"I'll try. Goodnight, Aida."

"Night," she said, but she didn't fall asleep. Her mind was far too awake for her body, her bad foot tapping in anxiety about her past.

She looked over at Lorian's sleeping body. She wanted to see their face again.

Their smile helped get her to sleep.

She remembered falling with her memories coming down with her. Their glass shards broke into so many pieces that she couldn't piece them back together. She'd spent hours gathering them from off the ground with Circa watching her, forgetting more with every handful she picked up.

Her time as a child, jumping between the Siinan and Roman Palace. She, excited about meeting Julia and pulling faces at King Julius II behind his back. She felt her mother's touch as she fell asleep in bed. She told Little Aida stories about history and magic. They were her favorite.

"You're our future," a voice said, *"and you're going to make a magnificent queen."*

She frantically palmed the covers for her love. "Lorian!"

Something hit her. "What? What?"

Her mind was awake before her eyes. She cradled her head. Already, the memories were leaving her. Circa and Eve, the Catacombs, nights spent with Lorian. It was like there was a leak in the back of her brain spilling out precious memories.

Lorian touched the middle of her back. "What's wrong? What do you need?"

She tried desperately to keep hold of what few memories remained. How could she've forgotten Lorian? It wasn't fair. She couldn't lose them. "I remember," she whispered. "Bits and pieces, but they're blurry." She pulled on her hair. Eve's face, Lorian's sister's name. The cottage they'd hidden away in, who owned it again?

"That's good, isn't it?"

"No. I'm losing them as quickly as I'm getting them back. It's like a dream I'm forgetting."

"Well, we'll fix this together. I know we will."

It'd been taken away so easily. Everything she'd learned about herself and Lorian, their families and how they were tied together.

Eve's family.

Her family.

Circa.

Something caught on the blankets: a handwoven bracelet embedded around a circle amulet.

The tiny stone within the bracelet had the letter "A" etched into it.

Snot rolled down to her upper lip. She remembered something. A face. A gentle hand touching her. But the memories were so faded.

She looked up at Lorian, her confidant she knew so well. Where had they met? It'd been in Roma City, right? At the academy she'd wanted so badly to attend? What was the name of it again?

"Aida?"

She tried calming down by taking deep breaths. She gulped back spit. "Lorian, they're there. My memories, I know they are."

"I know. I'm here."

She knew that already. They'd always been there, ever since...

Something about books.

What book series had she liked again?

"Does your head hurt?" Lorian asked.

"I think it's...broken," she said. "Very, very broken."

"Well, give it some time. I'm sure all of it will come back to you."

"I think time is the worst thing for me now. I can't remember anything from the past. I-I remember you, and Missus, Uh..." She shut her eyes harder to think. "Missus Sharma's place, but the farther it is, the less I..." She dropped her head on Lorian's chest. To have a moment with her own mother. That mother lived in Bĕlico, didn't she?

No. While she did have a mother in Bĕlico, there had been another.

In a dark space.

With Circa.

She kicked the blankets off of her.

"Aida?"

"I need to go," she said. "I need to talk to the king about something very important, or the Constable. Carmine—"

Her head wavered. His name. That little memory of him felt tethered on the thinnest fishing line. If she pulled on it too quickly, the memory would swim away.

Her body, from being moved too suddenly, gave out. Her knees buckled and she started going down.

So, as easily as breathing, she willed herself not to fall.

She hardly heard the electric *zap* that took all Visatorre away. She was so focused on herself that she couldn't. She ended up ten paces to the right, near the windows.

"Aida!"

Before she got too comfortable, she tried again. A jump to the left, close to the fireplace. She wasn't happy with her performance—she didn't hit her mental mark—so she tried for the bed and smacked into one of the posts.

"Your Highness?" The bedroom door unlocked from the outside to a constable standing watch—Carmine. "Is everything alright?"

Aida didn't know, but she wanted to try one more time. Without thinking, she touched Lorian's hand and took them away in a jump.

They dropped onto stone, cold against their bare feet.

Before them stretched out the magnificence of Roma City. Every building and road leading to it, thousands of years of history and a dozen years of modernity rolled into a city of nearly 250,000.

She'd travelled them to the top of the palace, atop the clock tower Lorian loved so. The rising Sun sparkled the mosaic glass beneath their feet.

Lorian clung tightly to Aida as they looked over the edge. A nervous smile tickled their lips. "Wow."

Aida's brain dribbled out of her ears, making her light-headed. It didn't hurt, but another two-dozen more jumps and she'd be seeing double.

But it wasn't bad. It wasn't seizures or convulsions or migraines. It was okay.

"This's incredible," Lorian said. "Terrifying and death-defying, but so wonderfully incredible. Does this mean that all your memories are coming back?"

Aida refocused her blurry eyesight. "Oh, a few. None too important."

Lorian laughed. "None at all?"

"None at all, but, uh, I think I need to talk to your mother about this. Like, right now. She's the reigning monarch, right? I don't need to talk to your dad about this?"

"...Well," they said with delay, "back before you left wherever you went, something happened to my family. I think it shattered."

"Shattered?"

They nodded. "Let's go see my parents."

"He *attacked* you?" Aida questioned. "He attacked *Beatrice*? That's your sister, right? That girl doesn't have a fighting bone in her—What the fuck is wrong with him? And you're their dad? That's—"

"*Language*," Carmine said. He was escorting them to the queen. He'd dressed down since they'd last met. That must've been embarrassing for him. "I can see that your memories are returning, but you need to be more diligent around Her Majesty."

"How is she?" Lorian asked.

"Hasn't slept a wink. We've been all over the palace signing documents, apologizing to both Aldaían and Bĕlican diplomats who saw the mess of last night unfurl. King Dimitri's in shambles not because his wife was attacked but from how this will sully his reputation. Bea got out of the infirmary this morning, Durante's in jail. Your mother willed it. That was the one thing she was resolute on." He fixed his cuffs. "That, and keeping me from the guillotine for what I did."

"I'd hope she wouldn't after you saved her kids," Aida said. "I can't believe you two boned."

Carmine tripped on nothing. "E-excuse me!?"

"*Aida*," Lorian chided.

"Now please, honestly!" Carmine fixed an ascot tie he wasn't wearing. "I know that you're injured and your head isn't in the right place, but we do *not* speak like that in front of the Royal Family!"

"Oh, much more's been said in front of royalty before."

"What's that supposed to—No, don't even answer that."

"Besides that," Lorian said, "Aida, when you left the ballroom, what happened to you? What did you see? How did you earn your double ring?"

"I have it now?" She rubbed down the marking to feel the second loop. "Right. Guess I took the final step."

Carmine opened a door guarded by three officers. "Your final step to what?"

Zaahir and Kadar were in the study waiting for them. Zaahir looked unperturbed, but Kadar, who was sitting down for the first time since Aida had seen him, looked horrible.

Black eye turning green, and his leg was bloated with bandages underneath his robes.

The queen looked fine. No amount of makeup could hide that she'd been crying, but she wasn't hiding it. She wore her emotions unapologetically.

She was holding Beatrice's hand. Her daughter was accompanied by two maids who were pouring her tea. Her dress was quite pretty for this morning, nothing elaborate like what she'd been wearing the night prior.

The absent sleeves showed off her left arm, or what was left of it. It'd been cut off beneath the elbow, leaving behind a healing stump around thick stitches.

"Good morning," the queen said. "Are you well?"

"No," Aida said, and told them her history.

The longer they spoke, the more advisors came in to document this historic meeting.

Aida told them about the Catacombs, Eve, and Circa. Explaining her existence was the hardest part of the story. How did one prove the existence of a Goddess when a maid was asking you what biscuits you preferred with your tea?

Lorian had her back, even when she told them about a two-meter-tall Goddess who enjoyed the world's misery as much as its happiness. It helped that both Beatrice and Zaahir had seen Eve in the Catacombs. This only left the queen and Carmine to persuade.

Or Queen Rosalia and King Carmine.

They didn't know yet. They'd never dealt with a king's abdication in their history.

As of right now, the entirety of Roma was under the rule of Queen Rosalia Romano and her lover and two children, one of whom might've been renouncing their title that day.

And Aida, the last surviving heir to the country of Siina.

Carmine ran a hand through his hair. "This'll be...not difficult, it'll be *impossible* to prove."

Prove?" Aida asked. They'd been talking for well over four hours. She'd gotten comfortable on her sofa beside Lorian, legs crossed, lap covered in cookie crumbs with a cigarette in her mouth. Lorian had taken their coffee black. They were on their fourth cup.

"We won't be able to prove that you were the child of Eve," Carmine said. "I didn't even know she had an heir before her death."

"That's because her history was wiped from the records. They didn't want anyone knowing a Roman king was murdered by a rival queen he slept with. Had relations with. Whatever. They rewrote it because they were the ones who survived to tell the story."

"You have my official statement of seeing her in the Catacombs," Zaahir said.

"And mine as well," Beatrice said.

"And while I wasn't there when Miss Aida saw Circa or Eve," Zaahir said, "from the marking on her forehead to the stories she's telling us, I don't have any reason to assume she's lying."

"This means she'd be a lost heir to a dead country," Carmine said.

"Not *dead*," Aida clarified. "Just buried and built upon by people who had no business building upon it.

"Look, putting all of that aside, I need to say something. There're thousands and *thousands* of Visatorre lost in Roma because of what my mother did. Most are homeless and struggling to get work and proper schooling that's just *given* to other non-Visatorre people simply because they act different. I know none of us in this room are fully responsible for their suffering. I know we want what's best for our countries and have been in shitty situations for years, fuck, *all* of our lives. But I want to see a difference happen now. Not in ten years from now, not until *this* heir gets married off and *this* alliance gets made. I want to start working on fixing this country now. Is that absurd, because I don't think it is."

"That's a large, unquantifiable project that'll take years to act on," Carmine said. "You can't change people overnight."

"But you can start it now."

"And *everyone* in this room has been working on improvements. It's only—"

"Because of Durante? Because you were scared of him? He's out of the picture now, ain't he? He was a coward and a traitor. We don't have to worry about that fucker anymore."

A few of the queen's advisors raised their heads.

"It's true. I know how ya'll thought about him. He tried running a dictatorship when the world runs on monarchies. For now."

"So you're saying you want to revive Siina?" Carmine asked.

"What? No. I'm saying I want the Visatorre and the...the Mediocris to live without hating each other."

"Mediocris?"

"It's something my future self called non-Visatorre people. Look, I don't have to be the goddamn ruler of a country that's still in ruins. Not...not now, at least."

Lorian looked over at her.

"Right now, I think we should focus on fixing the world. We have three heirs in this room that can change it. Zaahir, you're passionate about your love. You want everyone to have their voice heard, whether it's the smallest, weirdest, fucked-up girl with a limp, to the very royals sitting in this room. I respect that."

Zaahir bowed his head.

"And Beatrice, you're one of the most selfless rulers I've met. You deal with a scumbag of a husband in a cold and desolate country, yet you care so, so much for Lorian and your people. You lost your arm to protect them."

Beatrice looked to her lighter left side.

"I don't want to see these people get fucked over anymore. We deserve a spot at the table. We deserve to reclaim the history the crown stole from us."

Throughout Aida's talk, the queen had neither taken a bite of food nor sipped on the coffee and tea everyone had broken for. She'd listened to everyone's worries with a straight face, taking Aida's ramblings seriously. Aida applauded her for being so put together.

At the sudden silence, eyes drifted to the very woman who outclassed all of them.

Queen Rosalia closed her eyes before speaking. "I cannot imagine what you must be feeling after reliving such a past. I believe what you've said is true, but what's truer is that we *haven't* done enough to help the plight of these persecuted people. I hid behind my husband for years, yet you are correct.

I am the reigning monarch and should've had more impact on my people. I know that the Visatorre need a voice to speak for them, and you have done an excellent job in demonstrating that with us today.

"Right now, my advisors and I need to sort out the fate of our kingdom Durante has left us with. We also need to make sure Beatrice heals in a safe environment, and we need to annul Lorian's engagement with Prince Zaahir."

Lorian dropped the cup about to reach their lips.

"What?" Zaahir asked.

"I'm nullifying the engagement."

The two in question looked at one another.

"That is, if both of you want it nullified. I assume Lorian's opinion hasn't changed in the past ten hours, and I know you've engaged yourself with someone else."

Zaahir took Kadar's hand. "My...my mother—"

"I will speak with her. I haven't been able to due to Durante's...beliefs, but now, that's in the past." She smiled. "I see a bright future with all of you here. It makes me wish I'd grown up with such ideals, to be so independent. If I've learned anything this year, it's that our fates can change in the blink of an eye."

Lorian chuckled, but there was relief and tears in their voice.

Aida took their hand.

They wiped their eyes. "I'm sorry. That's just all I ever wanted, uhm..."

Their mother sat up and hugged Lorian. "I know, and now I can do my part as a mother and help keep my children safe." She turned to Beatrice. "Both of you."

"If you're expecting me to abdicate or get divorced or time travel into a war, I don't think I can do any of that." Beatrice swirled her tongue in her mouth. "For now."

One of the advisors bowed. "Your Majesty."

"I know. I apologize. I have a meeting with Carmine and my league advisors at eight."

"T-they want *me*?" Carmine asked. "Are you sure that's... I mean, I *can*, surely."

"Of course. Going forwards, you might need to accompany me to many more meetings. Is that alright?"

He got up and dusted off his clothes. "Of course! But I should change into something more..."

"Monarchical?"

He blushed. "More presentable, but, yes, of course. Course."

"Course," Aida repeated, because she liked seeing him sweat.

The queen turned to her. "Thank you for shedding some much needed light on us this morning. I cannot promise immediate change, but I can promise you this: I will do my best going forward to make Roma a safer, kinder country for everyone."

"Thank you."

After she and Carmine exited, Beatrice left to tell her daughter that she was alright. Zaahir insisted that Kadar needed to change his bandages, but he was so fidgety to be alone with his *amar* that Aida let him go. Before they left, she shared a look with Kadar. He winked at her with his good eye.

She and Lorian left last, holding back the maids and officers who wanted to stay with them. After talking and listening for so long, Aida needed Lorian Time.

They escaped to the clock tower through one of Aida's jumps. The morning light painted watercolors across the dusty wood. Her bedspread mess had been cleaned up, clearing the floor for them.

Lorian exhaled loudly and fanned their eyes with their hands.

"Okay, deep breaths now," Aida said. "What, are you having convulsions? Need to lie down, sleep for a week and miss all the royal drama?"

"Hush." They wiped away the stray tears. "I've been fighting this marriage all of my life, and I almost lost you and my sister. I lost my father and gained a new one. I watched him nearly die."

"And all that pain paid off. If you didn't argue it, you might've been married off and we wouldn't have met."

"And you wouldn't have met Eve. And Circa—Aida, Gods, how was it?"

"Strange. She never stops smiling. Like, ever. It's creepy."

"I guess if you're a Goddess who watches life go on, life into death, death into life, children dying, children saving lives, I guess all you could do is smile blissfully knowing it's going to happen."

"I'd fucking do something about it, the ass," Aida said.

"Don't badmouth a Goddess. Are you like your future self now? Can you jump anywhere, at any time?"

"I don't know. Gotta experiment a bit more."

"Be careful. I know you'll stay alive up until your future self, but between then and now, we don't know what can go wrong."

"We don't know what can go on, *period*." She twirled in a circle. "We have the next, what, ten years to figure out what happens next. So many things can go wrong."

"...Your Highness."

She gasped. "Hey, *no*." She pointed a finger at them. "I don't pull that shit with you, you ain't pulling that shit with me."

"I mean, things change."

She dropped her finger.

"I've been thinking. If I don't have to marry Zaahir... I mean, do you think I can try? Pick up the title again? I technically haven't abdicated. I just took a leap year."

Aida bit her lip. Her brain was spinning. "And if I, allegedly, of course—"

"Of course, this is all hypothetical."

"Right. Hypothetically, if I were to gather the masses, show them that I am royalty by, say, bringing valuables back from the past—"

"Nothing serious."

"Of course. And if I *happen* to recreate a palace of my own, get a few guards or officers in or, fuck, even *gladiators*, bring back the old words with new meanings..."

"That would be rather titillating."

"It'd be *grand*. Can you imagine, you and me, ruling a whole chunk of Roma as two monarchs? Bringing back *Siina*? And *me*? A *princess*? A *queen*? I have no class. I don't know how to create laws or suffer through budget meetings or council hearings. Who knows if the public will even accept me as an heir? So what, she brings back a few valuables and documents from the past? They still might hate me for what my future self's done."

"Or they might praise you for finally putting Durante behind bars."

"What if we abolish the whole monarchy entirely? Make something new. They couldn't stop us if we tried."

"Alright, now that's a little intense, even for you."

"We're royalty, Lorian. Nobody could stop us."

Lorian took her hand, and the two of them rekindled their previous dance together.

"I can teach you," they said as they led her, "how to be an heir in training. Just a warning, the budget meetings are dreadful."

"Oh, no. Budget meetings are dull? Great. Now all my plans have gone to the wind."

"I'm sure you can manage."

"Not unless I poke myself in the eyes first. I'm pissed that I can't remember shit about shit. It's like everything after last week has been covered in a dust storm and I'm stuck digging out the pieces jutting out from the sand. I can't even remember how we met, Lorian."

"Well, I heroically saved you from a pumpkin patch."

"Yeah, right." She eyed them. "Did you?"

They waltzed with her. "It's a shame that no one has written down your extensive thoughts in some kind of journal, something that might happen to be at my favorite elderly woman's cottage that we can sift through."

She stared at their stupidly pretty face. They had freckles. They were pretty.

"You *have*," they said. "I was thinking about it last night. You've written essays about what you know and everything that's happened in our lives."

"I have?"

"Yes! Goodness, Aida, we have so much to work on. Have we restarted from square one? Do you even remember why you like me?"

Aida studied them, really studied them. While many of her memories were buried, something that always stuck out from the sand was this blond little head, loving her even with all of her faults.

Bringing them down, Aida stood up on her tiptoes and kissed them.

A shocked "oomph" silenced Lorian and their teasing.

Aida pulled back. "Yeah, I remember," she said. "I don't think I'd ever forget all of you."

Lorian smirked that smirk of theirs, the one that'd captured Aida the moment they met. "That's all I can ask from you."

"*Ew!*"

A metal latch undid itself, and two curious, nosy, irritable heads poked out from the top of the clock.

Future Aida and Future Lorian were watching from above. Future Aida plopped down on the Roman numeral twelve while Future Lorian lounged within the curve of the clock. Upon being spotted, Future Aida stuck out her tongue. "*Ew,*" she repeated. "Find a more private place to confess your love, you dramatic lovebirds!"

Aida groaned. "You're still here?" she called out. "I thought we got rid of you."

"The silence was so nice while it lasted," Lorian said.

"Is *that* how you're taught to speak to your elders?" Future Aida asked. "Hey, are you happy I kept everything a surprise till the very end? Wasn't it worth it? Wasn't it a fun story?"

Aida glared the woman down.

If she squinted, from a distance, she saw that she was beginning to look like her.

Aida gave her future self a bow. "A marvellous performance, I agree, though the dramatic flair was a bit unnecessary, don't you think?"

Her future self, mirroring her, bowed back. "Who do you think I get it from?"

Acknowledgements

First of all, I want to thank all of my amazing Kickstarter backers for helping to support the printing of this novel! I simply wouldn't have been able to make it this far if not for all of ya'll. TIME TRAVELLER came from a wonderful fantasy dream I had back in March of 2018, so thank you for helping my dream come true!

As always, thank you for my family and their continued support in my writing and endless ramblings of ancient queens, dreams of going to Italy, time travelling, and softest kisses. I don't know how they put up with me, but I thank them regardless for listening.

And finally, thank you to my beautiful girlfriend, Mari, who travelled into my life the week I started posting TTT to the internet. She taught me how to love myself and others. So much of her devotion and patience morphed into the love Lorian and Aida share, and I cannot begin to express how grateful I am for her.

I can't wait to see all of you in the future!
Thank you for reading!

Melissa

Thank you to all my wonderful Kickstarter backers!

Aerylaance
Akeea Fox
Alastair
  August Mathews
Alex Haynes
Alexis Winstanley
Alison N
Ally P
Alynne. E
Alysha Lancaster
Amara
Amethyst Holden
Amy Kleman
Anais Effort
Anaxphone
Andi Kent
Andromeda
  Taylor-Wallace
Angel Demain-Leavey
Anonymous
Anonymous
Anonymous H.
APaleLily
Ariana
Arianne B.
ARNELA BEKTAS
ashes
Ashleigh H.
Ashley Kelly

Ava Dickerson
Ava Metz
Avery "AJ" Gragg
Ayo Akinyemi
B Annsa
Bad Artist Bri
Briseis
BRoberts
Brooke Brite
Brooks Moses
Camielle Adams
Candice J. Brown
Carerra
Carisa Bjorngaard
Cassie Brice
Cathy Green
Chickadee
Citro
clov3r
Cole Lopez
Connor Cassie
Connor Lee
Courtny Fenrich
Crissiel May Turqueza
CrystalRose Fales
Danielle Garnica
Demitri Beltran :3
Derek Frerichs

Desiree Jung
DiAnne
Dominica May
Donna Flint
Dr. Serenity Serseción
E. M. Dash
Echo
Eliana Dimopoulos
Elizabeth Sargent
Ellen Mellor
Ergane
Erin Yarborough
Erisol
Estelle Martinez
ET
Felix Fong
Fermin Serena Hortas
G Murray
Gabriel Hernandez
Gad Andromeda
Galactus and Calypso
  Schroeder
genxia
H. Baxter
Hannah Carter
Hikaru_wins
Holden Fra
Hyper Harebell
I McClure
IronRequiem
Isabel Lagunes—

@callalilycomics
Jackie Turley
Jason Kimble
JC Carlo
JD
Jennifer Lopez
Jenny Woods
Jillian M
Johanna J
Jon Wasik
Jonathan
  "ChessboardMan"
  Barrett
Joshua M Dreher
JT
K. Scarlett Lucas
Kaitlynn Leary
Kal Keckler
Karen M. Clay
Katherine R
Kendall T.
killjoyprince
Kit Farmer
Koda
Kynerae
Kædan Lior Clockwork
LB Fliegel
Leah R. Cruz
Leea
Leishycat
Linda S. Webb

Luce F

Lucy Dembski

LumineSomnium

lyric apted

M. Wagner

Maddie Flynt

Maia Lune

Malachi

Marie Oak

Marten van der Leij

mary crauderueff

Matthew Beckham

Meghan McCusker

Melissa Capriglione

Meredith Nudo

Mia Tylia

Micaela Godfrey

Mikayla Philp

Miss Mari <333

Moonflower

Morgan Tupper

MythSigh

N/A

N/A

Nanija

Naruto cullen

Nat Withers

Natasha Acuña

Nic Mercado

Nicole Norrington

Nina Silver Ch.

Octavia King

Olivia Montoya

Pate

Phantommilkshake

Phillip A

Quinn Keating

R. Joseph Snyder

R. Tori Fraser

Ranielle G

Rebecca Valente

Rich Cloud

Ritski

Robyn

Rollie Hinz

Rose Robinson

Ross Emery

Samantha Yigdal

Sarah Joy

Sekinat Adekanbi

Serena Avalar

Serena Z

Sergey Kochergan

Shaelei

Shakyra Dunn

Shihachi

Sigurd

Siobhan Wright

Skywings14

Socheata Chan

Sophie C

Stacey Appelt

Stephanie Leacock
Susan Hamm
Susan S.
The Blerd Newsletter
The Unwanted Moth
Trip Space-Parasite
Victoria Ingram Closser

Victoria McRae
Void Critter
WhiteRabbitND
William C. Tracy
WrathOfSlytherin
Xena Hiwatari
Xuxa Rosado

Melissa Sweeney grew up in a small farm town in Connecticut and got her B.A. in English at Central Connecticut State University in 2017. Before, during, and after that time, she drew and wrote about her characters as a dubious coping mechanism for her anxiety. She currently lives with her cats Pumpkin and Spice and continues battling on which story to write next. You can follow her on Instagram (@melissanovels) or on her website melissanovels.com.